Wrathful Empathies
The Second Raid on Harpers Ferry

This book is dedicated to Christine E.

Acknowledgements

This book would not be possible without the invaluable suggestions from J&J Editing and Michaelle Scanlon.

Take me to the chasms
of beasts and the unwanted

let me walk among the lost
in the great confusion

the unknown.

Waiting for the wave
to fade us away

hand in hand we wait
as the wave grows hungry
swallowing the sky
the sun will be consumed
and the water will claim its throne

the children play
while skeletons lay

as we all wait for the day

where the lost will become found
and the beasts will shed their skin

stop. Rinse. Repeat.

A poem by Lauren Ewing

PROLOGUE

T he old man awoke to a whisper whose angelic voice echoed from deep within the Blue Ridge Mountains slumbering in view of his roughhewn log cabin.

> *The morning comes, the night decays, the watchmen leave*
> *their stations:*
> *The grave is burst, the spices shed, the linen wrapped up:*
> *The bones of death, the cov'ring clay, the sinews shrunk & dry'd*
> *Reviving shake, inspiring move, breathing! awakening!*[1]

He rose from the woolen blankets covering his straw bed into the freezing air. He kindled a small fire in the hearth and dressed himself by the glow of the flames. Smoke curled from the chimney upward toward the long cold winter moon, which lurked just above Massanutten mountain. Looking down from the summit, the snow laden Shenandoah Valley spread far to the north. His republican dwelling was the sole mark of civilization to be seen for miles. With dawn still an hour away, Thomas Fairfax, 6th Lord of Cameron, born at Leeds Castle, in Kent, England, sole inheritor of over 5 million acres of land in colonial Virginia, pondered the meaning of the message. He thought about the voice that awoke him. It had come to him every night for weeks. It was at once familiar yet alien. The voice sounded like an Old Testament prophecy but from a bible unknown to him. He found the words ominous and commanding. Was he to do something? He only wanted to silence it. He spent his life walking a

---

[1] Blake, William. *The Complete Illuminated Books* (New York, NY: Thames and Hudson, 2000), 420

fine line between crown and colony. Clearly, a choice was before him. A great upheaval surrounded his farmstead now more than ever before. He had lived through tumultuous times but this was different. To the surprise of the world, the American revolution was victorious. Everything about his life hung in the balance. While genealogies meticulously documented his noble birth and position of wealth, he loved the wild places, which provided neither comfort nor security. He quietly stood by as his friends and neighbors rebelled against the authority of the King. They formed a new nation of free people. A republic unlike any other in history was born. He had not fought for the revolution but was sympathetic to its pursuit of liberty. The war was over but clearly an enemy remained on the field. The young nation writhed unprotected in its crib. He heard its congested breath. Should he help or let it die? Could he even help? Everything hung in the balance, most importantly his vast land holdings. Even now, an old authority was slowly reasserting itself. Its hidden hands were pulling the baby's swaddling clothes tight around its neck. An afterbirth lay next to the child not dead but alive and growing. It was slowly taking on a life of its own. So much was at stake. Finally, he named the prophecy that the angelic voice spoke of. It was America. The young republic born of a fervor for liberty was being suffocated at the hands of a new tyrant.

Thus, he rose and prepared to leave. He turned the iron latch on the heavy wooden door and swung it open. Its leather hinges croaked and sagged with the weight of gravity. The old man stepped outside into the frozen darkness of a vast wilderness. Having rebuked the ostentatious life of Williamsburg, the woodland Baron reflected on his position. For the better part of forty years, he chose to live on the wild side of the Blue Ridge. Despite his vast inheritance, he pursued a simple life in the Virginia frontier. In the maintenance of his vast estate, he strove to be fair-minded to all. There were grumblings of his loyalty to the crown but no harm had ever come to him. He fought for the colony in its savage battle against the French and Indians when King and colony were still one. He had even mentored the revolutionary general and preeminent statesman of the new nation.

In his eighty-ninth year, he could feel the coldness of death invade his body. He felt his life force ebbing away. Maybe because of his weakening state, a recurring image haunted his dreams in addition to the angelic voices. It was a vision of a closed gate on an expansive plain. Each night it appeared to him. A powerful, yet silent, vision. Now, the voices added auditory instruction to his dreams. Was he to open the gate? He sensed this act was as dangerous as it was essential. Looking across the dark sullen waters of the Shenandoah river flowing silently under the moonlight, he felt guilt and regret for his part in conquering the land and its people. He spent his life underwriting an insatiable desire. He watched the Virginia colony expand its frontier beyond his Blue Ridge home and deep into the far Ohio River Valley. It was a violent and bloody adventure into the wilderness. Was the prophecy offering him a chance to obtain absolution for his part in it?

Mounting his horse, he extended two hands from a thick woolen coat and gripped the reins so hard that his veins and tendons were indistinguishable from the leather braids of the halter. Lord Fairfax nudged his horse forward. The pair plodded down the valley that fateful morning. He was headed to the Land Title office twelve miles away in Winchester. For some reason, he felt an urgent obligation to review a patent held by his lawyer. He felt it a matter of grave importance. A vague sense overwhelmed him that it could somehow change the fate of the new republic. Why or how he didn't know. Travelling down the valley, his eyes contemplated the crimson dawn that bled over the Blue Ridge. He wondered what strange fires raged deep behind the mountains to create such an ominous sight. In the greyness of dawn, he glimpsed a comet streak through the sky above him. It faded into oblivion as quickly as it had come. Too quickly, it vanished from the heavens. In its celestial transit, he saw the glorious blaze of the new republic. These were all bad signs. He remembered the King of England once feared the same premonitions. Looking westward from his throne, the King saw the fiery dawn of a revolutionary spirit burning within the American colonies. The King's worst fears came true.

A pain in his chest hurt deeply. It was serious and could no longer be ignored. He would visit the town doctor after examining the land deed in question. Leaning forward over the pommel of his saddle, the worst of the bitter cold was effectively blocked. Still, the bitter cold penetrated his coat and gloves. He desperately searched the horizon for the familiar church steeples of Winchester. His watery eyes fluttered open, staring into the icy winds for markers along the way. The horse knew instinctively the destination. It made its way toward a familiar warm stable along Main Street with little guidance from its master. Many local people saw Lord Fairfax as he strode along the path on the last day of his life.

"Good morning your Lordship." Greeted a local woodsman who was out early collecting firewood for sale.

"I must ensure the boundaries." He replied to a question not asked.

"Have a good day, Sir," hailed a cattle drover taking a small herd to a winter pasture where hay was stored.

"The patent does not include it" he muttered in response.

"May you journey well," prayed a native elder emerging from his shelter along the road.

"A gate is closed, it must be open," he stammered.

Pausing his horse at a crossroads, he grimaced at the sight of a furrowed wagon road that ran the length of the Shenandoah Valley. It was an ugly scar on the land, gouged by the turning wheels of countless pilgrim wagons. He felt remorse for his role enticing them to this wild place. Generations had committed themselves to a hazardous journey, abandoning everything in search of wealth and prosperity. With hindsight, he knew the siren call that lured them into the wilderness was instead a warning.

Pangs of guilt gripped his heart. His land needed improvement to realize profit and he needed people to populate it. His life had been spent matching patents to parcels. Over decades he labored until his five-million-acre inheritance gradually transformed into thousands of lines on parchment. All of them were duly registered with legal officialdom and collecting dust on darkened shelves in the Winchester law office. He realized much too late that this process of matching desire with resource was fundamentally flawed. The Native Americans, forgotten in the transactions, materialized from the dark woods with hatchet in hand. They fought the invasion to the last man of their tribe. The ensuing battle for possession bathed the land in blood. Their effort was in vain. An endless stream of pilgrims replaced the fallen. An army of surveyors continued relentlessly drawing lines on paper, dividing and subdividing the frontier into smaller and smaller tracts. Ultimately, the last empty space where people had lived free for eons disappeared completely with the stroke of a pen.

His heart was beating weaker and weaker as each mile passed. His breaths drew shallow as the knot of pain tightened in his chest. He sensed death coming closer with each aching beat. Then it happened. The physical pain transformed into a spiritual ache. He was suddenly granted transcendence. With his new vision, psychic lines appeared across the valley before him. These same lines became superimposed across all the patents he ever granted in life. Whose hand carried the quill he did not know. Nonetheless, the hidden scribe dipped it in a cosmic inkwell and scratched on parchment the heretofore undocumented trauma associated with each parcel. He wondered if the mournful lines were permanent. Could they be erased? If so, how could his deeds be cleansed? What redemptive waters would remove the stains? Hallucinations increasingly invaded his consciousness. He thought he knew where to find the source of such a cleansing spring. Prophecies, revelations, apparitions occupied his mind. Were they all just dreams, or was someone, something, speaking to him? He wasn't sure.

Finally, he glimpsed the church steeples of Winchester, glinting in the rising sun. He wanted to atone for his role in the coming day of his reckoning. The burden of guilt weighed heavy. He stared across the wide valley and pondered.

"So much pain and suffering. Where does it all go?"

In response to his silent question, a sparkling river materialized in the morning mist. Its azure water overflowed its banks and began to submerge the land. Dipping his hand in the waters, he swallowed a universal empathy. It was then he realized the drainage of this spiritual concourse was a liquid that could not be viewed by the eye, but only with the soul. Closing his eyes, he again saw the vision but this time the magical water was seeping into the earth. He saw it disappear into a dark, deep cistern within a mountain.

"My God, there must be enough miseries to fill it up," he announced to the cold winter sky.

He had spent the last days of his life pondering such visions. In fact, he feared the mysterious cistern might be a secret cavern that only he knew of. It lay within the mountain at the juncture of the Shenandoah and Potomac Rivers. Serving as the collective drainage for the great valley where all cosmic waters passed through its portal.

Rocking forward in the saddle and squeezing his calves, he urged the horse toward the town. After plodding several more miles along the central road, the frozen pair crossed a primitive bridge over a small stream. He stared at the clear water below and beheld the limestone rocks protruding from deep within the earth. The sunlight fractured the crystalline water and reflected off the stony scales. He imagined something gigantic below the surface. Only its spine appeared through the earth's crust. The pattern spread across the width of the Shenandoah Valley. Transfixed by the glittering sight, he glimpsed the stones shiver and turn over. He shook his head to clear his vision. His breath caught in his throat at the thought of a great serpent coiled deep within the earth readying to strike. He shuddered at the thought. His heart contracted again and paralyzed his left arm. He just needed a little more time to finish one last act of atonement. A passing cloud interrupted the dazzling light and broke his trance. Regaining his faculties, he once again spurred the horse forward. He was close to town now, but, once again, his mind wandered within the rhythm of the horse's stride.

The signpost read, "Winchester Town: Est. by authority of the Governor of Virginia Colony."

He turned his horse onto the town thoroughfare. People stirred in the shops and streets as the sun rose in the sky. A final blast of snowy wind took his breath away. He brought the horse to a stop in front of the law office of Esquire Hamilton, district magistrate. He descended painfully. As his jackboots struck the frozen ground, an immense pain reverberated through his body. It shocked his heart into a final spasm. His journey was over. The town doctor saw him collapse. He ran across the street to render treatment. Quickly enough, he realized he could offer no relief. The great Lord Fairfax slumped to the ground. With a last ounce of strength, he uttered an inexplicable plea.

"Tell Mr. Harper it was not part of the patent," gasped the old man.

"Your lordship, Sir, of what are you talking about?" the doctor asked.

He held the dying man in his arms and bent over to hear his gulps for breath.

"I want to declare officially that it is not part of the patent."

"Sir, what patent?"

"You must tell Esquire Hamilton that it is not part of it!"

"I don't know what patent you speak of."

"The falls at Shenandoah River..." He wheezed.

"Then you speak of Harpers Ferry, what is not part of the patent, Sir?"

Another surge of pain overwhelmed him. The old man fell back flat on the ground. The doctor kneeled closer to Lord Fairfax, lowered his head, and turned his ear to hear the muffled last words. Nearby residents of Winchester gathered around to witness his death. They fully realized his passing marked an end to a momentous period of Virginia history. They were witness to the literal death of monarchy. Some murmured thanks for his fair pricing and leniency with rents. A few cursed his loyalty to the crown. Most remembered him as a man of principles and decency. Everyone prayed for his soul. Lord Fairfax's lips parted one last time, mouthing a few silent words. It was then obvious to all witnesses that his life's energy had left the body. He had passed on. The doctor closed the eyes of the deceased and rested his head on the dirt ground of Cameron Street. He stood and faced the growing crowd of Winchester denizens.

"What did he say at the end?" a shopkeeper inquired.

The doctor turned to walk away but stopped and shook his head in confusion. Exasperated, he finally responded to the inquisition of the crowd. The last words Lord Fairfax conveyed to the crowd that day are still subject to debate among historians.

"The caverns, the caverns." Replied the doctor.

After directing several strong men in the crowd to take the body to his office, the doctor headed toward the office of Esquire

Hamilton.   He stepped through a burst of leaves uplifted by the winter wind. He watched as they swirled within an invisible current, never falling back to earth but floating away down the great valley. Gathering his senses, the doctor strode purposefully toward the law office of the district magistrate of Frederick County, Virginia with the final desperate words of a clearly disordered mind.

Meanwhile, the soul of Lord Thomas Fairfax escaped its physical form and floated upward. It saw the Valley below in three distinct dimensions. Each one crisscrossed by lines of transit. The first was the physical world he just left where living persons wandered. The second was a spiritual world where souls walked along paths in search of reincarnation. It was dark and ominous. The last dimension was special because it crossed back and forth between the two others. Travelers in this dimension were free from time and space. They journeyed along golden paths where past, present and future could be visited. The three dimensions had one thing in common; all were haunted by ghosts. Tom Fairfax flew through a windy vortex. He descended onto a golden hued trail that was etched along the high ridges of the Blue Ridge under which he had lived his entire life.

Chapter One

David Bartholomew Cooper, or DB to his friends, passed through the open door and descended into the darkened cellar. He immediately smelled the musty stink of decay. For a moment, he held his breath, worried the mold particles he inhaled would implant themselves in his brain. He thought he heard a voice. With misgiving, he reached into the blackness and felt for a light switch along the wall. Finding it, he turned it on. He cringed at the sight before him. He was in the cellar of the Friends of the Great Trail Headquarters building in Harpers Ferry, West Virginia. Eight fluorescent fixtures hung in three parallel lines from a low wooden ceiling. Below their dusty diffusers, a cold blue light illuminated mountainous piles of journals. Initially stacked in neat columns, many leaned precariously while others toppled at mid height. The columns near the front of the room had collapsed completely and spilled onto the floor. His boot accidently kicked one journal back into the pile. A light flickered off plunging one corner of the storage room into darkness. He sensed something hiding in the shadows. A few journals fell from their column pinnacles, tumbling to the floor as if disturbed by an invisible hand. DB thought he heard a voice again, this time from outside.

Despondent at his employment decision, he turned around, and climbed up the narrow stairs. He emerged with relief into the bright noonday sun of the Bolivar Heights. He was standing on top of one of three mountains that formed the triangular boundaries of the Harpers Ferry. Stepping onto the grassy lawn, DB looked back toward the closed wooden storm doors. He sighed and wiped his sweaty brow. A feeling of doubt crept deep into his heart. A summer spent hiking the surrounding mountains and rafting the cool, frothing waters of the Potomac flashed before his eyes. Instead, he would spend three months in a dank basement hunched over endless moldy journals, squinting into the blinding light of a digitization machine. His job converting thousands, probably millions, of hand written notes into digital data seemed excessively boring.

He even doubted his main objective of the internship: An impressive self-directed historical research project. Would anyone be impressed by this three months on his resume? This summer before college graduation was critical. It would be his last chance to get noticed by faculty. After months of effort, his accomplishment might only amount to dozens of thumb drives containing electronically converted content. He feared that result would not be the pinnacle of scholarly achievement he needed. Hopefully, his analysis of hiker entries would develop into a great human-interest story that would be published. If he was lucky, the *Great Trail Magazine*, or *GT Magazine* as it was called, would pick it up. In his wildest dreams, other circulations would catch the eye of even bigger media outlets.

"History major gets scholarly paper printed in the *Washington Post*," DB said in a serious voice to the empty yard.

He daydreamed the headline might even appear in his Department newsletter with his fellow students rushing to congratulate him. He desperately wanted to be accepted to the Master's Degree program of Civil War History. After that, he hoped to pursue a PhD based on a thesis he had been secretly mulling in his mind. He dared not speak of it yet because it sounded so crazy. First, he needed some evidence and facts to support it. In addition to digitizing countless journal pages, he would read each line, looking for anything that supported his idea. Somewhere deep in that pile of moldy journals, he hoped to discover an epiphany. He was sure some of these hikers experienced their own dark night of the soul. He was anxious to investigate what thoughts were scribbled upon the dirt-smudged pages. Being a solo long distance hiker himself, he knew there was plenty of time for introspection. Too much time, in fact. Whether you were hunkering down through a raging thunderstorm in an isolated shelter, dismissing the deafening silence facing your thoughts on an isolated mountain summit or ignoring the primordial sounds of animals crying out in the dead of night, hikers sooner or later begin an internal conversation that leads them to uncharted destinations. It reminded him of Nietzsche's famous quote, *And when you gaze long into an abyss, the abyss gazes also into you.* He would mine for such reflections among the scribbled journal entries. Certainly, not all long-distance hikers were capable of such insight. A few, especially, the loners, held out that possibility. That would be a treasure indeed.

Pondering his future, DB glanced toward the Maryland Heights. It was the largest of three mountains that formed the confluence of the Potomac and Shenandoah Rivers. Its soaring rock cliff never ceased to amaze him. He let his eyes drift down toward the cluster of houses in the lower town of Harpers Ferry. They looked frightened in its presence clutching tightly to the opposite side of the river. He watched a line of cars creeping along Route 340 to the south of town. During the summer season, traffic backed up all the way to the bridge into Maryland. Hundreds of these metal boxes idled in the sun-dappled lanes. DB empathized with the people trapped inside. He swore he would never subject himself to such misery. Yes, it was fun to career through rapids barely afloat on an oversized inner tube, but these were temporary diversions for him and not worthy of hours in traffic.

What he found fascinating to the point of obsession was the history of America at war with itself. Harpers Ferry was ground zero for such an investigation. He looked toward the cellar door again. Forty years of journals rotting in the basement suddenly fired his imagination. He was in a race with time to discover their secrets before the pages literally disintegrated before his eyes. The thought sent a chill down the back of his neck. He quickly turned to survey the surrounding mountain ridges. He sensed something was watching him from those heights. Something very old and even eternal was observing him from across time and space. He intuited something more than he saw, smelled, or touched. He hesitated to give it a name. It was unseen, unheard, and unfelt, although present all around him. In fact, he was confident an abundance of clues were moldering beneath and between the woods and crags scattered across the mountain ridges.

It was a waste of time to just start looking unless you were sure of finding something valuable. Clues could be anywhere and nowhere. Fortunately, his summer in Harpers Ferry posed a great location for such an investigation. Its history was uniquely formed by geography, economics, and social events. He suspected spiritual entities played a role even if they were invisible to the untrained eye. One such ghost still haunted this town. DB was intrigued by John Brown's life and death. This historic figure was denied a formal military rank but was nonetheless an unrecognized general in the battle against slavery. He planned an uprising despite the legal authority underpinning human slavery. DB was as amazed by John Brown's raid, as well as, his plan afterwards. It was epic. Brown envisioned the entire chain of the Alleghenies serving as a Great Black Way. It would offer a defensible path upon which his slave army could march south while transiting freed slaves north.

John Brown knew that mountains were shaped by water, wind, and eons of pressure. Unique to his own thinking, DB thought John Brown also sensed spiritual trauma left its marks as well. From the Mason Dixon Line, down to the Iron Mountains in the southern highlands, DB knew every crest, fold, and gap of the Blue Ridge by heart. He could walk its trails with his eyes closed. These were old mountains, some of the oldest on earth. To the average eye, they lay sleeping, but he saw their concealed energies. At first, he didn't acknowledge his visions. Then, after it happened enough times, he stopped questioning. Occasionally, the mountains shivered. He acknowledged it sounded crazy. DB figured it was due to the extreme forces that formed them eons ago slipping loose for a split second. Not only were these energies still present, they obviously left a supernatural ghost that occasionally revealed itself. Until he could understand his vision better, DB kept it to himself. Clearly, these old hills of the Blue Ridge were not what they appeared. While time had worn them down, their spirits still soared to heights unseen by the normal eye. Surely, John Brown was planning to tap into these forces as well.

"You must be the new journal keeper," declared a voice behind him.

DB swung around. He saw before him a short, gaunt elderly man. DB immediately judged his withered appearance not only reflected old age but an unseen burden. His long grey hair was tamped down around his crown as if a hat was recently removed. The man stroked a lengthy gray beard, which was entangled with small twigs and spider webs. DB tried not to stare. His knobby knees and elbows protruded through worn out pants and shirtsleeves. Sweat stains traced past exertions across his flannel shirt. The man reminded him of his favorite fictional story. It was as if Rip Van Wrinkle had woken up from a slumber lasting 100 years, walked down off the mountain and struck up a conversation.

"Oh, sorry. I'm David Cooper. I left a message saying that I would stopping by today." Trying not to sound defensive, DB added more explanation.

"The front door was locked, so I came around to the side door. I guess I shouldn't have let myself into the cellar, but I thought I heard voices down there."

"I have been waiting for you," said the old man.

"Well, I'm very excited about this opportunity and can't wait to get started" DB replied.

"At first, I thought you might be another thru-hiker looking for a place to pitch a tent. We get that every year you know, all kinds of expectations of travelers here. I suspect you'll probably see that for yourself over the summer. I will leave you alone mostly. My time is spent doing whatever needs to be done, but mostly I keep some records myself. I'm not your boss, so don't bother trying to impress me. That is Leo Davis. He's assistant to the director of the GT. I'm basically a full-time trail angel, purveyor of candy to sugar-deprived hikers and all around denizen of these hills."

DB waited for the man to stick out his hand to shake. He felt awkward as the old man's gaze trailed off to the nearby heights of Maryland and Virginia.

"Well, hello again. It's nice to meet you. I was told to report here for duty and I left a voicemail." DB explained a bit impatiently.

"That phone number belongs to the general manager up in the office and gift store. Don't feel bad if nobody got back to you. They're busy maintaining two thousand miles of trail," the old man replied.

"So, is it just me or are there others on this project?" DB asked.

"You'll be working alone down there. So, it'll be just you and the ghosts," he laughed.

"Ah man, don't say stuff like that on my first day," DB responded.

He tried to hide his real fear of spirits while glancing at the partially open basement doors. He tried to remember if they were closed or open when he came up.

"You're one brave soul. I've been, I mean, *we* have been, anxious to turn this responsibility over for years. Just waiting for someone curious enough to take it on."

"Well, that would be me!" DB exclaimed.

The old hiker shook his head.

"No, I mean it. This is going to test your determination not to mention your sleuthing abilities. You may, at some point, think it's a thankless job. I can assure you that it is not. We admire your willingness to help us out. This journal collection has gotten completely out hand. They gave up trying to keep any semblance of order years ago."

"Oh, I'm actually looking forward to it." DB replied as he glanced toward the basement door again. They were now fully open. He waived his hands in a circular motion in the air for emphasis trying desperately not to let his growing anxiety show. It must be the wind, he thought to himself.

"I mean, there are decades of stories in those journals about trekking from Georgia to Maine. I can't imagine the commitment and perseverance it must take to complete a thru-hike of the GT," he continued.

"Well, I see you have convinced yourself, so I won't tell you otherwise. Working down there is going to be dirty, musty, and uncomfortable. But I know you'll find the truth," the old hiker said.

"The truth?" DB questioned.

"Yes. Look very carefully and you will find the truth between those pages. People seeking solitude gain insight not accessible to others who decide to sit in front of TVs and computers."

DB noticed the old hiker was getting more solemn with each statement.

"Those who lighten their load to only what is essential, push beyond comfort, overcome fear, and endure loneliness are the ones who receive the gift of insight. Don't get me wrong, not all long-distance hikers totally let go. Some carry their dogmas all the way to the terminus. It's the ones who take the middle way, abandoning all preconceptions, cast eyes across their own internal vistas. I found that the mountains of mindfulness surpass in beauty anything you will see from the trail. It is not a simple task. It takes determination and commitment to achieve that inner vision.

The old man made eye contact with DB for emphasis.

"You must will yourself over those mountains, mile after mile, up and down, rain or shine." He said pointing to the horizon.

DB looked in the direction he was pointing and suddenly realized he wasn't sure if the old man was talking about the physical Blue Ridge Mountains or his own mental images.

"Sir, are you talking about real mountains or something else?" DB asked.

Ignoring his question, or, simply disregarding it, the old man kept talking. DB started to wonder about his sanity.

"They breathe rarefied air up on those peaks and drink from their own eternal spring down in the hollows. These journals record the observations of truth seekers. Some of them document their moment of enlightenment. Look for those passages. Also, be alert for a conspiracy to question, challenge, and assault narratives forced upon us. You may even see a few hikers develop some kindred of sorts. That's important." He winked.

"Sounds a bit more challenging than I anticipated," DB stammered.

"Yep, you should find truth somewhere in those pages," he concluded.

"Sounds exciting," DB replied. He tried to hide his confusion about his job but smiled and shook his head in agreement.

"You can start today if you want," the old man proposed.

"I guess there is no time to lose. Speaking of which, do you know what time it is?" DB asked.

The old man looked at the cracked lens of his wristwatch and shook it.

"Sorry, my watched stopped keeping time years ago, I just wear it out of habit."

"No problem, I left mine at home. I must meet someone for lunch but that should still give me a couple of hours to work. I guess now is as good a time as any to start. Like they say a trip of a thousand miles begins with one step."

"I suggest you start at the beginning with the first shelter in the direction of a Northbound journey" he suggested.

"I just hope I can be finished before summer is over," DB responded.

"I have a feeling you will," The old man stated confidently.

Reaching into this pocket, he pulled something out and closed the distance between them.

"Here you go. You are now officially the keeper of the truth." Stretching out his hand, he offered DB an antique iron key that was attached to a faded leather band. DB accepted the gift and looked it over. It was heavy in his hand but felt familiar and good. He didn't want to mention the basement door was unlocked. He got the vague sense that maybe the old timer had been down there before him that morning.

"Feel free to come and go as you please. That key only gets you access to the storage room and won't work to the GT building itself." The old volunteer turned to walk away but called out over his shoulder.

"Help yourself to sodas and candy bars whenever the gift shop is open. They have a room in the back that's stocked for thru-hikers. You'll feel like you've hiked the GT a thousand times after you finish reading those journals." His voice trailed off.

"Not a problem, but I don't see why I should need to come upstairs much. Thanks, and nice meeting you!" DB shouted.

Just as quickly as he appeared, the mysterious character was gone.

Like any good historian, well, like a very odd historian, DB corrected himself, he wanted to shine a light into events and people that were tucked away in the dark corners of time. He realized we hear a certain narrative from the past, usually whoever talked the loudest. He knew that was not the voice of the Native American, the poor of Appalachia, or the slave in chains. The shelter journals would give him experience to practice his skill. He believed many long-distance hikers were simply nonconformists. Their tales, therefore, were never heard beyond the small hiking community. He would do it for them. Sifting through the journals, he would find the true essence of this human experience. He knew the scribblings of minds adrift in the extrasensory currents of wind and woods would prove revelatory.

What is past is prologue, DB once read on a federal building in Washington, DC. To the annoyance of everyone in his history classes, including most of his professors, DB questioned that statement. He often recited a different version. *Who controls the past controls the future; who controls the present controls the past.* It was from Orwell's novel *1984.* His curiosity and second-guessing of events earned him a disparaging nickname: The Conspirator. It wasn't too far off the mark he admitted to himself. He didn't understand why people just accepted what they read, what they were told. In fact, DB often believed the exact opposite. History was anything but settled. He fashioned himself a rebel fighting a guerilla war. It was a war between truth and lies. Most people didn't even know it was being waged. He wasn't sure who he was struggling against. He had no doubts, however, the battle was on. He saw it in the historical accounts of John Brown and the raid on Harpers Ferry. The truth behind that event was surely being managed to keep his dangerous insubordination in check. Once he realized this historical sleight of hand, he became intrigued as to the reason. He wanted desperately to find out why.

CHAPTER TWO

L ost Mungo straightened his aching back and reached for his water
bottle. He gulped down several mouthfuls, straining pine needles
and other forest detritus through his teeth. His parched throat
seared with pain as he swallowed the cold liquid. *Gotta drink more often.*
The thought crossed his mind as he wet his blistered lips. He realized
that he had not eaten since dawn either. The beauty of the mountains
distracted him from even basic human nourishment. It was twelve
days ago that he left Harpers Ferry. Hiking straight through with little
break to McEwen's Knob left him exhausted as hell. He had set a
blistering pace along the GT. He felt the punishment only when he
stopped each night. He slipped slowly out of his backpack and slid it
to the ground. Catching his breath, the exhaustion of pushing himself
so hard sank in. His knees buckled and he leaned on his trekking poles
to keep standing.

Finally, he could rest at one of his favorite spots: The summit
of Mount Catawba. He approached the rocky cliff's edge and braced
himself against the ferocious wind. Despite the stinging gusts in his
eyes, he gazed straight into the torrent. He was in awe, again. From
his vista, he took in the view. It never failed to take his breath away.
A bucolic pastoral valley stretched out far below. The Alleghenies rose
abruptly in a great dark wall a few miles to the west. Stroking his
flowing red beard, he stared into the dark folds of the mirroring
mountains. Their presence could be either uplifting or threatening.
Sometimes, their silent dark mass appeared distant and disinterested.
Today, he found them staring back into the shadow of his own soul.
He was ashamed of what they might see.

To the other visitors lingering on the knob that evening, he
appeared an eccentric thru-hiker. A grimy British pith helmet strapped
tightly over his black balaclava was guaranteed to give that impression.
To be sure, he stuck a long peacock feather into his hatband for added

effect. His long hair escaped from underneath the helmet in wild tassels. He hadn't had a proper haircut in years. On the streets of any major city, people would assume he was a homeless person struggling with mental illness or substance abuse. On the trail, however, his peculiar behavior was easily recognizable. He would overhear people say, "There's a thru-hiker." They assumed he was another long-distance hiker in the midst of a 2,100-mile journey. Except he wasn't. Not in the sense they meant. While he walked in the mist of this hiker community, he was really a stealth traveler. His real community was hidden. He admired those hiking the long trail, but he kept his distance. They were his camouflage and nothing more. Sometimes, his loneliness allowed him to interact, especially with a few of the most ardent. These hikers abandoned materialism and eschewed normality. They hiked for the journey not the destination. A few lingered on the trail and its small communities. They reveled in defying society and belonged to their own tribe. They proudly called themselves *Hiker Trash*. And yes, a few were crazy.

Standing on the rock ledge, Lost Mungo began talking to the sky. His arms gesticulated an extravagant story to an invisible audience. His conversation with the ether seemed genuine especially when he paused to hear a silent response. Observers said he gossiped with angels while others assumed he was eating mushrooms. Whatever they wanted to believe was fine with him as long as it wasn't the truth. His was in disguise operating behind enemy lines. A soldier in an underground movement, he used the trail deliberately for his assignments. It was common for the curious to eavesdrop on his conversations but they only heard the wind reply. He alone knew the conversation was meaningless and therefore harmless. The only thing of value to his mission lay buried in the bottom of his backpack.

The rest of his attire was more functional. His sweat stained clothes were visibly layered through his half-zipped anorak. His hiker pants were filthy with mud. Mungo, as he was known on the trail, was short and slight but weathered beyond his middle-aged years. His friends claimed sand from the African desert still clung to the creases in his face. Burnt by the equatorial sun, he endured every ailment that bad water, insects, malnutrition, and hungry animals could inflict. And that was in addition to warfare. His face revealed a survivor of not only physical hardship but emotional and psychological trauma. Indeed, his constant furtive glances hinted at a fugitive. Only he knew the horror that pursued him still.

His eyes betrayed his clownish appearance. These reflected a serious, vigilant, and focused mind. He peered north and followed the long, undulating brown ridgeline for several miles until the quartz rocks of Citadel Cliffs broke free. He looked beyond the horizon, and in his mind followed the invisible ridge that he knew curved northeast for several more miles before abruptly descending into a small trail town. From there, the GT traversed the Shenandoah Valley before meandering northward again. He saw the narrow trail navigating gaps, rivers, and ridges until finally penetrating the sublime Shenandoah Mountains. Mentally, he calculated the elevation changes that lay between where he stood and his destination several hundred miles away. The steps he would take to hike over and around these peaks, however, were better left untallied.

A fierce wind buffeted him back from the cliff face, swirling him around in an unbalanced circle. He balanced precariously until finding his footing again.

"So, that's the way you want to play it, huh?" He smirked as he raised his fists and began jabbing at an invisible foe directly in front of him.

"I got more where this came from, you devil. Nobody pushes the Mungo off the knob, unless I be wanting to go."

He defiantly danced an Irish jig before beating a hasty retreat from the edge. He glanced around to see if anyone was watching. Spying two day hikers heading the opposite direction, he continued his monologue.

"And I will finish our conversation later, my eternals," he said. Turning for one last glance at his astral audience, he touched the brim of his pith helmet in respectful farewell. The young college students shook their heads at the eccentric, disheveled trekker.

"I think he has been out here a little too long," one of the coeds said.

"You think?" replied the other.

"It will be dark soon. We want to reach the car before nightfall. I think we should get going.," the first offered.

They both looked at Lost Mungo and nodded in silent agreement. They didn't want to be alone on the mountain with him. Another gust of wind brought with it the first flakes of snow. Realizing there was no time to waste, they hurried south to the parking lot. Mungo turned north. Descending steeply down the trail that lead off the summit, he maneuvered over a cascade of boulders. He grasped for handholds when gravity unexpectedly pulled down on the full weight of his pack. Letting his body react instinctively to the trail, he let his mind reminisce.

While his GT hiking seemed aimless, he was really a refugee from violence. He stepped off the battlefield ten years ago and never stopped walking. He was ex-special services. His missions didn't exist in the public domain. They were above top secret. Staying alive meant making his own rules of engagement. Secrecy meant he could not be detected. Anyone that saw his unit became the enemy. Achieving his objectives meant people died. Was it war or massacre, he wasn't sure anymore. At the frontier of the American realm it didn't seem to matter. Except to him. He chose not to re-enlist despite honors, medals, and promotion. While he left the battlefield, it didn't leave him. A memory played endlessly in his mind. A hot gun barrel sizzled with the sweat dripping off his brow while gun smoke filled his nostrils. The heat of the Angolan desert and wind-driven sand stung his eyes. He squinted with pain but not from the elements. It was the sight of the bloody carnage before him. A family lay heaped in disjointed embrace. Even in death, they sought the protection unique to parents and children. The vision had become his nightmare.

He was the apocalypse every loving household fears. He had done it so easily and efficiently. He didn't even have to change ammo clips. It was the end of a long counterinsurgency campaign that increased in barbarity with each brown hill breached and dusty valley conquered. Operating in silence, his unit destabilized one region after another. He ended his service when he realized the wars would go on forever. He no longer believed the ends justified his means.

His unit was called the Lost Legion, after Kipling's poem of the same name. They were first to the battle and gone before anyone knew who was fighting. This was the first part of his trail name. Mungo came from the 18th century Scottish explorer who disappeared under the flowing waters of the Niger River trying to escape angry tribesman. Just like the doomed explorer, he had no business invading lands where he was not welcome.

Quitting and returning home was supposed to offer relief. Instead, he found it intensified his remorse. Seeking to confess his sins, he was granted absolution too easily. He had done nothing wrong they said. Instinctively, they understood it was part of the burden of a global power. Mastering disobedient or defiant nations came with added benefits. Suddenly, markets and natural resources were open that once were closed. Of course, it was always easier if your finger didn't pull the trigger. Yes, he wanted absolution from his sins but he rejected the congratulatory remarks. They rang hollow. He had killed pure and simple. Even the term murder was accurate in some cases. He did what anyone would do to survive. At least that is what he told himself. He didn't know why it took so long to realize that he could leave it all. Just get out of the cruel game. But how was he to clean the stain on his soul? Talking about it didn't work. Quickly, he realized his story was better left unseen and unheard, preferably forgotten if he would just let it go.

Not knowing where else to turn, he passed through a narrow gate into the wilderness. He was in self-imposed exile from society. Nature could assist his transformation. He began wandering the wilderness trails of the great Eastern forests and its ancient mountain chain: The Appalachians. One dark winter night, he stumbled upon a ceremony deep in the woods. To his surprise, the small group of people knew of him and his journey. He was invited into their circle around the fire. They too had escaped something immoral. That night, he learned their secrets. Suddenly, the crazy geo politics of world events made sense. His suspicion of government deception was confirmed. He learned the real reason why armies go to war. It was about maintaining power pure and simple. As the embers of the fire glimmered in the dawn light, the mysterious group asked him to join. They called themselves the Kindred. Before long, he was a soldier again. This time he didn't carry a gun.

Working his way down the trail, the site of a shelter appeared through the woods. Reflexively, he sighed with relief. Turning off the main trail, he followed the blue blaze to the shelter. It was a well-worn path, at once welcoming and familiar. While all GT shelters were different, the feeling of respite they offered was uniform. He hurried the last couple of yards, closing the distance quickly. He stumbled under the burden of his heavy pack into the clearing. Standing before the shelter, he braced himself for yet another bitterly cold night. As blue evening surrendered to black night, he slung his battered backpack onto the empty shelter floor. Taking off his wool gloves, he retrieved a spiral journal hanging from the interior wall. It was the shelter journal and would be the focus of his concentration for the next several hours. They were ubiquitous along the entire GT. Every shelter had one, usually, a tattered thin cardboard cover, smudged with hundreds of sweaty hands. Their purpose was to allow hikers an opportunity to record their visits. Often, their simple, lined, white paper pages were full of sophomoric inscriptions, cryptic symbols, and inside jokes. Each hiking season, they were replaced anew. The old journals began what could best be described as haphazard collection and shipment to Harpers Ferry for permanent record keeping.

He grabbed a pen between his frozen fingers to write an entry. The tip yielded no ink so he shook it several times to release the liquid. Once the ink flowed, he found the last journal entry and added his notation: *Lost Mungo, December 20, 1974, Northbound.* He had seen no other hikers on the trail that day and he expected none to come this late at night. He would share the open faced wooden shelter with only the howling winter wind. The weather reports of snow must have scared other hikers away. Indeed, the storm, which had begun moments ago, with a few flakes, had picked up into a driving force. If the snow accumulated as predicted, he would have several days to research all the entries from the entire spring, summer, and fall hiking seasons. Any northbound or southbound hiker was sure to leave some mark of their passage.

Reaching into his pack, he retrieved his own personal journal. Encased in leather, the jacket covering was roughened and cracked from exposure to the sun, wind, and rain. A small rusted metal plate was anchored with tiny bolts to the front. A scrawled engraving revealed its title: *The Genealogies of the Wrathful Empathies.* The contents were not sewn into the binding so much as stuffed randomly inside the rawhide sarcophagus. His fingers delicately removed several individual parchments. Each page was illustrated with an exquisitely detailed family tree. They traced descendants over extended generations from a single patriarch or matriarch. The starting point of each tree began the same year. The date was October 18, 1859.

Lost Mungo carefully sat his leather-bound documents next to the spiral journal. A cautious glance into the woods confirmed he was alone. It was now safe to concentrate on the work at hand. He thumbed through page after page of the hikers' entries until he noted an important piece of information, which he then dutifully scribbled onto the appropriate family tree. Snow fell and drifted as he worked.

It glimmered in ghostly orbs as his headlamp periodically penetrated the dark woods. After several hours of work, he closed the shelter journal. Packing away the parchment of each family, he lovingly touched the last genealogy with trembling hands. It was of a different origin date and much shorter. The family tree traced only three generations before it abruptly ended on a single person. It was of an African family. It started with the first-generation patriarch and his wife, descending to the second-generation children and followed by third generation grandchildren. The fourth generation terminated in a single person. Pasted into that space was the faded military ID of Lost Mungo.

Through the blurred vision of moistened eyes, he carefully returned the paper to the leather manuscript. It resumed its place of protection deep in his pack. He realized dawn was approaching. Yet another night without sleep had slipped by. He felt the strain of his pack straps as his sore shoulders laid down. While the sleeping bag was toasty warm, he felt a stinging cold deep inside his chest. He shivered uncontrollably. His heart felt frozen. Hugging his core helped to control these tremors. One day, he feared his soul would break off like an icicle hanging from the shelter entrance. He used to fall asleep with fatigue but no more. His soul was tired and it never slept. Closing his eyes, he listened to the snow fall in the deep woods. It had a ghostly lightness to it. Each snowflake was a little white apparition dancing its way down from heaven. Did they come for redemption or revenge, he wondered? Zipping the sleeping bag tight, he turned off his headlamp and finally fitfully slumbered for several minutes.

When he awoke, the sun was out and the snow had stopped. It had accumulated over a foot and drifted much more in certain spots. In a couple of days, the snow would melt down to a manageable depth and he would start hiking again. He must maintain his schedule. A date was set for a very important event. The Kindred had requested his presence in Battletown, Virginia.

Their name was nervously whispered by locals who were outside the organization. People knew enough not to talk too loudly lest they be suspected of being a member or supporter. The Authority had spies everywhere who listened closely for this rebel name. If they thought you knew of the organization, it meant trouble. If the person next to you at dinner was a soldier of the movement, you were in trouble as well. Every civil war is the same. The people in the middle must take care not to show favorites. You never know who you are talking to.

He knew exactly how this hike would end. He would journey the last distance under a full moon. Standing in the darkness of an empty trailhead parking lot, he would quietly wait for a car to arrive at midnight. He would enter and take a seat in silence. Stealth was still required as they travelled the backroads. Sheriffs' deputies and spies scrutinized anything suspicious. The more rural the road the better. No words would be exchanged until they safely reached a dirt drive at the edge of pastoral oblivion. Slowly bouncing up a rocky road, he would exit as the car came to a halt beside a stone barn with a rusted roof. Trespassing, he would open a creaking door and break through cobwebs as he climbed a shaky wooden ladder warped with age. He would emerge into a candle lit loft. A meeting of the Kindred would ensue as others emerged from the darkness to greet him. His commander would solemnly begin with a prayer. They were assembled again.

Epochs left them unchanged in purpose; human liberty was still their cause. A band of rebels once again risking their lives against terrible odds. Resurrected from the mists of history, these men stepped from myth to reality. They always were ready and waiting. Each mission took its toll. Since being turned away from the first fateful raid, they never gave up but just disappeared. Hiding in plain sight generation after generation. Once again, in yet another stone farmhouse, not far from Harpers Ferry, a plot was taking shape.

The solitude of winter hiking would offer him its own concealment. The trail would be mostly deserted for long stretches. Roads could safely be crossed during the long dark winter night. These conditions would allow him to continue his journal research at countless isolated shelters along the way. He was given no details of the gathering. The Kindred were cryptic that way. Their messages revealed as little information as possible. He suspected they planned something big. The Authority was growing in strength. He knew it must be challenged before it became too strong to overcome. His contacts along the trail whispered of a strange new battlefield. His assignment for many years was to document Kindred deaths and recruit replacements from the next unknowing generation. He feared whatever lay ahead would keep him very busy.

CHAPTER THREE

Washington, DC, December 20, 1974

T he father was getting anxious despite seeing the white of the
Capitol dome hovering above the skyline. Its image was reassuring. It
was his North Star for orientation. He was not completely lost if he
could still see it. The American flag snapping in the wind on top of the
rooftop pole assured him that they lived in a republic that protected its
citizens. At the same time, this symbol was uncomfortably far away
from where his family found themselves. The area around him was
effectively cut off from its promised safety. In fact, he feared his
family was in immediate jeopardy. The blighted street before him was
empty of any people. It was a world away from Capitol Hill. Instead
of symmetrically designed green parks, purposeful workers scurrying
between important meetings, beleaguered tourists staring slack-jawed
at statues, and a bristling phalanx of stern-faced armed security guards,
he was now in an urban wasteland.

On either side of the street stood brutal looking monstrosities.
He saw no inviting tourist shops or any stores at all for that matter.
Where were all the boulevard cafes DC was famous for? Worse,
somehow, he managed to find a street with no discernable exit. It was
choked with overpasses that could not be reached. He saw no
intersections offering a way off the corridor of concrete. He paused to
consider their predicament. Through a series of wrong turns from the
Metro station, he fatefully led his family, block after block, further off
track. When he realized his mistake, he couldn't remember the way
back.

He wanted desperately to get off the trash-strewn, pothole
filled street he had irresponsibly lead his wife and two kids onto. He
looked around for a street address. None of the buildings had a
discernable entrance door except for one. It was very odd. He

scanned the street for a pay phone but saw none. One building caught his eye for all the wrong reasons. It exuded a menacing appearance more than the others. He couldn't imagine what occurred inside and didn't want to. In keeping with the height restrictions of the nation's capital, it reached only seven stories, but leaned inward, giving it the appearance of a bunker. He sat his family on the steps outside its mirrored green glass entrance and studied the city map again.

"Daddy, I'm hot and thirsty," cried his daughter.

"I know, sweetie, we'll be there soon," her father replied.

He exhaled his cigarette. The smoke was pushed out with added exasperation about his situation. Adjusting it between his lips, he used both hands to extend the map onto the dirty marble step.

"Are we lost again?" complained his wife.

She juggled the crying newborn on her hips while searching for its bottle in her purse.

"We'll be there soon. I just need to get my bearings. Not sure where we got lost," he replied.

His waning confidence dripped along with the sweat falling from his brow. He caught the reflection of his family in the mirrored door. They were a pitiful sight. He sensed someone looking at them from inside. A sense of dread overtook him. He suddenly realized they were better off anywhere but right there. To his shock, he realized he had verbalized his thoughts. His wife shot him a terrified look. Trying to lighten the atmosphere, he changed the subject. He blew the smoke out and watched as it quickly was dragged between the front doors. An eerie green glow pulsating from a crevice in the doorframe caught his eye.

"Well, that's interesting." He said flicking the ashes from his cigarette.

"What is it daddy?" The girl asked.

"This building has negative air pressure. Look how it is drawing in the smoke from my cigarette."

"What does that mean?" she asked.

"It means the building is pulling air in. Most buildings push out air out," he replied.

Gazing upward, to his brief relief, he glimpsed a person glaring down at them from the top floor. Upon closer inspection, the father grew concerned by what he saw. The figure appeared to be eight feet tall with the mass of a weightlifter. Frightened, the father looked away. Whatever stood in the window did not look like a normal human being. His face was ancient yet his physique was super human. The father was more desperate than ever to escape their predicament. Whatever that nasty piece of work was, he sensed it had no sympathy for his family. Turning toward the street, he searched again for a way out. They should get going in any direction, the sooner the better. He didn't want to give that cold-hearted watchman any time to confront them. Before he could even speak his thoughts, a black van screeched to the curb. Within seconds and a few muffled screams, he and his family were snatched off the street.

*   *   *

Standing alone in his corner office, George Urizen looked away from the ill-fated family below. He turned his attention to the city skyline. Stroking his graceful white beard, he ruminated over the architecture of the government buildings. Smirking at the pretentious choices, he was surprised more people didn't see the irony before them. Why would a republic replicate empirical Egypt, Rome, and Napoleonic France to represent their government authority? It was, after all, a government of the people, by the people, for the people. It should not be impersonating history's greatest empires. The architectural choices should have been a clarion call to the citizenry.

"You can't have empires without complete obedience of the citizens. Their constitutional republic was sacrificed at the altar of power. Some day they will all wake up to that fact," he said to an empty office.

Occasionally, someone did notice the obvious contradiction and speak in protest. It was his job to track them down and terminate their voice. The government operated according to a secret set of guiding principles. There were seven in total. While other agencies implemented principles directed at mind control through manipulation of history and current events, his guiding principle was repression. He thoroughly enjoyed it. Fortunately, opportunities arose endlessly. Just this morning, he executed a rebel. He struggled to remember the prisoner's last word. Tapping his forehead with a semi-automatic pistol in concentration, he finally remembered. It was clever. The victim was a poet of sorts or he emulated a poet. He wasn't sure which. The little speech was defiant. *This city is filled with dark satanic mills belching out polluted laws that choke our liberty.*

He roared with laughter reciting his words again. Of course, they did. Why else bother to enact them? This rebel was awake to the deception. That made him a clear threat. Even more reason to silence him. The rebel carried no gun but only a book. Urizen picked it up off his desk. Turning over a blood-stained William Blake portable reader, he smiled to himself.

"What fools are poets. Words against bullets. They never stand a chance."

He had to admit, the rebel was right. These buildings were facades of a republic that ceased to exist. His department lay hidden in plain sight. Its location in the decayed quadrant of the capital meant everyone assumed his building possessed no power. The appearance was effective. It was the exact opposite. His agency's mission was the best-kept secret of government. Most officials knew nothing of its existence. Its budget was black and off the books. It abided by no federal regulations. It had free reign to terrorize. Its very existence was, in fact, a matter of national security. Urizen smiled to himself at the thought of his power. A ringing phone broke his concentration. It was a special line set up by his employers.

"Hello," he answered.

The annoyance in his voice was difficult to mask. A soft and unhurried voice responded.

"You have been causing us problems."

"How so?" Urizen questioned.

"I think you know. Too much public display. Our usual complaint."

The voice on the line was calm and detached, unafraid of Urizen. The person was simply relaying a message. There were limitations to his power. It was a reminder call, nothing more.

"What has drawn your attention today?"

"The family. Be more creative. You could have invited them in the building for a tour. Once they are out of view, then arrest them."

"I understand," Urizen answered. No apology followed.

"You must be more discrete," the caller insisted.

Before Urizen could respond, the phone line went dead. The call was over. Free to vent his frustration, he slammed the phone down onto the receiver.

"They still don't understand. Fear is good. Terror is preemptive. We should be less discrete." Urizen said to an empty office.

Choking at his tightened collar, Urizen once again contemplated his power. Yes, he reluctantly reported to a shadowy group. Mostly, they gave him latitude in all matters. The only limitation was in spilling blood. It must be done correctly. Discretion was best, but if necessary, a cover story was used. If the public saw their government killing civilians, it should be justified. Terrorism worked well as an excuse. Sometimes, it was true that state sponsored terror groups did something. Or, there was the occasional lone wolf. Regardless, none of these were real threats. Only the awakened citizens really scared them. These actors had to be dealt with and in ways that did not amplify their message. In these cases, inventiveness was brought to bear. Stories were concocted to explain overt federal actions. A compliant media, of course, was essential in assisting his narrative. Unfortunately, his unelected masters preferred not to step over dead bodies. Urizen was forced to find new tactics to control the population in ways that were as invisible as they were enduring.

What could be more discrete than the new approach he was testing he thought to himself? The question reminded him of the family. He decided to begin with them. Urizen had no qualms about people knowing the truth; it was just their stupid objections that annoyed him. Initially, enslaving minds was optional, while silencing dissent was necessary. Citizens have freedom in their everyday lives but are not allowed to ask questions. Over the years, advances in technology increased his capabilities. He could monitor the citizenry's physical actions anywhere and everywhere but now he could follow their souls. However, this required implanting fears in their minds that lasted beyond death. Recently, he gained the tools to detect and control their transcendent movements. Even a soul could not hide from him. The development was thrilling. He was on the verge of controlling citizens for an eternity. There was a slight blind spot, which bothered him immensely. Somehow a few manage to slip his net and disappear. He wanted to find that hole in his web.

In this case of the family, the father merely noticing building operations was a minor criminal offense. The secrecy of the building's tenants must be maintained. Whether tourist or rebel, it made no difference. One could not be too cautious in reacting to threats. Either the father was conducting surveillance for freedom fighters or he was just a perplexed tourist. It didn't matter. Either way, their deaths would benefit the Authority. All prisoners were valuable for multiple reasons and this family was no different. If they were plotting sedition, their networks could be exposed through interrogation. If innocent, the horror of their deaths could be exploited for his new tactical program. The souls of these family members would be the subject of experiments as they wandered the dark plain of the In-Between. He would strike them again in their most vulnerable state of confusion. It was called the in-between time. The short period immediately after death but before reincarnation. It would be a test of his new technology.

Guards pushed the family out of the van and into the darkened parking garage. Blood dripped down the father's face and tears stained the mother's makeup. The daughter cried softly while the baby's bawling echoed through the cavernous space. The father got a terrifyingly close look at what dwelled inside the green-mirrored doors. He yelled defiantly at his captors but to no avail. He grabbed his daughter's hand. Staring into her eyes, he tried to calm her fears.

"Don't be afraid, I will protect you," he whispered.

"This is scary for me, daddy," she replied.

"Be quite and stay close to me," he instructed.

The father blinked through dripping blood and looked with growing horror at the building interior. There was an odd mist falling from the ceiling, the floor was coated in a slick gel, guards were hidden behind respirator masks. His anger welled up at the sight of his miserable family. He wrenched free of the black-clad guards and confronted them.

"What do you want from us? We've done nothing wrong," he protested.

A baton quickly crushed his head knocking him unconscious. The daughter sank down to her knees seeking his comfort and security. There was a memory she always cherished. Her father standing by her bed when she awoke from nightmares. In the darkness, surrounded by monsters, his presence was strong, and protective. But not now. He lay lifeless on the cold concrete floor. She felt an unrelenting fear. The monsters of her dreams were present all around her. She was without protection. Pulling on her father's sleeve, she repeated the same sentence repeatedly.

"This is scary for me, daddy."

In cruel response, she heard only the laughter of the masked men all around her. Hugging the body of her motionless father, she sought protection in vain. Peering through the strands of her tear stained hair, she spied an approaching monster. Its long grey mane flowed with every step.

"This is scary for me."

The men surrounding her were unmoved by her cries. The mother screamed as a hand reached out and slit her throat. The baby fell with her body. It lay in her spreading pool of blood. Once again, the daughter screamed.

"This is scary for me!"

Watching the child's response, Urizen jabbed his finger in the air and looked at employees gathered around him.

"Textbook! That is exactly the fear we want," he shouted.

Switching to a falsetto voice, he pretended to be a desperate child.

"This is scary for me," he mimicked.

The gathered men laughed uproariously.

"Get the CCTV recording of her statement, duplicate, and transmit the video across the entire organization. I want it to be mandatory training to watch it. It is our goal to reduce all citizens to that level of childlike fear," he commanded.

Urizen's voice trailed off as he turned and swept back down the long hallway. He disappeared in a green tinted mist.

"This is scary for me...," his voiced echoed.

Chapter Four

Sky Meadows, VA, December 20, 1974

Bret was turning 16 tomorrow. His birthday fell on the same day as his cousin Orc. That meant another boring trip to his cousin's farm in the upper reaches of the Shenandoah Valley. Visiting the Blue Ridge wasn't so bad. He just didn't like country people. He was awkwardly welcomed by them and he returned the feeling. Clearly an outsider, he felt a chasm existed between them that couldn't be crossed. His cousin Orc lived with his Aunt Sarah in a small farmhouse at the edge of a national forest. The drive meant travelling up the Shenandoah Valley along Interstate 81 for what seemed like eternity. His mom talked to him the whole way but she never paid attention to his responses. He soon retreated into another world all his own. Staring out the window, he fantasied about walking atop the endless mountain ridgelines that ran parallel to the interstate.

Finally, they exited the highway and entered sleepy Battletown, Virginia. It was a languid world in sharp contrast to the city where he lived in a townhouse. Even though he visited only once or twice a year, these townsfolk reminded him of his family's Christmas ornaments. They were oddly familiar despite long periods of absence. Leaving town, his mom steered the car onto a secluded country lane. Shadowed by ancient oaks and lined by miles of mortar less stone walls, he easily imagined himself in an older Virginia. He was sure some of these old oaks were here during the civil war. He didn't doubt that the stone walls dated back to colonial times. The further off the interstate they drove, the more he thought time rolled backward. The relics of old Virginia refused to pass away. Bret realized he liked it that way. Finally, the asphalt lane turned to gravel. At this point in the trip, Bret always looked for his favorite landmark. It was a signal the journey was about to end. Just beyond it lay his relatives' farmhouse.

After creeping past the last mailbox, he saw the rusted sign erected by the Virginia Highway Administration. While it was meant to warn drivers that the road surface was officially no longer maintained from that point further, Bret saw it quite differently. The government officially relinquished its responsibilities beyond the sign. Travelers were now on their own. He found the notification a liberating demarcation line. He appreciated its symbolic, if unintended, declaration of freedom. It read, "End State Maintenance." He couldn't agree more with its emphatic message: Take control of your own life.

Pulling onto the front lawn, the creaking blue station wagon sank into the grass, exhausted from its journey. The Blue Ridge Mountains loomed just beyond the farm. Bret's mom jarred him back to consciousness. She was reminding him to unpack the suitcases. He saw his aunt and cousin waiting on the front porch. He opened the car door and felt the warm sun upon his skin. It was a great feeling to be out of the concrete canyons of the city. He stood straight while stretching his arms and legs as he eyed his cousin's house. Rustic was too nice a word to describe it. The place was decrepit. He thought the decay had really accelerated with the death of his uncle.

He enjoyed his relatives well enough even if he didn't feel comfortable with their mountain ways. Despite his annual outings to the country, he never got used to the pungent smell of animal dung and sweat from manual labor. Also, he was shocked at the coarseness of their vocabulary. No matter how hard he tried, he always seemed like a city slicker among these hardened mountain people. They were alien to him in every way, especially his cousin Orc.

Bret wasn't sure how Orc got his nickname. Nobody seemed to know its exact meaning. Over the years, he'd heard stories about Orc's parents. Had they really abandoned him? He assumed that's how he ended up with Aunt Sarah. Orc's father was arrested and disappeared within the federal prison system, losing custody of his son in the process. Bret wasn't completely clear on the story of Orc's mother. Rumors were that she either disappeared because of a broken heart, ran off with another, or both, in either order. Rumors were abundant if he listened close enough during family reunions.

Nobody was quite sure why Orc's father was arrested and it didn't seem smart to ask. All Bret knew was that his relatives despised local law enforcement and law enforcement reciprocated in kind. The whole community was secretive in its behavior. Everyone seemed on guard against something unseen. It was a strange and intriguing place to visit. Bret always suspected he was not being told something important. His mom said that these mountain relatives had as many secrets as there were caverns in the mountains. Bret, being an outsider, was not trusted to know any of them. All he knew for sure was his aunt and uncle adopted Orc. Why Orc was abandoned remained a mystery that he never expected to be explained. To an outsider like him, anyway.

His uncle volunteered to raise Orc. Apparently, he accepted the responsibility as a commitment that could not be broken. Orc was treated as his own son. When he died in a bizarre accident, the commitment fell upon Orc's aunt. She made it clear he was not her offspring. Orc became increasingly isolated growing up. He only felt kinship to the surrounding mountains, which he wandered aimlessly. Before long, they would take him in.

Standing on the porch, Orc stared contemptuously at his cousin from the city. He prepared again to be asked about his odd name. Unlike anyone else, he knew exactly where his name came from. It was his business and nobody else's. He had never divulged it to anyone but the incident was emotional baggage he carried for all to see. After yet another beating at the bus stop, his uncle soothed his sores by telling him a story of the most fearsome beast in the sea. He described an orca, which hunted whales and devoured sharks. His uncle said he was like that creature. Both black and white, he was strong and fearless. Orc never forgot that image. He saw himself as a solitary orca patrolling the ocean, fearlessly swimming among monsters. Within days of that talk, his uncle was dead. He was gone just like his parents. In his dreams, Orc swam toward the ocean surface while his parents became leviathans that swam into the deep dark abyss never to be seen again.

Bret carried the suitcases into the house. As he passed his mother and aunt talking in the kitchen he overheard them whispering about finances.

"Has the money come in this month?" his mother asked.

Bret didn't hear the response but surmised it had not yet come.

"Oh, I'm sure it will. They have been paying for so long, I don't see why it would stop. Unless, it's because the boy is turning sixteen tomorrow. Do you think that has anything to do with it?"

Again, Bret did not hear the response. They had travelled to celebrate both boys' sweet sixteen birthdays. Some celebration. Hicks in the sticks. He didn't see any birthday cake, just clear bottles of moonshine stacked on the kitchen table ready for a scruffy band of visitors to straggle in from a stream of pick-up trucks. Bret wondered if Orc's benefactors would finally reveal themselves at his 16th birthday party. Bret didn't know who *they* were exactly, and it didn't seem like his mom or aunt did either. It was just another thing to gossip about. Who sent the money and was it of honest origin? One thing was clear; money came from somewhere to help raise his cousin. His mom had mentioned a mysterious relative or relatives who watched the boy grow up from afar. While they didn't take an active role in his upbringing, it was their duty to see he was taken care of financially. Bret suspected this same group was behind his aunt taking over as the surrogate mother. One thing he knew for sure, she didn't want any part of their activity, but was not able to argue.

The two women were now strolling across the front lawn. Bret's mom shot a glance over her shoulder to see if he was listening. He wasn't sure who they were talking about but suspected it was him.

"He's a sensitive boy, Ruth, that's all." Bret's mother said. "After what he's been through, you can't blame him for being a little off. I mean, the divorce came as a shock to him even though all we did was fight."

"I guess he just thought married couples were supposed to be unhappy," Ruth replied.

They met eyes again and this time Bret's mom cast Bret an apologetic expression before taking another long drag on her cigarette. Bret tried to eavesdrop while he carried stuff back and forth from the car.

"I know, right? Anyway, it's good for him to come back to the mountains and see his people occasionally," his mother said. She shook her head to offer sympathy or condescension. He couldn't tell which.

"He just needs to get some fresh air and to be with a real boy. There's nobody in his school that he's friends with. And he spends too much time alone doing whatever he does. Looks like he's thinking or something all the time. What kind of kid just stares out the window like he's pondering the meaning of life?" his mom asked.

She glanced with despair at Bret. Bret feared he had become yet another disappointment in her life. He made the best of her dissatisfaction by diving deeper into his own thoughts. He wasn't sure his mom cared for him at all really. It was obvious she was fulfilling an obligation. Maybe she did love him. Why should a kid have to wonder? That was the question he asked himself. It fit his life. He didn't fit anywhere. He was neither popular nor despised, just nonexistent.

Except, of course, when he was alone in nature. Only there could he escape the doubt, indifference, and pain. Only there did he feel no judgment. He was accepted for simply being. Invisible arms embraced him. He connected to, no *joined with*, something bigger. It went beyond life. It was easiest to get to this place when he walked alone in the woods or simply stared at the clouds. He became uplifted. Disconnected from his physical body, he saw the world through the eyes of the forest. He didn't know what he joined exactly. It was beyond just thoughts and feelings. Whatever he experienced, it felt real and welcoming. He dared not describe it to anyone. He realized that nobody ever talked about such things.

The experience always surprised him because it came after he felt the most irrelevant. He went from feeling insignificant before the limitless universe to suddenly transforming into a single entity without time, place, or identity. In silent conversation, he could hear the trees speak to him. *Join us. We are one.*

His mother's voice jarred him back from his thoughts. She was yelling at him to finish unpacking the blue station wagon. From behind the barn, Orc came speeding up to the car on a mud splattered ATV. Bret tried to hide his excitement at the chance to ride it. Orc offered him a second helmet and slapped the back seat.

"Let's go for a ride."

"Maybe later, my mom wants me to unpack the car." Bret responded.

"I got a new trail. Runs through Sky Meadows. Kicks ass."
As an afterthought, Orc used an always-effective adolescent challenge.

"Come on, don't be a pussy."

Bret forgot his cousin's intensity. There was no denying his invitation now. Orc would not stop the insults until he climbed onboard. Bret preferred the freedom of driving himself, but knew he must give the obligatory first ride to Orc. Bret eyed Orc's clothing and realized he forgot to pack his hunting clothes. He would really look out of place now. After all, his aunt gave him hunting apparel each Christmas. She would be hurt that he didn't wear them. Of course, Orc was covered in camouflage from head to toe. Bret scrutinized his attire closely. Why do country bumpkins ignore the obvious? Clearly, the winter woodland pants contrasted with waterfowl reed pattern. *Make up your mind already*, he thought to himself. *Are you hunting deer or duck?* He wasn't sure if country people were too lazy to change or just too poor to afford matching designs. At some point, they must assume it doesn't matter. If you reflect bark, leaves, or reeds, it was all nature. Animals can't be that discriminating.

He shook his head and marveled at these people. Their lifestyle was functional and comfortable. Just as piney hollows trickled forth clear spring waters, Bret realized nature filtered out the conflicts of life. His high school psychology teacher could expound on their gestalt properties as a common-sense approach to living life without despair. It would be useless to explain his begrudging admiration to Orc for this feat of psychology. Besides, he wouldn't understand words like gestalt anyway. So, Bret just took the helmet from his cousin's outstretched hand.

Both boys climbed onto the ATV. Orc steered it toward the high pasture that spread out across the mountain plateau. Bret gripped the seat frame tightly. He leaned forward with anticipation for the bumps and turns as they picked up speed. Another reason Bret accepted the invitation to ride with Orc was that it would take him to the beautiful high meadows just beyond the family property. He wished he could drive himself and be alone up there but being with his cousin made his mom and aunt happy. All that talk about being around a real boy and having friends made him laugh aloud. Never mind Bret thought the farm dog was smarter and more interesting than Orc, but dogs don't drive ATVs.

Bret leaned into the first corner of the trail. They broke cover at the plateau. The view stunned him anew. He never tired of seeing it. The eastern Piedmont spread out below. Squinting his eyes, Bret searched the far horizon. He wondered if he could see the glittering waters of the Chesapeake Bay. The shimmering mirage was probably just haze but he swore he could smell salt in the air. The open meadow at the mountain top was punctuated with tall, swaying oaks. Looking up, Bret was so close to the sky, he reached out to touch it. He imagined himself floating on a sky meadow adrift from the valley floor. As they coasted through the air, Bret forgot his life down below. Just then, the motor sputtered and died. His beautiful image evaporated as he choked on gas fumes. Both boys climbed off and surveyed the machine.

"Must be out of gas," Orc said. He kicked the tire once. He cursed and kicked it again.

"That sucks," Bret replied.

He didn't want to walk down the mountain because that would mean carrying a full gas can back up.

"I'll wait for you here, in case anyone tries to steal it," Bret offered.

"Ain't nobody gonna steal an ATV without gas," said Orc. He looked at Bret with a mixture of disdain and pity. "Besides, how they would get it off the mountain?" he concluded.

Bret didn't bother to answer. He could imagine someone pushing the ATV down the trail easy enough, but wasn't sure the brakes would work. Either way, he didn't want to argue even if he believed theft was possible if not practical.

"You are in better shape than me. I don't think I could carry a gas can up here. Even if I could, you would be waiting for a long time before I could manage it." Bret explained.

Orc thought it over. He looked toward the house far below, glowered one last time at Bret and then started walking. Bret watched him kicking up dirt and cussing as he marched down the trail. With a respite from the Orc and the noise of the ATV engine, Bret could now relax and enjoy his solitude.

At last, he was alone in his favorite spot and probably would be for a while. He watched and listened to the wind crash upon the tall oak trees. Their canopies exploded with each wave of wind. Mesmerized, Bret's heart swam within the breezy currents of the shifting tall meadow grasses. The smell of snow was in the air. Within seconds, the tossing leaves mixed with the first flakes of snow. Ominous clouds were building on the horizon promising to bring a full throttled winter storm. He envied the tall trees swaying in unison with the breeze. Listening to each leaf shutter and brush against another in the wind made him listen intently for any secrets they whispered. Bret felt reunited with long lost friends. The earth fell off to either side of the mountain and the open sky was within his grasp. A giant knot of clouds began to slowly untie itself. He felt his body dissolving, atoms breaking apart at the cellular level and intermingling with nature all around him. All things in the world were loosening. He was sinking into blissful nothingness and he didn't care if he ever came back.

The experience was intruded upon by a deafening roar. A swirl of wind surrounded him and suddenly he was inside a blinding light.

Orc was just emerging over the cusp of the hill when he saw his cousin disappear into thin air. He dropped his gas can and ran screaming back down the mountain trail.

CHAPTER FIVE

Battletown, VA, December 20, 1974

Zoa ran faster and deeper into the pastoral countryside that marked the edge of Battletown, Virginia. She was escaping the smothering peer pressure of the Clarke County High School Christmas dance. It was an impulsive act that made her anxiety worse. She had no idea where to run but, right now, the act of running was enough. She simply fled the gymnasium without telling anyone where she was going. The winter air was a shock. Even though she was wearing her cowboy boots, a midnight frost moistened the bottom of her red dress and started to seep into the leather.

Try as she might, fitting in to the small town high school clique was impossible. Nothing she did or said seemed acceptably cool. She was playing a game with hundreds of people but everyone knew the rules except her. Her final social disgrace occurred with a simple request to the DJ. *Could he play a country line dance song?* He laughed in her face and told the audience over the loudspeakers of her request. Not wanting to disappoint a cool DC-based entertainer, the rural crowd of insecure teens jeered their disapproval. Taunts and laughter followed. Her classmates shouted for disco, which is what the DJ came to play. Her loudest assailants were the most desperate to be anything but rural kids from a poor pocket of the Blue Ridge.

An alien species from somewhere deep in the universe would find it easier to fit in with her classmates. Nothing they did or said made the least bit of sense. She didn't have any vanity nor was she self-absorbed. At least, that is what her counselor said. That put her in the minority of the teenage population. Silliness did not come naturally to her. She only laughed if she found something genuinely funny. She could only converse if the subject was of interest. She simply could not fake her feelings. When she tried to feign enthusiasm, it always proved disastrous. Her words came out awkwardly and her jokes fell flat. People could see her straining uncomfortably to fit in. She not only failed in every attempt, but looked too desperate. The politer kids excused themselves and put distance between her. The meanest kids openly mocked her and sought others to join in the derision. Her high school had an anti-Zoa club of which she was an unwilling member.

As the circle of ridicule formed around the dance floor, she sensed a panic attack coming on. The peer pressure was squeezing air from her lungs. Her awkwardness only intensified the chasm between her and everyone else. It was not high school hyperbole to say she could not catch her breath. Her social anxiety was like a weight crushing her chest. That is when she fled. She hoped nobody would notice as she grabbed her father's hunting jacket and said she needed a smoke. In fact, her panicked exit sent all the kids chin wagging. Her social demise was now complete. She had ruined everything. There was no turning back. She felt like a freak. The suffocating sensation threatened to overcome her. She'd experienced it before, but nothing like this. She would drown in the open air if she thought anymore about what people were saying back in the gym.

Desperate to escape the judgment of the crowd, she escaped to the only place where she felt genuinely welcome: outside in the open, under the sky with space to move freely. The fear loosened its grip but only slightly. She could still hear mocking voices in her mind. The lights of the school parking lot were visible but growing distant. Had anyone followed her? She stopped to listen. She heard nothing but wind blowing in the trees. The scars of that night were deep and painful. She would have to walk a long way before being healed.

Getting her bearings was easy. She was a child of the Valley. The snow-laden clouds brightened the night sky enough to let her get her bearings. She could see dark mountain ridgelines to the east and west. This gave her an easy and familiar sense of place. She knew her whereabouts not by the stars, but by the recognizable peaks and gaps she grew up seeing every day. Stretching north and south, they were old friends that guided her now. She loved them because they alone didn't judge her but stood silently like protective gods.

Heading due south across pastures, she passed through woods, keeping the Shenandoah River to her left. It felt comfortable to have it within striking distance of 100 yards or less. It flowed ribbon-like along the base of the eastern ridge, mimicking the mountain's contours. She visualized earth and water in romantic embrace across eons of time. She wondered if nature had such a love in store for her. Years of fishing the river with her father meant she knew a protective screen of trees bounded its banks. Her dad taught her how to use this cover to hide from view. In his case, this meant evading the DNR agents during illegal fishing trips. Surveying the pasture land, she spied a copse of low trees. She would huddle under them until dawn. It proved comfortable in a primitive way. The low branches embraced the ground deflecting the chilling night breeze and sheltering her from the cold morning dew.

With the first hint of grey light, she decided to risk crossing the barren fields. Purposely zigzagging between rocky outcroppings, she hid behind them while scanning for the next shielded spot. This method of travelling meant she did not move as quickly as possible. Assuming her parents were looking for her, maybe even the local police, she continued to hopscotch across the valley. It had its drawbacks. Bending low to enter islands of brushy seclusion, her red dress was ripped by thorny branches. Thistle weeds stabbed her hands whenever she crouched low. She realized that she must look as wild as those crazy hikers that stumbled off the Great Trail each spring.

Bewildered at what to do next, she thought about the night before. She fled the homecoming dance into the dark December night without any real plan. Shivering in the cold now, she cursed her impulsiveness. What was the alternative? She could not go on living such a painful life. She regretted her decision but realized she couldn't face her classmates. They must be talking about the hick girl who ran away. While she had contemplated escaping, or more honestly committing suicide, she wasn't prepared for her decision when she finally acted. Escaping without a plan meant she had no destination. Surely, the oblivion of nature was welcoming, but eventually life-threatening. If she decided life was worth living, she faced the very real problem of finding shelter, food, clothing, and, most daunting of all, money. She decided there was no turning back. What lay ahead could not be any worse than life back in Battletown. For once, she felt liberated from her fears. All she had to do was keep walking until a plan formed in her mind. In the meantime, it couldn't hurt to get as far away as possible. She silently admitted one thing to herself. Being lost, cold, and bleeding was a damn site better than being on that dance floor.

Exhausted from hours trudging through wood and field, she finally cried out her feelings. Salty tears stung the scratches on her face. She had been walking for almost 24 hours. *Toughen up*. She heard her father's voice say. She dried her tears on the sleeves of his coat. She could smell his cigarettes and sweat. It was familiar and comforting. She instinctually embraced the night. In the darkness, she was comfortable. Mostly, because she was invisible. Unlike most people who projected monsters and ghosts into the darkness, she saw an empty void. Her scary places were well lit and full of people.

Standing on a small hill, she saw the sun peek over the Blue Ridge. Contemplating her next move, she enjoyed a moment of deep perception. This was the real world. What she left behind was just a performance. A sensation of warmth enveloped her. It was not a southern breeze, but something coming from within. Suddenly, a vortex of wind surrounded her and a brilliant white light blinded her eyes. Just as quickly as it appeared, it was gone. Stunned, she stood back and marveled at the vision. At its brightest zenith, someone stepped forward from within the light. She shook her head in disbelief. The image was gone along with the wind and light. For an instance, right in front of her, she swore a young man reached out to her.

CHAPTER SIX

Washington, DC, December 20, 1974

The cafeteria located in the basement of the Headquarters building was where Agent Valle got coffee each morning. An elevator bank was just outside its doors but the wait at lunchtime was too long for Agent Valle. He preferred to run down the dimly lit stairwell and take the gloomy service hallway to beat the crowds eager for their morning coffee. The only drawback with this route was the off chance of running across a prisoner escort.

"God, why do they drag those wretches through here?" the agent murmured to himself.

He couldn't help but glance at the group this morning. The wailing child was especially discomforting. In fact, this group looked especially pitiful. He wondered what threat a little girl could possibly be to the Authority. The brutality of his agency seemed unjustified at times. He knew better than to complain. That would only be a sign of disloyalty. Remembering his shift was starting in minutes, he hurried to buy coffee and run back to his desk.

Agent Valle returned to his computer screen. Picking up his paper cup, he sipped its hot contents carefully while scrutinizing the image before him. It was a holographic spinning globe. The sensors in the system continually searched for a rare event when both a soul and physical body jumped to another dimension. The Authority called this a transit. It was his job to rule out any potential anomalies. This step required scrutinizing the measurements to ensure it wasn't a physical death. His awareness heightened, he examined the latest detection data extremely closely. Realizing there was no other possibility, he stood up, and punched a button on his console. He quickly fixed its coordinates and waited for his phone to ring. Someone had just transit body and soul together.

His computer was tied into the sprawling underground complex of Mount Storm. Satellites, which orbited at various levels of altitude and angle to the Earth, provided surface movement detection. As good as they were, they didn't and couldn't detect a transit with accuracy. He suspected this was the reason the Authority spent decades building the underground complex just outside Battletown.

The facility was connected to a hypersensitive subterranean network that monitored all activity on the surface at the most minute levels. At least, that's what he was told. He never got access to the schematic diagram. Instead, his supervisor joked it was like a giant coiled serpent encircling the Earth's bedrock. Its flickering tongue constantly sensing human essence. Any change in the air might signal a soul passing by. Of course, as a computer programmer, Agent Valle did not appreciate this voodoo explanation. It was pure nonsense. He tried to fathom the instrumentation and algorithms required to detect a spirit leaving the body but not escaping the physical world. It would have been a monumental breakthrough in computing. The sheer magnitude of data required for the measurements, calibration, and analytics was equal to all the sand crystals from every beach in the world. The computing power of the processors was enormous and would have required eight football field-size caverns. His clearance didn't allow him access to all levels of Mount Storm but he really was curious about what was there deep in the mountain. It didn't matter how it worked, only that it did work miraculously well. The system could calculate if the soul weight vanished and the body weight remained, which indicated a physical death had occurred. If both weights disappeared from sensor detection, it represented an intolerable threat.

The agent stood up from his desk and looked around anxiously. He hoped his alarm was right in both its detection of a transit and the exact location. He realized his alert would result in the notification of the Agency Director. They called him the Master of Death because he had no tolerance for failure. Agent Valle knew a death squad was at this very moment being dispatched to the coordinates he transmitted. Whoever they found there would be killed. The Authority did not want witnesses to such transits. Essentially, this was treated as a prison break. Anyone nearby the transit location was deemed co-conspirators to the security breach.

On another computer screen in Urizen's office, a blinking red light flashed along with a chirping sound. He turned his giant figure from the window and looked toward his monitor. Unlike everyone else in the building, Urizen took no precautions against contamination. In fact, he wore no protective attire whatsoever. Instead, he dressed in coarse robes. He looked more like an ascetic monk than a senior executive of a sprawling bureaucracy. His muscular frame was capable of much more violence than even the most athletic special force member of his death squads.

His eyes scanned the transmission. Without a moment's hesitation, he gripped a telephone and brought it to his snarling mouth.

"Transit detected at Grid coordinates 32.32.32 by 44.33.22."

His finger traced the sector on a computer-generated 3D map.

"I am authorizing a full enclosure team ASAP." He repeated the last order twice.

He looked closely at the map displayed on his screen and manipulated some dials on his dashboard. He was ordering a satellite image of the location minutes before the transit. A grainy image materialized on his screen. It revealed two men, maybe even boys, on a mechanized vehicle crossing an open field. Thinking there was more to this transit than usual. He spoke into the phone again.

"No witnesses. Full obfuscation protocols and public quarantine for 48 hours until it is determined if the door is still open."

Urizen studied the image again as he stroked his beard.

"Unusual. Why only a single transit when there are two conspirators? Which one of you is more of a danger to me?" He wondered.

He lifted his finger from the map, revealing the secondary identification coordinates of the transit: One-mile east of Crosby Gap and two miles south. Right at the base of the Tomkins Wildlife refuge near Linden, Virginia.

Having launched a deadly assault against the location, Urizen returned the phone to its receiver. Whoever just slipped his net posed a serious threat to the Authority. They were now beyond his reach. Neither his monitoring system nor his agents were effective anymore. In fact, the threshold was impossible for the Authority to pass through. It was a spiritual passage. His power did not extend to the path where these spirits tread. All he could do was destroy any evidence of their successful escape. If people became aware of holes in his net, chaos would be unleashed. He couldn't maintain order if people escaped his complex grid system.

Urizen walked away from his desk and across his office. His footsteps echoed off the concrete pillars and bounced off the high bare ceilings. Stopping before his office window he stared out across the capital. A disoriented pigeon flew into the glass. It bounced off and fell to the street, leaving a splattering of gore and feathers on the glass. He gazed through dripping blood toward the Washington Monument. He thought of the captured family and again smiled at their mistake. He turned away from the window and approached the only object in his office except his desk. It resembled a bank vault, fortified with layers of metal doors, each lined with steel bars. A small window of bulletproof glass provided the only view into the dimly lit interior.

He peered inside. "Good job, my friend," he whispered. "We couldn't do this without you."

A grey shadow moved inside toward the darkest corner of the vault. Urizen thumped his fist on the window before walking to an elevator. As the door opened, he sprinted to catch a ride up to the rooftop helicopter pad.

CHAPTER SEVEN

Harpers Ferry, WV, May 18, 2016

V*engeful spirits lurk on a darkened plain in another dimension. A far off bright light beckons them. Confused, lost, and angry, they step toward it. It is cast from an open door. On the other side, DB anxiously waits for them to pass through.* This was one of many strange fears that forced their way into DB's mind. He couldn't stop them. They came from another place and made their way to him without invitation. While ghost sightings were not new to him, he had never actually seen one pass through a door. Therefore, he couldn't explain this very specific recurring image in his mind. He assumed it was just a phobia. It made his life a bit tough. He could not sit in any room with an open door. He always sensed something on the other side, slowly approaching. With some difficulty, he tried to subtly close any door in a room without drawing too much attention to himself. If someone noticed, he would blame it on cold drafts, noise, or something else. That was the least of his concerns.

Fortunately, the basement of the GT building basement had just the single entrance and no windows. That was one thing he checked on his first visit.

Once, he visited a mental health counselor on campus. After answering all the substance abuse questions, his deepest fears were searched. Within 30 minutes of questioning, they arrived at a conclusion. Not bad for just one visit he thought. Instead of physical doors, the discussion centered on psychic doors in the dark alcoves of his mind. They were ajar and open to his deepest fears. Through these openings, something could enter his consciousness undetected. Instead of a simple door to another part of the house or building, he detected a susceptible threshold crossed by spiritual entities. The door was actual a portal between life and death.

While the session was productive in explaining his phobia, it really didn't stop the vision. He resigned himself to just living in fear of open doors.

DB blamed it on his girlfriend. She recommended he read the Tibetan Book of the Dead. He could never get the image of bardo out of his head. DB imagined that place between life and rebirth as darkened plains, where recently deceased souls journey free of physical bodies. They were confused about their existence and afraid of not having a body. Striving to find escape from the nightmare of unattached existence, they sought reincarnation into a body, any physical body. Forgoing an opportunity to realize their true condition of being part of something greater, they reacted in fear. To their horror, other spirits existed alongside them. Some of the spirits were malevolent. Known as wrathful deities, they confront the souls in terrifying images. In fact, they were just reflections of the soul's worse fears, nothing more. Too confused to confront their own fears, these wrathful projections hound the unready back into lesser states of existence and understanding of reality.

DB felt a little guilty every time he closed a door. A braver soul would fling it wide open, barge into the darkness, and guide lost souls to the light.

Don't freak out. Keep moving. He imagined himself saying to the shadowy beings.

If he really felt brave, he would confront the hungry entities that stalked them. As much as DB didn't want to come face-to-face with a human-eating demon, he knew it would be the heroic thing to do. Whether these entities pass through the doorway in search of rescue or revenge, he realized was of no matter. Regardless of their nature, he knew whoever or whatever came through these open doors was probably pissed off at their experience in the bardo. He didn't want to be the first person they saw but resigned himself to the eventual confrontation. For now, he just closed open doors.

Standing alone in the basement storage room, DB suddenly feared something much worse than wrathful entities. He was late for lunch with his girlfriend, Lyn. He collected the last remaining journals scattered across the floor and stacked them into piles. Standing back, he surveyed the columns arranged by year and state. He left little aisles to allow for access to each. Turning toward the stairs, he flicked off the lights and stooped low to climb the steep stairs.

Lyn was expecting him for lunch. She wouldn't appreciate his tardiness. She claimed it reflected her status in his life. He knew better. Call it attention-deficient disorder or good old-fashioned absent-mindedness, he simply could never focus on the here and now. Since that was where she existed, he admitted to himself she was right to complain.

He latched the basement storm door, secured the lock, and jogged the three blocks across of Bolivar Heights to his rendezvous. Stopping across the street from the bar, his worst fear materialized. Lyn was already sitting at a café table sipping a drink and staring at the menu.

"How angry are you?" DB said. He assumed the worse.

"Don't be afraid. I'm early. As much as it surprises me to say it, you're not late," Lyn replied. Dropping her menu, she leaned forward over the table. Glancing around the café, she settled her eyes back onto DB. "So, tell me about your new job. Did you discover anything in your journals today?" Picking up her wine glass, she sipped it and waited expectantly for his response.

"Actually, I didn't get a chance to start reading them yet. I am still in the organizing process. Hopefully, I should be able to jump into the entries this afternoon. There is something creepy about being surrounded by thousands of people's thoughts penned on decaying paper," DB admitted.

"Well, you are qualified on multiple levels for this job. I mean you are always talking about ghosts in the closets," she laughed. Raising her arms, she moved them back and forth, pretending to be a floating specter.

"I don't see ghosts in the closets. In fact, I regret ever telling you about my phobia of open doors." DB defended himself by picking up the menu and hiding behind it. He started reading but forgot her insult and launched into another topic.

"Anymore, there is only one thing I am certain of. I can't accept anything at face value. You know how I feel about American history." He looked at her for some support.

"I know," she said, reciting his creed. "*Why are some figures heroes and other villains?*"

"Wow, you do listen to me." He praised her but then frowned. "Can you say it without the sarcasm next time?"

"Sorry. I do think you got everything you've ever wanted with this summer job," she continued.

DB looked back toward the lower town and admitted to himself that she was right. Harpers Ferry *was* a great place to look for answers. He had the perfect opportunity to explore the town and dig deep into its past.

"Apology accepted. You can help me to keep on schedule. This internship only gives me three months. You know how easily I go off the rails. This town may prove too distracting with all its odd characters."

"Especially, your mysterious man from history, that guy, you know, John Brown," she finally remembered.

DB nodded his head in agreement. Without John Brown's raid, Harpers Ferry would be just another forgotten river town. DB loved to imagine America's alternative history had the raid succeeded. John Brown and his rag tag band stuck out like a sore thumb from America's historical narrative. Refusing to accept slavery as a legal institution, John Brown struck violently at the heart of a democratic government. He didn't care if slavery was lawful. Besides, if slaves could vote, they would have ended it a century earlier. The nation was shocked at his bloodshed. A controversial figure in his life, DB was curious why the passage of time never transformed Brown to hero status.

"You're right about that, I couldn't be in a better place to find answers." Lowering his voice, he leaned across the table and whispered. "You know, John Brown was made an example for all of us."

"Oh, there you go with your conspiracies again! I swear, DB, you sound crazy sometimes. There isn't a deep, dark "State" out there watching us and plotting across generations." She rolled her eyes.

He was thankful when their waitress arrived. He could use a drink. DB sat back in his chair and ordered his favorite craft beer: a Hefeweizen from a local Maryland brewery.

"Hey, I was in the lower town today running an errand and just couldn't resist," he said with a sheepish grin.

"Oh, no," Lyn said. "You didn't harass those poor National Park Rangers again, did you? DB, they're going to report you one of these days. Not because there's some secret conspiracy, but because you come across as crazy."

"I can't help myself. It's like they're reading from a script."

Leaning forward, he prepared to describe the entire conversation. He could see she had heard it many times and braced herself for one more story. He could also see her relief when his drink was delivered. He smiled over his beer glass. He took a long thirsty draw. The white foamy head mingled into his mustache making him look silly. Lyn laughed and he felt emboldened to continue. It was one of his quirks. He never tired of posing questions to the National Park Service ranger at the John Brown Museum.

"They started each monologue with the same false choice: Was John Brown a terrorist or a hero?" DB proffered.

"Ok, so what does that prove exactly?" Lyn asked.

She impatiently perused the menu regretting she ever mentioned John Brown.

"The park ranger at Mt. Vernon doesn't follow the same narrative. Why does George Washington get a free pass when he owned slaves? Sure, he did lots of great stuff...," DB trailed off realizing his vulnerability.

"Yeah, like win the revolution. Be the first president. That kinda stuff" Lyn retorted.

"Yes, but does that excuse the other stuff, owning slaves, single handedly starting the French and Indian war, as well as, being ruthless toward Native Americans. People live their lives along a spectrum with good and bad stuff. It's like you said, there are heroes and villains but nothing in between. Who decides which extreme they are placed on?" DB ended his question by clinking his glass against Lyn's. He ordered another round. Lyn could see he was on a roll and retreated into the menu again. She placed an order for lunch.

"And another thing that bothers me is the focus on the spectacular failure of the raid. It's an overt accusation upon John Brown's sanity. *He had to be crazy to think his plan would work.* According to the NPS, the raid on Harpers Ferry was...," DB stopped when Lyn interrupted him.

"…a disastrous blunder carried out with tactical ineptitude in pursuit of a deeply flawed objective," Lyn finished by rolling her eyes. She had heard the words a hundred times.

"Exactly! That focus obscured the morality of the action itself. You know like giving slaves the means to fight for their freedom," he clarified.

Lyn cleared her throat as her sandwich arrived. "Are you finished? I'm going to eat some food if this dissertation is going to continue much longer," she complained.

"Go ahead, and I'm almost finished. I believe the simplicity of his position was blindingly clear. Only massive revisionist history could erase its morality. Somewhere the description of his attack was changed. Gone was any mention of a slave revolt," DB explained.

He paused long enough for Lyn to take a bite of her sandwich before asking, "What is your opinion?"

Lyn frowned struggling to swallow her food. She tried to change the topic after a sip of wine.

"DB, please promise me you won't go the dark side. It is out of the ordinary behavior. Don't let your conspiracy theories impact your summer internship. Remember, you want this project to be taken seriously for future employment. Keep your focus on getting a good reference. Hopefully, you can get your findings published. This is your future. Besides, having a good job is a prerequisite if you ever want to marry me."

"Assuming I ask, right dear?" he smirked.

Taking another sip of his beer, DB admitted she was right. However, in the back of his mind, he knew many people were fascinated by John Brown. His ghost haunted Harpers Ferry to this day and people liked that. After all, a huge attraction of Harpers Ferry was its ghostly creepiness.

"It's this place Lyn. Something about it is different. I feel like it is a magnet for the supernatural. I'm sure that I am not the only one who can feel it."

"Oh, my God, can we talk about something else now?" she said losing her patience with him.

DB nodded his head and tried to think of something normal to talk about. Lyn got up to go to the bathroom. He felt lucky that he had time to find a suitable topic. She met a friend inside and talked for a couple of minutes. Sensing a brief reprieve from her skepticism, he indulged his thoughts while she chatted away.

DB wondered why Harpers Ferry was such a mystical portal. He theorized it resulted from a combination of geology and psychic activity. Did it have anything to do with the confluence of rivers and being surrounded by mountain ridges? Was John Brown drawn here merely because of its strategic military significance, or did he sense another element that could advance civilization?

"Earth to DB! Let's bring it back to 12:30 lunchtime with me," Lyn called out.

DB saw her looking at him and her mouth moving. He realized she was asking him something. Struggling to swim back out of his thoughts, he tried very hard to concentrate on what she was saying.

"DB, are you drunk? Or, are you just lost in your own thoughts again? Either way, I'm here and can help you back to this world," she scolded.

"Thanks for your concern Lyn. Sorry, if I escape to another place while you're socializing. No, I'm not drunk, only buzzed, and yes I was having a profound thought, the kind you like to describe as a mental seizure," he replied.

"Glad to have you back. I'm afraid to ask, but what was your scholarly idea this time?"

DB paused to judge her sincerity. He wasn't quite sure if she really wanted to hear more of his ramblings.

"I was just curious what would have happened had his plan succeeded," he offered.

"Whose plan?" She seemed genuinely confused.

"John Brown's! Imagine a successful raid liberating a huge federal arsenal and distributing arms to an ever-growing army of revolting slaves," he replied with growing excitement.

DB saw the regret on Lyn's face but kept going.

"There's evidence that small numbers of people spontaneously joined the raid only to be crushed in the streets or repelled back into

59

the nearby mountains. Just imagine it. How would Lincoln have reacted to a well-armed slave army fighting its way south, gaining size and momentum with each liberated plantation?"

"I don't follow you," she replied after careful consideration.

"They would have shit their pants, maybe, who knows. John Brown would have been the Spartacus of his time. Instead of rampaging through the Roman countryside, he would have been an out of control force rioting along the spine of the Alleghenies. He even had a name for this war path: The Great Black Way. His plan was to strike down into slave country, liberate slaves, and retreat to the fortified crags. This mountain highway would allow the army to march south and return freed slaves north."

"Check mate! That does sound like an awesome plan. Why haven't I heard it described that way?" she asked.

"Good question. It would have been a significant military campaign possibly negating the entire civil war," he responded.

"I am sure it would have been supported by the federal government, right?" she asked.

"That is the provocative question. Problem is, nobody seems to be asking it. Surely, Lincoln would not have sanctioned such a rogue force either explicitly or even tacitly. He certainly didn't in bloody Kansas."

"And I suspect this has something to do with your post graduate plans?" She asked.

"Well, I've already sketched out this very proposition for my PhD thesis."

"Assuming you graduate from college, of course."

"Thanks for that vote of confidence. I believe the federal government would have dealt with the successful slave revolt the same way it reacted to the raid on Harpers Ferry."

"You mean send in the Marines?" She asked.

"Oh, a much bigger scale. Think of Marines storming the mountains, army cannons barricading the gaps, and an archipelago of U.S. Army units defending slave plantations throughout the South."

"That sounds like an alternative war itself," she realized.

"With the failure of the raid at Harpers Ferry, the world never saw John Brown's master plan. The insurrection was quashed in its infancy. With the state of Virginia conducting the court trial and public execution, the federal government even got to keep its hand clean of his death. Eventually, the South seceded and attacked fort at Sumter Island. Lincoln reacted to yet another assault on federal authority and invaded. The ensuing bloodbath obscured its hypothetical significance with all the other blood being spilt" DB explained.

"So, you're really asking who keeps the image of John Brown, 'the mad lunatic driven to extremes,' at the forefront of history?" Lyn clarified.

"Exactly. Again, you're following my thought process while still mocking my sanity. Neat trick," DB exclaimed.

"As scary as it is for me to admit, I follow your line of thinking." She conceded. "But violence is never the answer in a democratic republic. Now, can we finish our lunch and figure out American history later?" she beseeched.

"Of course, thanks for listening to my rant."

He realized he never ordered food and snatched some fries off Lyn's plate. He had squandered his entire lunch hour. Why did his curiosity take control of his life so much? Frustrated as he was, DB couldn't stop thinking about John Brown, the raid, and the aftermath. He came to Harpers Ferry for answers.

CHAPTER EIGHT

Washington, DC, December 20, 1974

Before her father was killed, she saw several floors of the building as their captors dragged her down countless hallways and through one darkened room after another. She made eye contact with her father several times. Even though he appeared hurt and sleepy, he was trying to speak to her. There was so much noise from the men yelling and laughing she wasn't sure of his words. She thought he said *don't be afraid*. Passing through locked doors, she noticed people wearing strange devices and clothes. The floor was slippery. It reminded her of the bathtub when she spilled shampoo. There was a blue light that made everyone look like ghosts. Another set of big metal doors opened to a long gray hallway. She noticed colored lines on the floors and more guards. These guards carried big rifles. Plastic shields covered their faces. The last room scared her the most. It was like a gymnasium. Except instead of playing sports in shirts and shorts, there were aisles of workstations and everyone wore suits that covered their entire bodies. They breathed through tubes, which made funny noises. A mist dropped down from the ceiling. She didn't understand how it could be raining inside.

Nothing made any sense. Why were they wearing these suits and breathing through masks? Was the air poisoned? She wondered what were these people afraid of? Was she going to get sick herself? Along each of the many aisles within this room, people were hunched before desks. As she was dragged down one aisle she got a better view of their activity. Wearing rubber clothes and breathing through respirators, hundreds of people scanned mini TV screens before them. The workstations stretched the length of the entire floor. At one screen, an employee leaned forward to view a spinning planet. It looked exactly like earth. As he watched the image, he punched his fingers into what looked like rows of buttons. She saw other TV screens with nothing but streaming numbers. She didn't understand those either. One worker, however, got very excited at what he saw.

Further down the aisle, she overheard two workers talking about sensors and detection. Finally, she figured out all these people were watching something on the planet Earth.

A jerk on her arm pulled her forward. A pair of men were dragging her father along the floor in front of her. She hadn't seen her little brother since her mother was hurt. She wanted to wake up from this nightmare and find her dad standing next to her bed, protecting her from these monsters. Instead, he needed help himself. She decided in that moment to be strong for him. No more crying. They would not get any more fear out of her. She was just a little girl and there was nothing she could probably do to save them, but at least she would show these people how brave she could be.

Chapter Nine

Los was halfway through the roller coaster section of the GT. He had to get through its seven miles of continuous rocky summits before nightfall. As soon as he scrambled up 500 feet, he just as rapidly descended an equal amount. Only to start the pattern all over again. To make matters worse, the trail was one long boulder field. He traversed it, however, with the agility of a billy goat. His long gnarly beard balanced him as he hiked along the jagged path. He was a backpacker who carried only what was essential. His wiry physique was lean but tough. He crossed countless miles of trail at blistering speed. Standing almost seven feet tall, he used his long legs to stride over large swaths of ground. His long arms pulled hard against his trekking poles propelling him up steep hills. Getting old didn't mean slowing down just feeling more pain. He could still hike further and faster than much younger backpackers. Frost laden mornings stiffened his joints severely but he didn't expect to live without pain anymore, physical, or emotional. The trail had hardened him and its toil. He looked years older than his actual years.

One day, it struck like a thunderbolt. His reflection in a window shocked him. It happened as he took a day off trail or what hikers call a zero day. He couldn't stand the stink of his clothes any longer. Stopping in a trail town, he walked into a Laundromat. As he approached the glass door, he saw his father staring back at him. He swore that he would never look like his old man. But, he did. The image didn't lie. It was one thing to have a piece of gear fall off his pack and not realize it was missing until reaching camp miles up the trail. It was another thing to lose decades and not realize it until staring at your unrecognizable face in a Laundromat window. He was shocked to see deep wrinkles crease his face. Disoriented, he turned away and headed out of town to the trailhead. In that moment, he regretted his life choice. Between the trail and prison, he was a shell of his former self. Surviving day to day, he lived a hardscrabble life. He spent most days and nights alone. Sixteen years had passed. The ten years in prison were the worst because he could not communicate with Enith. He prayed every day that Lord Jim told her of his arrest. Since being released, he re-joined the Kindred and spent six years as a loyal soldier in their cause.

The thought of losing her and not the glare of setting sun made him squint. His red-rimmed eyes dropped a tear along with beads of sweat from his forehead. Memories of her stuck to his mind like the dirt on his denim overalls. Neither had been clean for years. Part of him didn't want to wash up ever again. Worse, hiking gave him time to think and remember. Winding up a serpentine trail, he reached a blue blaze cutoff near the summit. The sign read, "vista .3 miles." The romantic in him couldn't resist the detour. He knew the view would reopen old wounds but he liked the pain. Standing astride a rocky bluff, he spied a stone farmhouse far below in the valley. It reminded him of a home they once shared, at least in a dream. The old scar still remembered the pain of the cut. He looked away but quickly looked back. If he could just see it clearly, he might find an answer to the question that had dogged him for sixteen years: Whatever happened to them?

"Why did you just disappear without saying goodbye?" he asked the empty sky. The December sun was brighter than his faded memories. That was another source of pain entirely. He couldn't stand the thought of losing her images too. In the stillness of his mind, he stored visions of her. He brought them out in moments of quiet solitude like worn photos from a box. Her faded smile still burst like dawn over the mountains and caused him to squint again.

As he stood staring down at the farmhouse, he replayed all his mistakes over again in his mind. He knew the view of the lonely farmhouse in the valley would trigger his thoughts this way but he didn't care. They were all he had left. It had started with so much promise. He rented the farmhouse as a vacation home to seduce her out of the city. Only after signing the lease, did he realize his mistake. The mountain views did not mesmerize her. Quite the opposite, she found the rural tranquility a prison. What was meant to be a lifeline for their relationship was just another weight dragging them under. They did not spend weekends exploring the Valley and nearby mountain peaks as expected. She visited less and less. Finally, she just stopped coming altogether.

As winter set in, the starkness of the valley and brown mountains mirrored his dying hope. Still, he spent every spare moment staring out the windows of the farmhouse, hoping to see her car coming up the drive. Eventually, she stopped answering her phone. He was driving through Battletown on his way to see her back in the city when the siren of a police car changed his life forever.

Imprisoned, there was no opportunity to contact her or anyone for that matter. The federal agents used the term, "terrorist" in his paperwork. His court appearance was rushed with no legal representation. Within a day, he was just one of hundreds of political prisoners in his cellblock. He would spend the next ten years enduring deprivations and interrogations. Only after the beatings and questioning showed no effect did they finally give up on his confession. Just as suddenly as he was arrested, he found himself dumped back into freedom.

Luckily, the Authority never realized his identity. He successfully concealed his role with the Kindred. As far as they knew, a simple rube that couldn't read or write was set free. He was classified as no threat to the Authority. Stumbling along back roads and forested trails, he arrived at their farmhouse. His heart leaped when he saw the grass was cut and firewood stacked. He picked up a bouquet of dried flowers laying on the porch. Nobody answered the door. The house was dark and quiet. He forced his way in by breaking the lock. He switched on the light but the rooms remained dark. There was no electricity service. Day and night passed. He sat alone in each room breathing in memories. Cobwebs nested in every corner of the ceiling. He opened the flue to the fireplace in the living room and laid some logs down. Striking a match, he put it to the kindling and blew on the flame until it caught. He added some wood, opened the curtains, and stared out into the yard. The drive lay dark and empty in the moonlight. Los went into the kitchen and reached deep into a high cupboard above the refrigerator. Pushing aside some pans, he retrieved a dusty half bottle of bourbon. Returning to the fire, he pulled up a recliner and settled in for a night of numbness. He would never forget the morning he found out the truth.

The sunlight streaming through the window woke him up. He heard dishes clinking in the kitchen. Trying to stand up, he found himself covered with a thick wool blanket. An empty bottle of Buffalo Trace fell over and rolled across the floor.

"About time you woke up?" Came a female voice from the other room.

"Enith?" Los murmured hopefully.

"No son, it's just us." A deep male voice responded.

Around the corner came a gray-haired man wearing cowboy boots and denim overalls. His trucker cap tilted to one side revealed a concerned face. A calloused hand handed Los a steaming cup of coffee.

"You been mowing the grass and weeding all these years?' Los asked with a wry smile.

"Yes sir, I figure I can retire on what you owe me." The old man said in a stern voice.

They both laughed.

"Well, Herb, I mightily appreciate that. I hope you didn't plow the snow all those winters. I doubt anyone ever came here."

Carrying a wooden tray with a large plate of fried eggs and bacon, a matronly woman entered the living room.

"You fill up on some food. It don't look like they fed you too well," she said while wiping away something from her eye.

"There ain't nothing like country neighbors. I thank you kindly for taking care of the grounds, not to mention the hot coffee and breakfast," Los said.

He stared down at the plate of food embarrassed by their generosity.

"Nothing you wouldn't do for us if we got locked up. Hell, our horses would keep you much busier," Judy said sounding a bit too sympathetic.

"I guess Enith never came by?" Los said looking around at the dust.

"Well, not that we saw," Herb said with a frankness that shocked Judy.

"What he means to say, Los, is that she was never neighborly to us before you got arrested. So, if she was here, we were not on her visitation list," said Judy casting a harsh glance at Herb.

"She never came by, ever?" Los asked again.

"Son, she was seen but not here. The boys working maintenance at Mount Storm started seeing her up there of all places." Herb took off his cap and fidgeted with the band in his hands.

"Mount Storm! What would she be being doing up there? Los asked, putting down his coffee cup.

"Herb just heard rumors from worthless boys. It could have been anyone," Judy offered.

"No sir, those boys know Enith and they saw her there in the company of an agent," Herb added to the misery of Judy.

"What's that supposed to mean? Not sure what you're getting at Herb," Los said raising his voice.

"It's plain to see Los. She don't have your back," Herb blurted.

"What Herb is trying to say, Los, is that Enith moved on after you left."

"I lost my appetite," Los said pushing the tray aside.

"Other people, your friends, stopped by. They settled with Herb for the ground maintenance so don't have to buy him any scotch." She glared at Herb to keep quiet.

"Also, I get the feeling your friends, you know, those bearded men I see coming and going across the field late at night, will be in touch. I see them, you know, when I am out walking my dogs down the lane early in the morning. I see them coming or going. Scare the hell out of me, big bearded men, all serious and such. Not my business but they look dangerous. You might want to think again about why Enith left. She might not have liked you getting involved with the likes of them," Judy suggested.

"She believed in the cause," Los replied angrily.

"I think we should be going, Judy." Herb grabbed her arm.

"I am sorry. You guys are great people. I am just confused and need time to think," Los apologized.

"Sure son, we are just down the lane. Let us know what you need. Judy would be happy to run errands or clean up around here." Herb said looking at the mess.

"It would be my pleasure to help in anyway, Los. Don't think twice. I may even bring some supplies from the country store by later. If you don't mind that is," Judy offered.

"It may be best if you guys stay away. I am not sure the Authority is done with me yet. Just leave me alone for a while," Los replied.

"We will keep an eye out for any strangers poking about," Herb offered.

"Just be careful, son," Judy pleaded.

"Let me know if you hear anything about Enith," Los replied.

"We will. You just remember we are here for you," Judy reminded.

"Thank you, guys, please stay away. It's for your own good. I wouldn't want you to be dragged into this stuff."

"I fought over in Korea and that was bad, but I think you're facing a much more dangerous enemy. Watch yourself. I only wish we had the Kindred when I was in the mountains." Herb winked.

Los escorted the old couple to the door and watched them walk down the drive. Their five dogs circling them in a moving band of loyalty. He realized they knew more about the Kindred than they felt safe to say. Certainly, everyone in the Valley feared the Authority and wanted no part of the underground. Los had seen it before. People knew when to look away, what not hear, and why they should not question a request. Los would not ever return to prison. They would not take him alive next time.

There was no reason to go anywhere. The Kindred would be in touch after they confirmed he was safe again and not being observed. He spent those days ambling through empty rooms. Cleaning house and doing chores kept him busy but he hated it. At last, a chalk drawing of mountain peaks appeared on the barn door. It was time. That night, under a full moon, he passed through the storage hut and swung open the gate to the pasture. He hiked across the field to the next farm, hopped a fence, and repeated the process for almost an hour. Finally, he spied a familiar copse of trees tucked into a depression of the pasture before the river. He recognized the odd illumination coming from within. A solitary figure greeted him in the pale moonlight.

Los passed the sentry and walked toward the blazing fire in the center. The circle of people parted as he approached. Los re-joined the ranks of the Kindred that dated back to 1859. Hard-edged stares of committed warriors met his gaze. Silently, he acknowledged each man and woman present. Sparks popped from the combusting soft wood in the fire. Staring heavenward, he followed the rising embers. The meeting started when an old man stepped from the circle toward the fire. The last six years hiking the mountains had been a blur.

Los came back to the present from his dreams when his arm brushed against the heavy revolver strapped to his chest. Death had a way of focusing his mind. Enough of what could have been. It was time to focus on his mission tonight. He slipped his hands through the straps of his hiking poles and turned away from the view. He still had several miles of hiking to his destination.

Chapter Ten

Bret turned around in circles. He had been transported to a strange looking path. It stretched for miles ahead and for miles behind, but on either side of him there was a thick wall of mist. In one direction, the path ascended gradually upward on what must be a ridgeline. In the other direction, the path stretched far across a plain before disappearing into the horizon. He stood transfixed by the glow of the path. It seemed illuminated from below the ground from a hidden light source within the mountain. He detected a faint pulsation. Looking ahead, he followed the glowing line as it traversed the mountain ridge and crossed over the summit. Bret didn't recognize the mountain. Trying hard to contain his growing fear, he grasped for some sense of direction. Was this the mountain beyond the high pasture at his cousin's farm? How did he get here? What had happened?

"Hey, is anyone there?" he yelled.

There was no response, only the sound of wind sweeping through the trees. He was entirely alone on the mountain. It was a strange but familiar feeling. That was it. He recognized it now. He was completely alone. He ran down the trail for several minutes yelling again and again. Each time he was met with silence. He stepped off into the mist but became blinded, unable to see his hand in front of his face. He didn't know what lay beyond. Maybe it dropped off suddenly. Fearing he would tumble over a hidden cliff, he decided not to test the mist but wait for it to clear. He looked up and down the path to decide which direction to walk. He could head further down or he could hike toward the summit. Neither one looked especially promising.

Below, the trail declined into what looked like a wide valley. It went on for at least ten miles before disappearing into the far mountains that formed its western rim. He couldn't imagine walking that far just to find out what was there. What if it was more nothingness? No, he would head up the trail first. It seemed to disappear over a ridge in less than a mile and he knew that some ridges had fire roads built on them. If he could just get to a road that would give him a way off the mountain that led to something, anything.

Bret was amazed at the velvet green grass he trod upon. The path was clear of rocks and roots and never ascended more than an inch per step. Its grade was magically inconsistent with the elevation change of the ridgeline. He wondered how could the path be so clean and smoothly sculpted? Who had built it? What toil had wrought such a beautiful avenue? Was it worn smooth by footsteps of countless hikers before him? If so, it must be ancient.

He sat down to rest. Brilliant white tentacles of lightening traced outward from a single explosion in the sky followed by booming thunder. He fell to the ground and clutched the earth for security. He felt exposed up on the bald and cursed himself for not descending the trail. A wind picked up that froze the sweat on his skin. The mist on either side of the trail appeared phosphorescent. He then heard something strange.

Floating on the wind came the sound of bells jingling, clinging, and clanging. He cocked his head to listen then shook his head in disbelief at another noise that was wafting through the air. Was it possible that someone was signing? He looked down the trail in the direction of the sound. Far below, he could see a lighted object moving up the trail toward him. He started to run the opposite direction and then stopped. He could go further up the trail but it would just follow him. He thought again of diving into the mist on either side. He decided that was a bit premature. Maybe whatever was coming his way wasn't so bad. He decided to face whatever it was head on by standing right in the middle of the trail.

"Don't worry. It's just Magda and her food wagon," came a voice from behind him.

"Who's there?" Bret turned around in circles, his outstretched arms sweeping the mist.

"It's me, Tom," replied a child's voice.

Out of the mist, Bret saw a small figure emerge. It was a handsome young boy of eight or nine years of age. He was dressed in the clothes of a different time and place. The boy looked like he had stepped out of a history book. He wore knee length breeches, a wool vest, and a cotton shirt.

"It's just Magda. Don't worry," Tom repeated.

"And who is Magda?" Bret studied the boy and glanced back at the approaching object.

"She travels the path feeding the travelers. Don't be afraid."

"I am not scared just lost," Bret replied.

"Then I will be your guide."

Tom walked toward Bret and grabbed his hand. They stood together and watched the object approach. Through the darkness, the outline took shape. He was dazzled by its fantastic lights. Creaking up the trail was a four-wheeled carriage painted a bright white. Its door and windows were trimmed with bright blue and red accents. It had one large door, off-center toward the front, from which descended a red stepladder. There were three windows and a door on each long side. The windows were made of glass that looked like his mom's holiday crystal goblets. Each window was opaque but etched with colorful decorations of stars and crescent moons. The stars were yellow but the moon was blue. They were beaming colorfully in the night from a bright interior light. Bret realized it was a chuck wagon of sorts. A little metal chimney stack jutted from the curved wooden tiled roof. It gently puffed out a soft, white, fragrant smoke. As if that wasn't strange enough, the entire wagon was pulled by two massive beasts. Bret struggled to identify them. They had long, low slung horns and were very furry. Finally, it dawned on him where he had seen them before. It was in his social studies class at High School. He was sure of it now. For some reason, Himalayan Yaks were pulling a food wagon through the Blue Ridge Mountains. The wagon came to an abrupt stop in a little clearing off the trail that Bret didn't remember being there a minute ago. An elderly woman tied the reins to an iron ring before stepping inside the wagon. Bret only saw her for a moment, but she reminded him of a gypsy fortune-teller.

Tom entered the wagon and emerged with two steaming plates of stew. Bret tasted a small amount from his spoon and found it delicious. After eating his fill, Bret returned his plate to the open wagon door. He set it down on the top ladder step and quickly retreated. Tom was kneeling in the clearing. He was planting something. Bret saw that it was a bundle of twigs wrapped up in a small cotton bag and tied with a piece of twine. Tom watered it from his cup and stood back. Within seconds the twigs grew into branches. They wove themselves together and started to from a shelter. The twine bound the branches together and the cotton cloth became a large canvas doorway. He peered inside and saw a mixture of wool blankets and fur pellets covering the floor. He then heard the rhythmic beating of drums between gusts of wind outside. It grew louder as he focused on its cadence. Layered between drum strokes were faint voices singing in unison. Bret stepped from the shelter to discover night had magically fallen in the few seconds he was inside. He turned and walked toward the sound.

Alone against the blackness was a ghostly figure sitting at the edge of an eerie blue fire. It was an old man whose long, gray hair blew in the nighttime breeze. Bret watched his feeble hands beat the drum, crossing one hand over another. In concert with this rhythmic movement, he began to chant. Without stopping his chant, the elderly man acknowledged Bret's presence. His milky eyes were the saddest Bret had ever seen. Bret realized the apparition before him was a Native American who most assuredly was a distinguished elder of his tribe long since gone. He motioned for Bret to take a seat next to him by the fire. The man produced an intricately carved wooden pipe. It was already lit and smoking heavily. Taking a long draw from the pipe, he handed it to Bret in a solemn motion that seemed rehearsed from many campfire evenings. Bret approached the device cautiously. He thought the Elder deserved his polite attempt to smoke. The pipe obviously carried some meaning, maybe an offering. Bret could feel its heaviness in his hands. If a blessing was being bestowed upon him, he felt desperate enough to receive it.

He lifted the pipe to his mouth and took a long draw. The sensation was intoxicating. He felt anxiety leave his body. Time appeared to stand still and his mind went quiet. As he handed back the pipe, his hand grazed the leathery gray hand of the Elder. As it did, he felt an electric charge go through his body. He then heard conversations inside his head. The voices spoke a language he didn't recognize. The words became images, which revealed the history of a vibrant tribe. He didn't understand at first, but the Elder gestured at the images insistently. Bret grasped that the people the Elder once lead were no more. He was the last of his kind. It was in these very mountains that a great injustice had occurred to this man and his people. It had left an indelible image in the spirit world. A psychic trauma was being revealed. It was seeping through the sacred ground and into view of Bret's consciousness. He alone was witness to their sorrow. The Elder mimed that his people still wander the spirit world seeking their homeland. They were tired and wanted to rest.

Bret nodded his understanding. The voices and images stopped. The Elder lay down on his furs. Bret felt the conversation was over. He stood to leave and started to wave goodbye. The Elder evaporated before his eyes. The blue fire lifted off the ground and floated upward into the night sky. Its flames became glowing white embers that mingled with the stars.

Walking back to the shelter, which Tom now was calling a wickiup, Bret stopped in his tracks. Dirt, leaves and grass formed in a vortex that crossed onto the path before him. From within the whirlwind, he saw the image of a beautiful young woman. She seemed desperate to escape something behind her. He reached out his hand toward her. She vanished along with the dust devil as quickly as it had appeared.

CHAPTER ELEVEN

Sky Meadows, VA, December 20, 1974

Orc ran faster than his feet could carry him. Tumbling down the trail, he cut his forehead and scraped his hands. Thistle scratched his face as he plowed into the dirt. Hitting the ground knocked the air out of his lungs but could not erase the vision of what he had just seen. Bret had vanished into thin air. Kneeling and panting for breath, he looked back up the hill. Still no sign of his cousin. Was it a lighting strike maybe? Whatever it was, he had to tell his mom and aunt. Maybe they could call for help. He didn't know what to tell them exactly. He shook his head in disbelief. He sprinted forward, this time keeping his feet in front of him. Holding his arms out to either side, he flew down the mountain.

He saw his mother and aunt talking in the weak winter sun just off the front porch. They were sipping coffee and smoking cigarettes. He felt a churning in his stomach at the news he was bringing. At the top of his lungs, in a voice he didn't recognize, he yelled.

"Help!"

Gasping for breath, he managed to put more words together as he almost fell again.

"Bret is gone!"

He saw them step off the porch at the sound of his voice. He was halfway down the mountain but still far away. He was yelling as loud as he could. He tried to make more sense.

"Something happened to Bret!"

He saw his aunt drop her cigarette and spill her coffee onto the ground. Both women ran toward him. He barreled through the brush at the bottom of the meadow trail, clutching the gate at the bottom to stop his freefall. His mom grabbed his arm and nearly shook it off.

"What the hell is going on up there? Where is Bret?" she shrieked.

"Bret was there and then gone, just like that," Orc stammered. Sarah's eyes went wide with fear. She ran past them toward the mountain screaming out Bret's name.

"Orc, I'm going tan your hide. This isn't a bit funny," his mother warned him.

Orc looked toward the high pasture and then squarely into his mother's eyes.

"Bret is gone," he repeated.

"If I go up there and find out this is a game, there will be no more riding that ATV, for both of you." Her anger was growing with each word that Orc spoke.

"I promise it ain't. He was there one minute and then gone."

"We got to take the truck up there and look for ourselves," His aunt demanded.

"Should we call the police?" Ruth asked Sarah. "And say that he's lost or something like that?" She completed her thought not knowing what the emergency was exactly.

"I'm still not sure what these kids are up to." His aunt replied. She glanced at Orc to gauge his sincerity.

The two hurried across the yard to the truck. Orc suddenly worried Bret was playing a trick on him and sprinted back up the hill. He wanted to make sure his cousin wasn't lying low laughing at him. He could hear his mom turning the engine over. It wouldn't catch. She tried again and the motor revved up. As he summited the rim of the meadow he heard a different sound. He turned back toward his mom's truck, mystified that it would be making so much noise. The truck was slowing turning around in the front yard. He followed the noise. It came from the direction of the rural lane. Fear shot through him. Three black SUVs driving too fast and too close together were turning into their drive. He watched as they made a beeline toward the farmhouse at alarming speed, bumper to bumper, throwing off gravel in every direction. They didn't look like any law enforcement he had ever seen.

Orc didn't like the look of the cars or the men inside. They didn't look like they were there to help. Besides, how did they even know what was going on? He was far enough up the hill to be out of their line of sight. It was clear they had their eyes on his mom and aunt in the truck. He watched as his mom stopped the truck and rolled down the window. Orc saw his aunt get out of the passenger side of the truck and walk toward the oncoming SUVs. She began to wave. The SUVs veered off the lane and careened across the yard. Orc felt a calm relief that professional men would help find Bret. Their doors flew open and black suited men exited with guns drawn. He saw his aunt's face change. Her hopeful expression turned into a confused gaze. Like Orc, she didn't understand why guns were pointed at her. She was in the middle of saying something when the men took final aim through their scopes and fired. A slow-motion nightmare played out before Orc. Puffs of smoke, red and orange flashes and the crack of gunfire ripped the air apart. His aunt's body collapsed into the yard. His mom screamed and raced back toward the house. Again, Orc saw muzzles flash and heard multiple shots reverberate through the still December air. His mom's back exploded with red bursts of blood. Orc saw the bullets strike the house after they passed through her. He couldn't believe what he was seeing. Just minutes ago, they were talking over coffee and cigarettes. Now his mom and aunt lay dead in the grass.

"No!" he screamed out.

The men turned their guns toward the sound. It only took them seconds to aim and fire. Orc ducked behind a lone oak tree as bullets exploded the bark and ripped the ground all around him. The agents remounted their SUVs. The engines roared and wheels spun in the grass, kicking up mud. Orc ran toward the thick tree line at the opposite end of the meadow. Two SUVs bounded up the pasture while the third turned back to the county road and positioned itself to block the private lane. As the SUVs followed the contours of the hill, the steep grade didn't allow them to accelerate at full throttle due to the sheer weight of the vehicles. This gave Orc a couple more seconds to put trees and boulders between him and his pursuers. His hunting camouflage obscured his outline as he ran further into the trees.

The SUVs reached a point where they couldn't go any farther. Doors flung open and the angry men leapt from inside and hit the ground running. He saw them closing the distance across the pasture with incredible speed. Soon, he heard men crashing through the tree line and their boots crushing branches behind him. Through the dappled light of the forest, he saw the glint of metal barrels. He tried to keep trees between him and the killers. Explosions of bark littered the air as bullets raked the forest. His pursuers were silent and methodical. He realized they were leading their target when a tree exploded directly in front of him. Orc drew from his own memory of hunting and became a rabbit darting back and forth, no longer taking a predictable path. The whole time, he wanted to return to his mom and comfort her bleeding body. He knew it was useless. She was torn apart and gone forever. He decided at once, he would get revenge on these murdering bastards.

"Damn it! Kill that kid!" screamed one agent to another. The other three men kept running and shooting while he stopped and pulled out his phone.

"We have a runner at the same coordinates," he announced to someone on the other end and waited for a reply.

"Place this sector under martial law. Order residents to shelter in place until we eliminate all witnesses. Kill anyone in the immediate transit zone. Black out all media. Issue a HAZMAT spill alert. Activate drones and bring in the dogs," a scary voice replied.

Orc ran until he could not breathe. He grabbed a small tree limb and stumbled to the top of a ridge. The noises from the men were growing distant. Shadows in the forest cut different angles than they had when he entered. He realized the sun had moved significantly across the sky. As best he could figure, he had been running for almost two hours. The exertion of his escape was finally catching up. He sank to his knees and felt his adrenaline subside. He could now see quite far down either side of the mountain. There were no signs of his pursuers. Finally, he felt safe enough to stop. Like a fox in briar den, he could afford to rest and lick his wounds. He lay down on the ground to eliminate his profile. The gunshots were growing more distant. They were getting further away. The killers had followed the hollow the opposite direction.

He slowed his breathing to listen more intently. He didn't understand why they had killed his mom and aunt. What had the women done to deserve being killed? He wondered if it had anything to do with Bret's disappearance. He'd heard other kids talk about this kind of stuff at school, men in suits with guns who hunted the mysterious men of the Kindred. He'd never paid much attention before. Now he understood that the kids at school were right. These men were pure evil. They killed two defenseless women in cold blood. They wanted to kill him and almost did. He was in real danger and he didn't know why.

As the sounds of the men faded, he thought about his next move. Should he stay where he was or retreat deeper into the woods? He realized he would have to move eventually and it made sense to keep moving away from their voices. The woods were growing dark but the sun still had another couple of hours before setting. The hollow where he was hidden offered protection but not for long. They were bound to double back and head in his direction. He was dead if he waited too long to move. Orc scratched his head in distracted thought. Where should he go?

He wanted revenge. The Authority had started a blood war and he would return the favor. His only regret was that his rifle was back at the house. He knew he couldn't go back to retrieve it as the farm was probably full of more bad men by now. Besides, he couldn't stand looking at the bodies of his mom and aunt on the lawn. He figured these men were not local law enforcement. The SUVs looked like the same government-issue he saw driving in and out of the Mount Storm complex. If so, he figured the local Battletown police and county sheriff were probably not able to help. They all seemed suddenly suspect. He no longer trusted anyone. Except for his kin.

He remembered his uncles' den. In the dark side of the mountain, the structure was built stone on top of stone by unknown hands. Before any of his family came to the Blue Ridge, it was hidden and waiting for them to discover. A perfect place to cook up something that his uncles didn't want anyone to see. He could get there by reckoning but it would take some bushwhacking. All he had to do was come down the mountain, cross the narrow hollow, and then head up the next ridge. He would find his uncles there. They would be pissed he came. Especially, with agents in pursuit. He would explain what happened. They had lots of guns and ammo and would know what to do next. If nothing else, they would give the killers something to think about. Orc imagined their reaction and knew they would not be the least bit afraid of the women-killing agents. They hated all law enforcement anyway. He just had to get close enough to talk to his uncles without being shot. The men in black suits had picked a fight with the wrong folk. He could feel anger take over his fear. They would pay for what they had done. He figured Bret was out there somewhere and smart enough to take care of himself. Maybe he would find his way back from wherever he was. Orc decided he would let all his anger, rage, and hatred for the parents that abandoned him be released upon those agents and whoever sent them.

Chapter Twelve

Loudon Heights, VA, December 20, 1974

The Sun sank quickly behind the Allegany Mountains. Once again, Los walked among shadows of the deep woods. They were his familiar friends. His clothes were tattered and dirty. Mud clogged his boots and straggly brown hair fell in greasy strands over his face and shoulders. Since rejoining the Kindred, he had live mostly on the Great Trail. Under the sky and stars, exposed constantly to the cold, heat, wind, and sun, Los was recognized for his hard-bitten trail ethos. He had reached something of hiker celebrity status. The sinuous Great Trail community intersected countless small towns, shelters, trail heads, parking lots, dive bars, and second-hand festivals. This community admired Los for his authentic desire to live free. His appearance inspired some to embrace his lifestyle and sometimes repulsed those who encountered him. The constant hunger, thirst, and exertion of his existence gave him the appearance of a scarecrow. His physical agility however contrasted his age. People talked in hushed tones about what the trail had done to him. Only he knew that his ultimate deprivation wasn't externally inflicted.

His destination was about an hour away. The roller coaster section of the Great Trail was now complete. His feet were sore but his legs still fresh. Los reckoned he would reach his surveillance spot well after dark. Not easy to do when every footstep would be treacherous with a snow storm brewing and cold wind picking up. It had to be done and quickly. His hike to the summit of Loudon Heights was essential. It was in direct response to the murder of two women earlier in the day. The Kindred could not confirm who died nor who escaped. The media spun the usual misdirection: *Two women tragically killed as part of a domestic abuse incident in bucolic rural Virginia.* Despite the fake news, the Kindred knew the real killers. The Authority was to blame. Los was desperate to find out the names of the murdered women. It looked to him and everyone else in the

Kindred that the killings were a transit cleanup operation. Los overheard rumors that one of the women was Enith. He desperately sought to find out the truth as painful as that may be.

So far, he knew that a boy had disappeared into thin air and that another fled into the wilderness. The general vicinity and vague description of the victims was strikingly familiar. His suspicions became an overwhelming fear. He had pieced together some of the story since his release from prison. His brother Floyd adopted a baby just after Los' arrest. The child was being raised by his sister-in-law, Ruth, after Floyd's death. They lived alone in a small cottage at the base of the Blue Ridge Mountains. Until yesterday. Los was grieved to hear his brother passed about five years before he was released. Now, his sister-in-law was gone too. That meant his nephew was one of the two missing boys. Whether he escaped into the woods or transited, he did not know. Regardless, he was without a mother now. Los wondered who the other woman could be. She was still not identified by the Kindred. He thought that very strange. Was it Enith? How could she have a child? The thought of her having a son with another man made him dizzy. He could forgive much but that would be hard to swallow. If it was her, she was dead now. That meant he had no choice but to cross over himself. He would need help to navigate the In-Between. He had one last chance to find her. If she accepted him, they could spend eternity together. For now, he had to focus on his mission. Lord Jim had ordered him to observe activity around Harpers Ferry. Specifically, he was to study the train activity through the Maryland Heights tunnel. Los guessed that whatever he observed tonight would decide the time and date of the second raid on Harpers Ferry.

To make his hike more difficult, a winter lightning storm with snow unleashed in the sky above. His red-rimmed eyes focused on the forest path as he carefully placed each foot. His body didn't register fear regardless of the raging storm nor the slick stony path. His persistent and resolute stride cut large swaths of trail beneath him as he looked to the summit looming above. Gusting wind broke off huge branches from the tree canopy constantly throwing obstacles across his path. Undeterred, Los pulled a large cloak over his head and backpack. Its construction was unusual. It was only worn while he was on a mission and exposed to open sky. Reaching to his knees, the camo pattern hid his presence to the eye while the inside was coated with a shiny metallic lining. He fastened it securely to fit snugly around his pack and torso.

He could see his breath as he cleared the tree line. At the summit, the full force of the winter wind assaulted him. Like a frozen ghost passing through walls, no amount of layered clothes could keep it out. The cold became his companion in the woods. When he stopped hiking, his sweat froze on his skin. He had hiked for three hours to reach the ridge summit. Now, he wanted off. He couldn't stop shivering. Getting a grip of his senses, Los began his reconnaissance.

Lightening backlit racing clouds above him. His cloak served a dual purpose for his mission. It camouflaged his presence to satellites. He doubted Authority spies would be out in this storm. However, the eyes in the sky never slept. The internal lining of his cloak prevented satellites from detecting his infrared image. No longer under the protective canopy of forest, he was vulnerable to hunters like a deer emerging onto a meadow. He preferred the dangers of falling trees to exposure on the cliff face. The squall didn't bother him, but the wrath of the Authority did.

Los could barely see in the waning light. He was utterly alone on the rocky cliff. Nevertheless, he stood with the ghosts of his memories. He could still see her running ahead of him. An endless projection playing a cruel loop through his mind. He remembered every aspect of that day. It was burned into his retina. She laughed with childlike innocence as he chased her. Constellations of brilliant white trillium along the path framed her raw, natural beauty. Finally, catching her, they collapsed onto a bed of ferns and crowsfoot.

He closed his eyes to hold onto the vision. It evaporated as quickly as it had come. His hands reached out to grab hold, but she was gone. Her laughter echoed faintly off in the dense woods. Turning in all directions, he searched for her in the dusk. It was a vision that tortured him many times. It always ended the same way. She suddenly disappeared like so many years ago.

A thunderbolt brought him back to reality. The storm that gathered as he climbed finally broke open during his dream. A blanket of snow fell upon the woods. Bizarrely, lightning streaked across the sky and reached down to strike the ground. A tree behind him erupted into flames. The thunder clapped him on the back. The bright flash blinded him. He teetered on the cliff ledge. He felt intense heat from behind. Regaining his vision, he raised his hands to block the glare of the swirling inferno. He was in the middle of a cataclysm. It seemed like all the forces of the universe were focused on his destruction. Crouching low, he flicked on his headlight to find a safe space until the storm passed. The fire dampened and then was extinguished to smoldering red coals. It was going to be a long night of surveillance.

He knew the storm raging in this physical world also raged in the spiritual realm. The Kindred needed to know if a portal had opened between the two. Wild rumors circulated among people who wandered the woods late at night. There was a dark mountain where strange things happened. The Kindred listened to the tales and sent Los to investigate. He was to watch for trains that disappeared into tunnels within tunnels. Even stranger, he was to find a mysterious cavern where an underground lake glowed with ghostly specters. Like all Kindred, Los was a denizen of the dark, wild places. Nobody could travel unseen through the mountains better than Los. He was to find the truth behind these rumors without alerting the Authority. If the tales were real, the Kindred wanted Los to start a battle on this new front. Their mountain trails were of no use on this spiritual battlefield.

From the cliff ledge, Los would have the best vantage point to view the dark mountain. It lay directly across the Potomac River. He could see its entire southern face hulking in the darkness. Settling in for the night, he adjusted his jacket hood to block the cold wind but frame the base of the mountain in view. He could not fall asleep. The Kindred had maintained its vigilance for over a hundred years and he was not going to let them down. An army of anonymous soldiers, they kept the resistance alive when all other citizens succumbed to the anesthesia of the Authority. The spirit of liberty burned in each and everyone one of their hearts. John Brown had awoken it. The resulting battle against slavery eventually consumed a nation. It all started in sleepy Harpers Ferry. Nothing had really changed in his mind. The Authority still enslaved people through their thought control programs. If anyone broke free, they were terminated just like John Brown. Los wondered if any of the survivors of the first raid escaped to this rocky ledge. Did they witness the violent, climatic end of the raiding party from here? He could feel their spirits everywhere. Defiant in the face of overwhelming force, his ancestors showed him how to face danger.

Although most people never read it in the history books, many slaves and free men did respond to the Brown's call for insurrection. While most townspeople of Harpers Ferry reacted with anger at the thought of liberating slaves, a few decided in the moment to join the cause. They believed in liberty and were willing to personally risk everything. Some were stopped before reaching the raiders, but others slipped through the enraged mob of townsfolk who clamored to kill the abolitionists.

Realizing his fate, John Brown ordered a select few to take flight again. The men slipped back into the night, climbed the surrounding steep ridges, and huddled with other thwarted rebels. From their mountain summits, they looked down at the furious final assault by the United States Marine Corps. Afterwards, their anonymous faces were among the crowds as John Brown was tried in court for his crimes. Mingling within the overflowing angry crowds, they watched again as their fellow raiders were hung. The survivors took a solemn pledge. They would continue John Brown's cause for as many generations as it took until all men were free.

If a new battlefield called him, Los would march onto it. While he was there, he would search for Enith.

Over the passing years, the organization met clandestinely at night in desolate wild places. Between meetings, they communicated using the mountain trails of Appalachia. Hidden in plain sight, they watched as the Authority's power become absolute. Their commitment never waned. With each passing generation, they passed on their responsibilities. They watched in horror as the Authority's propaganda twisted history, distorting John Brown's morality to that of a terrorist who believed in violence for the sake of violence. Unlike other citizens, the Kindred were fortified from mind control. They saw evil for what it was. The Authority did not tolerate dissent and pursued them relentlessly. It would never forget acts of rebellion even across eons of time and space.

The shrill sound of a train whistle broke the stillness of the night. It echoed between the mountains. He gave up trying to determine what direction the train was travelling. All he cared about was the tunnel running through the mountain directly across from his cliff. Eventually, trains would make their way along the river banks to enter from either side. He would be watching to see if it came out the other side.

CHAPTER THIRTEEN

Bears Den, VA, December 20, 1974

Inside a dark cavern deep below the surface of the Mt. Frazier, a dozen rat snakes lay entwined in a bundle of scales. In another corner of the underground lair, half a dozen copperheads bunched their bodies to maintain whatever warmth they could. Alone in the middle of the cavern, away from the dripping wet walls, was a massively coiled timber rattlesnake that maintained a low vibrating hum with its tail. Licking the air, its head swiveled constantly, ready to strike any living creature that mistakenly passed too close. Its hooded yellow eyes pulsed. It could kill, eat, and digest with little movement. Beside it lay several clumps of bones—its unfortunate victims. The timber rattlesnake was larger than nature alone could produce. Some other force had contributed to its massive size.

The snake was the length of a small boy. Its sickly patchwork of green and yellow scales shined supernaturally in the dark cavern. It used its club-like rattler in a peculiar manner that was different from normal rattlesnakes. Instead of shaking the beads as a warning threat when provoked, the creature fell silent when approached. It did not want to avoid confrontation, but sought the opportunity to sink its deadly venom into its victims. It would pursue its stricken prey to add more venom until the animal suffered paralysis.

Residing within this snake was the soul of a reincarnated human. It was the lowest level of rebirth possible. The result was a creature that possessed the deadliness of a venomous reptile plus the human capacity for blind hatred. Imprisoned within its scaly body was the soul of an angry human that entered the In-Between confused, fearful, and desperate. The result was a monster unleashed upon the earth.

A normal snake waited for the warmth of the sun to exit its winter hibernation. Only then would it begin hunting in the open air. This snake was different. Its taste for blood overruled its biology. It slithered through the jumble of rocks at the mouth of the small cave and emerged into the flinty light of a cold December day. It craved the taste of human flesh. It's tongue flicked about the frigid wind. Light snowfall covered its V-shaped crossbands.

Chapter Fourteen

Near Paris Mountain, VA, December 20, 1974

Orc could see the stone shelter nestled into the mountain at the end of a piney hollow. It was located deep enough in the national forest. Nobody knew it was there except for a few locals. All other frontier homesteads in that stretch of mountains had been condemned and forcibly vacated when the federal government decided they wanted the area depopulated. Only a few signs of human habitation remained. Orc scrambled over a crumbling stone wall that once kept free range hogs from wandering off the mountain. He passed solitary stone chimneys that stood idly in the woods. He paused to think of families that gathered round these hearths through countless long winters. Lastly, he tiptoed over small family burial sites that had not been visited for generations. His uncle blamed it on condemnation. It is a legal trick the government uses to take whatever it wants. He complained that if the rest of us tried to steal like that we'd go to jail. Orc understood intuitively that mountain people were a little too free for the government. Up here, hardy people lived off the land with nature providing their heat, food, and medicine. All of it unregulated and untaxed.

Orc saw blue smoke curling from the cabin chimney. Trash was strewn down the steep hillside. Over the front door of the stone cabin, a large deer skull peered eyeless into the forest. It was not a welcoming sight, even for Orc. He cautiously picked his way through the woods and quietly approached the cabin. Before he got within fifty yards, a voice called out to him.

"Stop there, boy. Don't come any closer."

The voice was accented with an Appalachian twang that was even stronger than his.

"Uncle Jubal. It's Ma and Aunt Sarah. They are dead. A swarm of men drove right up to the house and started firing. Then they started shooting at me. They chased me into the woods. I don't think they're following me anymore because I lost them by switching hollows." Orc breathed hard between sentences.

"Now slow down son. You say your ma is dead?"

"Yes sir. Shot down by these men that came to our house in dark SUVs, all dressed in black."

"Okay, boy. Now, just slow down and tell me again. Did you say they are following you?"

"They might be, but I swore I lost them."

"What have I told you about coming here? You know we got shit going on here that nobody needs to see," his uncle said with growing anger.

"But they killed Ma and Aunt Sarah and they started shooting at me. Where am I supposed to go?" Orc shouted back.

"You go anyplace but here, dumbass."

"If you don't want to help me, at least give me a rifle. They ain't going to get me without a fight."

"Well, the damage is done. How many were chasing you?"

"I guess it was three."

Orc sat down in the dirt and clasped his arms around his knees. His jeans were covered in burrs and his hands scratched red by briars. He was shivering from fear and cold. His uncle took pity on the boy and gave him his coat. He surveilled the woods and listened for movement. His livelihood was at stake and he needed to protect it. Plus, he wasn't going to prison again. Satisfied nobody was in immediate pursuit, Uncle Jubal casually strode into the stone shelter. Orc heard him rummaging around for something. Emerging with a rifle, he began loading as he walked toward the far end of the hollow.

"I got to look for the sons of bitches and see if they found your trail. Your mom and aunt may be gone but we are very much alive and I plan to keep it that way."

"I'm sorry I came here. I didn't know where else to go. They followed me into the woods but couldn't keep up. Why do you think they were shooting at everyone?" Orc felt like crying but stopped himself.

"This must have something to do with the Kindred. Damn their rebellion. Life is hard enough without picking a fight with the Authority," his uncle declared.

"Now that I think of it, they came right after Bret disappeared.... I don't think they're ever going to find him," Orc mumbled.

His uncle stopped in his tracks and swirled.

"What do you mean by, 'disappeared?'"

Shocked by his reaction, Orc wished he hadn't said anything.

"I have no idea what the hell happened, but Bret just vanished into thin air. Right in front of me."

"Oh shit, that is another thing altogether. They ain't going to stop until they kill everyone who can give witness to that...," Uncle Jubal's words trailed off unfinished.

Orc realized what he was saying and stood up and prepared himself for a fight.

"What can I do?"

"First things first. I got to see if they're following you. You need to keep heading south. Take this bag and stay hidden. It has lots of essentials I keep for a quick escape. Don't expose yourself to anyone. You got to move silently and swiftly," Jubal instructed.

With a wave of his hand, his uncle dismissed him.

Orc hung his head and lifted the small pack onto his back. Jubal transferred the binoculars from around his neck to Orc's. He pushed the kid off and watched him drag along the path out of the hollow.

"Use those binoculars to scan ahead of you. Now, move your ass, boy!" Jubal yelled.

He then pulled a walkie-talkie from the cargo pockets on his army pants.

"Hey Eddy, this is Jubal, we going to need to light it up. Switch it over to our secondary channel over when you're done. Big shit coming down right now and we need the diversion sooner rather than later. Over and out."

Five miles away, a similar device squawked with a burst of static. The message from Jubal Mosby was noted with the nod of a head that sported long hair that spilled out from under a grease stained truckers cap. A pair of dirty fingers clicked a confirmation response. Eddy filled a battered metal can full of gasoline and placed it under a blue canoe that jutted precariously from the open bed of a rusted pickup truck. The figure climbed into the cab and pulled his cap down over his eyes. He exited the service bay of Big Daddy's Auto and steered onto Main Street in Battletown. Just before entering Highway 17, he pulled over to pick up a lone figure waiting near the curb. A couple more miles further and the truck turned onto a rural road that wound its way down to the Shenandoah River. After several miles kicking up dust, the driver parked in a small lot adjacent to a boat launch. The two men unloaded the gas can and canoe. They placed the can inside the canoe and carried it to the riverbank. One figure entered the canoe while the other pushed him wordlessly into the fast-moving current.

The canoeist paddled toward a large island in the middle of the river and breasted the canoe on its bank. He jumped out and sloshed up the sandy beach carrying the gas can. In the middle of the small island was a massive logjam. They had watched this wood pile grow for years. He emptied half the gas can and set it inside the pyre. Without looking back, he lit a flare and threw over his shoulder. Trudging back to the canoe, he shoved off once again into the current. The canoe slipped silently downstream toward the stair-step rapids of Harpers Ferry miles downriver. The blaze crackled in the background until it exploded. Over the roar, he could faintly hear the volunteer fire sirens begin to wail in Battletown.

Emergency frequencies up and down the valley erupted into a frenzied call for assistance. Calls went out to all deputy sheriff cars in Clarke and neighboring counties. Fire stations as far away as Strasburg and Charlestown responded to the alarm. The message repeated the same information: Devil's Island was aflame. The diversion was successful and Uncle Jubal could start his hunt.

Back at the cabin, Jubal removed his fingerprints from the cooking equipment. Going against these sons of bitches meant trouble. It wasn't about making drugs anymore. This was bigger. Kin had been murdered, and relations still meant something to him. The Authority didn't want any part of his clan if they knew what was good for them. He made his money and was self-sufficient. Illegal or not, it didn't matter to him anymore. He watched in silence as the country got as corrupt as the hellholes he fought in overseas. Coming back had opened his eyes. So be it. Rich men get richer and the rest get by. He didn't like trafficking poison. While he didn't use himself, he felt nothing for the weak who did. He figured he was no different than the Authority. They made their poison too. It did not harm the strong but only the weak and ignorant. Unlike the Kindred, he had no empathy for those that were infected.

Unfortunately, they had done the one thing that he couldn't ignore. Murdered his harmless kinfolk. Even though he kept a distance from the Kindred, he knew Orc was special to them. While his little operation was illegal and by necessity covert, it didn't compare to the Kindred's organization. After all, theirs was a brotherhood that had operated in secret since 1859. Their network was tight and wrathful. He wanted to be on the right side of this battle.

He stepped outside and broke off a large juniper branch from its base. He followed Orc's trail backwards and used the bush's wiry leaves to wipe away all tracks. He worked his way to the bottom edge of the hollow where it opened to the creek. He stared intently and listened for any pursuers.

"Good boy. You must have thrown them off your track. All those years of poaching in the woods paid off," he whispered.

Jubal climbed the summit of the nearest ridge like a panther chasing a fawn. He moved silently across the ridgeline before stopping as it dropped off into the next hollow. He scanned again for pursuers. Hearing no dogs, he concluded Orc's pursuers were not local law enforcement, but probably federal agents of the Authority. He knew they despised public attention. They preferred to operate covertly. Murdering the women could be written off as a domestic abuse or something. The flaming island in the middle of the Shenandoah was an event everyone could see with their own eyes. It would take the Authority a little time to manage that spectacle. Also, the smoke and haze from the conflagration would provide temporary cover from aerial surveillance.

He made his way back to the stone shelter and sat before a short-wave radio. He clicked the mic button in a pre-arranged morse

code sequence of dots and dashes that signified danger: − · − ·   − −
· −   − · ·. He lit a Marlboro while he waited for a reply. As he
exhaled, his calloused fingers trembled slightly. This was serious.
Killing women in cold blood was not something the Authority did
every day. Sure, people showed up dead in these mountains from all
kinds of things, but this was different. The fact they were shooting at
Orc confirmed the boy had seen a transit. That explained why the
women were gunned down.

    Jubal picked his way across the dimly lit room. He bent down
in front of large green metal locker and spun the padlock. Opening it,
he pulled out a M-16 and several ammo clips. He fastened a flak vest
over his flannel shirt and coveralls. He went ahead and chambered a
round. He was securing the walkie-talkie to his ammo vest when
several clicks sounded. He responded with more of his own. They'd
done this before when local DEA agents came sniffing around. He
knew the elite squad following Orc were probably better trained and
armed. He wasn't worried. His clan had all served together in
Vietnam special forces. Coupled with their deep knowledge of the
Blue Ridge Mountains, they were a formidable force to be reckoned
with.

    Jubal knew command and control over his widely-dispersed
men would be a challenge. Communications could make them
vulnerable if they didn't have secrecy in their blood. Dating back to
Mosby's Raiders, the men of these mountains knew a thing about
subterfuge. He took one last draw of this cigarette and flicked it to the
ground. They would be running north to south along 26 miles of
ridgeline from Harpers Ferry to Linden.

    "Let's see how you fight men instead of women and children."

    He ran out of the shelter and immediately worked his way
around the hollow and straight up the ridgeline. He climbed with little
effort and no noise. His breath didn't come hard despite years of
smoking. His sinewy frame broke free onto the summit. The wind
cooled him down. He listened for any noise that it carried up to his
position.

    Like a predator, he scanned the woods below. He adjusted his
night vision googles until he saw shadows moving toward his position
silently and effortlessly. It was his two brothers and three cousins.
They came ready to fight. They knew exactly where to rendezvous and

had made good time getting there. All the men were outfitted with M-16s and had extra clips stashed in their military-grade fatigues.

"Sup brother?" Seth spit a stream of tobacco as he looked into Jubal's eyes.

There was an unspoken communication between the two hardened warriors. They had spent three tours of duty in the mountains and jungles of Indochina.

"Got some bad news. Ruth and Sarah were killed by Authority agents. They tried to kill Orc but he escaped here. He says they are following him. Sounds like his cousin, Bret, was a transit."

"Where are these agents now exactly?" his brother Clay asked.

"Not sure I know the answer to that. I reckon they must be Authority though. Judging by the description Orc gave me. The fact they couldn't catch him means they ain't from around here. They couldn't even catch a 16-year-old boy," Jubal responded.

"Or, you ain't giving him enough credit," Seth replied as he adjusted his metal sight on the rifle barrel.

"Anyhow, we think we got a pack of them coming this direction from the north and east. I suspect there are more heading this way from the south. We need to set up a little welcoming party," Jubal replied.

"What he means to say is they ain't coming out of these mountains," Seth said.

He made eye contact with each man in the small warrior unit for confirmation.

CHAPTER FIFTEEN

Harpers Ferry, WV, May 21, 2016

H is growing eagerness to explore the journals surprised DB. What seemed like a thankless boring job on the way to lunch, now gnawed at him. A begrudging fascination with the cluttered basement was taking hold of his imagination. He wondered about the authors. Who were they? What did they see? Where were they now? As he walked along its quiet sidewalks, he sensed the mystery of Harpers Ferry enveloping his consciousness. He wondered how a town that experienced so much intrigue could be tucked away in near isolation. The town was asleep but with one eye open. His perceived a subliminal pulsing through the air and from the ground. He felt like he had tripped a wire that set off sensors in some dark place and was now being watched. Beginning to see conspirators behind every door and window, DB quickened his pace.

It struck him that Harpers Ferry was a small bone shard protruding from the wasteland of modernity. This relic of the past was hastily glimpsed by travelers motoring along highway 340. A brief sight of church spires jutting above a shroud of foliage might catch the travelers eye. Like an apparition that appears for mere seconds, it quickly disappears again into the mist of time. It can't be seen from the rear-view window. The terrestrial fissure where two rivers meet three mountains closed the landscape up as quickly as it opened. Few motorists have time to contemplate its importance. Fewer still comprehend the swirling passions unleashed on its streets by a rogue band of rebels. Yet, the ghost of John Brown still stalks it shadowy alleys. DB saw the spirits wandering among the tourists. Unlike hundreds of other small river towns that quietly sank into irrelevance, DB believed Harpers Ferry was preserved as a federal mausoleum. It drew pilgrims who paid homage to an omnipotent authority. Its history was kept on display like an embalmed cadaver. Hordes of tourists come each summer to glimpse the seamier side of violence. The raid on Harpers Ferry had been reduced to a carnival freak show in wax. Its fateful actors engaged in anarchy every 20 minutes on a movie reel in a darkened theater. The bloodshed on display reminded visitors what happens when government authority is challenged. The atmosphere was lurid. For all DB knew, tourists probably thought Jack the Ripper lurked in its quiet cobblestone streets. There was no other reason to visit. After all, the town had no modern dining, shopping or entertainment franchise chains. It just offered history and scary history at that. Only a few imaginative minds conjured up the story behind the artifact. Where most observers saw a bleached fragment of bone, he saw the colossal creature moldering beneath the ground. DB relished the idea of having all this history to himself and his imagination.

Back at the storage room, he sat amid the silent journals. He imagined the wild adventures they contained. DB was convinced that among the multitude of people skirting the edge of civilized society along a 2,100-mile trail, a few must have written down phenomenal, and, heretofore, untold insights. He was looking for a hiker with the eye of a modern-day Herodotus who saw and documented strange anomalies while travelling beyond the matrix of society. After several hours of digitizing and reading, DB decided to go upstairs to the GT visitors center. He especially enjoyed scrutinizing the 3D map that displayed elevation of the trail across thirteen states. He was greeted with a friendly voice as soon as he entered the front door.

"Look who has emerged from the dismal and dank basement!" A plump man announced. It was Leo Davis the GT Deputy Director of the Friends organization.

The store was full of staff, hikers, and tourists. All of them were now staring expectedly at DB.

"It is not that bad," DB replied.

He looked around at the strange faces and became self-conscious of his dusty clothes. Hoping nobody noticed, he brushed off spider webs from his hair to the amusement of everyone. He wished he had stayed downstairs.

"Truly, I tell you, this hero of summer descends daily into Hades where hiker memories go to die," Leo continued.

The room of people became silent, captivated by DB's odyssey.

"You make it sound like a Greek tragedy," DB replied.

Nobody was laughing at the joke but himself.

"Nonetheless, let's hail our summer hero. Please give a big trail welcome to Daniel Bartholomew Cooper." Leo started clapping his hands and the assembled crowd joined the applause.

"I am nowhere near finished," DB blushed.

He was starting to get annoyed with the spectacle Leo was making of him. He wondered if there wasn't a hint of sarcasm somewhere in his speech.

"Forgotten adventures will rise like Lazarus under his gaze," Leo concluded with a wink.

"That was quite the introduction, I am not sure I will live up to it."

"Nonsense, it was your idea for the summer project. We wouldn't have even contemplated such a huge undertaking in so short a time," Leo explained.

"Well, I can't take credit for the project. I just responded to your advertisement. This wasn't my idea," DB clarified.

He tried to come across as modest but really wanted to cover his ass. He wanted Leo and everyone watching to know that the project was certainly not his idea. In the back of his mind, he didn't want to be held responsible for missing expectations of whoever devised the project.

Without excusing himself, Leo left the store front and disappeared into his back office. DB was left alone with the throng of inquiring visitors who pressed him with multiple requests for details on his methods and findings.

"So, how is your research shaping up?" One tourist inquired.

"Kinda getting my arms around it. Thinking of a strategy to do it on time and on budget," DB replied.

"You better figure it out fast. There will be another thousand journals coming in after this hiking season," said a grungy hiker munching on a chocolate candy bar.

"Oh, no worries, I am making progress, finding some very interesting entries," DB defended himself.

"I bet. Hikers can be an eccentric lot," chirped an elderly female tourist who seemed to reminisce about her past hiking exploits.

"Of course, no doubt," DB was starting to get annoyed at the attention.

"Most importantly, I would think you need to organize things first then begin converting everything to digital files," she directed.

"That's a brilliant idea," DB answered hoping his sarcasm was not as evident as Leo's.

"Move the journals offsite for better long-term storage. That would give qualified historians access to their contents for further research," a middle-aged man pontificated. His boorish manner put DB off. No wonder why the basement had become such a mess. Everyone had ideas but nobody did anything themselves.

"Just try to not to damage the originals when you handle them. They have been protected for such a long time. It would be a shame if something happened to them now," the boor said loud enough for everyone to hear. His blotchy face had a bulbous veiny nose, which DB suspected was from swilling too much free wine at the GT charity events.

Suddenly, DB realized why Leo disappeared into the back office. These people were annoying as shit.

"Sounds like everyone is an expert around here," DB muttered.

Looking for a reason to leave, DB asked a question of the group.

"Hey, I was wondering if there was coffee brewing in the back. I mean, if there isn't, I can run up to Bolivar and get some. And in that case, I would be taking orders." DB was desperate to get back to the basement and work by himself.

Before anyone could respond, Leo emerged from his office with two steaming cups of coffee. He extended his hand to DB.

"Thank you. It's time I get back downstairs. It's not the most exciting reading so far but I found some passages interesting." DB sipped the coffee and looked nervously around the gift shop collection of books.

"Do you need anything for your research?" Leo asked.

"Now that you mention it, yes. If you could recommend a good book on the history of the trail, that would be great. For example, I am little confused about what date it was built. I am not even clear where the concept of a long continuous trail came from. Stuff like that."

"Well, that would be this book right over there. I call it *the Bible*. It has the entire history of the Great Trail." Leo handed him the oversized hardcover.

"Perfect. Thank you." DB took the book and tried to hide his shock at the price tag.

"There is a 10% discount if you have a GT Friends membership. If not, we can sign you up right here."

Leo pulled out a membership form and handed DB a pen. DB blushed and admitted he wasn't. He signed the membership form then began scanning the table of contents.

It troubled him that the dates provided in the book didn't seem old enough. Certainly, there were people walking ancient paths across these mountains long before the GT concept was envisioned. DB read somewhere else that the Cherokees in the southern Appalachians had extensive trail networks. Also, he knew John Brown had envisioned a secretive path through the mountains as part of the Underground Railroad. He wondered why these earlier trails were not documented in the history book. DB thought to himself that the old geezer he met on his first day could recommend a better book. He looked around for the eccentric character but didn't see him.

"Leo, where is the really old volunteer with a long beard. He kind of looks like Rip Van Winkle and calls himself the unofficial mayor of Harpers Ferry?"

"Not sure anyone fits that description who works here. It might have been a tourist or maybe one of the many hikers that visit," Leo responded. He seemed genuinely perplexed by DB's description.

"Ok, that's strange. He certainly worked here in some capacity."

DB gave up looking for the old man who gave him the key. He tucked the book under his arm and left. Walking outside, he descended the steps, turned the corner, and approached the cellar door. Holding the hot, steaming cup of coffee, he sipped it carefully to avoid burning his mouth. The cool evening air was already relieving the oppressive heat of the day. He looked at the book cover and was mesmerized by the beautiful picture of a secluded trail winding through a green forest. The prominent GT white blaze on a large tree focused his attention. He imagined hiking into the picture and touching the bark as he passed. He wondered how many people had walked that very stretch of trail. From the GT building's position at the top of the ridge, he could see the historic river town far below him. The surrounding mountains had already cast shadows over its buildings and streets. The emerald green waters of the Potomac sparkled with phosphorus where rapids formed.

DB had worked up a thirst after finishing work for the day. He decided hitting a bar after a long day in the musty basement would be his daily reward. His favorite was the Conspirators Tavern. Locals just called it *The Hole*. It was hidden from the main street, only accessible from a small alleyway that came to an apparent dead end. From there, adventurous patrons crossed under a small stone archway to the right that lead to a wooden footbridge which presented half a dozen stone steps before abruptly ending before a black metal door. He opened it and stepped inside. There were only a few drinkers clutched around a single table. The rest of the tavern was empty.

No wonder business was slow, this place is impossible to find. DB thought to himself.

Despite its rundown state, DB saw The Hole as a sanctuary from his toils. The food was decent, fresh local draft beer flowed from the taps and, most importantly, was free of tourists or townies late at night. DB loved the tavern's palpable sense of intrigue. History breathed through its walls and he even sensed a malevolence seeping up from its floorboards. He shuddered at the thought of what crawled within its basement. The Hole was to become his second home.

While the beer was refreshing, DB needed to fortify his courage with spirits for the last leg of his walk home. It was the last couple of blocks before reaching his apartment that always spooked him. Footsteps echoed off the quiet stone walls. They seemed to follow him, especially as he crossed in front of an infamous alley. At this spot, he often heard a strange whistling. His courage would only allow furtive glances over his shoulder toward the sound, several times glimpsing what appeared to be a moving shadow where there should be none.

One night it stepped into plain view. It wasn't a shadow at all, but a middle aged black man in baggy pants and a slouch hat. His throat had a gaping slit that spurted blood with each breath. A whistling sound escaped from it as his mouth issued a silent plea. The ghost crossed the street ahead of him, spotted him, and then approached. In horror, DB watched as the man's body disintegrated within a swirl of smaller beastly shadows. They made a frightening squealing sound as they devoured the larger ghost.

He'd heard stories of slaves joining John Brown's raid only to be murdered and mutilated by local townsfolk. DB wondered if this was a ghost of someone who had been caught defenseless. If John Brown miscalculated one important consideration in planning his raid, it was the venomous reaction of the citizens of Harpers Ferry. Their response to news of the raid was swift and ferocious. Brown never saw it coming. Slaves rallying to his cause, which some accounts say numbered in the dozens, were cut down mercilessly by the enraged mob. Enveloping the raiders within minutes of church bells ringing the alarm, the locals effectively locked down the town until federal troops could arrive. Had the denizens of Harpers Ferry stayed in their beds, the raiders would have earned valuable time to free the armory of its contents, delivering the munitions, as planned to nearby mountain hiding places. DB wondered if the ghastly silent plea was a request for help or an accusation of complicity. Without realizing it, DB had opened a door that would transit him through time and space.

Chapter Sixteen

Shenandoah, VA, December 22, 1974

Zoa awoke with a sudden spasm. Her blanket of leaves exploded into the air. She had curled up in the crook of a hollow sycamore tree and fallen asleep. She passed the night fitfully, awaking to strange noises. Whenever she got close to dreaming, an aching pain from the frigid ground woke her up.

She welcomed dawn even if it was still a slow transition from black to gray. Regardless, it faced her with a realization. She needed to run to a destination not just away from Battletown. The woods offered protection during the night but daylight would bring things into sharper contrast. She would be much more visible now. She briefly weighed returning home and just living with the insults and taunts of her classmates. Like the dark woods, she could always retreat further into her social isolation. She quickly decided they wouldn't leave her alone after the spectacle at the dance. Abusing her seemed to be the only entertainment in Battletown. At least, her parents loved her unconditionally. She felt bad for them. Having a social outcast as a daughter in a small town meant they could never be anonymous. She didn't want to be their lifelong embarrassment. No, she decided, there was no going back until she figured out her life and her purpose on this earth. There had to be more than pain and suffering. She wanted something else. She dreamed of a world where she would be embraced not be ridiculed.

She trembled at the thought of what lay before her. She shivered, too, in the near-freezing December air. While she had complained about her cold loft bedroom over the garage, she now dreamed of being in her bed. Her dad tried to fix it up but couldn't afford to extend the central heating. Winter nights were spent under layers of quilts and blankets next to the small electric radiator. Even though she kept it at maximum heat, it was no match to the cold drafts sweeping through the uninsulated floor and attic. She shook the image from her mind and focused. One thing she needed for this adventure was proper clothing.

She pushed away the leaves and climbed out of the hollow tree trunk. Thick snowflakes were falling. Now was the best time for her to get moving. In the gray light, she creeped through the morning mist along the river road. She listened carefully for the sound of a car, ready to jump behind a tree at the slightest sound of a distant engine. After about a mile, she came across three old shacks perched on the riverbank. She recognized them from long drives her dad would take her on scouting for wild turkey. They had been abandoned most of her life, but recently, one cottage had been used by immigrant fieldworkers during fall harvest of a nearby farm. She checked the doors— all were locked—but she pried open a window at the rear. She climbed inside and thudded to the floor. Her muddy boots slid across the moldy linoleum floor.

It was hard to discern trash from anything of value, but she did locate a thick flannel shirt, and pairs of leather gloves. Two mismatched shoes, both a size too big, did not offer any improvement to her cowboy boots. Finally, she found a trucker's cap bearing an American eagle. She beat the dust from it and pulled her long hair through the back. She rummaged around a rusted metal kitchen cabinet for anything to eat. The last tenants left very little. Mice had eaten through most dry goods, but she did find three cans of chili. They appeared in good shape. She popped them open and ate the contents cold. She grabbed a blue canvas Walmart shopping bag and packed it with a cheap, green plastic poncho, a large piece of Tyvek she ripped off the wall, and a plastic gallon jug that she could fill with river water. She climbed back out the window and carefully replaced the screen and shutter.

She decided to head toward a remote spot between farms where she once rode during horseback riding lessons. She remembered thinking that it was the loneliest place she had ever seen. Now, that isolation was exactly what she needed. Horse trails crisscrossed the valley floor and she used these to ease her escape. It took hours, but running these lines eventually brought her to the spot she remembered from years ago. It looked much the same, but everything was a bit overgrown and even more abandoned than before.

The chains on the gates separating pastures were rusted with only the barest sign of use. Maybe some kind of farm vehicle had passed this way seasons ago, but it was an old track. She dropped her bag and considered the spot a short-term home. Nobody knew she was there but the half wild cattle huddled in the thick bush. Suddenly, her anxiety swelled again into waves and threatened to drown her under their forceful under tow. Why had she run away? Had it all been a huge mistake? Could she go back or had she just dug herself deeper into a black hole?

"Could they commit me to a psych ward for just running away? Maybe send me to a home for troubled juveniles?" she asked the cattle who stared at her while munching mouthfuls of grass. A calf who had approached her to investigate leaped away at the sound of her voice.

Just when she saw a wave of worry cresting over her head, a breeze rustled through the high branches of the sycamores. The emerging sunlight dappled the rivulets in the stream nearby. The sound was soothing and familiar. It was almost like the trees were speaking to her. She could hear them say, *calm down, be in the moment, there is nothing of this world you need to fear. All is in place and you only must find your place.*

She tried to gather her thoughts, which were scattered about like debris from a shipwreck at sea. She was suddenly floundering in the water, sometimes at the surface and sometimes underneath. She saw images of her life floating around her. Memories from her childhood, adolescence, painful looks of her parents and the ugly faces of her tormentors were suspended on the surface. She looked around as she struggled to tread water. There was a distant shore in one direction and an expanding sea in the other. Far from offering safe buoyancy, these objects threatened to cling to her and dragged her to the dark depths. To escape them, she swam below the surface and watched as they floated in the current above. Losing breath, she came up for air only to have the memory flotsam come rushing toward her again. Finally, she forcefully pushed them back and swam away from the shore toward open water. Eventually, all the debris of her life ceased to follow her and floated away in the opposite direction. She found herself suspended in the water with no sensation of up or down neither drowning nor struggling. There was no anxiety or fear just peace. She saw a dazzling white light that beckoned her from the black depths below. Its brightness awoke her from the daydream. She must have fainted onto the ground. Opening her eyes, she found herself staring into the reflection of the noonday sun off the plastic jug of water.

Sitting up, she leaned her back against the base of a giant oak tree. She was alone in the wild spot of her childhood not adrift at sea. Zoa felt contentment for the first time she could remember.

"I am on the right path," she admitted.

The cows stopped grazing and looked up at her. The small, curious calf haltingly approached again. Zoa smiled and cried a tear of joy. She was determined more than ever not to quit but to see this quest through. She wrapped the Tyvek around her and lay on the poncho. The flannel shirt warmed her and she could smell the sweat of the laborer who wore it last. As she dozed off, she dreamed of the handsome young man she saw in another dream reaching out to her from inside a vortex.

Chapter Seventeen

Loudon Heights, December 21, 1974

O nce a transit slips through the net of the Authority, it is beyond further monitoring. Los wanted his Tibetan friend to confirm that his mission would be just as invisible. By assaulting the Kindred family, the Authority had forced Los' hand. He wasn't sure how long he could wait for the monk. His mission had to start if the rumor about Enith was true. Lord Jim certainly believed it could be her. He said the second woman's identity would be confirmed within hours. Her soul could be approaching the gates of oblivion even now. She never shared his beliefs in reincarnation and would certainly be confused and afraid to find her body less soul wandering the In-Between. As he hiked through the night back to the farmhouse, he heard a voice calling out for him. He saw her in the glare of his headlamps pacing next to him. She was lost and calling his name. Was he hallucinating? He switched off his lamp. The image was gone. It must have just been a trick of the light.

He started hiking again. After a dozen footsteps, his mind went into a trance again. He was now hiking across the darkened plain of the In-Between. He was searching for her. Years studying and preparing for this moment prepared him for the journey. He knew what to expect. His greatest fears would assault him in the form of countless wrathful deities. He knew they were just images of his own creation, emerging from deep within his consciousness. They would not divert him from the mission. The Kindred had chosen him for exactly for this reason. He was truly a warrior soul. For added protection, Los called in a favor from his friend. The monk had agreed to come and conduct the Tibetan prayer for the dying. He wondered if his friend could detect his search for Enith? If so, would he keep his secret?

Los looked up into the starry night and smiled. They used to look at the same sky and plan for a life of adventures and romance.

He felt elation at the thought of seeing her again. A decision would have to be made soon. He could not wait anymore if Enith had crossed over. Time was of the essence. He felt no fear of death nor what lay beyond. Besides, he would not be alone. The monk would be watching his back.

His old friend was completing a long journey across mountains and cultures to be his spiritual guide. From the snow-covered peaks of Tibet to the forested mountains of the Alleghenies, Los would receive his instructional prayers on how to navigate the In-Between.

They had met years ago, before Enith, when he was trekking ancient Tibetan trails and stumbled upon a small monastery. A young monk befriended Los and began instructing him on Tibetan Buddhism. The new friendship became a lasting bond between the monk and convert. While their lifestyles were different in many ways, they bonded in their belief in reincarnation. When the time came for Los to leave, oaths of eternal friendship were taken. If ever called upon, they would come to each other's aid. If the monk needed sanctuary away from his troubled homeland, Los would arrange his passage to Virginia. If Los needed spiritual support in his fight against the Authority, the monk would answer his call.

Reunited once again, the two would comprise an unusual team conducting a raid unlike any before in history. Los had volunteered to destroy an essential part of the Authority's net where the physical and spiritual worlds were woven together. Here, the Authority's surveillance system was weakest. In this twilight world between dimensions he could look for her.

Los was aware that Buddhist belief limited passage through the In-Between to just 42 days. After that period, the soul would be forced to reincarnate. The trick was to find the best reincarnation possible in that short time. Each passing day exposed the wandering soul to howling, fang toothed, blood drinking, monsters. These wrathful deities confronted each soul with their own worst fears. Many souls fled in terror into the darkest depths of the In-Between. As they were pursued further and further away from awareness of their state of existence, they diminished their chances of a positive reincarnation. The longer a soul spent wandering, the more it risked suffering an eternity of pain and grief. Those spirits reincarnating into higher forms contribute to the elevation of all human society in the next life. Adversely, confused and fearful souls become so desperate to reincarnate that they choose entities in descending levels of ignorance. The Kindred suspected the Authority was manipulating this experience so that successive generations possess diminished capacity for awareness. Each new reincarnated generation being more ignorant than the last. Eventually, the citizenry would evolve beyond a point of no return. The Kindred had to guide slaves out of this bondage before it was too late. Certainly, the In-Between was no place to linger but that was exactly what Los planned to do. He was getting ahead of himself. That journey was ahead. Tonight, Los had to focus on surveillance.

CHAPTER EIGHTEEN

Harpers Ferry, WV, June 1, 2016

Sinking to his knees, DB picked up the one of many books that he was to handle that summer. He decided to start at the beginning— 1973—with a journal stored adjacent to the rear wall of the basement. Not surprisingly, 1973 journals were in the worst state of disintegration. The crusted cover made a crackling sound as DB opened it. He wiped away dust and turned the first page.

As DB read dozens and dozens of journals, he became intrigued with specific hiker trail names. These characters appeared different than the others. He could not explain their entries. It became obvious and undeniable that they were involved in much more than hiking a long-distance trail. They appeared to be co-conspirators in an intricate plot of some kind. He could not place it exactly. Every time he thought he figured out what they were doing, it led to an unbelievable conclusion. DB believed he had discovered activities that were leading him into a sinister world. He changed his mind again about the entries. They were not telling a story but revealing the communications of a cult. Or something like a cult. He did not know what else to call it. A secretive group of people communicating, plotting, fighting, and dying over generations. Everything he thought he knew about the nearby mountains, the GT, American history and its politics was turned upside down. He skipped ahead years to follow one author. It confirmed the incredible. Each journal entry by Lost Mungo across forty years wove a family record of members of this cult. He still could not describe their association to each other. He decided they were not a cult, but more like a tribe or, more accurately, a clan. These people traced their common lineage even if it was not a blood line to a single person. They were more like descendants of an event. Except this event was at once a historic occurrence and a continuous way of life. It was as if they were united in the bloodshed of a cause that endured for decades.

DB kept digitizing the journals but also transcribing his own notes of names, places, and events of this underground group. He began to live vicariously through their cloak-and-dagger existence. DB imagined he was hiking besides them under the moonlight between distant shelters along lonely mountain ridges in the stark winter months. DB was as tough and lean in his imagination as Lost Mungo. He even stopped shaving to resemble these mysterious mountain men. As he lay in bed at night, if he listened carefully, he could make out shouts from these rebels. Their voices cascaded down from the mountain ridges and echoed through the cobblestone streets of sleepy Harpers Ferry. Lyn said it was just the wind stirring the leaves high up in the trees and the rest was his imagination. DB wondered if such warriors carried forth that force into the next spiritual life. After falling asleep, DB dreamed of countless souls leaching from the earth with each rainfall. Their spiritual plasma mingled with small streams before emptying into the winding Shenandoah and Potomac Rivers. The geologic confinement of Harpers Ferry received this tearful deluge. It flowed into a vortex of anguish whose mists swirl up over the riverbanks, eventually climbing up the Maryland and Virginia Heights. It didn't crest the ridgeline but seeped back into the hole gouged out by two rivers over a millennium and filled up the dreams of permeable minds like DB's. Emerging from the mists were the ghosts who had not yet crossed over.

DB awoke in a cold sweat. He was not sure if he had had a nightmare or a vision. His hand hurt as if it was punctured. He turned on the light on the bed stand to see what was causing him pain. In his sleep, he had gripped the cellar door tightly to keep an army of ghost from attacking him. Awake, he opened his tightened fist to reveal the iron key. Blood now flowed from the cut in his palm. Quietly, he went to the bathroom to get a Band-Aid. He suppressed a curse when he saw blood had stained the bedsheet. Lyn would not be happy since she just bought this new set to complete their bedroom decorations. He made a mental note to clean it with bleach in the morning. She didn't need to know about his strange dream, his self-inflicted wound, or the bloodied sheet. They would all be his secrets.

CHAPTER NINETEEN

Washington DC, December 21, 1974

The military helicopter had barely touched down on the roof of the Headquarters for Safety building when a bent figure sprinted to its open door. Within seconds of the figure jumping in, it lifted off and veered westward. Grabbing the handholds on either side of the door, Urizen leaned out into space. From below, he looked every inch his nickname: The Lord of Death. Clenching his teeth with rage, he screamed at the crewman behind him.

"Give me a gun, now!"

"Yes, sir!" There was a flourish of activity that produced an M-16 rifle.

"Six clips of ammo, and get me some night vision goggles!" His hands quickly checking the gun's functions.

"Yes sir!" shouted the crewman again. This time he fumbled with the clips and dropped one onto the steel plated floor. It quickly slid across the deck before flying out the door and disappearing into the dusk. The crewman froze in pure terror and slowly raised his eyes to meet the Deputy Director's glare.

"Go get that clip, soldier."

"Sir, get the clip? It fell out the door. How am I to get it?"

"Come here son." He said with a more subdued tone. The pilot and co-pilot looked at each other and grimaced. The young soldier grasped the interior netting and walked toward Urizen, careful not to let go of one handhold before grasping another. When he was face to face, he stuttered in defense.

"Sir, there are plenty of ammo clips onboard. Can I retrieve one from stowage, sir?"

"You can retrieve the one that went out the door."

"Sir, I don't understand." He started to shake before the withering gaze of pure malevolence.

"Let go of that netting soldier." Urizen stated softly and calmly.

"Yes, sir. But we do have extra clips on board."

"I don't want extra clips. I want the one that went out the door. And you are going to get it for me. I am going to teach you a lesson in discipline."

With a flash of his arm, he grasped the soldier by his uniform collar. With his immense power, a simple jerk was all that Urizen needed to hurl the soldier out of the helicopter. His screams descended with his body as he plunged toward the earth. The remaining crew cringed but silently kept about their business. Both the pilot and co-pilot exchanged glances but returned their stares toward the instrumentation panel before them.

"The lesson in discipline was not for him but you and everyone else under my command. I don't tolerate incompetence. In fact, if you don't get me to the drop zone by dark, you'll not be happy with my lesson in improving your piloting skills."

He pounded each magazine clip against the inside of the metal helicopter flight deck to ensure it was fully loaded and aligned, placing each tested clip into an ammo vest harnessed securely to his torso.

"Incompetence is weakness of the mind. We can't run a nation on weakness," he said.

The crew and soldiers avoided eye contact with each other. He thought to himself that only strength could exist at his level for government to work effectively. After all, he advanced his way up the organization, or more accurately, terrorized his way to the top. His process was simple: Find weakness in successive levels of management and throw the weak out of their positions by sheer intimidation. His management mantra was succinct: targeted brutality on weaker individuals. Not only did it remove the person he wanted to replace but it terrorized into submission others who decided not to risk their own jobs or lives for a fellow employee. Quickly, Urizen rose to the top of the Authority. He strengthened its power over decades. He applied his targeted brutality to a nation of citizens in every segment of society. A few deaths went far in controlling the narrative of society, including its history and current affairs. With such tactics, Urizen enslaved everyone on a virtual plantation, without the need for chains.

Occasionally, a slave escaped. He would respond by unleashing his hounds, tracking them down, and destroying them. Urizen was about to target this brutality against the witnesses of today's transit. For good measure, he would terrorize an ever-widening circle of Battletown citizens. It wasn't often he took to the field to get involved in operations, but he had a feeling about this cluster of transits. Something was happening in the Northern Valley and he needed to deal with it firsthand. He sensed something emerging. It was a new powerful force coiling to strike at the Authority.

As the helicopter touched down onto the front yard of the rural farmhouse, he leapt to the ground. Without breaking stride, he approached a group of black-clad forces milling near two corpses.

"Is this all you can accomplish? Killing two unarmed women?" Urizen glared at the elite squad of assassins.

"Sir, something strange happened out there." The squad leader motioned toward the forest.

"Besides two children escaping a quick reaction force?"

"Sir, we found two of our squad dead of…" his voice trailed off.

"It's bad enough that they are dead. I really don't care how they died, you idiot."

"But, sir, they appeared to die from snake bites to the neck and face. It appears the jugular was even targeted." The squad leader unconsciously raised his hand to his throat in fear.

"Are you saying we are dealing with snake boys?" Urizen laughed in his face.

"Sir, I am just saying that they died terrible deaths without firing any shots."

"So, we are to give up the because of some snakes in the woods. My God, the Authority should just collapse for lack of anti-venom?"

The leader of the squad looked at his watch and then chambered his gun. He scanned the faces of his men and summoned the courage to explain himself.

"Sir, I just want to be clear that all units going into action should be advised that boys are not our only enemy in those woods."

"You better be on the lookout for me. Being bitten on the ass by a snake is preferable to how you'd die at my hands. Do I make myself understood?" Urizen glared around at all the men standing before him."

"Yes, sir. Understood, sir."

The Lord of Death gazed toward the setting sun that bled across the western sky. He started the timer on his watch.

"I will personally lead a squad in search of the escapees. They have a couple of hours lead but that is of no matter. I want them tracked down within 60 minutes or else. This is a search and destroy mission. My rules of engagement are simple. You are authorized to kill anyone in those mountains. Do I make myself clear? You are authorized to kill anyone who crosses your path, and that includes snake people."

The gathered men silently nodded their understanding.

"Now, take me to the operation site. I want as much intel as possible."

"Sir, we will drive you to where the trail went cold."

An SUV pulled up and Urizen sat down in the passenger seat. The driver was clearly frightened by who was riding shotgun. He accelerated out of the front yard, sped down the drive and squealed the tires onto the road.

CHAPTER TWENTY

At a confluence of two trails, Los left the white-blazed trail and turned down the blue-blazed way. A small wooden sign read, *Dark Hollow Shelter .4 miles.* He followed the side trail until he saw the shelter looming before him as a shadow darker than the night. As he approached, his headlamp illuminated its three-sided frame and cast its glow into its open-faced interior. He immediately spied something unusual. A warning sign posted on the front of the shelter caught his eye.

"*WARNING, an extremely large timber rattlesnake has been sighted on this section of trail. Several hikers have reported its very aggressive behavior. Give this creature an extremely wide berth as it has been known to pursue hikers.*"

Los nodded his head and put the warning in context with what he was about to do. A pissed off rattlesnake was probably not something he wanted to cross just hours from his mission. Taking note of the warning, Los climbed the steps into the shelter and scanned its interior for movement. Most importantly, he listened carefully for the telltale rattle. Hearing and seeing nothing suspicious, he walked through leaves scattered across the wooden floor. He grabbed a broom standing in the corner and immediately swept a circle around his feet. To his relief, no snake lurked below. He began slowly and carefully sweeping the entire wooden shelter, making sure to keep the broom head a safe distance away. He hoped the snake wasn't as big as described in the posted warning. The cleaning was necessary but didn't reveal anything but a mouse nest. That was a good sign. Snakes eat mice and this place had mice. Thrusting with the broom, he inspected every inch of the floor where it met the shelter wall carefully for holes. He also checked the rafters above. Satisfied, the snake was somewhere out in the woods and not in the shelter he got down to business. He reached up to a shelf mounted on the interior wall. Here, stacked upright inside a small box, he retrieved a battered spiral notebook. It was a trail log that visitors to the shelter signed and dated. Some hikers who felt inspired left a left a more descriptive statement. Functionally, these trail logs served as an essential method of communication for long distant hikers traversing the 2,100-mile Great Trail. One could leave messages of importance to those behind or coming the other way. These messages were nourishment to isolated, tired, and lonely hikers.

Los removed his gloves and took the pen out of the spiral notebook and wrote:

> *"To Wobbly: Come to the old stone farmhouse. It is starting. You know the way. Where State Maintenance Ends!* ☺ *Be safe. See ya soon. Los."*

Los closed the notebook, replaced the pen, and restored it to the shelf. He knew Wobbly would see his message and follow his instructions.

As the crow flies, the old stone farmhouse was only about nine miles away. Following Kindred security rules, Wobbly would need most of the day to reach it. The closer he got to the HQ location, the more surreptitious his route would become. First, Wobbly would stick to character as a thru-hiker whenever in public. Second, he would search for cover and follow secret paths to close the last couple of miles. The locals at Raven Rocks were accustomed to seeing dirty, bedraggled figures loitering around the parking lot at the crest of the mountain gap. These characters were often seen ambling across the divided highway burdened with heavy packs. Sometimes, they stuck out their thumbs to hitch into town. Los knew a ride would be offered to Wobbly eventually despite his appearance. He might only have to wait an hour for a driver brave enough to stop his car and pick up the chubby, flannel clad, fuzzy red head.

Wobbly would first need to hike the 3.7 miles from the shelter down the trail to the highway. The free ride from Snickers Gap into Battletown was about six miles. From Main Street, Wobbly would hike along the railroad tracks for about three miles until he saw the old stone chapel. He would descend from the tracks and walk past the deserted house of worship. A sign noted its historical significance as a place where Lord Fairfax occasionally attended services. The cemetery behind the chapel held graves of generations of Virginians. Among the tombstones, engraved dates marked the lives of colonial pioneers to fallen defenders of the Confederacy. From there, Wobbly would go under the train trestle and follow a country lane until it abruptly turned to gravel. At its terminus, a Virginia Department of Transportation sign notified the traveler that its authority had reached a boundary with the declaration: *End State Maintenance*. A rock-strewn dirt drive began under private ownership. Passing a stone barn after a couple steps, Wobbly would see a two-story stone farmhouse built in 1891. He would receive his orders once inside. He committed the route to memory.

Los left the shelter and went into the darkness. He headed back to the main trail, following the cone of light from his head lamp. As he walked, he thought to himself about the types of hikers on the trial. There were three kinds: the lost, the seekers, and the guides. It had taken him years to discover that there were different types of trails as well. Try as he might, he could never transit to the Golden Path. Not while living anyway. In death, he might be able to see it.

CHAPTER TWENTY-ONE

Bluemont, VA, December 22, 1974

W obbly slung his backpack into the Adirondack shelter and stepped out of the rain. The sudden loss of the heavy pack threw him off balance. He swayed too far in compensation and had to steady himself against the shelter to keep from falling. Befitting his trail name, Wobbly struggled in many ways to right himself. He was soaked through. His many layers of clothing were dripping wet; the outer layer from rain and the inner from sweat. The breathable rain gear probably worked well under normal circumstances, but humping up 2,000 feet in less than two miles with a full pack left him drenched from exertion. He stripped off the rain shell and carefully removed his boots so as not to tramp mud all over the floor. The dampness of his clothes immediately chilled him in the 31-degree ambient atmosphere. He was always shocked how fast hyperthermia set in. Stopping for a couple of seconds meant his core could no longer maintain enough heat to negate the wet clothing. The ambient temperature now assaulted his wet clothes. He quickly changed clothing and started to warm back up.

Snickers Gap was still 3.7 miles away, but he was too tired to hike any further. He decided to spend the night and be glad for its basic protections. Even though these shelters were bare bones and open on one side, he appreciated the strong walls. It was hard to get a good night's sleep in a tent when the wind ripped through the forests. At least the shelter offered some protection against falling trees. Most importantly, the shelter had a roof to keep him dry when it rained. A simple pleasure people often overlooked, he thought, is dry clothes. Maybe he could manage a fire in the fire pit out front if he had the energy to find dry kindling. He loved the sense of security a fire produced out in the dark, scary woods.

Wobbly assessed his home for the night. First, he took note of a strange warning about a rattlesnake. This was something he had never seen before. He thought the information bizarre. Trying to picture the actions of an aggressive rattlesnake, he shook his head in confusion. Snakes don't chase people. The warning made no sense. Second, he started cleaning the communal, but empty, shelter. He spied around for the broom and swept up old debris and any dirt he tracked in. Next, he laid out his gear and prioritized which clothes to dry. From the bottom of his pack, he tugged free his food bag and cook kit. It would be dark soon. He scavenged through his messy pack, found his headlamp, and secured it on his forehead. He struck a match and lit a fuel tab that he then placed within his unfolded metal stove. He placed a titanium cup half-full of water on the growing flame and dropped in a sachet of green tea. Waiting for the water to boil, he had time to do some real work.

He looked around for the trail journal. It was stuffed into a cupboard hanging from the wall. He reached for the notebook and opened it to the last few pages of entries. He scanned the lettering for signs of a coded message.

"Los, my man!" Wobbly yelled aloud to the eerily silent eight-person shelter. His voice echoed back from the mist-shrouded woods.

"Oh man, warm fire and cold beer here I come," he said.

He duly scrawled a symbol indicating his acknowledgement of the message. He thought about copying the message and decided against it. If he was stopped by the Authority, any correspondence on his possession would be thoroughly scrutinized. His memory was not very good, neither short nor long term. He read the instructions three more times before closing the trail journal. He knew Los had taken a great chance in leaving that message. Even in remote places like Dark Hollow Shelter, the Authority had its spies. They searched constantly for people like Los and Lord Jim. They might pose as thru-hikers, but their general cleanliness and military bearing always gave them away.

Wobbly lived between trail shelters and trail towns. Unlike other long distance hikers whose objectives were to hike the trail from end to end, his was to be part of the trail community continuously. His hike had no end. His mission was to carry information, educate, recruit, and organize, but most importantly, earn money for the Kindred. His contribution to the cause, however limited, was selling weed to whoever would buy it. His supply was from deep in the national forests where select parcels of wilderness were secretly cultivated. He kept enough money to maintain body and soul and dropped the rest at designated locations where money transactions were hard to trace.

In addition to financially supporting the Kindred, he was a defunct member of the Wobblies, an outlawed union known for its radicalized approach to civil disobedience. Decades ago, his father was one of its most fiery leaders. His grandfather had been a member of the International Workers Union back in the 20s and Wobbly took his trail name in his honor. Talk about roughing it. Those guys travelled the rails relentlessly to confront mine owners wherever wages and safety conditions were being challenged. Those radicals battled cops and union busters, before fleeing arrest and disappearing back into the wild.

Although the Wobblies were still active, it had become a shadow of its former self. No longer did it fight with police and company thugs in open warfare. Over time, a coordinated assault on the rebel union left their numbers decimated and the rugged lifestyle drove away many who were still active. No longer did they ride the rails and hitchhike across the country as they did during the first Great Depression.

As the union's rogue actions disappeared into memory, Wobbly heard from fellow trekkers of another secret organization. It started with whispered rumors in remote shelters. Someone told stories to another who passed them on again about a strange traveler on the trail. Eventually, more details emerged and finally he had an actual first hand contact. He was invited to attend a clandestine meeting of this underground organization.

What he saw blew his mind. He couldn't fathom its incongruity. It went against everything he knew of history and physics. First, there were the Kindred who traced their lineage from survivors of John Brown's raid on Harpers Ferry. A long line of descendants fought to protect individual rights enshrined in the U.S. Constitution. Next, he learned of travelers along the golden path. They were a mystic group who allegedly could transit back and forth into a different dimension. He understood this group less. Certainly, he had never met any of them, at least, that he knew. He just heard about their abilities. He couldn't get his mind wrapped around it. How could someone transport his or her mind, body, and soul into another dimension? Lastly, he was given a vague description of Wrathful Empathies. They were neither Kindred nor Line Walkers, but transformational entities that existed nowhere yet everywhere.

His personal experience was limited to the Kindred. He joined them in the dark of night. It was a fateful decision. The life he now lived was dirty, dangerous, and deprived of most human comforts. There were no love interests and that troubled him. What woman would put up with this lifestyle? He felt like a priest, but without the benefits of a warm bed and free dinners. His contribution was strictly financial. He sold weed and turned over all profits. At times, he thought of quitting but always came back to the reason he joined in the first place: The Authority was growing stronger in its grasp and control of human existence. There was no escaping it by pretending it didn't matter. Someone had to fight back and he felt compelled to carry on his family tradition of speaking truth to power and taking direct action.

His first formal meeting of the Kindred was held near the summit of the Iron Mountains in the Virginia Highlands. The group gathered in a bald, at the base of huge boulders that protected them from view. As an added precaution, men with shotguns stood watch, strategically surrounding the small audience atop the natural cairn. A stern man dressed in black lead the meeting. He preached a message of empathy, self-introspection, and, most importantly, awakening from the lies of the Authority. His followers were not concerned about their next meal, but their next life. The Wobblies had fought for improved conditions in this world while the Kindred fought for the same in the next.

Strict adherence to these secrecy protocols was a matter of life and death. Even the trail journals were subject to surveillance. The Kindred suspected that the battered and mouse eaten trail books from hundreds of shelters strewn across 13 states were being read on some basis. To be sure, not even the most isolated GT shelter was free from surveillance. Even more reason to maintain the pretense of living and talking like hiker trash. The lifestyle came naturally to Wobbly.

He was always on guard for anyone asking too many questions and others casting strange looks. He didn't let the paranoia ruin his time on the trail. There were more good people than bad hiking the GT. He travelled constantly, linking up one trail system with another. By switching between the GT and other mountain trail systems each season, he kept his network growing and made it harder for the Authority to set traps. If he were being monitored, through journal entries or reports of drug dealing, he wouldn't be in the same place again for several years.

He shuffled toward the edge of the shelter and kneeled to shovel the scattered trail gear into his pack. A passerby would only see clutter and mud-splattered rags. He was a bit ashamed to admit that this apparent trash was all he possessed. The thought of his poverty only bothered him when he saw it in the harsh light of a headlight. He admitted to himself it looked somewhat miserable.

Dawn was about to break and he wanted to be on the trail before any day hikers or trail runners came by. He would sleep later. He cleared the shelter of any evidence that he had spent the night and lifted his pack onto his shoulders. The feeling of the straps was all too familiar and signified it was time to hike out. One last glance at the shelter left him amazed that the Authority didn't close these things down. Surely, they wanted to maintain appearances of normalcy, but they must not have realized how much the trail system benefited their enemies.

The hiking that morning was easy since it was all downhill. He began to hear the rush of engines and knew he was close to the road. He took a cloth banner from his pocket and opened it up. It read, *To town*. Hitching was not as easy as it used to be, but rural back roads and byways had a greater than average number of cool people driving them. Within minutes, a pick-up pulled off and he climbed in the back.

"Battletown?" he indicated by pointing west down the road.

"I can drop you off at the edge of town," came the reply.

The driver was a bleary-eyed worker returning from a midnight shift in Washington DC.

Within minutes, wind was ripping through his hair as his ride sped down the mountain pass.

CHAPTER TWENTY-TWO

L os held back before descending the river bank. He was afraid to
leave the protection of the forest. Deer could not have been more
cautious in approaching the water's edge. He had chosen a
secluded but wide stretch of the Shenandoah to wade across. The
Authority was ever vigilant, using all manners of surveillance ranging
from the most sophisticated technology to human intelligence. What
frightened Los the most were human informants posing as a friend, or,
in his case, a neighbor.

Posted yellow signs declared the very edge of the riverbank
private property and strictly forbade trespassing. Los lamented the fact
that the universe had succumbed to this but invaded anyway. He
visualized the land squared, measured, parsed, and tallied precisely into
place. Not a square foot of land had been left unaccounted for even
the land where he stood. Standing behind a sycamore, he scanned the
deserted sandy banks of the Shenandoah River. All land was held as
property by someone, their ownership documented on a piece of paper
filed away on a dusty shelf. As he owned no property, he was in a
constant state of trespass. Just walking across the land made him a
criminal. He realized it was only a matter of time before human
thought was similarly seized. Why should individuals expect to possess
freedom of intellect separate from property rights? This is what he
was fighting against.

As he crept toward the bank, the trees bordering the river
became increasingly dense. Securely placing his boot before each step,
he traversed the last yards near the river bank. Before reaching the
river, he came across a small stream running perpendicular to the river.
It tumbled down the ridge behind him joyfully careening its way
through a briar patch. Splashing into white froth as it jumped past
rocks daring to block its way to the river. He found the sight
reassuring and hopeful. If water flows to the ocean following a course
ordained by gravity, regardless of property rights, what force could
hinder human consciousness from seeking truth? But Los knew of

one: The Authority. It was attempting to gather souls in its net before they could fold into the greater consciousness. He just had to figure out how exactly they planned to do it.

Punching his staff through the ice at the edge of the water, Los waded into the river. He set a course along a line of submerged stones less than two feet under water. The invisible bridge ran the width of the river from bank to bank. As the current pushed against him, he adjusted his staff downstream to brace against the force. A numbing coldness crept up his legs. He carefully searched for his foot placement among the slippery, submerged stones. He traversed slowly but surely, pushing off each step only after securing his next.

Whenever he strode upon this natural bridge, it reminded him of the spine of a giant serpent. He feared his footsteps might awaken the creature from its slumber deep within the earth. One day it would surely wreak havoc and hopefully his boot would not be the cause. But that was a silly thought when so many real dangers were all around him.

Finally, he approached the opposite bank before losing ability to walk due to the numbness of his feet. He emerged from the ice-cold water with barely a splash. He ascended the incline and plunged into the forest, confronting a dirt road that paralleled the coiled river. Again, more posted signs forbid his presence. Stay hidden, he thought, seek cover. A farmer might see him from his tractor crossing a field or his wife hanging laundry in the backyard. They did not support the Authority but feared it. If terrorists were found to be crossing their land, it could be seized through condemnation. Surely, if seen, his violation of this invisible property line would be reported. Woods offered the best cover but did not reach all the way to the stone farmhouse. This meant he would take more time to navigate. Instead, he traversed the rural landscape. It was a patchwork of cultivated fields, animal pastures, and woods. The farmland was sculpted smooth and cleared of debris primed for planting. By contrast, the expansive and desolate animal pastures followed a wilder contour. It was punctuated by rocks and scattered with massive oak trees. Kindred instructions came instinctively to mind. *All fields should be crossed only if necessary and then as quickly as possible. Observation is key. Wait for the enemy to show himself. If something seems out of place—a noise, smell, or movement — react with silence and stillness.*

He approached a rural road. He stopped to listen for cars. He looked both ways before stepping into sight. As he crossed the width of the road, he sensed something just out of sight. To his left, dark shadows emerged from the dense foliage and crossed the road in tandem. He froze out of fear at the spectacle. No matter how many times he had witnessed these apparitions, it always took his breath away. Three huddled figures, opaque but shimmering from an interior light, emerged from the brush. With trepidation, they ventured onto the road, carrying bundles in their arms. All three cocked their heads at a sound, but it was not coming from his direction. He heard it too: the bark of hounds, hooves of horses, and yells of slave catchers echoed from a distant space and time. He knew their plight and it pained him. These lost souls still travelled the Underground Railroad in search of freedom. Never reaching their destination in life, they would pursue it for eternity. There was nothing he could do for them now. They could not see nor hear him. In fact, they did not exist in any sense other than psychic scars imprinted on the land. At one time, runaway slaves escaped along this road. Their emotional trauma imprinted like the tracks of a person. There was nothing to be done to free these visions. They were faint traces of the human experience. Like a falling star in the dark night sky, they traced faintly behind the movement of a soul. Los adjusted his pack and slipped through a narrow opening between two fence posts. He set eyes upon the light of a distant farmhouse. With a look of grim determination, he began the final trek across the last mile of pastureland.

He was on his way to tell Lord Jim the intelligence reports were accurate. There was a disappearing train, which meant there was a hidden tunnel. Whatever was happening inside the Maryland Heights, it must be extremely important due to its secrecy. As leader of the Kindred, Los would need his approval for the 49-day transit into the spirit realm. As the leader of the Kindred, Lord Jim had lived in hiding for decades. Age had begun to slow him down. While his toughness was legendary, he now preferred a roof to sleeping under the stars and a hearth to a campfire. He found the last winter in the wild as cold as a tomb. It nearly killed him. While his zeal to lead burned brightly, the fierce winter winds were more than he could bare.

Los knew his way to the Kindred farmhouse even in the dark of night. Over three more pastures and just as many barbed wire fences was an old stone farmhouse. Los could see the warm glow of the windows now only half a mile away. He had one last rocky pasture to cross before reaching the farmyard. He crouched to his knees to look in all directions. Catching a lone rebel would be good for the Authority, but Lord Jim was a greater prize. A single barbed wired fence was now his last barrier to cross. He rose and advanced toward a small wooden shed that straddled the fence line. Open to the pasture on the eastern side, a rusted chain was all that held a metal gate closed to its interior. Once inside, he crossed a small animal pen. Los passed through the manger part of the shed into a small storage room. A final door exited into the farmyard. Its weathered wood hung from leather hinges.

Transiting this final passage required spinning a small piece of wood that was secured to the door with a single rusty nail. He always marveled at the mystery of this simple fabrication. It would take only a slight brush to shift its position and open the door. Los laughed at the simplicity of the device. The flimsy contraption made him laugh. *If the cows only knew how easily they could affect release from their domesticated existence.*

He spun the wooden dial and pushed open the door. From the other side, he spun the wooden block back in place. As he crossed the lawn, he looked back to make sure the door stayed closed. As he climbed the stairs to the front porch, Los looked inside the small living room window. He saw a black bearded barrel chested man sitting before the fire. A shadow emerged from the corner of the porch. A shotgun barrel was leveled at his chest.

"Were you seen?" a whispered voice asked.

CHAPTER TWENTY-THREE

Bret roused from his sleep but didn't want to leave the warm shelter. He was content to stare up through its hole in the ceiling. Blue sky stretched beyond the twig woven opening. He glanced over at young Tom. To his surprise the boy appeared to have aged 10 years during the night. Bret shook his head and rubbed his eyes. He looked again, this time studying the boy's face. Yes, Tom now appeared a teen ager.

"This is crazy. Yesterday, I walked a path that exists along its own invisible contours. I talked to the ghost of a Native American. I ate dinner from a magical chuck wagon pulled by Himalayan yaks. At night, the entire path turned blue and I slept in a Wickiup that sprang up from a bundle of twigs. Perfectly normal," Bret laughed.

Crawling out into the morning sun, he stepped onto the grassy path. It ran in a straight line as far as he could see in both directions. Only the path was visible, nothing else. It existed in its own golden-hued tunnel of foliage on either side. A big sky arched overhead. Sun, clouds, stars, and moon passed by above disconnected from the narrow path. Bret realized he was in a world within a world. It was set apart and left behind.

"Why can't someone age ten years overnight?" he asked several pilgrim travelers passing by.

This made him wonder about how long he had been sleeping. Was it just one night or had ten years passed? Tom emerged into the morning light. He stood almost six feet tall. Both young men studied the other.

"Another day on the trail," Tom stated.

"Yes, I have to decide what do with myself. Do I stay here or start hiking?" Bret replied. "Why are we here?" Bret asked.

"Why indeed! I have unfinished business that requires me to transit."

"Transit? That's a weird word," Bret replied.

"How else would you describe it?"

"Transit sounds like I purposely travelled here. In fact, I have no idea what happened."

"Give yourself more credit. You are the vessel within which you travel. Don't forget you have a mind that can transport you anywhere you want to go."

Bret looked at Tom very carefully. The two shivered in the cold dawn light. Pains of hunger made him look for the colorfully decorated food wagon. He saw its colorful lanterns twinkling far away down the trail. He hoped breakfast would be as good as dinner. Returning his attention to Tom he decided this strange person knew more about the path than he was letting on.

"I never felt at home in the other world. It didn't fit me. I knew there must be something beyond it. That's all I know," said Bret.

"I remember travelling somewhere. It was important that I talk to someone. I was trying to prevent something. A pain in my chest was my last memory. I awoke on the path." Tom said.

He acted differently now than yesterday. Bret thought it was more than just being older. His bearing was official and serious. He was anxious to travel.

"What direction should we go?" Bret asked.

"I definitely need to go that way," Tom replied. He pointed in the direction away from where Bret had emerged on the trail the day before.

"Do you know where it leads?" Bret asked.

"Yes, I do. My memory is coming back to me now. I was witness to something extremely grand. It was something that the whole world watched. Expectations were so high, but alas, the young republic struggled almost immediately. I could have done more to help. I believe that direction will afford me the opportunity to do so."

"Does your mission have something to do with your clothes?" Bret asked. "I mean, you do kind of look like you're from another time and place."

"I'm here to set things right. It was the purpose of my journey all those years ago." Tom looked remorseful.

"Are you talking about the American revolution? That was so long ago. How could you have been part of that?"

"I was there. I watched the whole thing. I remember now. There was a property that I sold to a Mr. Harper at the convergence of two rivers. That was my life you see, I sold parcels to rich and poor at a fair price. It was surveyed by a young man I hired who went on to do great things."

"If you remember all this, I suspect you are very different than me. This shouldn't come as a surprise, but what you are saying is impossible. How could you be here now?" Bret stood back to create some distance with what he suspected was a specter.

"I am here the same as you. I exist on this trail and must make the best of it. One of my first deeds is to investigate what I could have done."

Tom seemed aged by the burden of his duty. Another ten years had been added to his face during their conversation. His hair was now in a ponytail and was flecked with grey. His body no longer had youthful vigor, but the denseness of age

"You are not making any sense, Tom."

Bret felt nervous in the presence of a person who aged years in the span of minutes. He didn't feel comfortable calling him Tom anymore. Maybe, "Sir" or "Thomas" was more appropriate.

They decided to fold up the blankets and prepare for the day. They emerged from the Wickiup back into blazing sunlight. Magda was there to greet them with two hot cups of tea, sweetened and with the perfect touch of cream. They gulped down the steaming beverages and tore into buttered biscuits. The Wickiup unwound itself, reducing into a bundle of twigs. Magda wrapped it up in a canvas bag and stowed it in box under the wagon. The wagon lurched forward. Its smokestack coughed out soft, white clouds as the yaks, once again, pulled it onto the trail. Bret turned to Tom and inquired about his direction on the path.

"So, I don't know why I am here or what I am supposed to do on this path.

"I can only speak for myself but I have much to set right. You see, I owned most of northern Virginia back before the nation was even founded. My grant stretched all the way to what I believe you call West Virginia today. Back then, the land was a wilderness. I needed to map it and inventory my parcels for sale."

"You've got to be kidding me! You sound famous. What is your full name again?"

"I was the sixth Baron of Cameron Lord Thomas Fairfax. I came to the Virginia frontier to administer my inheritance. However, the beauty of the mountains, rivers, and valleys changed me."

"I am afraid I've never heard of you. Sorry, I didn't pay too much attention in history class. Do you have a destination in mind? Bret asked.

"It is not so much a place as a time. I plan to visit an old friend. He must be warned of dangers to the republic."

"This path can take us back in time?"

"Yes, but we must be on guard. The misty barrier between dimensions is thin. We are safe while on the path but there is danger just beyond its veils. Not only is it dangerous to step off but we open a hole every time we do. There are monsters patrolling the darkness searching for doorways to invade the path. Whatever happens, you must be prepared to fight."

Tom looked around at the wavering wall of mist. He saw travelers far off in the distance. They were making their way along the trail. Another day was starting on the path.

"Wow, this is a lot more exciting than high school. I really don't know what else to do. Do you mind if I travel with you?" Bret asked

"But, of course. The more the merrier. We are not alone on this path. Maybe you will meet someone your age."

Thomas pointed toward pilgrims approaching. All these travelers are searching for something. You can join any of them but I would enjoy your company. Please feel free to join me."

"Sir, I got no other plan," Bret replied.

"It's agreed. Let's walk. The past awaits us."

Thomas smiled and nodded. He grabbed a wooden staff that was leaning against a tree and tapped it three times on the grassy path. Bret followed behind. He realized this could all be a figment of his imagination. Orc certainly would not fit in here. He would have done something by now to imperil them all. The thought of his cousin saddened him. What chaos had his disappearance caused back at Sky Meadows? Was his physical body lying dead in the grass? Or, did he simply vanish into thin air?

Bret laughed out loud as he imagined the look on Orc's face. Thomas cast him a weary glance over his shoulder. The pair mingled in with a stream of pilgrims. Bret wondered where they could all be going.

CHAPTER TWENTY-FOUR

Battletown, VA, December 22, 1974

Entering the front door of the stone farmhouse, Los followed the low light into the living room. A fire blazed in the hearth. A hulking figure stood before it. Lord Jim turned away from the crackling flames to greet Los. Steam rose from his clothes. The two men embraced. The old man was warm from the blazing fire in the hearth. Los could feel the cold fleeing his clothes from the contact. Los broke off the hug to get a good look at Lord Jim. He looked rough like a feral dog who just came back home from a year in the woods. His leather boots were scraped and gouged. His woolen trousers were patched in the knees and sprinkled with sticker burrs. A waxed canvas coat was missing buttons but secured with an improvised nylon cord. Pulling on his bushy black beard, Lord Jim pushed Los into the leather chair next to the fire. Los accepted the forced comfort and marveled at the mysterious old man. If the Kindred were a secret organization that lived in the shadows, Lord Jim was a black hole that no light could penetrate.

"Thought I might have to make a run for it. Too cold and wet for a man my age." Lord Jim declared.

He beamed a big smile that shone through his ruddy complexion. The two men stared into the flames. An unspoken communication told Lord Jim that Los had big news.

"So, you saw something I take it?" Lord Jim asked.

"Yes, clear as day," Los replied.

"Then it's time."

"Yes, I'm to transit as soon as the monk arrives."

"Listen to me." He placed his hands upon Los' shoulders. "Once you start this, there is no going back."

"Believe me, I know that."

"I know. I just had to say it."

The two men were alone in the small, isolated stone house.

"Well, take off your boots and stay for the night. No rush. The Authority will be swarming everything between Battletown and Bear's Den for the next day or so."

Lord Jim's hospitality ran deep. His roots in the Adirondack Mountains stripped bare any pretense. Growing up in the cold windswept ridges stunted Lord Jim's conversation like the trees on its slopes. He spoke tersely as if icy cold wind was taking each breath away. While Lord Jim's generosity was limitless, it came at a price. Los knew that he was honor bound to respect Lord Jim's leadership of the Kindred. His orders and decisions were unquestionable. The old man was stoic before, but Los had noticed a change since he returned from prison. He seemed more aloof and callous than ever.

His nostrils were suddenly filled with a foul smell. Los wondered if he smelled as bad as his companion. No doubt, their rough lifestyle contributed to the stink. He couldn't remember the last time he showered. Lord Jim abandoned modern sanitation years ago. He claimed it was an act of survival that allowed him to sniff out government agents in the woods simply by their soap, cologne, or shampoo before ever seeing them. Los thought Lord Jim had just gotten lazy and a bit eccentric in his old age. But, the old rebel was doing something right. His trail had gone cold for many years. The Authority stood no chance of catching him unless he wanted to be caught.

That didn't stop the Authority from searching. Clearly, they believed Lord Jim to still be a very dangerous man. His philosophical teachings liberated many a mind and soul. Los remembered the first time they met. It was on a winter's night. Los was one of dozens gathered to hear a rebel sermon. They stood, hushed, in the darkness in a shallow wooded depression in the middle of a vast field. Four somber watchmen stood guard. With their backs to the hidden group, their eyes scanned the horizon in all directions. Government patrols were constantly searching for such "teachings" as Lord Jim called them. The Authority had issued standing orders to arrest attendees and kill their leader.

He remembered Lord Jim addressing the huddled crowd that cold winter night. Sparks from the fire leaped into the sky. Lord Jim walked to the edge of the firelight and called out the name of their inspiration.

"John Brown is with us tonight in spirit and righteousness."

The group murmured a solemn, "amen," in response.

"Over a hundred years ago, John Brown gave his life so that all people could live free. He believed our republic could only be sustained if patriots defended the rights enshrined in its Constitution for all men. Now, we carry on his fight. These mountains are still the pathways. We travel them north and south, day and night, in all manner of weather. Faithful to his vision, we keep the trails open for both escape and invasion. We know the Authority has its secret facilities, brimming with its arsenals of despair. No doubt, its base of power is formidable. But remember, we have our own!" He pointed to the dark Alleghany mountains behind him.

"Our mission is to keep his truth alive. Generation after generation, we walk the same paths as the original raiders. Like them, we face a critical decision. Liberty is still threatened. Slavery was only abolished by the Authority in one dimension. Through its lies and murderousness, it threatens to wipe out all freedom for eternity. Our struggle is just as perilous as that faced by John Brown all those years ago. Like him, we are faced with a decision. We can no longer sit by and watch the chains of slavery become stronger. We cannot afford to watch from the darkness anymore. We have built a powerful force with which to do battle. Generations of warriors have been bred to fight in every manner and on every battlefield. The time is right to strike again at the very heart of the Authority. I need volunteers who are willing to sacrifice like our forefathers. It's time for the next generation to step forward and become outlaws, to live the rebel life and forsake all. Who will join me?"

Out of the darkness, Los had stepped forward. He joined the cause right then and there. He took the oath of the freedom league. This decision would mark the beginning of the end of his life with Enith. She would never understand his commitment.

Now, twenty years later, Los passed into the kitchen of the small stone farmhouse. A fire had been burning for most of the day and a bed of red-hot coals now consumed the fireplace. He planned to transit soon, but not before the monk arrived.   A knock on the front door made both men jump. The door opened and a messenger came in from the cold. He handed Lord Jim a letter. After reading it, the old man crushed it in his massive fists. He looked a Los and sighed.

"I have bad news. The murdered women have been identified." Lord Jim said solemnly.

"Who were they?" Los asked. He looked back to the fire.

"One was your brother's wife, Sarah."

"And the other?"

"I am afraid it was Enith." Lord Jim answered before throwing the letter into the fire.

"It can't be. She is not Kindred. They would have no reason to kill her," Los pleaded.

"Anyone who witnesses a transit is a threat. You know that as well as I do," said Lord Jim.

It changed everything. Until now, Los had not fully committed to the mission. He didn't really believe it would be necessary. Now, he realized there was no time to waste.

CHAPTER TWENTY-FIVE

Mt. Catawba, VA, December 23, 1974

Lost Mungo shivered in the cold dawn. He bent his gloved hands back and forth forcing their movement. His numb fingers cracked at each joint in painful reaction. Taking off his gloves, he rubbed his hands together one over the other hoping the friction on bare skin would bring back warmth. He wrote all night long until the ink ran dry from his pen. With only three sides, the shelter was open to the raw northern wind. The snow had drifted within two feet of his sleeping bag. He knew conditions on the trail would be even worse. It had been a while since he lashed together snowshoes and he concentrated on their design while gulping down the last of his morning tea. The snow was at least a foot deep and even higher where it drifted around boulders and tree trunks. He sat his titanium cup down on the wooden floor of the shelter. He adjusted the sleeping bag higher around his chest before he once again began studying the journals for ancestral clues of the Kindred.

A familiar sound echoed through the woods causing Lost Mungo to stop writing. Tilting his head, he looked out toward the trail to better hear the unique noise. Without a doubt, he was listening to the distinct sound known to all hikers: the clacking and scraping of metal spikes striking rocks. Someone was coming down the snow-laden trail with trekking poles swinging away. Lost Mungo couldn't imagine a hiker plowing through the seven miles of snow from the nearest shelter, especially, this early in the morning. Also, he thought it improbable they would have spent the night on the mountain top exposed to the howling winter snowstorm.

Who in their right mind would be hauling ass in these conditions? He squirmed out of his sleeping bag and ran to the edge of the shelter. Peering into the frozen woods, he spied an advancing mist of snow crystals. The advancing crystal storm swirled around something inside. Moving as effortlessly as a bear galloping through the forest, it quickly closed the distance toward the shelter. As the figure grew nearer, Lost

Mungo spied a large backpack set upon the shoulders of an even larger hiker. Arms flayed the snow with poles and snowshoes skimmed across its surface, propelling the figure between trees and boulders down the mountainside. Lost Mungo shook his head in disbelief and started to laugh in the empty shelter. He recognized the figure.

"Whiskeytown, you're bat shit crazy. What in the world are you doing out here?"

"Someone has to rescue your sorry ass, Mungo."

"Be careful! There's a small stream under the snow just before you."

"Won't be the first one I have fallen through; I haven't felt my feet for a couple miles now."

The moving mass of snow crystals stopped before the shelter and slowly dissolved into a mountain-sized man.

"I'll brew up some tea to help get you defrosted."

Lost Mungo bent down to light his hobo stove and struck several matches trying to ignite his Esbit tablets in the wind. Whiskeytown fidgeted in front of the shelter before he interrupted Mungo.

"That would hit the spot, but I am afraid we don't have time. You should get packed up."

"I don't like the sound of that," Lost responded standing up from his cook kit. He noticed Whiskeytown had not taken off his backpack or even let go of his poles. He could tell he was carrying an important message.

"Mungo, the Kindred sent me. I'm to break trail through the snow and shepherd you along as far as you need me."

"The Kindred, you say? Why are they in such a hurry? I'm not supposed to be at the gathering for another month."

Whiskeytown made direct eye contact with Lost Mungo.

"Things have taken a turn for the worse. I'm sorry to give you some bad news, but your Genealogies will need updating."

"What happened this time?"

"The Authority conducted a raid on some of ours. Its power of surveillance may have finally surpassed our ability to evade them. We know two sisters were killed. Some youngsters escaped but are being hunted as we speak. As best we can figure, one of the kids must have transited and the other is running like hell through the woods."

Lost Mungo looked around the shelter at his equipment scattered about on the floor. He picked up his titanium cup. Lost in contemplation, he stared at the remaining tea leaves at the bottom of his cup and wondered what forces stirred the lives of men. His divination skills had grown as cold as the dregs he was looking at but he decided to try to see into the future. Swirling the cup three times, he waited until the tea leaves settled. He stared at the results. No recognizable pattern appeared. He was about to discard the remains when he saw the letter M had formed along the cup wall.

"Hey, Whiskey, does that look like an M to you?"

"Take your pick, it's an M or a worm. Whatever makes you happy."

"Now, if I remember right, an M is the symbol for the serpent."

"And that means what exactly?"

"It means destruction for the sitter that I am divining."

"Is that me?" Whiskeytown looked at Mungo with a serious expression.

"No, I was trying to divine the future of the Authority. I also see the symbol for mountain, which I believe means journey."

"You should start to pack up. We've got to keep moving across these mountains ourselves. Hopefully, not to our destruction." Whiskeytown cast a last nervous glance inside the cup. He shook his head and stepped away from the troublesome cup.

"Do we know who passed?" Mungo asked.

"From what we can figure, Bret Cantwell was the one who transited. I am afraid his mother was killed. His cousin, Orc Patterson, escaped the Authority's response team. We cannot verify the identity of the other woman but we assume it was Orc's aunt. Of course, rumors are flying. One says it was Enith but she ain't really dead. It was all just a show to bring Los out. That explains how the Authority found the transit point so fast."

"The Kindred needs to stop whispering half-truths and stick to the facts," Mungo answered.

"It's not like she is trustworthy after what she did to Los."

"Never mind your rumors. Besides, I am not at all surprised that Los' son got away. He's so much like his dad. Shame if something were to happen to him before he found out who his real father was."

"From what I heard, he ain't no kin to Los."

"You don't know Enith and Los like I do," Mungo shot back.

"Well, it may not matter anymore. I wouldn't be surprised if Los has passed by now. He volunteered for a suicide mission the next day. I tell you Mungo, all hell is breaking loose up in those mountains."

With this news, Lost Mungo sat down on the floor of the shelter and pulled his knees up to his chest. Shaking his head back and forth, he refused to accept the news.

"That poor family. They never got to know the truth. I can't believe they could all be gone." Mungo looked up at the shelter ceiling for an answer.

"I only know what the Kindred wants me to know. And right now, all I know is they want you at Battletown within a week. That means we got lots of hiking to do. I hope you are not as old as you look."

"Don't worry about me. I have been hiking these mountains longer than you."

"Well, do what you've got to do. Pack things up and let's get going. Until this snow melts, it's my job to break trail for you."

"Let me make the proper notations, and then we can get a move on."

Lost Mungo became focused and purposeful in his movements. He sat down among his belongings and reached into his pack. Retrieving the leather-bound genealogies, he grabbed his pen and thumbed through the pages before finding the family tree of Bret's father and mother. He noted her death next to her husband's date three years earlier. He then turned to the Patterson family tree. He refused to believe Los, Enith, and Orc could all be dead. Their family story was tragic enough already. They at least deserved to know the truth about each other. Only two people knew that Orc was the son of Los and Enith and Lord Jim has sworn him to secrecy. The parents didn't even know why they were separated in the first place. It was all a big misunderstanding. Los' arrest cut the cord between everyone and Lord Jim made sure nobody talked since. That was another secret burning away within Mungo. He wanted the family to reunite and hoped he could let them know the truth. He also recognized that nobody survived the fury of the Authority's deadly response team. He started to enter a death date for the unfortunate trio but stopped and slammed the manuscript shut.

"They don't know what they got with Orc. He is the spirit of revolution itself. The prophecy is happening. He is the force that will bring down the Authority. They have bit off much more than they can chew this time."

Whiskeytown nodded in agreement even if he had no idea what Lost Mungo was saying. He helped the little man off the floor. The two prepared to depart.

"I am just leading you until the snow is gone. You don't need me to guide you anywhere. As soon as the trail clears, you are on your own again. I got better things to do than babysit you."

"Your concern is heartwarming" Lost Mungo muttered.

Within minutes, the flurry of snow was once again moving down the mountain amid the bundle of human force that was Whiskeytown. This time, there was a smaller hiker in tow moving much quicker with the trail broken before him.

CHAPTER TWENTY-SIX

Paris, VA, December 23, 1974

T he gravel trailhead parking lot was surrounded by dense forest on three sides. High ridgelines framed the view in all directions. Black SUVs clogged every inch of space. Military equipment was stacked high under temporary tarps. Electrified static filled the air as dark-uniformed men barked orders into a vast array of communication equipment. Bloody bandages littered the trailhead just below the GT blaze on a large oak tree where the dirt trail met gravel. Two bodies lay on the ground zipped into green plastic body bags. Urizen surveyed the scene with dismay. His head jerked up toward the high ridgeline at the sound of gunshots beyond the summit. He immediately knew his agents had engaged another force. The caliber of weapon was familiar but fired in a desperate pattern. He detected panic and fear. He stepped toward the black SUV and grabbed a walkie-talkie from the hand of the agent behind the wheel.

"Who the fuck is shooting?" he screamed across the radio band. He released the mic button and blood returned to his white fingers.

"We're trying to locate two agents, but there is no response," a subordinate replied. The voice crackled with a tension that betrayed fear even the most hardened agents experienced when addressing the Lord of Death.

"I don't like the sound coming from those mountains. It better be from some local rednecks and not agents," he replied.

Urizen flung the walkie-talkie through the SUV's open window and pulled his automatic pistol from its sheath. He fired three quick shots into the air and glared at everyone around him.

"Sir, the team is not responding. The communications appear dead."

"Whoever those motherfuckers are out there, I want them dead. Nobody challenge's the Authority and lives to tell about it," Urizen bellowed.

Spittle coursed down his chin. The assembled units fell silent. Agents stood still as the parking lot darkened with the fading sunlight. The sound of gas-fired generators hummed at the entrance near the access road. Artificial lights illuminated the operation casting the forest into stark blackness. Urizen fired three more ferocious shots into the night sky. He swung his head and torso in a loosely controlled duet of madness. The warning shots echoed through the hills. There was no response.

"Call for Deputy Director Urizen coming through the communication link." The radio operator emerged from inside the operations tent with another handheld radio set.

"It better be the Director himself. I don't want any bureaucratic interference; do you hear me? I will personally kill anyone in my command that thinks a politician is more important than the mission." He grabbed the phone and extended the antenna.

"What the fuck is it?" Urizen said.

"George, this is Director Taylor. It's my understanding that citizens have been killed rather sloppily. A breach of transit is serious but your response must be balanced."

"And your point is exactly?"

"You should show greater discretion about who is killed and how."

Director Taylor was superior only in title. He spoke in the calm voice of a man holding the leash of a monster. Only confidence could keep the violent animal under control. He just regretted his hand held the leash.

"Well, we can deal with insurrection in this life or the next, but it must be dealt with eventually. Now or later. Your choice, Director."

"You don't want to face the whole council. Keep things under control."

"I can assure you that as soon as I deal with these treasonous rebels, I will pay a little visit to the council and remind them who actually runs this country." Urizen slammed the microphone down without waiting for a response.

He looked toward the darkening hills and strapped his ammo vest tighter to his torso. He struggled to insert his hands into his tactical gloves, not because of their fit, but because of his impatience to start the hunt. The assembled men now numbered about two hundred. Urizen selected his own team of twelve. He picked the meanest and most physically fit. He knew they would still be no match to his strength, endurance, and lust for blood. With a simple hand gesture, his team followed him toward the tree line. The men cast nervous glances at each other. Urizen's body twitched and contorted like that of a rabid dog. He began salivating white foam. The frightening sight made several men slow their pace. They wanted some distance between themselves and the possessed demon leading them into the woods. He seemed truly possessed. His violent spasms intensified as he approached the forest. Urizen sprinted further ahead of his squad before crashing headfirst through the underbrush of the forest. Once inside, he maneuvered like an alpha wolf leading his pack. The taste of blood was in the air and he would not stop until the prey was writhing between his jaws, his teeth sunk into its veins. He was more animal than human. The soldiers in his unit began barking. Just like a pack, their supplication to the alpha wolf was complete. They were no longer afraid of anything before them but their leader himself.

Back at the assembly area, the remaining soldiers listened to the animalistic howls from Urizen and his unit. The baying echoed through the night air. Slowly, the black clad units set off in different directions, each man careful to give Urizen's route a wide berth.

CHAPTER TWENTY-SEVEN

Harpers Ferry, WV, June 7, 2016

DB settled into a comfortable cross-legged position on the floor and began to read. Each page held all sorts of scribblings, usually short passages announcing the author's presence, where he came from, and where he was going next. Many were simply expressions of facts and observations of the climate and geography, such as, "Hot as hell today! Three Ridges is a bitch of a climb!" These entries fell in to a recognizable pattern. Some of their authors had straightforward trail names like, "Blisters," "Wander," "Neo," or "Trail Rot." Others, while more creative, reflected meanings only known to the authors.

The nature of the short declarative entries punctuated by expletives and humorous drawings became monotonous in their repetition. This format allowed DB to mechanically digitize page after page without much interest in its content, duly notating each file by category of date, shelter number, and volunteer trail association. His work was off to a promising if dull start.

Except, on occasion, a break in the pattern appeared. After weeks of reviewing entries, DB noticed certain passages that were stylistically and substantively different. These unique entries started in November of 1973 at Mollies Ridge shelter in the depths of the Great Smoky Mountain National Park. It struck him that the hiking season was over at that time and not too many thru-hikers should be on the trail—especially in the Great Smoky National Park amid the darkest days of winter—and hiking north. The entries themselves were different from anything he had seen. Their script was eccentric, like calligraphy, reminiscent of the format one might see in historical records. The content reminded him of an old church almanac. It had no relation to hiking, nature, or weather. It simply listed births, marriages, and deaths of individuals, most of whom appeared related due to the recurring surnames. This discovery slowed his digitization process considerably as he began to read every new entry with care. Each was notated with a symbol and a signature. DB soon realized that hundreds of trail names had authored genealogical events over decades, but, strangely, the name notating each was always the same: Lost Mungo. DB found this strange name repeatedly. It appeared all along the 2,300-mile trail year after year, decade after decade.

Soon, he started to notice other unique entries. These were not long passages in a peculiar script and format, but obtuse communications that made little sense. Obviously, they were between distinct parties on the trail. They obfuscated more than they reveled. DB could discern that these people were not hiking north or south, but lingering on the same section of trail for long periods of time. While entries by Lost Mungo were simple notations, almost as if someone was checking off his work, the shorter communications had a sense of intimacy and immediacy that didn't dissipate with the passage of time. These people were amid something perilous, so palpable it came across through the years of musty journals. DB realized these authors must be part of an underground movement. The person who appeared to direct the clandestine group went by the name Lord Jim. He was the central character in a plan that included hundreds of names.

His digitizing work had now come to a complete stop due to his distraction over these secretive and fascinating entries. He read the diaries, but didn't have the patience to digitize each journal, skipping through to find writings of this subversive group. One thing he was sure of, these people were living intense lives and were involved in a desperate struggle. Their voices leaped from the pages and captured his imagination even though their entries occurred 42 years ago. They were obviously using the trail journal system to document compelling and urgent messages. He had stumbled upon two distinct voices, one that was documenting genealogy, mystical in its nature and the other, a secretive alliance bent on uprising.

He looked over his shoulder reflexively, into the dark corners of his apartment living room. He sensed he was being watched and perceived an invading danger. He collected the journals in a cardboard box and carried them to the couch. Flicking on every light in the room, he tried to push back his fears with the warm glow of incandescent lights. There was something inherently perilous in these posts. His old nightmare came to mind. A door was open. It cast a light upon an infinite dark plain.

He couldn't think who would be threatened by these messages. Obviously, he reassured himself, nothing ever happened with these characters. Had there been a rebellion against the government, he certainly would have read about it. He wracked his brain but couldn't connect these authors to any historical event. If their activities really did amount to nothing, why did he feel alarm reading them decades later?

It was late at night and a full moon shone blue through low clouds driving across the sky. DB's apartment occupied the entire second floor of an old Civil War-era house that was only accessible by a creaky, exterior wooden staircase. The house clung precariously to the valley side of the steep ridge road that served as the main street from the lower river town to the upper village of Bolivar Heights.

"Hey, come over here for a second." DB took Lyn's hand and led her to their threadbare couch. He sat her down by applying gentle pressure to her shoulders—she should be sitting down for this he thought—and handed her a dirt smudged and thoroughly-worn journal.

"Read this and see what I am talking about."

"Oh, is this one of your mysterious passages? You know, the weird ones that have caused you to totally fall behind in your job?"

"It's bizarre I tell you. This isn't like anything I typically find in the journals."

"What do you mean?"

"This is the exact opposite of what you would expect from someone struggling under a heavy pack up a thousand-foot elevation. Even a thru-hiker going light and fast across 30 miles of trail would still mention something about his physical experience. You know, mostly, 'my feet hurt,' or 'my chafing is driving me crazy,' but not," he stretched out his arms for emphasis, "John the Baptist admonishing society from the edge of the wilderness. I'm telling you, this stuff is weird in a way I can't define. It isn't exactly menacing, but something in its tone and voice seems alarming."

DB opened to a page and pointed to a sentence with his index finger. Lyn scoffed and rolled her eyes.

"Seriously, you want me to read journal entries from 42 years ago on a Saturday night? Can we at least go to the Conspirators Tavern and get a drink?"

DB stood up and paced the floor. "Maybe we should just tell the GT Director what I found. He can decide what to do. Maybe he can go to the National Park Service and say something."

"Like what, tell the park service that weirdos were on the trail, or inform the Conservancy that people might be using the journals and shelters to elicit family reunions?" she laughed.

DB looked out the window of the living room into the night. He could see the wet rock face of Maryland Heights glistening in the moonlight. A train emerged from the tunnel and began crossing the Potomac River Bridge toward Harpers Ferry. The distant hum of the engine and shrieking train whistle made him stop. He handed her another moldy journal with a serious expression on his face she had not seen before. In a hushed voice, he said, "Here, just read this passage from November 1974. It was posted in the Catawba shelter by someone named Lost Mungo. Tell me what kind of person would document ancestries in a desolate shelter on top of a mountain in the middle of winter."

"Ok, obviously, something has you spooked. I promise not to laugh until I at least get through the first paragraph."

She took the book and opened it to the page where his finger pointed toward an entry. She immediately noticed that this entry was unique. The name of the author was at the beginning, unlike all the other entries, and it was neatly written with a carefully constructed format. No misspellings or breaks in the calligraphy. It was written perfectly the first time. It wasn't long before the voice of the narrator had her deeply entranced with his story.

Chapter Twenty-Eight

Lord Jim had burnt all the firewood in the house. Los volunteered to bring in more from the barn. As he pushed a wheel barrel full of split wood back across the lawn, he looked at the inviting glow of lamplight coming from the stone farmhouse. He breathed heavy at the memory of the day his life fell apart. He would never forget the phone call. It came just before his arrest. Enith had stopped coming to the farm, making a series of excuses for why she couldn't get out of the city. Summer had passed into fall. Soon the mountains would be in glorious color. Blazed with orange, red, gold, and yellow, the entire chain of the Blue Ridge would transform in to a spectacular, but fleeting, scene. And she would miss it all. He had tried to keep himself busy by readying firewood for winter. He even went for long runs down country lanes and along dirt roads, but nothing could take his mind off her. He accepted things had changed between them and came to terms that she was never coming home. The phone call confirmed his worse fear. Enith sounded like she had rehearsed what she was going to say and loaded it with triggers.

"Why are you separating from us?" She started.

"What do you mean?"

"I mean exactly what I said. You're off doing your own thing."

"I don't know what you are talking about. This was supposed to be our place."

"I can't stop my life to come out there."

"My plans are all about protecting us from the Authority."

"That is exactly what I am talking about. Even when you are here, your mind is somewhere else, plotting for a rebellion that may never happen."

"I have a responsibility to serve. You know my family history."

"What about our family history? When does that start?"

"That's not fair. The Authority will invade our lives either way."

"Los, even if the Authority does emerge as the all-encompassing evil in your fantasy, I don't want to exist in the woods living like an animal."

"You make the farmhouse sound so primitive. It's a bit rustic I admit."

"Let's live the life we have now and let the future be whatever it is. If we truly love each other, we can survive anything. There's no preparation or planning or plotting in the world that can save us if there's no love."

"But there is love and I'm preparing for a future where we can survive. Do you want to die of starvation while we hold hands and stare at each other so deep in love?"

"Maybe I do. All I want is love. That's all that should matter."

"But what about what I want? We can be together when everyone else is lost and confused. We will be protected."

"Without love, there's nothing to protect. I no longer feel any love from you, just anger. I want to live now, not wait."

"Is it too late for us? I can fix it."

"There's been too much damage, Los. All these years preparing for some great battle that never comes. It's too late. You've lost me."

"No. Don't say that. It's never too late."

"Your apocalypse is self-created. You destroyed everything you love in your compulsion to survive the future. Do you think I will want to be with you at that time? I don't even know who you are anymore."

"We should stand up to it before it is too late. We can't depend on others to fight this battle."

"Why do you care about humanity more than us?"

"We are humanity."

"Are you willing to give up our life to save some faceless humanity!"

"Someone must sacrifice. I need to be part of this struggle."

"I want you in our lives now, not tomorrow. If you want to wait until tomorrow, I can't promise I'll be there."

"You say that now but when things get bad, you'll appreciate what I'm doing for us, for our family, for our future."

"I'm just telling you how I feel. I would rather live today than for some distant future. I can take care of myself and will survive no matter what."

"So, you are leaving me?"

"You're the one who drove us apart with your righteous anger against the Authority. I am afraid of being on the wrong end of your wrath."

That was the last conversation Los ever had with Enith. She hung up the phone and disappeared from his life forever. Holding the phone in his hand, he listened to the dead call signal for several minutes. He hoped it might be possible she could come back on line. Finally, he hung up the receiver and dialed her number. He listened as the phone rang endlessly but was never answered. Desperate to understand where it all went wrong, Los stared at the empty kitchen. The silence of the country house now taunted him. He was so far away from her in the city. He wanted to hold her and make it all go away. Looking around him for answers, Los grimaced at the cheap curtains with which he decorated the windows. He picked up them up at Family General as well as the bedspread. He realized it was a lame attempt to dress up the 250-year-old stone farmhouse. He admitted to himself the place was old, uncomfortable and even a bit primitive but inhabitable. He caught himself thinking how sad that sounded. She was right. Why did he expect her to accept this house and a life of isolation? He immediately decided to make the trip into the capital tomorrow. He would never make it.

CHAPTER TWENTY-NINE

White Post, VA, December 23, 1974

Standing among a grove of Sycamores, Zoa heard gunshots behind Fletcher Hill across the Shenandoah river. The sound was not uncommon in these parts of the Valley, especially so close to the Blue Ridge during hunting season. But these shots sounded different. They rang out sharper and faster than the single-shot hunting rifle. They came in bursts of three, controlled and evenly paced. She crouched low and scanned the forest for movement.

The sound of a woman's muffled scream was distinct but short lived. Zoa was sure someone had just been shot. She slinked through a narrow band of trees up river to put some distance between her and whoever was shooting. Her plan to follow the river south had worked well until now. A large stream flowed into the river from inland. Its banks were steep and muddy. The water flowed quickly with a combination of dark pools and small waterfalls. The last thing she needed was to get soaking wet. Instead, she turned inland and followed the tributary into the forest. A dirt trail along the high bank made her way easier. As she walked along, she glimpsed someone walking toward her from the other side of the stream. The figure appeared and then disappeared as brush and trees obscured her view. Finally, she got a good look. It was a young woman. Zoa couldn't believe her eyes. The girl looked like her. Zoa stopped in her tracks. Was this a real person or an apparition? For some reason, Zoa no longer trusted her senses. The forest felt very different than a minute ago. Her anxiety melted away. She felt one with woods, river, and sky. Her legs glided above the ground. Her arms swam through a vapor of stars. The sun and the moon rested on either shoulder. It all seemed impossible.

Her other was staring at her from across the stream. They were parallel now. At the same moment, they both hailed each other.

Their eyes met with a deep awareness and recognition. It was her—an exact replica—walking downstream as she walked upstream. It was as if she was staring in a mirror. She asked her twin a question.

"How is it possible that I am on both sides of the stream at once?"

Zoa felt faint at the thought of what she was experiencing. She had met herself along its spectrum from birth to this point and watched the other Zoa reverse from death toward this moment. Both Zoas opened their mouths and spoke identical words simultaneously.

"I have been where you are going. You will be okay. Just keep pushing on."

The communication made her dizzier with its ramifications. Time did not exist as she thought. Her yesterday was confronting her tomorrow in a single moment of now. Then she was alone again. A mist enveloped her and she felt a force pressing at her back. A violent wind propelled her forward through an opening. She traveled from one world to another. On the other side, there was a grassy path. It was surreal in its smoothness; cleared of all rocks, roots, leaves and branches. She stepped forward onto its subtle gradient. She felt the shackles of gravity fall off. She was enveloped by a warm breeze. It was not winter here. This place, wherever it was, felt safe and welcoming. The sky above was a pool of deep blue sprinkled with stars. They appeared to float on the rippling surface of time.

Suddenly, she sensed a presence next to her. Turning around, she saw a young, handsome boy. He gazed at her with equal parts befuddlement and interest. Finally, he held out his hand.

"I am Bret. Welcome to the craziest place in the world," he laughed.

She grabbed his hand and shook it. For some reason, she felt relief at meeting him. He felt like a long, lost friend. Their reunion made her smile.

CHAPTER THIRTY

Leo Davis stood at the top of the cellar stairs and stared down into the dimly lit basement. He looked back at the two men in dark suits standing behind him in the lawn. Their barrel chests, muscular shoulders, and thick necks strained at the confines of business attire. Leo could not judge their emotions behind their sunglasses. They stared coldly at him. No emotion gave away their intent. They reminded him of sharks swimming along a boat waiting for their prey to fall into the water. Leo crossed his arms and rubbed his elbows. He didn't want any part of their business but realized DB must have done something to cause their visit. He hoped it had nothing to do with the Great Trail activities.

"Hey, DB. You have visitors," he yelled.

"Gentlemen, if you will excuse me now, I have to get back to the shop. DB will be with you shortly."

Leo hurried away leaving them alone waiting for DB. Once inside the GT visitor center, he watched them through the window.

DB brushed off the dust and spider webs from his clothes. Hauling dirty trail manuals off shelves and moving them around a moldy basement was indeed dirty work. He couldn't imagine what visitors he could possibly have waiting for him. He climbed the stairs and emerged into the overcast afternoon. The two men standing in the lawn immediately sent alarm signals to his brain. They didn't belong in Harpers Ferry. Both were dressed in black business suits that perfectly fit their tall muscular frames.

"David Cooper?"

"Uh, yes, that's me. I go by DB, actually."

"Is that some kind of joke?" The dark haired one responded.

"You're David Bartholomew Cooper of 1232 Main Street, apartment 102, Harpers Ferry, West Virginia?" The other balding man asked.

"Uh yeah, that's me alright. Is this about the parking tickets at campus? I can explain."

I'm Special Agent Michael Faroe and this is Special Agent John Burnt of the Federal Bureau of Investigation. We have some questions for you."

"Yeah, well, I'm DB Cooper, special volunteer, Great Trail Center Headquarters. What's this all about?"

"It's come to our attention you've made inflammatory anti-government remarks to an official of a federal agency in the conduct of his mission. Is that true?"

"Well, that's quite the allegation. Am I really supposed to understand why you might be saying that?"

"We have a complaint from the United States National Park Service ranger station in the Harpers Ferry Historic National Park. They have lodged a formal complaint that you repeatedly harassed federal agents in the conduct of their official duties. Also, have you ever made any statements supporting anarchy?'

"Harassment? Really? If you mean my questions about John Brown, then I would say someone has got thin skin. Jesus, harassing a federal official?"

"So, you admit to this charge?"

"No! I'm not admitting to harassment. When did asking a park ranger history questions become harassment?"

"We're the ones asking the question, asshole. You better be respectful, or we can do this another way."

DB looked beyond the menacing agents to see if anyone from the GT office was watching his interrogation. He knew questioning rangers was not a federal offense. He was less sure if he ever mentioned anarchy. He might have gotten carried away but he couldn't remember. He began backing up toward the cellar door.

"I don't think I have anything else to say to you guys. Good luck with your little investigation."

"Did you ever make comments advocating violent insurrection against the U.S. government?"

"Of course not. I just stated the obvious, that violence is okay when the government does it."

"We have witness testimony that you said violence against tyranny is justified. Are you denying you made these statements?"

"You know, I'm done talking. There's been some kind of misunderstanding about my historical interest in John Brown's raid on Harpers Ferry and the issue of slavery."

"Do you think violent insurrection against the U.S. government is a way to solve social issues?"

"You call slavery a social issue? Seriously?"

DB felt trapped by their questions and even worse when he spied Leo Davis watching the encounter from the upstairs window. Now, his job was at stake. Had he only listened to Lyn and kept his mouth shut, he wouldn't be in this trouble.

"Keep a civil tone young man. You disrespect us and you are disrespecting the federal government of the United States of America. Or, maybe that is what you really want to say, isn't it?"

"You know what? This is bullshit. You guys are putting words in my mouth. I'm not going to debate the evil of slavery with you. It wasn't a social issue and that's my main problem with the bullshit narrative coming out of the NPS. As a historian, I will tell the truth and not bend it to assuage the guilt of the U.S. government."

"So, you're advocating violent insurrection against the U.S. government."

"You guys are like a broken record. Arrest me or leave me alone. I'm done here."

"Can we see your identification to verify your identity?"

DB knew this tactic. They were trying to escalate a voluntary encounter in to a criminal reaction. He didn't fall for it.

"Sure, fellas. Here ya go. Just to be clear, I go by DB Cooper and not David or David Bartholomew."

"Are you offering us an alias?"

"I'm simply stating my preferred nickname, which I guess is sort of an alias if you look at it that way."

"Listen, Mr. Bartholomew…."

"DB," he interrupted.

"Please don't interrupt us. Mr. Bartholomew, we're investigating an accusation that you pose a threat to national security. Please be advised that any misleading information you provide us can amount to a criminal act. Now, please answer the question. Have you made statements threatening the constitutional authority of the United States government?"

By this time, DB's head was swirling with a combination of fear and rage. He knew he stood no chance in the federal court system. For the first time, he felt what John Brown must have experienced going against not only the institution of slavery but a federal government that legitimized it.

"Hey asshole. Are you going to make us ask you again?"

"Listen, I showed you my identification and now I have to get back to work. If you want to ask me any further questions, I'll seek legal counsel with my current employer. I'm on contract to research and document the contents of official Great Trail records. If I'm correct, they are a quasi-federal agency authorized under USC 641 that receives federal monies. So, if I have questions about the history of Harpers Ferry, it's pursuant to federal research activities. Therefore, you should really be in contact with the Office of General Counsel of the U.S. Forest Service, and specifically, the National Park Service for any additional questions. If anything, the National Park Service should be investigating the park ranger in question for his obstruction of the will of Congress to comply with my requests for information."

With that, he turned and walked away.

The agents looked at each other quizzically, neither one wanting to admit their complete confusion about what DB had just said.

"We need to take this up the chain. If necessary, we may have to issue a subpoena for his records to find out exactly what his research has produced. Maybe there is a connection to domestic terrorism we missed. This could be much bigger than we ever realized.

Not a lone wolf situation but an actual underground network of extremists."

"Do you think he was making fun of us when he insisted we call him DB? I mean, doesn't he know who DB Cooper is and what an embarrassment he was to the Bureau?"

"He's just another asshole who thinks his freedoms trump national security. He wouldn't last a day on the run like the real DB Cooper."

"I thought he died in the parachute jump? Are you saying he survived?"

"No, just forget about it. This asshole has us all confused."

CHAPTER THIRTY-ONE

Bolivar Heights, WV, December 23, 1974 4:30 PM

Before he started the mission, there was one important friend he had to visit. And ask a favor of. The fire had gone cold by dawn. The old man was snoring away in his chair. Los walked out of the farmhouse for his truck carrying a manila envelope. He drove for 20 minutes and parked in a visitor lot. Los strode into the student union building of Storer College. He wore a maintenance uniform and looked every bit like he was responding to a service call. Nobody paid him the least bit of attention, exactly as he wanted. He hadn't been on this campus for years, since his days as a student, and was navigating from memory. He was heading to the campus radio station. Students scurried about or lounged in groups and concentrated on their text books. He studied them carefully and despaired. Little did they know that the Authority approved of every bit of information in those texts. Far from being trained to think critically and objectively, these students were just another generation in a long-running psychological operation. The Authority saw to it that all subjects in the curriculum, from art to zoology, supported an altered narrative. Nothing was left up to interpretation. Every door to the curious mind was firmly shut.

Colleges and universities were no place to question the Authority and these young minds had already been deeply conditioned by its satanic mills. Would they ever be free of the invisible chains that bound them? Los was not optimistic. The Authority would crush their potential for independent thought before they had even their first glimmers of doubt. Unless, the Kindred took drastic action. This was his main reason for visiting the campus today.

Los shook his head in disgust. The thought of poisoning these young minds made him sick. He descended a flight of stairs, turned into a long corridor, and walked until he came to a blinking red light above set of metal double doors. He burst inside and saw a large, denim-clad figure pawing at a keyboard with two index fingers. His long black hair was tied neatly into a ponytail with a lengthy cord of leather.

"Oh, my God, when did they let you off the reservation?" Los's entrance broke the quiet of the windowless room.

"I never went to the reservation, motherfucker. Remember the Trail of Tears? We were told to walk to Indian Territory or die trying. Besides, my people just went deeper in the Catawba mountains."

Joseph Standing Bear pushed back his chair and stood to greet his visitor. The two shook hands, gripping tightly in a test of strength. Both laughed as neither could break the others will to quit.

"We shouldn't ever let go again brother," Standing Bear's expression turned serious. His eyes made direct contact with Los.

"I never let go of you in spirit. Besides, it wasn't my fault I got locked up for ten years."

"Well, it's good to see you in person. The Kindred kept me informed about your imprisonment. We were all thinking of you. Just couldn't write but you know that." Standing Bear looked at his feet, he struggled to control his emotions.

"Well, I am back now and standing in your studio with only one little favor to ask."

"You can't be serious? Just out of jail and you are already up to something."

"I gotta make up for lost time."

"Seriously, you have to be more careful Los. Just like my namesake, I stand up and look around from time to time. Don't like what I see. The Authority seems to be tightening its grip everywhere I look."

"And that is exactly why I'm here." Los winked at Standing Bear.

Los' face became serious and he motioned for his friend to close the door to his office.

"I'm going to transit and I'll need your help."

"Sounds ominous. What do you need from me?"

"There's going to be a shit storm when I cross over. I need a force multiplier to really punch multiple holes in the Authority's net. They need to see us coming at them from every direction. Here is the deal. The Kindred is launching an operation in tandem with my transit. We're going right for the jugular of this mind control crap. From how they've operated in the past, we know the Authority will quarantine the transit area and shut down all local media reports. I need you to send out a message when they do that."

He handed Joseph the large envelope sealed with tape. Joseph looked at Los with a questioning expression.

"And who is this message intended for exactly?" he asked.

"Let's just say we have multiple audiences. The Kindred has deep cover moles in of every facet of society. These spies tell us the Authority is vulnerable to leaks and whistle blowers. While there are many paid shills who couldn't care less about the republic, others are buried deep in various elements of the vast network. Right now, these people are isolated and alone. They want to speak out against the mind control programs but want their inevitable sacrifice to be part of something bigger. Best case scenario, we can leverage them as part of our planned uprising."

"You still haven't told me what my role is." Standing Bear could sense his own sacrifice was on the table.

"We want to reach the key people operating within the Authority—representatives in government, military, law enforcement, media, entertainment, religion—and give them the spark to act and throw a wrench in the gears of control. Again, they must feel part of something bigger than themselves and be assured their sacrifice won't be wasted. Let's not forget the work we could do right here on campus. If professors can wake up these fertile minds and help them break free, we can score a major victory. Remember what Lincoln said to Harriet Beecher Stowe?"

"*'So, you're the little woman who wrote the book that started this Great War.'*"

"She definitely helped the army recruit, at least in the North," Standing Bear nodded his head in agreement.

"Exactly, narratives matter. Who knows if the federal government could have fought the war without her."

"She helped to create a wrathful army," Standing Bear concurred.

"This transcript I hope will have the same effect. It is a manifesto. A call to arms. It outlines exactly how to change society's complicit behavior." Los stabbed his finger at the envelope.

"It sounds like a blueprint for revolution.

"We're going to hit the Authority where it is weakest."

"When you say transit, why do I get the feeling this isn't a trip to the path and back? It sounds a little more dangerous."

"There is no other way to do what needs to be done. Besides, I hope to find Enith."

"You guys are my family. I'll pray to the spirits to guide you to her. Can you tell me anything about this mission that makes it so special?"

"It is safer if you don't know, but you always said you wanted to help the Kindred." Los looked for understanding in Standing Bear's eyes.

Los looked around at the radio equipment.

"You said you have a college radio network that's willing to pick up and rebroadcast your show. When they do, just insert this cassette and play it over and over again. At least, as long as they let you. read exactly what I've written down. Say it repeatedly and again after each new station joins. If it keeps circulating in wider and wider circles, we stand a chance of creating momentum of resistance that will outlast us. The mainstream media will black it out, but if enough people hear it, the message may spread like a virus. They'll play their minds games and so will I."

He shook hands and gave a final hug to his old friend. He may have held on too tight because Standing Bear pushed away.

"Listen to me. We are brothers in this world and the next. I will be looking for you."

"As I will you."

They both looked down at their feet not knowing what to say next. Los ended the awkward moment by leaving the room without another word or even saying goodbye.

Standing Bear sat down in his chair and scrutinized the package. He laughed as he opened it. Los must know he couldn't resist. Inside were several typed pages. He recognized them immediately as Solzhenitsyn's "Spiritual Death Has…Touched Us All." He began reading the document aloud practicing the text for his broadcast.

At one time we dared not even to whisper. Now we write and read samizdat, and sometimes when we gather in the smoking room at the Science Institute, we complain frankly to one another: What kind of tricks are they playing on us, and where are they dragging us? Gratuitous boasting of cosmic achievements while there is poverty and destruction at home. Propping up remote, uncivilized regimes. Fanning up civil war. And we recklessly fostered Mao Tse-tung at our expense—and it will be we who are sent to war against him, and will have to go. Is there any way out? And they put on trial anybody they want and they put sane people in asylums—always they, and we are powerless.

Things have almost reached rock bottom. A universal spiritual death has already touched us all, and physical death will soon flare up and consume us both and our children—but as before we still smile in a cowardly way and mumble without tongues tied. But what can we do to stop it? We haven't the strength.

We have been so hopelessly dehumanized that for today's modest ration of food we are willing to abandon all our principles, our souls, and all the efforts of our predecessors and all opportunities for our descendants—but just don't disturb our fragile existence. We lack staunchness, pride and enthusiasm. We don't even fear universal nuclear death, and we don't fear a third world war. We have already taken refuge in the crevices. We just fear acts of civil courage.

We fear only to lag behind the herd and to take a step alone-and suddenly find ourselves without white bread, without heating gas and without a Moscow registration.

We have been indoctrinated in political courses, and in just the same way was fostered the idea to live comfortably, and all will be well for the rest of our lives. You can't escape your environment and social conditions. Everyday life defines consciousness. What does it have to do with us? We can't do anything about it?

But we can—everything. But we lie to ourselves for assurance. And it is not they who are to blame for everything—we ourselves, only we. One can object: But actually you can think anything you like. Gags have been stuffed into our mouths. Nobody wants to listen to us and nobody asks us. How can we force them to listen? It is impossible to change their minds.

It would be natural to vote them out of office—but there are not elections in our country. In the West people know about strikes and protest demonstrations—but we are too oppressed, and it is a horrible prospect for us: How can one suddenly renounce a job and take to the streets? Yet the other fatal paths probed during the past century by our bitter Russian history are, nevertheless, not for us, and truly we don't need them.

Now that the axes have done their work, when everything which was sown has sprouted anew, we can see that the young and presumptuous people who thought they would make out country just and happy through terror, bloody rebellion and civil war were themselves misled. No thanks, fathers of education! Now we know that infamous methods breed infamous results. Let our hands be clean!

The circle—is it closed? And is there really no way out? And is there only one thing left for us to do, to wait without taking action? Maybe something will happen by itself? It will never happen as long as we daily acknowledge, extol, and strengthen—and do not sever ourselves from the most perceptible of its aspects: Lies.

When violence intrudes into peaceful life, its face glows with self-confidence, as if it were carrying a banner and shouting: "I am violence. Run away, make way for me—I will crush you." But violence quickly grows old. And it has lost confidence in itself, and in order to maintain a respectable face it summons falsehood as its ally—since violence lays its ponderous paw not every day and not on every shoulder. It demands from us only obedience to lies and daily participation in lies—all loyalty lies in that.

And the simplest and most accessible key to our self-neglected liberation lies right here: Personal non-participation in lies. Though lies conceal everything, though lies embrace everything, but not with any help from me.

This opens a breach in the imaginary encirclement caused by our inaction. It is the easiest thing to do for us, but the most devastating for the lies. Because when people renounce lies it simply cuts short their existence. Like an infection, they can exist only in a living organism.

We do not exhort ourselves. We have not sufficiently matured to march into the squares and shout the truth out loud or to express aloud what we think. It's not necessary.

It's dangerous. But let us refuse to say that which we do not think.

This is our path, the easiest and most accessible one, which takes into account our inherent cowardice, already well rooted. And it is much easier—it's dangerous even to say this—than the sort of civil disobedience which Gandhi advocated.

Our path is not to give conscious support to lies about anything whatsoever! And once we realize where lie the perimeters of falsehood, each sees them in his own way.

Our path is to walk away from the gangrenous boundary. If we did not paste together the dead bones and scales of ideology, if we did not sew together the rotting rags, we would be astonished how quickly the lies would be rendered helpless and subside.

That which should be naked would then really appear naked before the whole world.

So, in our timidity, let each of us make a choice: Whether consciously, to remain a servant of falsehood—of course, it is not out of inclination, but to feed one's family, that one raises his children in the spirit of lies—or to shrug off the lies and become an honest man worthy of respect both by one's children and contemporaries.

And from that day onward he:

- *Will not henceforth write, sign, or print in any way a single phrase which in his opinion distorts the truth.*
- *Will utter such a phrase neither in private conversation nor in the presence of many people, neither on his own behalf nor at the prompting of someone else, either in the role of agitator, teacher, educator, nor in a theatrical role.*

- *Will not depict, foster or broadcast a single idea which he can only see is false or a distortion of the truth whether it be in painting, sculpture, photography, technical science, or music.*
- *Will not cite out of context, either orally or written, a single quotation so as to please someone, to feather his own nest, to achieve success in his work, if he does not share completely the idea which is quoted, or if it does not accurately reflect the matter at issue.*
- *Will not allow himself to be compelled to attend demonstrations or meetings if they are contrary to his desire or will, will neither take into hand not raise into the air a poster or slogan which he does not completely accept.*
- *Will not raise his hand to vote for a proposal with which he does not sincerely sympathize, will vote neither openly nor secretly for a person whom he considers unworthy or of doubtful abilities.*
- *Will not allow himself to be dragged to a meeting where there can be expected a forced or distorted discussion of a question.*
- *Will immediately walk out of a meeting, session, lecture, performance or film showing if he hears a speaker tell lies, or purvey ideological nonsense or shameless propaganda.*
- *Will not subscribe to or buy a newspaper or magazine in which information is distorted and primary facts are concealed.*

Of course we have not listed all of the possible and necessary deviations from falsehood. But a person who purifies himself will easily distinguish other instances with his purified outlook.

No, it will not be the same for everybody at first. Some, at first, will lose their jobs. For young people who want to live with truth, this will, in the beginning, complicate their young lives very much, because the required recitations are stuffed with lies, and it is necessary to make a choice.

But there are no loopholes for anybody who wants to be honest. On any given day any one of us will be confronted with at least one of the above-mentioned choices even in the most secure of the technical sciences. Either truth or falsehood: Toward spiritual independence or toward spiritual servitude.

And he who is not sufficiently courageous even to defend his soul—don't let him be proud of his "progressive" views, don't let him boast that he is an academician or a people's artist, a merited figure, or a general—let him say to himself: I am in the herd, and a coward. It's all the same to me as long as I'm fed and warm.

Even this path, which is the most modest of all paths of resistance, will not be easy for us. But it is much easier than self-immolation or a hunger strike: The flames will not envelope your body, your eyeballs, will not burst from the heat, and brown bread and clean water will always be available to your family.

A great people of Europe, the Czechoslovaks, whom we betrayed and deceived: Haven't they shown us how a vulnerable breast can stand up even against tanks if there is a worthy heart within it?

You say it will not be easy? But it will be easiest of all possible resources. It will not be an easy choice for a body, but it is the only one for a soul. No, it is not an easy path. But there are already people, even dozens of them, who over the years have maintained all these points and live by the truth.

So you will not be the first to take this path, but will join those who have already taken it. This path will be easier and shorter for all of us if we take it by mutual efforts and in close rank. If there are thousands of us, they will not be able to do anything with us. If there are tens of thousands of us, then we would not even recognize our country.

If we are too frightened, then we should stop complaining that someone is suffocating us. We ourselves are doing it. Let us then bow down even more, let us wait, and our brothers the biologists will help to bring nearer the day when they are able to read our thoughts are worthless and hopeless.

And if we get cold feet, even taking this step, then we are worthless and hopeless, and the scorn of Pushkin should be directed to us:

Why should cattle have the gifts of freedom?
Their heritage from generation to generation is the belled yoke and the lash.

After reading the entire document, Standing Bear stowed it carefully behind thick files in his cabinet drawer. It was a call to arms to be sure. An impassioned voice of disobedience. He wondered if the audience would realize they were in the same situation as Soviet citizens. He kicked his feet up on his desk and crossed his arms. He couldn't believe his little college radio station could play a role in attacking the Authority. Up until now, Los kept him out of any danger. He realized a line would be crossed with any broadcast of this material. The Authority would react with all its fury. He knew how members of John Brown's raiding party must have felt as they plotted the raid on Harpers Ferry. There was no going back. Once again, a hornet's nest would be struck. The attacking swarm would be viscous. Standing Bear touched down the needle on the turn table and began playing a new song. He wondered to himself where exactly the Kindred would strike. Would it be against the Authority headquarters in Washington, DC? Maybe, Mount Storm and its underground complex was their target. If it was, he wondered if he would be able to see anything from the top of his university building sitting atop Bolivar Heights. It was only about ten miles south as the crow flies. Adjusting some dials on his mixing board, he visualized the battle that would unfold. He had no idea it would be so close to where he was sitting in a small college radio station in Harpers Ferry.

CHAPTER THIRTY-TWO

Battletown, VA, December 24, 1974

The small upstairs bedroom had two windows on opposite walls, both of which were open, letting in the winter wind. A small fireplace contained the remains of burnt logs and ash from flames that died out days before. A heavy wooden door was closed tightly to seal in the cold from the rest of the house. The body of Los lay on a twin mattress under one window. Four small medicine bottles of morphine lay next to the bed. They were empty. A needle was clasped in one hand. There was no movement of the chest as his last breath escaped minutes ago. Los had started his mission. He was to find the reincarnated soul of The Architect of the complex at Mount Storm. Only this person knew the vulnerabilities of the complex. The Kindred hoped his secrets would allow for its destruction. Los needed to travel between dimensions in his search. He didn't know in what form the soul had reincarnated. That was why he had to die first. Free from his physical form and not bound by time and space, Los could journey wherever his senses told him this soul was located. Only in the spirit state could Los find him and communicate the Kindred's need. The entire mission depended on this creature revealing the secrets from his previous life. Los' challenge was to find and communicate with this reincarnated spirit.

Los broke free from the last ties to his body. An image of Enith flashed before his eyes. She appeared as an angel clothed in bright white light. Her hair flowed in a noiseless wind. She was as beautiful as he remembered. The image vanished. He was now alone in the bedroom staring down at his body on the tattered mattress. He realized the vision was the last act of an oxygen starved brain. His soul rose and hovered close to the ceiling in the corner. He passed freely through the stone wall and floated outside into the dark night. The light emanating from the window felt bitter sweet. His life was over.

The separation from physical being to ethereal spirit was complete. The thought of never holding her again was unbearable. What would their lives as spirits be like? Could they experience love? He didn't know and didn't care. Being together was everything. Her mere presence was enough.

Enith, wait just a little longer. I will find you, he thought.

Los was free from his physical body. He sensed no gravity, just weightlessness. Movement was easy; he simply thought of a direction and his spirit traveled there. He felt less than the denseness of a breeze. He sensed a dark mass nearby. Flying closer, he saw it spread along the entire horizon. They were mountains. A gray light backlit their peaks and ridges. It was imposing but familiar.

He looked back once more and saw the porchlight of the stone farmhouse diminishing to an insignificant speck of light. Everything he knew in life was fading away. No doubt, his Kindred brothers and sisters were still gathering from the shadows. He visualized the priest at his bedside in the upper room chanting rhythmically. Downstairs he saw the irascible commander of the Kindred whose trail name reflected his role and more. Lord Jim was sitting before the fire in the living room dragging hard on his clay pipe. Los could see his thoughts. He was bracing for the endgame. Los sensed that visions of destruction and death swirled around the old man's soul. He was calm in the face of the coming storm.

Los travelled over fields and woods until he reached the bottom land before a river. He swerved through the high treetops of the sycamores and swooped low over the river. A reflection on its glassy surface revealed his translucent form. He saw shadowy apparitions far below him. They looked upward in despair and confusion. These souls were lost and confused. Wandering the In-Between, they struggled to achieve the self-realization he obtained instantaneously. He wanted to descend and lead them but had precious little time—42 days exactly—a to search for his target. That was the limit his Buddhist friend said he had to search the In-Between. After that, his soul would be reincarnated into a completely ignorant beast. It would have no memory of its previous life. That was his greatest fear. He would not find Enith before their memories were obliterated from existence.

As he flew, he focused his conscious mind on the murders at Sky Meadows. Within minutes of hearing the gun shots, the Kindred began investigating. Compiling public reports and inside intelligence, the identities of at least one victim was established but not the other. Whispers of the tragedy made its way to Los. The other woman was Enith. Lord Jim had alluded to it himself. If so, she could be lost in the In-Between. He wanted desperately to free her from the confusion and pain of death. He saw her fear drawing evil spirits. They stalked the dead and some ate their souls.

He flew for an eternity as the days passed. While the In-Between was faintly illuminated from an opaque sky, Los counted one distant sunrise and sunset pass by until he reached 30 days. He did not sense the spirits of The Architect or Enith below him. Growing desperate, he decided to fly along the top of the mountain. His instincts told him the soul might stay close to his master accomplishment; Mount Storm. The underground complex straddled the summit and ran its length for nearly half a mile. Images of dark holes repeatedly invaded his mind. The darkest nooks of the mountains beckoned him. He flew into the dark folds of the mountains and then into every black cave.

Chapter Thirty-three

Harpers Ferry, WV, June 20, 2016, 4:00 PM

Sitting at the kitchen table they bought for $5 at Goodwill, Lyn and DB took turns hitting a bottle of bourbon. There were no clean glasses to be found and the immediacy of their crisis could not wait for them to be washed. Drinking from the bottle seemed expedient. The 45% alcohol by volume Kentucky bourbon was DB's favorite. Lyn watched him take a long draw and frown. Something was obviously troubling him.

"Oh man, you wouldn't believe the bullshit at work today," DB replied.

Lyn rolled her eyes as she walked into the apartment carrying groceries.

"What happened that has you so upset?"

"Oh, just a visit from two FBI agents."

"DB, what the hell did you do?"

"Well, I think you were probably right when you said I should stop harassing the park ranger...."

"Oh, my God! What are they accusing you of? Why the hell is the FBI involved?"

"Hum. Seems like my questions have been construed as anti-government threats, which is not accurate of course. I was merely accusing the federal government of hypocrisy. Maybe questioning the immorality of federal laws sanctioning the legality of slavery, nothing else."

"DB! That's exactly what John Brown took to the next level with his violent raid. Of course, they would assume you're a threat! I told you to stop questioning those poor rangers. No matter how immoral a law is, it's still a law and not something we can just disobey."

"Yeah, well, I'm just saying we should be clear about who was in the right and who was in the wrong. History proved John Brown to be on both the moral and legal side of history. He was just defending our constitutional republic. You know the democratic process that protect the individual from mob rule. So, why am I treated like a criminal for clarifying history?"

Lyn stood up and left the kitchen. She walked to the window and stared out at the twinkling lights of Harpers Ferry. Obviously, thinking to herself, she shook her head in disagreement with DB. It was obvious, to her at least, that DB was missing something critical to common sense.

"You really need to cool it with the NPS. What else did they say?"

"Not much. I put a stop to the interrogation by citing my federal authority to ask such questions."

"What federal authority?"

"Oh, you know, my job as the official researcher of the GT journals."

"That hardly amounts to federal authorization, DB. I hope you didn't perjure yourself."

"Now who is being accusatory? Though they do seem interested in my research now...."

"Maybe you should get a lawyer."

"I directed them to the National Park Service Office of General Counsel for future questions."

"You did what? That's probably the office that got them involved with this in the first place! Oh, my God, would you just keep your mouth shut while I figure this out?"

Lyn paced around the apartment throwing her hands up in frustration at DB's stupidity. She couldn't believe what she was hearing. Thoughts ran through her head of DB being arrested and spending his life at Leavenworth prison. She would be a widow, of sorts, before she was even married.

"You're right. I need to secure my notes on the journal entries. It may not look too good that I've uncovered an underground rebel network, even if it's forty years old."

"I forgot all about that! What if it's still active? Or they did do something against the federal government? Oh shit! What if they're planning something as we speak and you are sitting on all this information?"

"Remember when I told you I felt like I was being watched or that I was peering into something dangerous? That could explain it. You're a genius!"

DB was being completely sincere in his compliment but didn't realize that he only pissed off Lyn even more. From her perspective, Lyn realized just how hopeless DB was when it came to appreciating his predicament. She made eye contact with DB to make sure he was paying attention to what she said next.

"But you, unfortunately, are not. What should we do? You've either got to turn that stuff in or get rid of it. Wait, have you showed it to anyone but me?"

"Nope. It's our secret. I was thinking though, what if this Lost Mungo character is still out there someplace? He seems like a nice guy. I mean I don't see anything dangerous about keeping family records. Should I try to warn him or something?"

"You've completely lost your mind. Warn him? Are you crazy? First off, he might not even exist. Second, if he did, he must have died years ago. And third, he could live anywhere along the 2,000 miles of trail or have moved on completely. How could you ever find him?"

"Well, I was thinking about that. From my review of the journals, all the characters I am reading about make routine visits to this town. Something about Harpers Ferry serves as a magnet to them. We need only to watch the summer thru-hikers this season and see if we spot anyone who looks suspicious."

"Seriously? Suspicious? Thru-hikers by their very nature look suspicious."

Lyn grabbed the bourbon bottle and drank deeply. DB looked on in awe. She was going to be completely drunk within minutes. Something about her desperate action made him think twice about the seriousness of his FBI interview. Faintly, it occurred to him that he may really be in trouble. As soon as she smashed the bottle down on the table, he picked it up and matched her.

Chapter Thirty-Four

Battletown, VA, December 24, 1974

The monk chanted over the deceased body of Los, his voice rising and falling as he gave repetitive instructions to the wandering soul traversing the In-Between. He had prayed these phrases a hundred times. The room was dimly lit by candles and smoke from incense wafted in circular patterns toward the ceiling. The body was turned east to facilitate its travels.

"Los, you will see a blue light. Do not approach it but walk away with confidence and no fear. You will see flashes in the sky and hear thunderous explosions. It's all sensory confusion. Walk away and keep to the path until you see a white light. Do not be afraid and do not desire your physical body back. Do not seek its familiarity. Your soul is free to wander and seek truth. Let go and follow the reality that presents itself. Do not collapse in fear. You have the opportunity for self-realization. Terrifying monsters will block your path. You must not fear them. They are only manifestations of your own fears. They do not exist. Look for empathetic deities. They will present themselves and serve as guides on this journey."

The priest could sense something unusual with this soul pilgrim. There was no fear, but only confidence. It was neither afraid nor surprised by its bodiless state. The monk was shocked it moved confidently across the In-Between. This was unlike any soul he ever prayed over. The spirit of Los was searching for something other than self-realization. The priest paused in his chants before he continued with urgency. He felt especially close to this soul. It was an endless spirit that had reincarnated multiple times before, even though it was fully self-realized. A tear streaked down his cheek with sheer joy. He was in the presence of a buddhavista, a pure enlightened soul who stayed during pain and suffering to protect fearful humans from their misery. Grasping his wooden prayer wheel, he raised his voice and spun it with increased devotion. Suddenly, he realized that he was playing a very small part in something immensely important to the human experience. He sensed countless souls were at stake.

A sense of purposeful searching came back through the ether. He now realized the buddhavista needed his help to find something specific that was lost: a soul was wandering the In-Between and he was witnessing its rescue. Something or someone was combating the darkest of all wrathful deities: The Authority. He would do what he could to help in this mission.

He had never seen such a strong spirit command the void in all directions. He looked down at the corpse of Los before him. He realized that he never knew his friend in life. Now, he truly understood why Los had invited him to the Shenandoah Valley. He was being taking along as a passenger with Los on a spiritual rescue mission. Images of Los flooded his mind. He saw the body of a large, middle-aged man, thin but strong with years of physical endeavor that bronzed his skin and weathered it like leather. He sensed great strength from the spirit but also great injury, even though there were no external scars. Whatever wounded this warrior was done deep inside the heart without penetration by any external object. By using his mind's eye, the priest peered into the core of the body to the damaged organ. The chambers and valves of the heart were physically sound, but a scar was obvious to his empathetic vision. A great betrayal had left a gaping hole. Misery bled from it even after death. Suddenly, the priest realized the spirit released from this body was searching for the cause of its pain. He didn't doubt this warrior spirit was joining the battle in the In-Between against the Authority but he felt it was also offering salvation to a soul.

The old monk kept these thoughts to himself and continued chanting instructions in the corpse before him.

CHAPTER THIRTY-FIVE

Standing on the path, the young couple stared together into the dense woods just beyond the translucent curtain of mist on either side. Bret realized he was falling in love with Zoa. He didn't understand why. She was just a stranger like all the other travelers. Why did she hold his attention so?

He sensed she was the same person who had appeared in the vortex. His hand had reached out to her without thinking. He had wanted to pull her through. There was no plea for help but she had appeared to be in peril. He had felt her condition was desperate but she had disappeared as the vortex closed. Realizing he might have interfered with her passage, Bret had hoped she could to make it through herself. Now, she was right next to him clutching his arm.

Ominous and strange sounds echoed through the air. Metal clashed against metal, hounds bayed and dogs barked off in the distance. An explosion brought Zoa into Bret's arms. It felt familiar and natural to hold her protectively. He remembered this embrace from some distant past. He heard his mom talk about soul mates. He wondered if this was the same sensation. He didn't want her to disappear back into the vortex of wind. He just wanted to be with her. He was content just being with her, on or off the path. She, however, was homesick. He decided to journey with her wherever she went.

Bret, Zoa, and the other younger travelers traded small talk as they rested along the trail. Rumors of a side trail that led back to the real world were repeated endlessly. It was not far from the clearing where they were spending the night. It supposedly led to a dismal bog that magically crossed through the impenetrable barrier. For some reason, the mist was thin there and passable. It was supposedly protected by a scary guard of some kind that blocked the way across the water. Bret heard that it could be bribed to let people pass. The only thing it accepted was Magda's food. Travelers suspected the guard was hungry because it lived in the isolated woods. There was no other way to physically cross back into the real world they left behind. Bret had watched helplessly as Zoa cried for hours about being in this strange place. She worried about never seeing her parents again. Bret didn't feel half as bad about not seeing his mother again but didn't want to mention it. So, with the hope Zoa would like him or at least need him, Bret talked of the secret crossing through the bog. To his satisfaction, she wanted to go and asked Bret to come with her. They planned their escape together while sitting around the fire beneath a starry sky. Young Tom was asleep under the wool blankets. They dared not tell anyone, especially Magda. She would probably be very upset if she heard their extra helpings were really going to feed a greedy guard. They had no idea how mad she would really be and why.

Waking up to another brilliant sunrise, Bret and Zoa packed up and roused Young Tom. He seemed strangely silent and not at all talkative. They started hiking along the path and quickly lost sight of Young Tom as other travelers joined the trek. Even though he could see hikers for miles up and down the path, they found themselves alone for long stretches of time.

Bret kept an eye out for signs of the secret side trail. He heard from other young people to watch out for a unique bend in the trail that temporarily obscured visibility of anyone on that section. He was to look for the telltale sign of thinning grass, a short stretch of dirt suddenly departing at a right angle in the middle of the bend exactly where a large oak tree half emerged from the mist. After hiking several hundred feet, Bret finally saw an oak tree that fit the description. As he walked past, he briefly saw what appeared to be an animal trail.

Bret grabbed Zoa's hand and pulled her off the golden path. He looked behind them to make sure their escape was unseen. He was confronted by a wall of mist that the narrow trail disappeared into. He tightened his grip on Zoa's hand.

"Are you sure you want to do this?" He asked.

"As long as you go first." She replied.

They went through one after the other. On the other side of the mist wall, they emerged into a dense forest.

"That is a good sign. The mist wall along the other parts of the trail are impassable." Bret said.

"Ok, what's next?" Zoa asked.

"We should be able to follow this trail to a bog or something, cross it and find our world on the other side."

"Something about a grumpy guard blocking our way?"

"That is why we brought the food. When he tells us we can't pass, we offer Magda's delights." Bret responded.

"Sounds too simple to be true but what is the worst that can happen?" Zoa said.

They followed the trail up and down several small hills and around several large boulders until the land became flat and muddy. Eventually, the trail ended at the banks of a dismal bog.

"I don't see any guard," Bret whispered.

"Let's try to get across before he sees us," Zoa said.

Black water filled the bog. Clumps of dead reeds poked through its slimy surface. Bret assumed nothing survived within its waters judging by the lack of any living vegetation along its banks. They stepped across the first of many large stones that stretched crookedly toward the opposite side. Their shoes slid on each oily stone. Through the mist, Bret could see a diffused light. They smiled at each other imagining this was the real world within reach.

As they reached the bog's center, a dark hulking figure sloshed toward them from within the mist. Zoa reached for Bret's hand. It was the sentinel. They could not see its face as it was robed from head to toe. A spear rose in its arm pointed directly at them. Their way was now blocked. The creature waited right next to the stepping stones. It screamed an indecipherable command. Bret stopped in mid step, balancing on one foot to avoid getting any closer. The creature extended a green hand from within its cloaked robe. Long pointed fingernails gleamed like razor blades in the dim light. Bret looked to Zoa for help.

"Do you think this is when we feed it?" Bret asked.

"Haven't you ever had a dog? It definitely wants to eat," Zoa replied.

What if it wants to eat me?" Bret asked.

"Don't be a pussy. Feed it or get out of my way so I can. This thing ain't stopping me from seeing my parents."

"You sound exactly like my cousin Orc. What is it with country people, no subtlety," Bret said.

"You better feed him or he will eat you," Zoa replied with a gentle nudge on his back.

Alarmed at the thought of being eaten and unsure of Zoa's patience, Bret placed the basket of food into the claw-like hand. The creature brought Magda's delights to its hooded face. The sounds of gnashing teeth tearing the basket apart stunned Bret.

"Run!" shouted Zoa.

She pushed hard onto Bret's back. The two skimmed across the wet stones – hardly touching down before leaping to the next – until they reached dry land.

"Holy shit! I can't believe we made it without falling in," Bret said.

"People can do amazing things when they're scared shitless," Zoa responded.

"I couldn't have put it better myself. Must mean I am becoming a redneck." Bret added with a slight Southern drawl.

The pair stood on the bank of the dismal bog. Bending over to catch his breath, Bret wondered aloud if the creature would pursue them. Zoa jerked her head back toward the mist to look for the guard. Seeing nothing, she patted Bret on the shoulder.

"Good job back there. I thought for sure he would take your hand with that basket."

"Now you tell me."

"I can see the trail leading away from the bank. It looks to disappear into that thicket of briar," Zoa said.

"Can't be any more dangerous than that hungry monster," Bret offered.

Zoa took the lead and followed the trail into the briar patch, which appeared dense and impenetrable. To their amazement, the trail zigzagged back and forth at sharp angles weaving its way through the wall of thorns. They emerged onto a deserted road.

"I recognize this," Zoa said.

"Could be a million country lanes if you ask me," Bret replied.

"Nope, I know exactly where we are. This is the perimeter road that runs just outside the town limits."

"But what town exactly?"

"Battletown!" Zoa yelled.

While she recognized the general area, it looked very different than she remembered. As they passed through the outer neighborhoods toward Main Street, Zoa became increasingly alarmed. Everything she saw was in a state of decay. Townsfolk shuffled about the yards and sidewalks seemingly oblivious to the destruction. Houses and buildings had partially collapsed, their bricks spilled into the streets. Bret and Zoa crossed what used to be a small town that was well on its way to becoming the ruins of a past civilization. When Zoa recognized her home in the debris, she started running. She jumped up the sagging wooden porch steps and pushed through the front door that barely hung on its hinges. Bret followed her into the living room and noticed that the clocks in the house had stopped working some time ago. Zoa's mother rose from the torn seat cushions of the sofa. She squealed with pleasure at seeing her daughter. A piece of rotted upholstery stuck to her pants. The sun shone through the absent roof.

"Goddam it Zoa, where have you been?"

"I am okay. Don't be mad Momma."

"We were worried sick about you. Your father has been out with the sheriff's deputies looking all night.

"Mom, I missed you. I'm sorry I made you worry. I love you but I don't think I can stay for Dad."

"You can't leave us again. This is where you belong."

"I just came back to tell you I am okay. My friend and I must get back. Something isn't right here. We need to find out what happened while we were gone."

"I don't know what you are saying. Everything is the same as when you left, dear. Except I cleaned up your bedroom, which I won't do again mind you."

Bret stepped forward and was about to introduce himself when Zoa turned and ran up the stairs just off the kitchen.

"Sorry, ma'am. It's nice to meet you. Your daughter is a nice person. Bret fidgeted but could not make himself disappear, try as he might.

"Mom, never mind him," Zoa yelled from the second floor. Bret followed her upstairs and stepped over fallen drywall in the hallway. He tiptoed into her bedroom just in time to see her sit on her bed. It instantaneously collapsed onto the floor.

"What the hell happened here?" Zoa pleaded.

"I forgot to tell you that Magda said we can never go back home. I mean that we will never see our homes the way they were. Once we leave the path, we see the things differently. Nothing has changed for people here. It is just our new vision that makes things look different."

"Like what does that mean?"

"I think anthropology would call it being thrice born. We are born once into this life where everything looks normal because it is all we know. Then we leave and learn another culture and see the world from a different perspective. When we come back home, we see our world as outsiders. I think that is what has happened. This world hasn't changed. We have."

"That is some crazy shit, Bret."

"Sorry, but that is better than believing your hometown is some kind of post-apocalyptic hell hole."

"Well, that makes me feel a little better. We must get back to the path either way. I want to figure out how to see things the way they were."

The two agreed and walked slowly down the stairs to say goodbye.

Chapter Thirty-Six

Battletown, VA, December 24, 1974

Lord Jim spread out the manuscripts on the scratched and tarnished kitchen table. He was sitting before the fireplace watching slender flames flicker faintly in the early morning darkness. The smoke from his pipe curled up toward the ceiling. He was alone in the house except for the monk chanting over the body of Los in the upstairs bedroom. At dawn, the second raid on Harpers Ferry would start. He would not participate in the main action but a diversionary action. There was no chance he would survive. For that reason, he wanted to inventory important documents in the possession of the Kindred. He felt compelled to notate each document. Sifting through the mound of papers, he closely examined each one under a small lamp. Before him lay a collection of official government memorandums, maps, illustrations, and detailed schematics. His hand gripped a pen that narrated a short message on each record. He did not know who would survive tomorrow's raid. The highest-ranking member still drawing breath tomorrow evening would be the new chief of the Kindred. He knew for sure it would not be him. Whoever it was, they would need help understanding the mission of organization and more importantly the enemy they faced.

He drew one illustrated document up to his eyes for closer examination. It depicted human existence in life, death, and the In-Between. Bodies and spirits in each realm had two things in common: They appeared to be in constant transit and continuously harassed by evil spirits. Lord Jim scratched an asterisk next to the spirits and at the bottom of the document wrote the words, "Authority Agents." Souls traveled between key milestones. They appeared in constant transit between life, death, and rebirth. Ever present was the Authority surveillance and manipulation of minds and souls. It constantly implanted fear subconsciously in the physical realm through its national emergency broadcast system.

From deep within Mount Storm, electrical pulses transmitted overt alerts of impending danger that interrupted radio and televisions. The threats included earthquakes, storms, floods, tornados, chemical accidents, crime sprees, or terrorism. In the same broadcasts, the Authority sent out subliminal messages in packets that were released upon death. The disembodied soul found itself wandering the In Between completely confused by its new existence. In this vulnerable state, the Authority messages were spontaneously released to frighten the soul even more.

Lord Jim heard the chanting upstairs stop and footsteps descend to the kitchen. The monk appeared in the doorway. He was bundled in a bulky coat and a sweater. His orange cloth robe reached just below his bare knees. Wool socks warmed his feet inside leather sandals.

"How is Los?" Lord Jim asked.

"He is journeying wide and far. Fearless in his search," the monk replied.

"I had no doubt he would transit like a soldier."

"There is something different. I have never seen it before. His spirit is fully conscious but won't leave the In-Between."

"He was unique." Lord Jim looked back to his papers.

"There is secrecy. He does not see something he is looking for. Do you know what it is?" The monk shifted his position in the doorway and cuddled an empty bowl. He stared at Lord Jim. An accusation had been given and he waited for the response.

"You have been in the cold too long. Fill up that thing with some hot tea."

"He doesn't know that Enith is still alive. You tricked him."

Waving his hand in the air, Lord Jim tried to push away the truth.

"He is simply different from the rest. Don't worry about him. He will reincarnate to a higher being but only after his mission is accomplished."

Lord Jim stood and walked to the stove. He placed a kettle on the range and turned on the electric element. Within seconds, it was glowing red. Without turning around, he continued the conversation.

"You know as well as I do that fear mongering is successful among the truly weak. Those souls who have not prepared to wander the In-Between seek shelter wherever it can be found. Out of fear, they abandon all aspirations to advance in the next life and simply cling to any physical presence, degrading with each reincarnation. That is exactly what the Authority wants. Los was always different. Nothing gave him fear."

"He feared losing Enith and I sense he fears not finding her."

"I don't know what you are talking about. She left him years ago."

"He will search for her in vain. Her spirit cannot be found because she is not dead. She is alive. You put him at great risk."

Lord Jim breathed heavily, a tear fell down his cheek. The whistling kettle broke the silence of the room. He took it off the stove and poured two cups of tea. He turned and offered one to the small monk who was now sitting at the kitchen table looking at his manuscripts.

"We needed a warrior spirit and Los was our best choice. You don't understand who we are up against. I make the tough decisions. Urizen must be stopped. Look at those documents carefully. He plans to terrorize generations of citizens. He will ensure millions of souls will never reincarnate into higher forms. Nobody will be permitted to exist outside of Urizen's net, even when cast beyond life itself."

The monk accepted the tea and cupped it with both hands. The warmth felt good and relieved the numbness in his fingers. He sipped the tea and leaned toward the fire.

"I understand the spiritual world my friend," said the monk. "Like any good plan, Urizen's is generational. I feel his presence everywhere in the In-Between. He attacks wandering souls relentlessly. I must tell you though, he fears transits more than anything. These souls are beyond his control. He finds that intolerable. His monitoring system can only detect a transit's departure. It cannot locate their travels along the golden path during the day or even as they pulsate blue at night. These souls were entirely off the grid. Urizen's worse fear was these travelers were going back in time. That was even more dangerous than reincarnation. Generations of his work could be undone. He has never planned for this action. If they corrected the past, his system of control in the physical dimension would be undermined completely. So, these time travelers can undo his work from the past."

"You know a lot for a lowly monk from a monastery at the rooftop of the world. No wonder Los wanted you here," Lord Jim said.

"Urizen is worried the Kindred will understand his spiritual manipulation. His confidence waivers. I sense other things as well. There is a new force that threatens him. Finally, I feel an unearthly force at work. It is different than anything I have ever detected. This force is strange, unknown to me. I feel it is alien to this world, to this planet."

The monk drained the last bit of his tea and stood to depart.

"I have to get back to my prayers. As strong as he is, Los is very much in danger. He needs my prayers."

The monk bowed with his hands clasped together. Lord Jim crossed himself in return.

"Let's pray for travelers across all realms this dawn. With the sunrise comes death." Lord Jim replied.

Lord Jim returned to the documents on the kitchen table. The fire was dead now. His pipe was cold. The first hints of light distinguished the barn in the front lawn from the black night. He listened to the footsteps of the monk ascend the stairs. He shuffled through documents and made several notations in the margins. Upstairs, the prayer chanting began again. He paused from his work and crossed himself again.

Chapter Thirty-Seven

Harpers Ferry, WV, June 20, 2016, 9:00 PM

The evening had advanced, tourists and adventure seekers exhausted and sunburnt fled back to their cars for their return trips to the real world. DB and Lyn sat silently for several minutes contemplating his predicament.

"I think we should get a bite to eat," DB said.

He hoped to calm Lyn down. She was still clearly frustrated about his visit from the FBI.

"What you need is a little humility and a good lawyer."

She shook her head at his attempt to change the topic but realized she was very hungry.

"I can't afford an attorney. If they pursue their investigation, I promise not to talk to them without a lawyer. I especially promise to stay away from the Park Service rangers," DB replied standing up from the table.

DB stroked her hair and rubbed her shoulders. He couldn't believe his life was spiraling downwards so fast. The last thing he wanted was to lose was Lyn.

"Why are you so consumed by your conspiracy theory? Just let it go and live your life! Clearly people are enjoying themselves, prospering, travelling, writing, and God knows what else! All under the scrutiny of 'the Authority' or whatever you call it." She threw her hands up in disgust.

"Lyn, we're free to exist and thrive as long as we don't question authority – small 'a' – but when we do, that's when the Authority – capital 'A' – gets upset and comes down to spank us back into line."

"Well, I guess I do need something to eat. I just can't process all this crap on an empty stomach. Seriously, sometimes I just want a normal boyfriend. Nobody can see the truth but you. OOOOH. Sounds scary but it's also borderline elitist. Why are you the only person who questions all of society? Why is nobody else doing the same?"

"That's exactly why we need to find this Lost Mungo character. He can tell us what the hell the secret group is up to and, by default, how much trouble I'm in."

Together, they left the apartment. Lyn's mind was on drinks while DB's was on Lost Mungo. They descended the rickety, wooden stairs affixed to the outside of the house and walked down Main Street to the bar. Lyn pushed open the door of the Secret Society Tavern ahead of DB. She was met with catcalls from the male patrons inside. She was probably the most beautiful woman in Harpers Ferry that summer, or at least the most beautiful to frequent this hole and these barflies were showing their appreciation.

"Alright, calm down you animals," DB protested.

"Either buy me a drink or shut up," Lyn chimed in.

One especially drunk acquaintance offered to buy her drinks all night for a closer inspection.

"That's enough!" said the bartender. "These guys actually pay their tabs, so the rest of you miscreants can shut the hell up."

"Thank you, good sir," said DB. "We appreciate your honor and decency." He spoke with faux formality and bowed his head.

"Enough of that shit. What are you drinking?" came the no nonsense reply.

"A glass of your finest wine for my lady and I shall have a cognac, aged not under 10 years." DB refused to give up his act.

"Okay. You can get yourself a six pack to go if you keep this shit up."

"Sorry. Two draft Mothman IPAs please," DB replied.

They took seats in a booth under a drawing of John Brown standing on the gallows awaiting his execution.

"Let's hope you have a happier ending," Lyn said.

"They don't hang people for ridiculing park rangers," DB laughed nervously.

Lyn grabbed a pen from her purse and began writing on a napkin. She was doing what attracted DB to her in the first place; organizing him out of a problem. As Lyn enumerated his transgressions and possible punishments, she clearly distinguished herself from any jeopardy. They didn't notice a middle-aged woman studying them with great interest. She didn't break her stare even as she took turns stroking a pair of obese Chesapeake Bay Retrievers wheezing heavily under her table. Looking every inch a workhand, she took large swigs from her pint glass before wiping away the foam from her lips. She wore canvas pants tucked into high, brown leather boots spackled with mud. Her long-sleeve cotton shirt was rolled to the elbow, exposing her tanned and muscular arms. A colorful bandana was tied around her neck and another held back her long, unruly hair. It hadn't seen a brush in a while, let alone shampoo. Large callouses were visible on both hands. She dug one of them into her pocket and produced an earring, silver and colored with gemstones. She threaded it through a hole, one of many on each ear. She wore a leather necklace with a single piece of bone tied in the center. A cloth bag rested on the seat across from her. It was half filled with tree saplings. She looked every inch a gypsy fortune teller.

"So, according to hiker descriptions recorded in the journals, we're looking for an eccentric man who dresses like a jester and wears a backpack." DB started the conversation.

"That could be half the people in Harpers Ferry during hiking season!" Lyn replied.

"I think we can narrow him down due to the eccentricity of his headgear. Look at this."

DB withdrew a wrinkled piece of Xerox paper from his chest pocket. He unfolded it and placed it squarely on the table between them.

"I saw this drawing in a journal after a hiker entry sometime back in 1985. He is listing several oddities of his hike that day, one of which was this description of an elderly man wearing a pith helmet."

"That's so weird. What makes you think its Lost Mungo?"

"Because the hiker wrote that he came upon an old guy in a shelter writing in a large, leather-bound book. He assumed it was the shelter journal. When he asked to see it when the old guy was done, supposedly, he snapped it shut and put it in his pack and hiked into the night. The hiker, of course, thought this behavior was extremely weird. When he found the real shelter journal and realized it wasn't what the old guy had been carrying, he tried to remember if he had seen anything written on the book's cover. Look here, underneath his sketch of the old guy."

"*The Genealogies of the Wrathful Empathies.* Are you kidding me? We've found him. That was 1985. Do you think he's alive today?" Lyn blurted out.

"I am not sure, but at least we've narrowed down our search. I mean, how many elderly men will be backpacking through town this summer wearing a pith helmet?"

"Fortunately, not more than five or six. We've got to set up a watch or something. I mean, with both of us working, we could miss him if he just breezes through on the trail and doesn't hang around."

DB leaned toward her and lowered his voice.

"I'll let my contacts know. I have my own secret network," he said only half joking.

"Well, what if he doesn't frequent bars? You may need more spies than a handful of bartenders."

"Hey, don't disparage my network!"

"I'm just saying, we may need to enroll some new contacts if we want to increase our chances of finding this mysterious Lost Mungo."

A pair of boots approached their table and a pair of scarred hands pulled out a chair. The gypsy woman thrust herself between them as she leaned over the table. Both DB and Lyn were speechless with her boldness.

"You're never going to find Lost Mungo! He's not stupid enough to waltz into this town in broad daylight."

Lyn looked the woman up and down and wondered if she was homeless. DB was the first to respond.

"Well, since you seem to be part of the conversation now, I guess you can be part of the planning. What do you know about Mungo and who the hell are you?"

"I'm Magda and those are my lazy dogs under the table over there." She pointed to the now-snoring retrievers.

"They are fat, lazy, and expect the world to feed them. Once upon a time, they were strong and mean, and put the fear in men and bears. Now they are just old and decrepit, but they provide me with companionship and can still muster up a growl if anyone enters our camp."

"Nice dogs. I'll try not to wake them," DB responded.

"What can you tell us about Lost Mungo and why don't you think we'll ever find him?" Lyn asked.

"Well, I never said, 'never.' You'll just have to go find him yourself instead of waiting for him to stumble past you."

Lyn moved over in the booth and offered Magda a seat. She sat down but knocked the table with her large girth sending both beers tumbling over.

"Sorry, about that. I fattened up for winter, ya know."

"No problem, I will order some more. Do you want anything?" DB offered.

"We should just get a pitcher or two. I am mighty thirsty. Been hauling saplings across mountains all day," she replied.

"Back to Mungo, I don't want to do anything to jeopardize the old guy. He seems like someone I would like to get to know. I think we have a lot in common. If anything, I'm probably in as much trouble as he is," DB let slip.

"Well, I happen to know these hills pretty good and can send you in the general direction. I met him a couple of times. Harmless enough old guy and I wouldn't want any mischief to come to him either. Tell me why you're so interested in meeting him."

"Sure, but before I say too much about us, maybe we should know more about you. I mean, the FBI interrogated me today and out of the blue you push yourself into our conversation. Who are you exactly?"

"FBI huh? Sounds like you and Lost Mungo keep the same company. Or have the same enemies, more likely," Magda replied.

"Just to be clear, they're interested in DB, not me. I'm just a material witness or whatever they call an innocent bystander," Lyn interrupted.

She put both her hands out to draw space between her and DB as if that helped to put distance between his criminality.

Magda eyed Lyn carefully.

"Well, like I said, I'm Magda. I plant trees. That bag over there was full of saplings when I started this morning. I reseeded the entire eastern slope of Sugarloaf Mountain today. Nasty case of ash borer beetles left the forest decimated. I work for the Civilian Conservation Corps and I reforest land all over the mid-Atlantic. It's just me and the dogs. We go wherever I get a contract and I sleep wherever I run out of saplings. End up most nights under the stars and when it gets cold, I sleep in my pickup truck. So, I'm in places where there aren't many people and not many trails. I make my own way up and down the mountains. Typically, I come across maintained trails that are blazed, but occasionally I stumble across hidden trails."

"Hidden trials, that sounds intriguing." DB looked at Lyn.

She rolled her eyes. "More secret worlds in plain sight. I really wish you'd never started this summer internship DB," she replied then drank deeply from her beer glass.

"We digress, Magda. Please continue," DB apologized.

Magda looked around the bar, gripped her beer, took a swig, swallowed hard, and leaned forward.

"There are trails and then there are trails. Ghost trails I call 'em. Left to the forest except they aren't really abandoned. Some hikers know of their existence, either from memory or by instinct. Why, every once in a while, I'll get on a ghost trail by mistake only to realize I made a wrong turn after about 20 yards or so. These ghost trails are mostly tracts of what was once the main trail, which has been abandoned. When new a trail section is opened, the old section is closed off at the junctions. New maps are printed and the old trails are erased completely from the record. Since the trail is hidden by brush and logs, people just walk past a four or five-mile section of old trail without being any wiser. Some reroutes are even longer. Without maintenance or activity, these trails are lost to the forest and to all but the memory of a few old veterans of the mountains. I suspect Lost Mungo is one of 'em old hikers with a long memory. What people don't realize is that these sections, in most cases, have the old shelters, too. And they are still intact."

"Let me guess. Ghost shelters?" Lyn piped in.

"Exactly. Ghost shelters, signs, springs, and trail depressions. It's all there if one has the eyes to see," Magda answered.

"I don't believe people can see ghost trails any more than I believe people can see ghosts." Lyn scoffed.

DB and Magda exchanged knowing glances. Magda tried again to explain the supernatural in a way Lyn could understand.

"Have you ever seen an animal trail when you were walking in the woods? Are they there or are you just imagining a path? Maybe you're just seeing random depressions in the ground, a series of unrelated spaces linked together by passages through forest detritus. Or maybe animal trails do exist and are evidence of inexplicable paths that animals choose to follow. Imagine the entire forest is open for you to move through, but you decide to stay on a path. Does it give you comfort, a sense of safety? Maybe it's just easy to stay out of the way of obstacles. Imagine these paths are built without the use of any tools or intentional maintenance; they just exist due to the countless animals that tread them. I say there's no difference between the feet of thousands of animals following the same path for centuries and the humans that hike the trails that mean something special to them. Unlike animals, the trail isn't implanted in our DNA but in our psyche. Once a trail has been walked, there's a spiritual imprint left behind. Only a few can see but even fewer choose to follow it."

"I know what she is talking about!" DB chimed in. "Occasionally, I'll keep hiking on a path even though there's a change-of-direction sign. Sure, I may have to step over and under some blowdown, but I can clearly see the path ahead of me. Its only after walking about fifty yards that I notice the blazes are extremely faded or even scratched off that it dawns on me. I'm on a ghost trail! I stop to turn back, but I swear I can see the path go on into the distance. It's physically obscured, but I can sense it."

"Seriously DB, you've got to get ahold of yourself," Lyn turned toward Magda. "And you need to stop encouraging him with your ghost trails and secret society of midnight hikers," Lyn wiggled her fingers in the air.

DB shooed her off.

"So, what you're saying is, throughout these mountains," DB raised his arms and waved them in every direction, "are secret hikers, using secret trails, spending the nights in secret shelters. Wow." DB stared at both women with eyes as wide as his gaping mouth.

"I don't know much about the secret groups or their activities, but there are ghost hikers on ghost trails and I've seen them. In fact, I saw your Lost Mungo not too long ago," Magda admitted.

Both Lyn and DB jumped up from their seats and yelled the same question.

"Where did you see him?"

"It was down near Peter's Mountain. There's a section of trail that was rerouted off private land into a state park. I was replanting the southern slope of the mountain, you know, the side that faces the industrial plant on the New River. It was that afternoon I saw him. I was squatting down in the bushes to pee when he came walking by on the ghost trail. Of course, my dogs were sound asleep on a bed of ferns and provided absolutely no warning. He was a strange looking dude. He had an enormous backpack on, bent him over at an angle. Maybe because it's heavy or maybe because he is so old. Either way, he didn't see me and just kept hiking. I went back to planting saplings until my bag was empty. Then I bushwhacked until I came upon a blue blaze that I recognized. It ran down to the trailhead parking lot. When I got to my truck, I lowered the tailgate and cooked dinner on my stove. After cleaning up, I settled down to spend the night in the truck cap. A couple hours went by. I think it was around midnight when a headlamp showed into my truck. It was him. He walked into the parking lot from a blue blaze trailhead. He was without a pack. I figure he left it at a ghost shelter. Anyway, he just stood there in the empty lot, turned off his light and waited. I watched him standing there, by himself, in the dark for about ten minutes. Finally, I heard a car engine and saw bright headlights pull in off the road. He climbed in without saying a word. The car drove away. Just before dawn the next morning, I heard a car door shut and I heard someone walk past my truck. One of my lazy dogs even mustered a growled. I could hear the footsteps cross the parking lot. This time, I grabbed my gun before I peeked out the cab window. Sure enough, it was him, hiking back up the trail.

"Are you sure it was him?"

"Well, how many people have a headlamp affixed to their pith helmet? Besides, I just figured he went into town to resupply or something, maybe drink a beer. Who knows. But, for sure, he left after sunset and returned before dawn. That's why I am saying you won't see him walking down Main Street Harpers Ferry in broad daylight."

"Okay, well that settles it. Either we stake out the streets at night or wander these ghost trails during the day. Take your pick," DB said.

He turned to Lyn excited to hear her choice. She shook her head no at either option.

"DB, seriously, I'm not wandering the woods on hidden trails and I'm not losing sleep waiting for this guy to make his ghost-like appearance in the middle of the night. I have a day job, remember?"

Magda once again inserted herself.

"Well, just don't waste your time looking for him in broad daylight in Harpers Ferry. He avoids police at all costs. Watch night traffic or find ghost trails during the day. That is your choice. Which reminds me, why are you so interested in him again?"

"I'm doing research for the GTC this summer and he keeps coming up in the journals. I connected these weird symbols to him after certain other hiker entries tipped me off to his presence in the shelter at the same time. A pattern developed. He was notating births and deaths of anonymous people. I really can't figure out why exactly, but there appears to be a correlation between him and another group that I'm still struggling to identify," DB explained.

He then grabbed his notes and searched lines of pages for a specific word.

"Found it. Have you ever heard of a group called the Kindred?" he asked.

Magda's face went white as a ghost at the question.

CHAPTER THIRTY-EIGHT

Battletown, VA, December 23, 1974

Wobbly shifted his feet and tried to look inconspicuous while standing at the corner of Main Street and Rout 340. His lips moved as he silently repeated the instructions Los had given him the night before. He stared into the window of the local grill, wanting so badly to eat, and feel the warmth of a cozy table inside. Not this time, he thought to himself. He had an important rendezvous with Los and Lord Jim. They had called a meeting of all the Kindred. He suspected something big was about to take place. What role he would play was a mystery to him. In the past, he was never trusted with anything important. Maybe this time things would be different. He wasn't sure if Lord Jim had finally accepted him as full member. After all, he was not part of the Kindred lineage but an adopted son. It was only because of his father's and grandfather's devotion to local coal miners, many of whom were Kindred members, that Lord Jim consented to let him into the organization. He wasn't treated as a real warrior but only trusted with non-secure roles. In his case, this meant serving as drug runner and messenger. His job was to take the weed grown deep in the Kindred-controlled forest of West Virginia, and sell it for profit in trail towns all along the GT. It turned out, he was a natural drug dealer. His secondary job was to disseminate and post critical messages as signaled by coded trail journals. The remaining communities of Wobblies helped him accomplish this task. In this way, he managed to reach far-flung audiences stretching across the nation. It seemed underground rebels were present wherever two backroads met. Los mentioned other networks would assist in this effort, but Wobbly didn't know who they were.

He was proud of his family's legacy. His grandfather was an early organizer of the coal miners' union from Kentucky to Pennsylvania. If the voiceless miner had royalty, his grandfather was a king. His father continued the tradition of direct action. He battled at the picket line, killed a man, and ran away from the cops and his family. Some say the State Highway Patrol caught him on a lonely back road and beat him to death. Wobbly liked that version of the story rather than believe he was abandoned by a union goon who was just avoiding a jail cell.

Maybe because he never knew his father beyond a distant memory, Wobbly fantasied about him as a virtuous Tom Joad punching a hired gun so hard he died. Wobbly saw it as his birthright to continue this legacy of disorderly conduct. Although his monetary inheritance was nothing more than a lucky rabbit's foot, he felt morally rich. He hoped the blood coursing through his veins was of a unique type that risked everything to fight injustice. Evaluating his reflection in the café window, Wobbly saw a very unheroic figure staring back. Where his father and grandfather were known to be physically imposing, Wobbly was short, corpulent, and not at all intimidating. Still, in his mind, he was a daring rebel who risked arrest at any minute. Even if it was just for selling weed.

The most exciting tales he remembered were of the old days. His mother told stories of his father and grandfather behaving like men possessed in bare knuckle fights. They even faced revolvers held by coal company thugs. These tales were handed down by family and friends. All completely out of sight of the newspapers and, of course, the history books. He wondered how many Americans today had ever heard of the Wobblies? Yes, they lost more fights than they won, especially toward the end of their movement. But despite the best efforts of the Authority, their deeds were not forgotten and couldn't be erased where it mattered most: in the hearts, minds, and souls of almost everyone who cared not for their own prosperity but for humanity.

The final straw for the Wobblies was the creation of the FBI. They took over for the hired company goons and truly professionalized intimidation. In truth, the first national police organization cut its teeth on suppressing political dissent. His grandfather and his father had fought at the very margins of society. Their struggle for a workers' utopia pitted them against a vast and highly organized force capable of immense violence. The real hallmark of the FBI was its creation of a federal surveillance state before the emergence of an electronic technology. Even with its role in the development of the modern surveillance society, the FBI still operated within Constitutional constraints. The Authority, of course, crossed the line where the FBI stopped. It completely disregarded the idea of a constitutional republic. As a result, a dark, sinister control matrix was now in control of reality. The Kindred were the last of the free thinkers and they were a target.

Walking down the sidewalk of yet another small trail town, Wobbly opened his wallet expecting the worse. He peered into the empty space where dollars should be and sighed with resignation. Wobbly suffered from an inconvenient downside of being a social reformer: extreme poverty. Stopping at the main intersection in Battletown, he took out his most valuable possession. It was a tattered photograph of his father. Being the son of such a famous underground figure had its privileges. Rarely did he buy his own beer, at least in certain taverns. Touching his finger to the defiant face in the picture, he hoped to gain some of his strength. He visualized himself standing at a picket line facing off across from a big company goon. Like anyone, he wondered whether he would be brave in the face of danger. His deep fear was he may not be cut of the same cloth as his ancestors.

He stuffed the photo back in his wallet and headed toward the local burger joint. It was time to make some money. His profits supported families who could not work due to the nature of their Kindred duties. Lucky for them, he had lots of customers who would pay good money for premium weed. As he approached the parking lot, he saw a group of teenagers who recognized him and eagerly started calling out their orders. He collected hundreds of dollars by unloading nature's tonic. He made great money selling to locals at each trail town and especially at the high schools. Teenagers were the same everywhere he went. It was a job that was truly mobile with no office hours or dress code. Best of all, he had no boss.

His next stop was the Christmas Eve Mass at St. Francis Catholic Church in Battletown. Wobbly shuffled in just as the Mass began. The crowd was small and sparsely seated. Seriously buzzing, he nodded off during the sermon, but woke just before the collection plate was passed down his aisle. He stuffed several hundred dollars into a church envelope and dropped the rather pregnant donation into the basket. The church attendant nodded knowingly as he received a collection much heavier than usual. Wobbly went back to sleep.

He awoke with the sound of singing and shuffling as people got up to take Communion. Dutifully, Wobbly got in line and proceeded to the alter. He held out his hands and the priest pressed a small piece of paper into his palms. Another successful drop and exchange of communications. The money from the collection basket would be distributed to Kindred families, hand-counted by the rebel priest, and placed in equal amounts in hand-addressed envelopes.

After the service, Wobbly walked back into town and toward his favorite joint. He felt satisfied that he had completed his duty for the day and looked forward to refreshments. People would eat and pay their bills this week thanks to him. It was important work if not heroic work. The Kindred could focus on what it needed to do: plan its next big raid against the Authority.

Wobbly lit a fresh joint and dragged deeply. He scanned Main Street in both directions. While he loved the freedom of his life, coming off the trail always left him hungry and with a powerful thirst. He had no money to satisfy either. Half his earnings went into the church envelope. The other half went to the local Kindred tavern. He hoped to scrounge a meal but knew he had earned at least a few free beers. If the right bartender was working, it could be more. At the point of despair, his eyes opened wide when he recognized an establishment two blocks away.

"When you ain't in chains, where ya going to go? Vagaries!" Wobbly shouted.

He turned an unsteady circle and started boogying down the road. Several townsfolk looked askance at the sight of the dirty, smelly hiker as he ambled past clever boutiques and trendy bistros. Wafting puffs of smoke as he shambled down the street, Wobbly turned right and crossed against oncoming traffic. Car horns blared as he danced in the middle of the street. Stumbling over the curb, he stopped in front of a dingy storefront. A blackboard sign hung at an angle from the covered porch. Someone had haphazardly scrawled the name of the establishment with thick yellow chalk: The Vagaries of Life Tavern. Half a dozen backpacks were lined up on the front porch. Empty beer cans littered the un-mowed grass between the broken sidewalk and the sagging wooden front steps.

Inside, faux-wood paneling lined most of the walls. Stained and broken ceiling tiles clung precariously overhead. A wall-mounted phone rang incessantly. Finally, provoking his ire, a scruffy man towering behind the bar pawed the phone to his ear.

"Vagaries," he growled. "No idea. Absurd happy hour starts when it starts. What the fuck don't you understand? I have no idea when it starts! Absurd happy hour happens when it happens. No time or end. Well, yeah not before 5 pm. That should be obvious. Only when a quorum of twelve drinkers, not including the bartender or barmaid, is present. And then the happy hour bell has to ring itself." He mangled the phone back onto its receiver. "Yeah, fuck you too," he replied as an afterthought.

Shaking his head in frustration, he turned to face Wobbly. With mock disgust, he announced to the bar crowd, "Even someone as clueless as Wobbly knows the obvious distinction between a normal hour and an absurd happy hour."

"Dude, where did you learn your customer skills? Maybe if you didn't piss everyone off, this bar could turn a profit," Wobbly countered to much laughter from the bar crowd.

"Not if everyone drinks like a bottomless shit hole like you."

"Ah Bigfoot, you really know how to talk to a girl."

Wobbly felt the weight on an enormous hand on his shoulders. He suddenly feared Vagaries got a bouncer since the last time he was here. He turned around to confront his fate and saw a huge bearded man towering over him.

"Whiskeytown!" Wobbly screamed at the top of his voice.

"Wobbly, you red headed piece of shit!" came the reply.

Before he could react, Wobbly was face first in the drunken embrace of a man-bear whose down jacket reeked of beer.

"Long time man. Good to see the legend. Whiskeytown making the scene at Vagaries. Classic," Wobbly said pushing away.

"Jesus, the Kindred must be pulling out all the stops to bring you here," Whiskeytown replied.

"Hey, someone has to pay for this beer. What are you doing out of the mountains? Are there no lost hikers to rescue?"

"As a matter of fact, I ferried Lost Mungo out of a bad snowstorm earlier this week."

"That's a bad sign. If the Kindred brought him in, then shit is about to hit fan."

"I know. Lost Mungo is the official recorder of dead raiders. They wanted the little guy here and I don't question my orders," Whiskeytown remarked considering his beer.

"Even more reason to drink our faces off tonight," Wobbly cheered.

His positivity generated a rebel yell from everyone in the bar. Pushing past two shabby and unstable patrons, he gently rested his two elbows on the bar and smiled angelically.

"One PBR draft please."

"Wobbly, you are paying for your beer today and I mean it this time."

"Bigfoot, you know the Kindred drink for free. I mean, this is a bar for the Kindred so stop hassling me. Besides, I'm here in official capacity. First order of my business is financial. Here is today's contribution on behalf of all Kindred drinkers in this fine establishment." Wobbly handed Bigfoot a wad of bills. "Second, I'm here to meet an important operative, so for Christ's sake, try not to look so fucking scary."

Bigfoot carefully counted the money and expressed dismay.

"Wobbly, your outstanding tab is almost $200. That means you can afford one beer and there is nothing left over for anyone else."

"Don't forget, I'm adding to the whole absurd happy hour head count, so I'm going to be drinking for free any minute. Please, Bigfoot, one for the cause. Besides, living on the run is thirsty business."

Before Wobbly even finished his plea, Bigfoot was drawing a Pabst Blue Ribbon, shaking his head at the lovable, disheveled, and portly renegade before him. Without any more argument, he pushed the foaming glass across the battered wooden bar top to Wobbly.

"All we need is one more for a quorum!" Bigfoot announced.

Eleven heads nodded in solemn agreement, including a bushy-haired red head that was chugging down his beer. A brass bell was secured to a post at one end of the bar. It would need to ring of its own accord once the twelfth drinker arrived. Only then would the absurd happy hour commence.

Far off, Wobbly heard a train whistle faintly sounding over Bob Marley's *No Woman, No Cry* playing softly from the battered jukebox in the corner. The door to the tavern opened and a very small man wrapped in an orange robe shuffled in on well-worn sandals. All heads rose toward the bell. Wobbly shambled over to the jukebox and dropped in a quarter.

"I feel a more appropriate song is in order, gentlemen." Wobbly manipulated the buttons until he was satisfied with his selection, turned and pretended to strike a power chord on an invisible guitar.

"And when I say appropriate, I mean fucking appropriate for what is about to happen." Raising his glass, he offered a toast to the new rock anthem released that year by Aerosmith. With the opening guitar lick, people stood up from their chairs. Everyone started signing aloud its refrain.

Well, on a train, I met a dame
She rather handsome, we kind looked the same
She was pretty, from New York City
I'm walking down that old fair lane
I'm in heat, I'm in love
But I just couldn't tell her so

The rumbling train thundered nearer. Its powerful engine could be heard above the music and the conversations of the patrons. Heads shifted away from their drinks and toward the bell affixed to the wall. As the hurling mass of metal neared, a dull tremble moved through the floor. Bottles and glasses behind the bar shuddered. The patrons grew closer to the bar.

I said, train kept a-rolling all night long
Train kept a-rolling all night long
Train kept a-rolling all night long
Train kept a-rolling all night long
With a heave, and a ho

The Buddhist monk sat down in the middle of the floor and started chanting, "Om Mani Padme Hum."

"Awesome! How cool is that? He has the whole astral projection thing going man. The bell will indeed ring tonight. Mark my words, Bigfoot," Wobbly said with glee.

"You're brilliant, Wobbly. But with or without Tibetan Buddhism, something tells me your right for once. "

With a crescendo, the heavy freight train clapped on the tracks right behind the bar. Its steel construction was built to haul the heaviest load of coal and its sheer weight and velocity shook the foundation of the wood-frame tavern. The stationary post bell attached to the bar began to oscillate. Finally, its clapper struck the sound bow and it rang loudly.

"Happy hour!" roared Bigfoot. He started pouring draft beer and handing out thick pint glasses as fast as his stout fingers could manage.

The previously surly patrons now surged the bar in joyous expectation of unlimited alcohol. Except the monk, who stood still and silent confused by the frenetic action. All drinks were free in this absurd moment of chance. A losing business strategy by any standard, but a long-standing tradition at Vagaries. A barroom of crazed patrons pummeled the shoulders of the diminutive Tibetan monk in celebration of his contribution to the quorum. Soon, he was clasping a cold beer glass in his small hands and grinning mischievously, his little sandaled feet tapping to the music.

Wobbly strode over to the jukebox and cranked up the volume by hitting its side panel—a trick only he knew—just in time for the guitar solo. The train passed beyond the tavern, but the sound of twelve men stomping their feet clanked the bell anew. Beer flowed freely for the hour. It was good to be hiker trash and even better to be Kindred.

Wobbly lifted his beer and sang at the top of his lungs in exultant celebration of living in the moment. The revelers formed a whirling mob of spinning flannel and long hair. The driving riff and repeating single note of the guitar propelled the dancers into a downward spiral until some knocked over tables as they crashed to the ground. Wobbly took an inglorious tumble over a chair and lay belly-up on the floor. He stared up in delight. Tacked above the bar, he saw an assortment of tattered Polaroid photographs of legendary patrons. One photo, faded with age, showed a young man staring at a beautiful woman. Her gaze was directed straight into the camera. It was Los and Enith. Wobbly loved this place, its denizens and their commitment to the cause.

Outside the tavern, parked in the alley under a flickering street light purred the high-powered engine of a Clarke County Sheriff Department pursuit car. The dark tinted windows obscured the driver, but the throttle of the engine scared away a feral dog that had come too close.

Chapter Thirty-nine

Battletown, VA, December 24, 1974

Downstairs, in the glowing light of the living room fireplace, Lord Jim glanced one last time at the document. He sighed and looked toward the flames dancing in the darkened room. The heat of the fire would warm him through the long, cold night. The upstairs windows were open and no fire burned. It was necessary to keep the room at least below thirty-two degrees. It would serve as a morgue for the next forty-two days.

It's the internal flame that keeps men living, he thought. The manifesto was essential fuel for the flickering fire within the world today. The Kindred would spread the word. The survival of the republic was at stake. A cancer was invading every feature of society. To combat it, everyone had a part to play in the great rebellion. The Authority would feel the heat of his raid from more than one fire this time. The surprise attack would be the penetration of whatever lay underneath Maryland Heights across from Harpers Ferry.

He folded the document and put it inside his jacket. Its warmth from the fire felt good. He thought of Los laying cold upstairs. John Brown made the ultimate sacrifice as did many good Kindred soldiers over the last 100 years. He made a solemn promise that Los' sacrifice would not be wasted. Lord Jim turned and walked across the creaking wood floor toward the front door. He placed his hand on the iron knob pausing to listen to the chanting coming from the upstairs room. It was mournful but rhythmic.

"That's right. Pace yourself, old man. It's going to be a while before you can stop. I have a feeling Los will take this to the very end in his search for Enith." Lord Jim said as he looked up the narrow stairs.

He turned the knob and heaved the wooden door. The weight of it strained his arm and spirit. He felt like he was leaving a tomb that held his dead friend. So many thoughts went through his head. He knew from the start why Los wanted the suicide mission. He was sick to his stomach that he lied to Los about Enith over the years and especially about the murders yesterday. He was almost certain she was not one of the women killed in the raid. It could be true but he doubted it. If his suspicion of her was correct, she was safe and sound in the capital city with her new husband.

He pulled all the harder and threw the door open, casting a small circle of light across the covered front porch. The moon was bright but caged behind dark clouds. He stepped onto the porch and paused to scan the front yard. Two shadows emerged from either side of the door. He could see many more silhouettes scattered throughout the farmyard. He looked directly at the two shadows of men on the front porch.

"Are you ready then?"

With a terseness of serious men on a dangerous mission, the shadows stepped into the small circle of light. Both men grasped shotguns in their large farm hands and nodded.

"Good. Let's get this started."

The two men fell in behind Lord Jim as he descended the stairs and marched across the farmyard toward the fencepost that marked the boundary of the adjoining pasture. He unlocked the wooden swivel on the shed and entered its darkened interior. The two men followed and closed the door from the inside. All three men traversed the interior rooms of the shed and emerged into the pasture. They strode across the undulating rocky ground toward a copse of tall trees that lay at the bottom of two hills. The glow of firelight illuminated their approach. The armed men stopped and took their positions. Their black barrels reflected the full moon.

Lord Jim went into the clearing among the trees. Embers from the fire floated skyward and lit up the faces of people gathered at the edge of the firelight. He withdrew the manuscript and began reading the sacred words to the assembled crowd. A wind whipped up as he started to speak. He braced himself and delivered his sermon with animated arms and hands, exclaiming his pronouncements with the fervor of a dervish. His voice tore through the wind and the racket of spinning leaves and thrashing branches. The people huddled close trying to block the bitter wind that dove down into the hollow. His message of self-realization was like that of the robed priest's inside the small room in the nearby farmhouse. The only difference was the state of the audience: one alive and the other dead. Nonetheless, both battles were for their souls.

CHAPTER FORTY

The pair agreed to split up. Their search would be more efficient and practical if they worked in shifts. Lyn would survey the relatively safe streets of Harpers Ferry at night when Lost Mungo would be most likely to pass through. Before dawn, DB would be at trailhead parking lots to catch him coming back from his trips to town. DB would also spend several hours each night working in the GT headquarters' basement storage room completing his internship duties. They both agreed this was a work shift that neither could maintain for long.

The first two weeks were a bust. Lyn stationed herself across the street from the GT headquarters where a steady stream of hikers and tourists visited to take pictures on the porch, check in, and grab some snacks or gifts. At night, it slowed to a few odd hikers, which, while promising, did not produce an old man in a pith helmet. DB visited a dozen ghost trails that Magda penciled on a map. All were within a hundred miles of Harpers Ferry. He had no luck either. The search took a physical and mental toll on them. Lyn got a sore butt sitting on the sidewalk night after night while DB strained every muscle in his legs, blistered each foot, and got a serious case of dehydration. They were going to give it one more chance before giving up on the entire project.

Today's search sent the pair in different directions. DB to a relatively close mountain, just a few miles down the ridgeline near Paris, Virginia. It was a section of trail rerouted when a much more scenic tract of land was converted to public access. If he timed it right, he could get to the trailhead before dawn when Lost Mungo was known to return from a resupply. Lyn reluctantly agreed to station herself in the lower town where the GT passed directly for those not interested in visiting the GT headquarters. DB recommended a specific spot that was only one block from the edge of town. Beyond that lay some parkland and the Shenandoah River. It was remote but that could work in their favor.

DB prepared to work a couple hours digitizing journals. Then he would head home and try to get some sleep so he could wake up early. This meant Lyn had first watch at the new spot. He kissed her goodnight and went to work.

Lyn grabbed her pepper spray and checked the battery on her cell phone. It was fully charged. She would use it to contact DB should she spot Lost Mungo. Hopefully, he was a nice old man. Her plan was to pose as a trail angel who just so happened to be sitting on Main Street at midnight with an ice chest full of alcoholic refreshment.

She would never forget her first thru-hike experience. She came out of the mountains to find an iced cooler sitting by a deserted crossroad. The gesture of kindness was as intoxicating as the cold beer. The memory made her thirsty. She lifted the cooler lid and popped the first can of the night. She hoped a buzz might take away some of her fear if not the embarrassment of her situation. She wasn't nearly as afraid of the old man as she was of drunken rowdies emptying the local bars. She figured an old man would not be as sex crazed as the young men spending their paychecks on a Friday night.

In addition to the countless thirsty thru-hikers, there was the assortment of semi-professional guides who worked the summer adventure industry. They spent hot summer days leading tourists across canopy zip lines, repelling sheer cliff faces or paddling rafts over Class I to III rapids. By the last bus ride back to the parking lot, they had built a powerful thirst that could only be quenched by copious amounts of beer. Without a doubt, these guides had beer radar that could detect freebies a mile away. After all, they were young, poor, and dehydrated.

Her headlamp swung back and forth as she looked up and down the street before setting up her trail magic sign and positioning her cooler. The occasional car passed, some drivers slowing down to give her thumbs up or to request a date. She was careful to only sip her beer when no cars were near. She situated herself under a streetlight to be visible for safety. She knew the Friday night party crowd might get rowdy. As suspected, her first customers were townies who stumbled past and praised her coolness at being the first night trail angel they had ever seen.

"Hey, what's in the cooler?"

Her answer always led to a free beer. Lyn told them she could only afford one round as she expected a group of Four State Challengers to come through. This excuse was received with genuine awe and understanding. Any thru-hiker attempting to leave Virginia, cross West Virginia and Maryland before ending, 24 hours later, in Pennsylvania deserved a cold beer for sure. After a few more attestations to her coolness, the townies moved on, beer in hand.

It was a few minutes short of midnight when she encountered the ghost. It started with a strange whistle. The sound came infrequently but grew louder as it approached her. She pointed her headlamp in the direction of the sound. It was coming from Pig Alley, which was one block down the street. Since Harpers Ferry alleys did not have street lamps, she could only stare into the darkness and try to discern what lurked in the shadows.

"Of course, there are no annoying young drunk men when you really need one!" Lyn whispered to the empty street.

She raised her voice in the direction and called out.

"I'm calling the cops. So, whoever is out there better cut the shit!" Lyn waived her cell phone in the air with one hand and a beer can in the other.

She wasn't sure what message she was sending but she hoped it would be confusing enough to make them back off.

"I can see you! I'll send your picture to the police so don't come any closer!"

Although she had only heard strange noises so far, whatever was out there didn't know she couldn't see it. The sound alone gave her the chills. She didn't want to think about what might cause the noise. She dialed DB's cell. It rang until it went to voicemail.

"Hello, you've reached Special Volunteer DB Cooper. Please leave a message if you're a friend and call my lawyer if you're with the FBI."

"You fucking idiot!"

She slammed the phone to her knee and cursed him again. She visualized him sound asleep on the couch while *X-Files* reruns played on the TV. This only infuriated her more. The whistle came clearer and closer. She stood up and crossed the street away from the sound and her beer chest. A mist was creeping up from the river and with it came a ghostly specter. She clasped her hands over her mouth to muffle a scream. She backpedaled all the way into the lighted doorway of a historic building. She pounded on its door and screamed for help. The ghost approached her from the darkness and entered the circle of artificial light.

"Let me in! Let me in! Somebody help!"

It was then she remembered that the historic lower town wasn't real but an empty shell. The historic buildings were just living museums owned by the National Park Service and occupied by re-enactors during operating hours. They were barren at night. No one could hear her screams. With horror, she realized her mistake in choosing this as the location of her trail angel beer stand. DB had suggested it. He failed to consider, or didn't think it important, that this place was completely abandoned after dark. Once the museum shops closed, it quite literally became a ghost town. She cursed him a third time for his crazy ideas.

She turned to confront the spirit and saw the apparition take a recognizable form. She took back what she had ever said about ghosts and crazy people who claimed to see them. In front of her now stood a middle-aged black man in baggy pants, muddy boots, a rough wool coat, and a slouch hat. The whistling was coming not from his mouth but from a deep gash in the throat. He mouthed silent words and held out a hand as if he were trying to communicate an urgent message. She sensed he was trying to warn her. He didn't appear menacing, but protective. His eyes darted left then right, looking for an invisible danger. His eyes pleaded caution. Lyn realized he was more afraid than her.

The sound of pigs squealing echoed through the murky night. Next, she heard scarping hooves across the cobblestone street. A wind picked up and swirled around her and the ghost. Beastly shadows rose with the wind and circled he pair. Lyn stepped away from the pitiful ghost. The snorting pigs from hell began tearing him apart.

"Jesus Christ, this is a crazy fucking night!" she shrieked.

The ghost swung about as he was attacked until he was dragged to the ground. As it writhed below her, Lyn saw razor teeth ripping him apart. The animal sounds mixed with the screams of a man being eaten alive. At least that's what she remembered before fainting.

Chapter Forty-One

Sky Meadows, VA, July 16, 2016 4:45 AM

DB pushed harder on the accelerator to maintain speed up the mountain. His Subaru had over 200,000 miles and strained to climb the grade. Even the windshield wipers seemed over-powered by the driving rain. The car headlights reflected off silver, swirling clouds of mist that came in bands and pushed the car toward the shoulder. He had only another mile or so before he reached the turn off for the trailhead parking lot. It always caught him off guard because it came with no warning and in the middle of a stretch of uninhabited forest. He was determined to be on the trail before first light. If Magda was right, that's when Lost Mungo was most likely to return from his resupply trips.

DB pulled the parking brake and climbed out of the car and into the dark night. He switched on his headlamp, located the trailhead, and swung on his daypack. He planned on being out until the afternoon before heading back to Harpers Ferry, Lyn, and a cold beer.

This was his thirteenth day hike along Magda's ghost trails. He crossed his fingers and hoped of success. Lyn was losing patience with his plan. As usual, she was right from the beginning. This search effort was extremely fatiguing. The lack of sleep and physical exhaustion were straining their relationship.

He stood silently on the trail just beyond the parking lot and listened for the sound of motors slowing down to pull off the highway onto the dirt side road. He waited until the first hint of grey to start his hike. If his memory was right, it was about three miles until the GT took off in a new direction. He would try to find the ghost trail. A double blaze indicated he should turn direction, but he sensed the presence of a trail continuing straight ahead. He ducked under blowdown and pushed through some branches that were placed strategically to obscure the path. Beyond, perceptible to the trained eye was a faint trace of a trail. Its form had decayed at the edges, but it was still intact. He stepped gingerly, not sure if he should trust his vision. After half a dozen steps, the ghost trail became clearer.

He followed it for over a mile. He traversed a ridge and spied the dilapidated roof of a shelter in a clearing on the other side. He approached it quietly and circled around until he could see its opening. It was dark inside, cluttered with leaves and hiker paraphernalia. He stepped closer to improve his view. His breath suddenly in his throat at the sight before him. A British pith helmet hung from a nail driven into the shelter post beam. A shadow rose from the dark interior corner. An old man was sitting up inside a sleeping bag on the dirty floor. DB slung off his backpack and dropped it to the ground. At last, he was going to confront Lost Mungo. DB called out a greeting that echoed in the silence of the trees.

"Hello, I'm DB Cooper. And you're Lost Mungo, I presume?" DB stammered.

Kicking himself that he didn't prepare for a better introduction. He simply blurted out the first thing that came into his mind. Now, he felt completely stupid mimicking Henry Stanley's first words to Dr. Livingstone after spending years looking for him in the African jungle.

The figure squirmed toward the interior wall to better support his sitting position. His hollow face was rimmed by a long beard and flowing hair. Both grew together into a mass of speckled grayness that covered his shoulders and chest. His veined temples showed a mental intensity above his tortoise shell glasses whose lenses were both sweat-stained and cracked. A pair of familiar eyes peered toward him. DB's jaw dropped when he recognized his face.

"Well, you finally found me." Lost Mungo replied.

"Holy shit! You were there my first day outside the basement. You gave me the key to the door. I don't understand. What's this all about?"

"I was expecting you to find me." He paused to stretch. "We were right about you. You've made great progress. You found the truth. Congratulations on gaining more insight over this summer than more people achieve in their lifetimes." There was a tinge of disappointment in his voice.

"We've been watching you. Your college papers impressed us."

"Who has been watching me?"

"We're called the Kindred and we are well placed throughout the Shenandoah Valley community. We've been waiting for someone like you for quite some time."

"Why me?"

"You're curious and display great empathy toward your fellow man like someone else we hold in our hearts."

"Who is that?" DB questioned.

"John Brown had a wrathful empathy for the enslaved and you are just as angry about lies that bind society." Lost Mungo winked.

"I am certainly no John Brown. First, I am an atheist. Second, I am a pacifist are you with the FBI?" DB suddenly felt exposed.

"Of course not. Your curiosity drove you to find the truth. In the process, you unveiled a great struggle between those who seek justice and those who deny it. Your heart caused you to search all those journals. You found what was always there, but invisible to others. You have awakened your wrathful empathy."

"How do you know I'm intolerant of the status quo?"

"It's obvious from your questions in class and your very first field trip to Harpers Ferry. Remember back to your freshman year? You had an epiphany when the park ranger asked if John Brown was a terrorist. It is time to use your qualities in a greater role. By speaking truth to power, you not only expose their lies, but educate people who are listening. We sense your anger at the fraud of history. It only needs an outlet to be productive. If you choose, a role in the struggle awaits you."

"I think you guys overestimate my wrath. I'm not revolutionary material. I am here to warn you that the FBI may be looking for you. I might have revealed your activities by mistake."

"Believe me, they know all about the Kindred. They just can't find us. We just needed to see you in action. I arranged your internship. You found me. You understand the danger but still speak truth to power. That's exactly what we're looking for. Not a rebel in the sense of any violence. Just documenting the Kindred so that those who descend from knowing insight can always be watched and approached when the time is right."

"So, that's why you trace genealogies of people dating back to…."

"Dating back to the first raid on Harpers Ferry."

"Oh, my God. I was right. There is a huge conspiracy. I knew it. Wait until I tell Lyn."

"Yes, we kept the truth alive, educated the descendants, observed, and planned. We dealt a great blow once and then another. I am afraid it was not enough."

DB took off his daypack and sat down at the picnic table in front of the shelter. He felt no danger from Lost Mungo. Instead, he felt like he was talking to his grandfather. The old man was impressive despite his age.

"How do you keep up this lifestyle? I got tired just doing some day hikes."

"Yes, I'm old and tired. My time is up. I need someone to replace me. You seemed to fit the bill, but we had to test you first."

"Test me? You mean going through all those journals?"

"That you found us. That was the test. Your ability to read between the lines and see something nobody else has ever seen."

"So, I passed a test that I didn't know I was taking. What now?"

"The Kindred needs a new genealogist. You came here for a purpose today whether you realized it or not."

"I wanted to find you. To confirm there's a secret underground society spanning generations that's still active today. I didn't have plans for another challenge," DB said backing away from accepting anything.

"The truth cannot be put back in those journals and filed away onto dusty shelves. Your eyes are open now. Your wildest suspicions are confirmed. There is a great evil that enslaves us once again. You cannot walk away from your discovery. Now, you must act out your anger at the injustice."

"It could be someone else. What if I hadn't been selected for the internship. Besides, how did you know I would get the internship? I applied to an announcement. It could have been anyone."

"I only sent it to you. Also, I wrote a letter to Leo Davis in your name offering to volunteer for the job. Everyone thought it was just another college intern dreaming up a project for college credit. No questions. It all worked without anyone being the wiser to my subterfuge. Remember, we have been doing this for decades."

"Certainly, I'm not the kind of person you want. Commitment is a word I really don't understand. Ask my girlfriend; she'll tell you. There's a big difference between a summer internship and doing what you've been doing for the past sixty years."

Lost Mungo dug in his pack and pulled out a leather-bound book—*The Genealogies*.

"The trail stops here for me. Please take this and guard it. Should you decide to accept this challenge, the Kindred will contact you."

His arm remained outstretched in the air. "I have very little time left, DB."

DB looked at the book but did not accept it.

"Listen, I'm impressed with your years of dedication. Your life mission in support of this Kindred is impressive, but I definitely don't think I'm up for it."

DB realized that he sounded cowardly and felt ashamed in front of this rebellious spirit who sacrificed everything. DB, however, cringed at the thought of living rough—enduring extremes of weather and physical exhaustion to hike endless mountains to collect records of some dead people he didn't even know about. He'd have to drink bad water, eat scant meals, and live clandestinely as a rebel on the run. Besides, Lyn would never choose this lifestyle.

"You're honorable, but I'm not you. I can't possibly give up my life. My research will be ready for publication in a couple more weeks. It can open doors for me. I feel like it can launch my professional career."

"I must ask you never to publish what you've discovered. It could destroy the Kindred and everything we've sacrificed for generations. There's no one else to challenge the Authority."

Lost Mungo traced his finger down a list of names in *The Genealogies*.

"There aren't many of us left, but we're close to striking a significant blow. If we don't, the future of humanity, I fear, is lost."

"But why strike again, when your numbers are low? Why wait all these years?"

DB stood up and paced before the shelter. Lost Mungo smiled at his question. He was happy to see DB's curiosity kicking in and decided to feed him as much information as he could absorb. It was a risk giving away so much detail but DB had a warrior soul and Lost Mungo knew the information would be protected. He suspected a few answers would convince the young man to make the commitment of a lifetime.

"The Authority has invaded the spiritual realm. They have captured cosmic waters drained from decades of human trauma. These waters have been diverted underneath Maryland Heights into a gigantic secret cavern. We discovered the waters are being pumped through tunnels to the underground complex at Mount Storm. We don't fully understand how they manipulate its characteristics, but somehow, they've amplified it and are sending it out to people's subconscious."

DB stopped pacing and scratched his head. He was thinking out loud now. To Lost Mungo's surprise he had already figured out the reason.

"This Authority you talk about is obviously some kind of hidden power behind the government. Exactly, what I suspected. They are obviously manipulating history and current events. No doubt about that." DB's voice was getting louder and his words were coming faster. "If you ask me, they are using these captured human traumas to project fear into the population. I have read that Mount Storm is where the government broadcasts the emergency messages that we hear on the radio and TV. I assume you know the messages came from Mouth Storm?"

"Yes, of course, but what does that have to do with the cosmic waters?"

"What if they figured out a way to extract that trauma from the cosmic water and then broadcast centuries of human fear and confusion to the population on a subconscious level. What if those fears follow them into the afterlife?"

"The Authority uses fear to control our minds so we cannot think clearly. I was told, the second raid on Harpers Ferry was really an attack on Mount Storm. I wasn't told anymore. My job is to just trace the lineage of Kindred descendants." Lost Mungo replied.

Lost Mungo zipped his sleeping bag up to block the cold wind that began blowing down the mountain. The forest had become noisy with the rushing wind through the leaves.

"It's one thing for the Authority to spread its net across our physical dimension, but we have no hope if it covers the In-Between." Lost Mungo stated with a slow and painful exhale of his breath.

Lost Mungo shivered and became pale. His strength drained perceptively. He lowered himself onto the floor. DB climbed into the shelter and placed his coat under the old man's head. Lost Mungo complained about the cold and shivered again.

"You can make the same decision I did many, many years ago. I've never once regretted it. One cannot live in compliance with the Authority. That is not a life, but a lie. At the very least, take The Genealogies with you. Protect it and think upon what life you want to live."

With that last sentence, Lost Mungo closed his eyes and became perfectly still. DB could not wake him, or what was left of him. A death rattle began to clog the old man's breath. Alarmed, DB pulled up Lost Mungo's coat sleeve to search for a pulse. It was barely detectable and erratic. The blueness of his skin shocked DB. He had watched his grandmother die in hospice and Lost Mungo looked exactly like she did in her final hours. Like her, he looked peaceful and content to let go. He made a silent oath not to abandon him.

A noise in the woods startled him from his thoughts. He glanced out of the shelter and saw a dozen men emerge from the tree line.

"It's okay to leave him. We'll carry him away at the proper time."

The leader of the group was dressed in a red flannel hunting coat. His long silver beard blew in the strong wind. All the men in the group moved mechanically but effortlessly through the brush and debris of the forest floor. The leader's blue eyes rested on Lost Mungo and then focused intently on DB.

"You have nothing to fear from us young man. I think Lost Mungo left you with a choice." He placed a hand on DB's shoulder.

DB tried not to appear afraid of these men. He straightened his shoulders, tried to control his breathing and stood as tall as he could. He still felt incredibly small as the men now surrounding the shelter were giants of the forest.

"Who are you exactly?" DB asked.

"They call me Lord Jim."

"You're the Kindred, aren't you?"

Lord Jim was silent.

"You guys aren't going to hold me prisoner or anything, are you?"

"You're free to decide your own fate. It's a core principle of ours."

"No offense to Lost Mungo. But this isn't exactly the lifestyle I would choose for myself."

"Take your time to think it over."

DB hesitated and looked at the puffs of air coming from Lost Mungo's mouth, growing fewer and farther between in the cold air.

"He wanted to die in the silent woods he knew so well. It was his final request and we shall honor it. Take the same trial back and tell no one of this place for at least twelve hours. By then, we'll see to it that Lost Mungo has been taken to a sacred place where he'll begin his next journey. Who knows, you may run into him again."

The twelve men then walked away before blending back into the forest.

DB stood quietly outside of the shelter. He no longer heard the men's footsteps in the woods. They disappeared like they had come, soundlessly. Now, he only heard the faint breathing of a dying man. DB figured he had only hours to live. He stepped back inside the shelter and knelt next to Lost Mungo. To his surprise, DB started to cry. He only met this person an hour ago but following his actions in the trail journals across four decades made him feel like family. He felt alone at the thought of Lost Mungo not being on in the mountains walking the Great Trail.

DB retraced his steps back down the ghost trail. He hiked for several miles until he stumbled through dense blowdown. He crawled over fallen tree trunks and large branches with *The Genealogies* carefully secured in his daypack. He entered back on to a white-blaze section of the Great Trail. He hiked along this main route for three miles before he recognized the blue-blaze side trail sign with an arrow pointing in the direction of the parking lot. He jogged the short distance to his car. He placed his daypack on the trunk and gently removed *The Genealogies of the Wrathful Empathies.* He laid it on the passenger seat and buckled it in for good measure.

"Lyn is going to die when I tell her about this."

As he drove out of the parking lot, a burly bearded backpacker hopped down from his observation post atop a gigantic boulder and bushwhacked through the woods. He moved rapidly, flailing the ground with his trekking poles. His speed created a whirlwind of leaves that swirled aloft and briefly trailed in his wake. If DB had still been listening in the quiet woods, he would have heard a voice calling out.

"Mungo, Whiskeytown is coming to get you off the mountain one last time."

Back at the ghost shelter, Lost Mungo had passed. Before his heart failed, he used his last bit of strength to take one last sip of cold tea. His grip loosened with death, releasing the dented titanium cup. It rolled across the shelter floor and dropped onto the dirt. Rain began falling. It pinged off the unoccupied metal shelter roof and filled the teacup until it overflowed.

"Well, ain't that a wonder!"

Whiskeytown picked up the cup and drained the clear water down his parched throat. He laughed softly and stepped into the shelter.

"Hey brother. I don't know what I am going to do without you. Nobody was as grateful for my help as you. I can say that you were never too heavy and I was proud to carry you. If you don't mind, I would like to take this cup and sip fine Kentucky bourbon in your memory."

The soft rain became a raging torrent but it didn't stop Whiskeytown from loading up Lost Mungo in his arms and ferrying his body to a very special place deeper in the woods.

CHAPTER FORTY-TWO

Battletown, VA, December 25, 1974, 1:59 AM

Lord Jim sat before the fire and sipped a single malt scotch. He listened to the monk softly chanting prayers between the crackling and popping of the fire. The stone farmhouse was bathed in black. He never remembered a darker day. His heart was heavy with despair at the low odds of their victory over the Authority. His heart felt a surge of pain at the wasted lives should the raid fail. He had played a part in destroying the happiness of his closet friend. Would it have changed anything if he just told Los the truth? Had he misjudged Enith? Because of his decision to protect operational security, the boy was raised without parents. All these ghosts came back to haunt him as he sat alone in the living room. The scotch did not chase them away. He had decided not to tell Los of the child. Enith had given birth months after he went to prison. It could have been Los' but it might not. Lord Jim never trusted her. Even worse, she was possibly collaborating with the Authority. For that reason, he also decided not to tell her of Los' arrest. He was relatively safe in prison if his identity was unknown. Yes, he would be tortured but that was up to Los to survive. He believed that Los would not reveal his membership in the Kindred. Certainly, Los would die before he gave up the secrets they harbored. Even as Los was wasting away in prison and asking for her, he didn't trust Enith. Likewise, he watched Enith search for Los, ask too many questions, and mourn for him. He watched as Enith gave up on Los and publically begin a new life. Within a year, she was married and living in the capital.

Just in case the boy was Los' son, the Kindred had him kidnapped. He was placed with Los' brother to raise. His identity was known only to the two men. Los's brother felt guilt in taking the child away from his mother. The action, however, did not seem extreme to Lord Jim. Their names matched the prophecy. Only he knew the identity and true relationship of all. Los, Enith and Orc matched the names and relationships identified in the prophecy. Nobody else knew the trinity had come to pass. He could not risk sharing the truth until Los was free. It was foretold in a poem by William Blake entitled America a Prophecy. In his mythology of the American revolution, the son of Los and Enith would lead a final rebellion. The child's name was Orc. The secret weighed heavy on Lord Jim. He accepted the painful burden in silence, being a hard ass for the sake of the world. The plan had to be carried out until the boy reached a certain age. They used a cover story to explain his presence. Under the guise of an adopted orphan, he would be raised as part of the Kindred community. Everyone knew of the guarantee to protect children and wives of Kindred soldiers killed in action. The arrangement would not be questioned. Sarah accepted the child reluctantly. The financial support from the Kindred for his upbringing relieved her protests. Lord Jim watched the boy grow up to see if he resembled Los. He instructed Lost Mungo to record Orc in *The Genealogies* as the son of Los and Enith with an asterisk. When he felt sure of his relationship, the boy would be informed of his identity.

Chapter Forty-Three

Battletown, VA, December 27, 1974

Enith drove her Mercedes sedan up the gutted dirt road toward the stone farmhouse. She shook her head in disbelief that Los ever thought she would give up everything and move there. It was 250 years old for God's sake. He may have dreamed they would live an enchanted rural existence but all she saw was spider webs, bugs, cramped space, poor plumbing, and small drafty rooms. She found everything about the farm lifestyle suffocating. Sixteen years had passed since she last drove up to its porch. She wanted it to be unchanged from her memory and unchanged by time.

What she saw broke her heart. Everything was unkempt and decayed. She rolled her window up as the Mercedes slowly crept over the rutted and rock strewn dirt road. The green lush lawn that she remembered was littered with trash both material and human. She tried not to stare at the people sprawled about the large front the lawn. It looked like a hobo camp. Dozens of men lingered about. Some stood around fires warming themselves. Others emerged from small tents only to watch her carefully. A silent alarm had alerted everyone to her approach. She drove the car through a grey haze of smoke and menace. Shabbily dressed men glared at her. They appeared to be an assortment of farmhands, woodsmen, and beggars. She hoped she passed judgement but wasn't sure what their evaluation entailed.

Small campfires struggled to stay lit in the bitterly cold wind. She assumed this motley group were welcomed by Los, which only made her angry. She struggled to understand what they were doing here. She realized Los must have launched the hiker hostel that he had always talked about. Now, he had contaminated his paradise. She slowed her Mercedes to get a better look at these people. It then dawned on her where she had seen these types of people before. She had flown passed them at mountain gaps with these miscreants sticking their thumbs up. They emerged from the woods or mist individually or in pairs, standing along the shoulders of the highway. They had looked harmless enough then, in their isolated desperation, but when grouped amass, their presence was intimidating.

She couldn't put a finger on it, but something about their choice of lifestyle was confrontational. Their dedication to the freedom of the trail evoked a passion that bordered on fierceness. As she drove closer to the house, several among them made eye contact with her. Their stares evoked intensity, forceful in its power and strength. If not outright accusatory, their gazes challenged her presence like a wild animal might question a human's intrusion in nature. She sensed more than she saw a capacity for violence in a select few. She locked her doors instinctively as she advanced up the rough drive.

She parked her car under the giant oak near the front porch. She pulled her coat tight around her and looked up at the second-floor bedroom. She saw a figure move back from the open window. She glanced over her shoulder at the scary men in the yard the whole way up the front porch steps. She was greeted by a different type of person at the front door. An elderly man met her. He was stern and disciplined in his movements. His physical strength could not be hidden by his thick wool coat. This man seemed focused and keenly attuned to her presence. He was tall and solidly built.

"What can I help you with?"

"I'm looking for Los."

"I'm afraid you missed him. He's not here anymore."

"Do I know you?"

She tried to push her way inside.

"You should not be here."

The old man blocked her way.

"Los!" Enith yelled.

"I don't believe we've had the pleasure."

Lord Jim offered his hand to shake. She didn't take it.

"Are you a friend of Los'?" Enith asked.

"Professional relationship would be more accurate," Lord Jim replied.

"Maybe you recognize me. I'm Enith. Los and I were married once. He might have mentioned that...."

He blinked inadvertently but quickly recovered his composure.

"Los told me about you. In fact, he's been looking for you for some time now. But, it's too late. Like I said, he has already gone."

"Do you know when he's coming back? I'd like to see him."

"Not sure I can answer that to your satisfaction. As for you seeing him again, well, that's out of my control."

Lord Jim stepped back from Enith to create space between them.

"Where did Los go and when do you expect him back? Can I at least get some answers?" Enith demanded.

She was growing angry. She promised her new husband she would find Los. Feeling totally blocked by Lord Jim, she worried that she would not accomplish her assignment.

"I'm afraid I don't know his exact whereabouts and that's an honest answer."

"It's strange that you're in his house and yet know nothing about where he is or what he's doing."

"Lass, I think we both know what he's doing. That's all I can speak about it. I'm sure you understand my silence."

"So, he's out battling the Authority again. Just like him. Never around for me but available to the world."

"Again, I'm afraid I can't be of help."

Enith turned to walk away and took a step down the porch stairs. She whirled around when she remembered the figure she had seen in the upstairs window while driving up to the house.

"I really need to use the phone. I'm sure Los would allow me that. I really don't know what all of this is." She pointed to the crowd on the lawn. "I'm pretty sure you aren't a simple hostel keeper. Something about this just doesn't strike me as Los being out for an errand. Are you going to let me in to use the phone?"

Enith looked Lord Jim dead in the eye.

"I suppose you can come into the kitchen. There are chores in the barn that I must get to. If you can make it quick I prefer to lock up myself. Not that I don't trust you, but I'm not as trusting as Los with all that trail trash out there."

Enith walked past the Lord Jim into the farmhouse. Without hesitation, Enith pushed him back through the threshold and slammed shut the interior wooden door and bolted the lock. She could see the knob turn but didn't hesitate at the sound of his pounding and shouts. With no intention of explaining herself, she ran toward the stairs. The fireplace in the small living room blazed orange, red, and yellow flames. The heat it produced escaped into the small foyer. It seemed unusually hot. She didn't think anything more before a cold draft struck her in the face as she climbed the stairs. The temperature plunged with each step she ascended. Down below, she heard the back door crash open. Lord Jim shouted for her to stop.

"Enith, stop! You don't want to see Los this way!"

She didn't understand. What way did he mean? She felt a gut-wrenching fear.

"Oh, my God, Los!"

The old man stopped at the bottom of the stairs and repeated himself. She dismissed his words as a desperate act of an old man. It was a mere diversion she hoped. As she reached the final step, a closed bedroom door muffled a voice inside. She threw open the bedroom door. A frigid blast of cold air struck her in the face. She screamed in horror.

Chapter Forty-Four

Near Spy Rock, VA, December 25, 1974

Lost Mungo sat on a flat rock in a tranquil clearing. A signpost consisting of three arrows pointing toward destinations marked by name and mileage distance. Two arrows pointed north and south respectively. They indicated the names of shelters from that position. The third arrow pointed to the west. A parking lot was 3.7 miles away. Taking his titanium cup of boiling water off his small hobo stove, Mungo dropped in a tea bag. The silence of the forest was broken by the noise of feet stumbling over loose rocks and trekking poles clicking metallically. Mungo quickly extinguished his stove flame, grabbed his freshly brewed cup of tea and receded back into the trees. He heard the faint strains of a song being sung by the approaching hiker. Listening carefully, he recognized it as a somber and ancient chant. He immediately stepped back into the sunshine. It was Whiskeytown.

"You look like an exhausted pilgrim returning from Jerusalem," Mungo said.

"Surely does seems like it," Whiskeytown replied.

"Then I wish you greetings Templar."

"Why are you always at the top of a ridge when I come looking for you? Just once, you could be down in a gap close to a road."

"It is less than four miles from the trailhead parking lot."

"And 2,000 feet," Whiskeytown replied.

"We can change jobs anytime. I am getting too old for this lifestyle," Mungo said.

Whiskeytown got straight to business. He was in no mood to joke.

"I got new orders for you."

"Aye, there have been wee whispers. Something about an insurrection. Hikers are talking about it but nobody knows what is going on for sure," Mungo replied.

"Yes, its spreading all along the mountains."

The pair sat down and shared the cup of tea. Whiskeytown described the attack at the Sky Meadows farm. Kindred had been murdered in cold blood. Lost Mungo heard the word massacre and knew revenge was in the air. It happened at a remote mountain farm so word trickled out slowly. Rumors spread up and down the trail. Agents of the Authority were turning up dead in the woods. Nobody knew exactly who was killing them.

"I am hearing wild tales about ghosts and snakes." Mungo raised his eyebrow.

"Yes, Mosby's raiders were seen riding under a full moon along the Blue Ridge again," Whiskeytown answered.

"Maybe his spirit was awakened to take revenge. Two women were killed and two boys disappeared. One family was a distant relation to Mosby. The other was related to Los." Whiskeytown explained.

"Now that is a hornet's nest best left alone."

Mungo shook his head and stared into the tea leaves.

"As far as the snake story goes, something is definitely poisoning its way along the GT. The mother of all timber rattlers has been scaring the shit of out hikers since spring. Maybe there is a connection. Weird thing though, only Authority agents are getting bit. And dying!"

Whiskeytown shook his head in disbelief. Mungo and Whiskeytown looked at their feet as the wind rustled the dead leaves on the forest floor. They both listened for the telltale rattle. Hearing nothing, they continued their discussion.

"There was also gossip of a double transit," Whiskeytown said.

"If so, that would explain why the Authority was cleansing the area," Mungo replied.

"So that brings me to the reason for hiking all the way up here to find you.'"

"I assumed you had orders for me," Mungo replied.

Whiskeytown repeated the communications given to him by the Kindred. Lost Mungo was to locate Orc and reveal to him the identity of his parents. Then, Mungo was to offer Orc membership into the Kindred. If Orc accepted, he was then authorized to reveal the secret prophecy.

"What do you think? Is the boy the one?" Whiskeytown asked.

Lost Mungo thought it over.

"He escaped a death squad. He has skills that are unexplained."

Whiskeytown stood up and prepared to leave.

"The boy is still running from them. Fortunately, he is headed right toward you. Intelligence reports that the Lord of Death has helicoptered in from the capital to join the hunt. That seems significant. Clearly, the boy is a threat beyond witnessing a mere transit."

Lost Mungo realized the boy might be fulfilling the prophecy from long ago. It dated way back before John Brown's raid and the Kindred's formation. A few survivors of the violence of the first raid at Harpers Ferry obviously belonged to a much older sect. How long the secret order had been in existence was a mystery, at least to Lost Mungo. He suspected Lord Jim knew much more than he ever revealed. His use of signs and symbols was at least masonic if not something earlier. Lost Mungo understood the importance of practicing operational security. Compartmental information was. He practiced it himself in the CIA a long time ago. He saw the same methods since joining the Kindred. Their practice was even stranger though. Instead of limiting physical intelligence, he suspected Lord Jim was controlling the revelation of the mythical prophecy. A unique couple would give birth to a special child. A destiny would be fulfilled. The prophecy spoke of revolution taking human form. His name was Orc and his parents were called Los and Enith. The boy would grow into a violent man who would break the chains enslaving all humanity. His first act would be to enlist the powers of nature, specifically, a giant serpent, by bending it to his will. Together, they would destroy Urizen. No wonder the Lord of Death was stalking the boy in the woods. He had no time to waste.

* * *

Hiking north, Lost Mungo picked up intel from hikers passing him in the other direction. Everyone was evacuating the spreading search grid of the Authority. Many innocent civilians had been questioned, detained, or worse. This cleansing operation was the most intense the Authority had ever executed. Apparently, all hell had broken loose. He stayed one step ahead of the roving search parties. Four days had passed since he started his search and rescue mission. Finally, he reached a long ridge line that ran for ten miles. It was the last place the boy had been seen. He feared capture but not for his life. *The Genealogies* could not fall into the hands of the Authority. He was taking a great risk by heading toward the danger zone. He contemplated hiding them but feared their discovery or his poor memory. His life's work was safest where it was—in his backpack riding on his sore shoulders.

Nobody will ever find Lost Mungo. I know better than anyone how to disappear. If I don't want to be found, then there's no finding me. Not bragging, just the truth. Hell, the real me hasn't existed for years, he thought.

He was getting closer now. He could hear the helicopters searching for the boy. Men's voices shouted in the distance and gunfire cracked through the air. Someone was killing and someone was dying in these cold blue mountains. The trail descended the undulating ridgeline. Someone was barking orders in the distance. The voice sounded official and military. It certainly wasn't the boy. Lost Mungo abandoned the GT and began bushwhacking through the forest. He came across three agents of the Authority. They were dead. Their bodies told a gruesome story. Their necks were punctured. The wounds had swollen black and oozed blood and puss. Their faces were frozen in silent screams. Whatever killed them had slithered away into the forest. He decided to ascend the next ridge to get a better view.

After an hour of vertical scrambling, he stopped to rest on the narrow summit. Deep in the cleft of the next mountain ridge, between two steep slopes, he spied Orc resting in a small clearing. Standing behind a tree, Lost Mungo watched him for several minutes. The boy was scared. Sitting on a log in a small clearing, Orc rubbed his knees and peered into the shadows of the loblolly pines that surrounded him. The noises of the forest obviously had him on edge. At the sound of every bird call, twisting branch in the wind, and snap of a twig underfoot of an animal, he would jump up ready for confrontation.

The elevation change between them was more significant than the actual distance. Lost Mungo realized he didn't have time to hike off the ridge in gradual descent.

"God dammit. I got to slide down there on my ass. No time to reach him any other way." Lost Mungo cursed out loud.

He accepted his fate with a curse and a grunt. The Kindred needed Orc and he was the only one here. Nobody else could help this kid except him. He felt exhausted from the search. He wanted nothing more than to sit down and rest or maybe even walk away. Nobody would know he was this close. He feared this boy but didn't know why. He sensed doom and chaos all around him. Despite his intuition, Lost Mungo started silently sliding down the mountain. His body felt every rock and stick as he just barely managed to keep from freefalling.

Lost Mungo saw the boy stand up and gaze into the surrounding forest. He sensed that someone was watching him. It sent chills down Lost Mungo's spine.

"How could he tell I was here?"

Lost Mungo froze fearing the boy would run off. He was too old and tired to race this young man through the woods.

"Show yourself!" Orc yelled.

He was looking exactly in the direction of Lost Mungo. Giving up any pretense of concealment, he ran down the remaining slope. Navigating through the pine trees, Lost Mungo stepped into the clearing. Holding out his empty hands, he tried to calm the boy down.

'Don't be afraid. I'm Lost Mungo. Do you know who you are?"

CHAPTER FORTY-FIVE

Harpers Ferry, WV, July 16, 2016, 9:05 PM

D B arrived back in Harpers Ferry distraught at the trouble he got himself into. First, the FBI and now the Kindred. He figured an apology to the park rangers might get the agents to shut down their investigation. He didn't think dealing with the Kindred would be so easy. They appeared to be in a life and death struggle. If he joined them, he would be crossing a line into real criminality. His mind was now reeling. One thing for sure, he had to secure his analysis of the journals. His discovery of the underground network waging war against the secret government was a real problem. That information was dangerous in too many ways. The Kindred didn't want to be exposed and neither did the Authority. He thought hard to remember where he left his manuscript. How stupid to lose the most important document of his life. The last place he remembered seeing it was on the small desk in the basement where he digitized journals. While he was confident he would not become the next genealogist for the Kindred, he was equally resigned to not publishing his great discovery. He wanted to make sure no one else would either. That was the least he could do to help the Kindred, and a way to avoid exposing himself to any danger.

"At least anymore danger than I'm already he in," he said to the empty parking lot at the GT Headquarters building.

He fumbled with the iron key to unlock the cellar door. To his surprise, it was already unlocked. The light was on in the basement. He edged down the steps slowly and silently. Only a few boards creaked. The storage room was in complete darkness. DB felt along the cinderblock wall for the light switch. He flicked it upward. The fluorescent lights buzzed and flickered on.

Leo was sitting upright, tied to a chair. Blood glistened from his mouth, ears and nose. Even his eyes were bloody holes.

"Holy shit, Leo!" DB yelled

He couldn't fathom what was before him. He approached his boss to shake him awake but recoiled in horror. He was dead.

The neat stacks of journals DB had spent the summer reorganizing were scattered across the floor. At Leo's feet was a handwritten letter. DB picked it up and started reading. It was addressed to the FBI, signed Leo Davis, concerning the research DB had produced. Leo stated his concern about the discovery of an underground cell operating on the Great Trail. He thought it posed a threat to national security and the Authority should be informed. Leo repeatedly made it clear throughout the letter that DB was not a part of the cell, but had only discovered it.

DB realized that whoever did this to Leo was looking for his notes. Leo must have reported their conversation. He remembered Leo asking when he would let him read his research paper. DB realized he didn't wait but was alarmed enough by what he was told. Lyn was right, he was an imbecile. He should have kept it secret, especially when he started piecing everything together.

DB searched frantically for his notebook in the mess of journals. Either the agents had it or had left to look for it someplace else. DB processed their next move in his mind if they hadn't found it yet.

"The apartment. Lyn!" he shouted.

He hoped Lyn was still in town doing beer magic.

He rushed up the stairs and bolted across the lawn to Main Street. He ran as fast as he could down the steep road. He was on the verge of losing his balance and tumbling head first with each step. He saw the house where they lived and the stairs leading to their third story apartment. As he reached the bottom of the staircase, he looked up and recoiled in horror. The front door was hanging on its hinges. He plunged up the stairs and through the threshold.

The apartment was in shambles worse than the basement at work. All the furniture was turned upside down. Clothing was scattered everywhere and kitchen plates and cups were shattered in a sign of extreme violence. Lyn was nowhere to be seen. He sighed in relief and then hit his forehead in disgust. Why didn't he think of calling her? He reached into his pocket and flipped open his cell. There were no messages. He dialed her number but only got a voicemail.

"Lyn, this is DB. You must listen to me and do everything I tell you. Things have gotten serious. Leo is dead, killed by some evil people. What they did to him...."

DB started crying into the phone.

"Lyn, it is really important you not come back to the apartment. They were here looking for my manuscript. I think this is because of my research on the trail journals. And, oh yeah, that secret group wants me to come work for them. I will tell you more about that later."

DB looked around the apartment and started planning their escape. The voicemail cut him off. He dialed her number again and picked up his voicemail where he left off.

"Lyn, I know I caused all this because of my stupid obsession about John Brown and history. Crazy thing is, I was right. Now, we've got to disappear. I know this sounds like the craziest idea I have ever had but we are safest with the Kindred. They can hide us from the Authority. Like my research showed, they apparently have been doing this for a long time. So, listen carefully. I want you to drive from wherever you are and go right to Battletown, Virginia. When you get there, slow down because there is only one traffic light. Ask locals for directions to a bar called, "Vagaries." Tell them Lord Jim sent you and mention that you are my girlfriend." DB ended the call and then immediately redialed her number. He patiently listened to her voice recording until it was over. "I forgot to mention I met Lost Mungo. He is dead now unfortunately but that is another story. Anyway, before he died he told me where we would be safe. It's a place called Vagaries Tavern in Battletown, Virginia. I admit a dive bar is not what I expected. See you there, I hope. Love you. Bye." DB paused and wondered if the message sounded stupid but decided it would have to do.

He ended the cell phone call and immediately second guessed himself. Should she mention his name. He didn't want them to think he was joining up or anything. He just wanted some protection. After all, they said he should take his time deciding. Time to these guys could be rather long he hoped.

Satisfied with the clarity of his message. DB jumped up and ran into the kitchen. He flung open the oven door and pulled out a pizza box. Lifting the grease-stained lid, he yelled out in triumph.

Inside was his notebook. Lyn had joked it would always be safe in the oven since they never cooked.

DB grabbed some clothes and camping gear and began stuffing everything into his backpack. He exited the apartment and clambered down the stairs, burdened with his load. He ran as fast as he could under the weight of the backpack to the GT office. In his concern about saving Lyn, he had left his car park there. *The Genealogies* that Lost Mungo had given him were in the back seat. This was even more important than his notebook. He loaded the leather-encased sheets of family trees into the top compartment of his pack. He got into his car and started the engine. The gas light came on indicating his tank was empty.

"Shit, shit, shit!" he screamed.

He reached for his wallet to see if he had money to fill up. Realizing he left it back at the apartment sent him into another cussing frenzy.

"God damn, shit, fuck! God, I am stupid!"

It was then DB realized he couldn't be too stupid or he would be dead. Abandoning his car, he looked around the empty street for ideas. Whoever killed Leo would be out there looking for him. They were probably prowling Harpers Ferry right now. He hoped Lyn was safely on her way to Battletown. Now, he had to get himself there.

Chapter Forty-Six

Battletown, VA, December 27, 1974

Subfreezing air passed through the open window and across the bed that contained the body of Los. The monk sat in a chair bundled against the cold. He rocked gently back and forth chanting prayers. His breath was visible in the coldness of the room. Though incense wafted through the small room, it could not hide the smell of death. It was day fifteen of the Tibetan ritual of guiding the dead through the In-Between. The monk was frustrated. The soul of Los was not cooperating. Now, there was a racket from downstairs. The monk heard yelling and someone rushing up the stairs.

Enith screamed at the sight of the decaying body. The monk tried to block her view by covering him up. She pushed him out of the way and rushed to Los' side. The body was lying on its side with its back toward her. She was too afraid to touch him.

The monk picked himself off the floor and continued chanting. He motioned for her to leave.

"What have you done to him?!" Enith shrieked.

"You mustn't interfere. Your presence here is dangerous for him."

She gathered the courage to lean over his body and look at his face. She barely recognized her ex-lover. His once handsome appearance was disfigured by death.

"It can't be! You bastards killed him!" she screamed loud enough to be heard outside the house. Tears flooded down her cheeks.

"The Kindred didn't do this. Los was solely responsible," the monk replied.

"What are you saying? He took his own life? You're lying! He'd never do such a thing."

"I'm sorry to say he did and willingly so."

Enith swung around to confront him. Her eyes were red with tears and pleading for understanding.

"But he would never take this way out. He would never surrender in this way. The fight against the Authority was his life."

The monk put his hand on her shoulder and spoke in a calm voice.

"As were you. Once a man loses all, there is nothing to keep him alive."

"How does this have anything to do with me? What do you know about his decision? Did he say anything, leave a note for anyone, maybe me?"

"I don't know. He passed away before I got here. If he had last words, it would have been to Lord Jim."

Enith's shoulders slumped. Lord Jim kept too many secrets between them. This was just one more. The thought that he was the last person Los spoke with only worsened her despair.

"He finally did it, didn't he? Finally sacrificed himself for the struggle. How selfish of him. Leaving me behind."

"He came back here to depart on his mission, rather than anywhere else. This is the last place he saw you and from here he wanted to start his last mission. He didn't leave you behind, but is searching for you right now."

"What are you talking about? Why would he do this to himself to find me?"

"Isn't it obvious? He never stopped loving you."

"We separated years ago. I told him he was losing me. I warned him we were drifting apart and then he disappeared."

"That doesn't sound final to me and it didn't to him either. For him, there's no distance that cannot be crossed. Love is a bridge. He's searching the In-Between this very moment."

"But I am not dead," Enith pleaded.

She sank into the chair and sobbed. The monk lit a stick of incense and stroked her long brown hair. Enith became visibly cold and he placed his coat over her shoulders.

"The Kindred has found a devastating weakness to the Authority."

"And, of course, Los had to volunteer."

"If it is any consolation, I don't think he would have volunteered for this mission had he known you were alive.

"Like you, he became tired of waiting. He wanted to be with you and mend your relationship. I believe he was told you were killed last week. We got news of a termination action by the Authority of witnesses to a transit."

The cold was becoming too intense. The monk lifted Enith up and ushered her into the hall. He closed the door behind them. She was numb from sadness.

"I still don't understand why he would do this. What could he possibly hope to achieve with his own suicide?"

"Los is journeying the In-Between as we speak. The Kindred gave him a mission that was a prelude to the second raid on Harpers Ferry. They believe there's a vulnerability within the mountain at Harpers Ferry."

"And how do I factor in to this?"

"Because he thinks you are dead and he is desperate to meet— I may even say rescue—your soul."

Enith became angry with his statement. She pushed him away and walked to the hall window. Outside she could see dozens of men milling about the fires in the front lawn. She remembered the first time they drove up the lane to the house. They were still very much in love.

"What happened to us? We could have made it." Why was she always competing for his time with the Authority? She slammed her fist on the transom.

"That man never cared about me in life and now he's suddenly searching for me in death."

"Sometimes love is not as evident as you think. He thinks if he finds you in the In-Between, you two can reincarnate together. The thought of losing you for an eternity was too much to bear."

"But I'm not there to be rescued. What does that do his mission?"

"It means he may spend his entire transit searching for you to no avail. This jeopardizes our greatest chance to attack the Authority. If I know him, he will forgo his duties until the last possible moment. And he may not reincarnate at all since he doesn't want to exist without you."

Enith grew perfectly calm and made eye contact with the diminutive monk for the first time.

"What can I do?"

"You can pray for him, to him. He is surely facing many wrathful deities in the In-Between."

"Do you really believe what you're doing will help him?"

The monk turned to the bedroom door and placed his hand on the doorknob.

"He's a very strong spirit, the strongest I've ever seen. I will pray for you as well."

Enith straightened up and descended the stairs. She did not want to see the body again. She wished she had never looked. That was not the Los she knew and loved. She heard the door open and close. The chanting started again. A plan formed in her mind as she crossed the foyer toward the front door.

CHAPTER FORTY-SEVEN

Charles Town, WV, July 17, 2016, 1:40 AM

The emergency room was sterile, white, and trimmed with stainless steel. The linoleum floor shined under the harsh fluorescent lighting. Lyn struggled to focus her eyes in the brightness. Her head pounded with pain. She lifted her hand to touch the source of the pain. A thick bandage was there instead of her hair. It was then she noticed her other arm had a tube connected to it. A clear bag dripped liquid that eventually made its way through a needle inserted into her wrist.

"Now, hon. Don't go touching anything," a nurse dressed in blue said as she entered her room.

"What happened to me? Where am I?" Lyn asked.

"It seems you fainted, maybe, 'passed out' would be a better term."

"Why would you say I, 'passed out?'"

"Well, dear, you were found collapsed in a doorway of Harpers Ferry with lots of beer around you."

The nurse let out a little laugh and checked the digital indicators on equipment reading her vital signs and then adjusted a device stuck over her finger.

"Well dear, you blood oxygen levels look good. In fact, everything looks normal.

"I remember now. There was somebody else there."

Lyn bolted upright in her bed and shrieked. She looked around the room to make sure the ghost was not there.

"You are safe here hon. Don't worry about anything. Besides some glass cuts on your legs, nothing else happened to you. Just a little bump on your head from fainting to the ground. Which means we need watch for signs of a concussion." The nurse said while patting her free arm.

"So, where am I exactly?" Lyn asked.

"You are in the emergency room of the Charles Town hospital."

"How did I get here again?"

"Well, an ambulance brought you here. I guess a Harpers Ferry couple saw you lying there and called 911."

Lyn looked around the room for her purse, which she saw sitting on a cabinet top across the room.

"Can you hand me my purse please? She asked.

The nurse picked up her purse and held her nose.

"This reeks of beer. Oh, I remember my years at nursing school. We partied pretty hard too."

Lyn searched her purse and retrieved her cell phone. She unlocked it and check for messages. She saw a voice mail was waiting for her to retrieve.

"Can I get something to drink please? My throat is dry. Maybe some ice chips would help."

"Sure thing, dear. I will be right back."

The nurse left the room. Lyn quickly listened to the voicemail. It was from DB. She didn't understand his words the first time and had to listen to it again. She gasped at the news of Leo's death and then clutched her bedsheet at his warning of her danger. Her room was windowless so she peered out through her room's open door. She slammed her fist down at this request that she immediately leave and head to Battletown.

"Why the hell would we meet at some dive bar? And, how the hell am I supposed to get there?"

She cursed DB louder than she wanted. His tone did scare her. He sounded serious like she had never heard him before. She slowly swung her legs over the bed. Her clothes were still on. All she had to do was grab her shoes and coat. First, she had to pull the needle out of her arm. It bled a little but stopped. She popped off the device on her thumb and stood up. She felt woozy but pretty good for being in the emergency room.

"Here ya go, hon," the nurse said bringing in a plastic cup full of ice water.

"Well, I'll be damned. Where did that child get off to?"

Lyn was already in the parking lot of the hospital by the time the nurse returned. She saw a taxi pull up to the hospital entrance. An elderly couple emerged and went into the front hospital glass doors. Lyn walked up to the taxi driver's window waving her hands in the air.

"Can you drive me to Battletown, sir?"

"That will cost you about thirty dollars. Can you afford it?"

"Yes, I can. I may need your help once we get there. I know where I am going but don't know the address exactly."

"Well, it is a pretty small town so that should not be too hard."

"Thank you so much," Lyn said as she carefully sat in the back seat.

The taxi made its way through Charles Town. Lyn looked through the back window to see if they were being followed. She hoped the nurse wasn't in any trouble for losing her patient but she was happy with her ability to sneak out undetected. She then searched her purse for her wallet. She hoped there was cash inside. DB always told her not to swipe a credit card if she wanted to off grid. How paranoid was he? She thought about it and looked out the back window again. All she saw were the quiet dark streets of Charles Town. The taxi then merged onto Route 340 and headed south to Battletown. A sign said it was only five miles away. She opened her wallet and saw two twenty dollar bills.

"Great, my last cash. Thanks DB."

"Excuse me ma'am?" the taxi driver said looking at her closely in the rear-view mirror.

"Oh, I was just saying the name of the place I am going. It's called, "Vagaries.""

"What a dump. Are you sure you want to go there?"

"I am afraid I don't have much choice," Lyn responded while gently feeling the Band-Aid on her head.

Chapter Forty-Eight

Battletown, VA, December 27, 1974

Enith ran from the farmhouse to her car. Her hands shook as she tried to open the door. The keys fumbled in her hands and dropped to the ground. Picking them up, she unlocked the door, slumped behind the steering wheel and cried. Gaining her composure, she closed the car door and turned the keys in the ignition. She was reluctant to drive away. This was the last place they were together. A flood of bitter-sweet memories overwhelmed her. She looked one last time at the open upstairs window. She thought of Los lying dead just below it. Shaking her head at what could have been, she sighed and hugged the wheel. Had she caused all this? She never wanted to share Los with the Kindred. The secret organization is what grew between them. It pried them apart.

Lord Jim appeared on the front porch. His eyes were without emotion. She silently cursed him. He should have tried harder to stop her from seeing Los. She decided Urizen himself could not have a darker heart. Desperately wanting to escape the painful memories, Enith started the engine and drove one last time away from their home. She vowed not to look back but caught the farmhouse in the side mirror. A candle flickered on an interior window ledge. She remembered how Los left one lit for her. She began to cry again.

Through the tears, she saw movement in the yard. The men were gathering along the drive. She worried they would prevent her from leaving. They lined up along each side all the way down to the gate. One by one, they raised their trekking poles to form a tunnel under which she slowly passed. She rolled down the car windows and made eye contact with as many men as she could. She mumbled quietly to each one.

"Thank you, thank you. I am sorry he is gone, too."

It was then she realized this spontaneous expression was as much for her as the widow of Los as it was in memory of him. She burst into tears. She finally saw the face of humanity. These fighters were about to face death and they stood in remembrance and honor. Los deserved it but not her. He had spoken many times of the universal spirit. It concerned him greatly. She doubted his sincerity. And now here it was, these people, suffering and sacrificing together. She hoped Los could somehow see it. The words of the monk came back to her. Los was searching for her. He was not here. Could they really be together again?

She circumvented a patchwork of dirt and gravel country roads until finally turning onto the asphalt lane that led to the highway. The further she got from the farm, the more determined her plan became. Driving the final three miles into Battletown took longer than usual with all the police road blocks. Her government issued credentials got her through with few questions. After turning into the parking lot of the town hall building, she parked her car. A man approached and got in. It was Todd. Her lover for the past eight years.

"Was he there?" he asked.

"No, but I know where he can be found."

"We never should have let him out of prison."

Enith blinked her eyes with the last statement. She tried not to act surprised by the information. Todd was obviously involved with the Authority to a greater degree than she ever knew.

"You never told me he was in jail."

Todd kissed her on the cheek and held her arm.

"You left him, remember? Why would you care what happened to him?"

Enith hid her confusion. So many thoughts were racing through her mind but she couldn't talk to him. She gave up on Los for good but only after he had disappeared. Things might have been different had she known he was in prison. She bit her lip at the realization that Lord Jim knew all along. He kept the truth from her. She was just a pawn in the game for him and his precious Kindred. She stifled her growing rage. Was Los just a pawn to Lord Jim too? What about Todd, was he using her also?

"Hey, don't freak out. The Authority will protect you. I was afraid of this. Now, that you agreed to lead me to Los, there is no going back."

Todd moved across the front seat to put his arm around her. He nuzzled her cheek with his nose. It was cold from being outside. Enith pulled back.

"We are so close to our dreams. If I can, I mean, if we catch Los it will mean great things for my career. I can get promoted to run an entire division. Imagine that. I would be a director reporting directly to high command. We can finally afford that house we bought. Our dreams are so close," Todd said. His voice was starting to get hard.

"What do you want me to do now?" Enith replied.

She dreaded the answer but braced for his instructions.

"The Authority wants you to take this device and get next to Los. We will track its electronic signal from Mount Storm. It was first used over in Vietnam. If it can penetrate those jungles, it should work in the forest. When you turn this green button on, it activates the beacon. When you meet Los, push this red button, which locks in your position. It will signal us you have made contact. They told me it is important for you to stay in the same spot. Don't move and stay very close to him. Depending on where you are, it will take up to 30 minutes for agents to arrive. He will be arrested and interrogated. Scummy rebel. Can you imagine fighting your own government? We need to take these vermin out and you can help us."

"I will help you out," Enith said.

"You will help *us* out." He corrected.

"I love you." She said.

Enith gazed into his eyes to gauge his sincerity.

"I love you too," he replied.

He kissed her one last time on the cheek and quickly looked out the window back toward town hall. A group of black-clad agents stood near the front door.

Enith accepted the bulky transmitter. Another kiss goodbye and she was alone. She set the device down on the passenger seat and started the car.

"I am going to find out who is telling me the truth. Once and for all, I will know who really loves me," she said to the empty car.

About an hour later, she pulled into the trailhead parking lot. The Kindred had eyes everywhere. The Authority knew they could not simply follow her. Todd had set a delicate trap. His bait was Enith.

Enith flicked on the device as instructed and put it in her purse. It blinked red next to her wallet and lipstick. She wasn't dressed for the outdoors, but she wouldn't be outside for long. Leaving behind her car, she started walking up the trail. Her brand new expensive shoes quickly sank into the mud. Her favorite new dress caught on a branch and snagged. Her flimsy blazer added no warmth and offered no protection against the cold wind. She walked through the woods almost a mile before approaching a signpost. It pointed to a blue blaze side trail called, "Angels Overlook." It led out onto a narrow ridge that ran like a finger away from the hand of the mountain plateau, narrowing considerably before terminating in a rocky bluff. She walked along its spine, touching pine tree boughs and pushing through rhododendron bushes. Memories flooded through her mind. Los had chased her here. They both laughed, ran, fell, laughed, and ran until they reached the end. He finally caught her. Hugging each other, they collapsed into a soft bed of trillium. Now, she was alone. The fleeting image of Los evaporated. She gripped the beacon device. The moment of truth arrived. She pushed the red button. If agents arrived in 30 minutes, then she knew she knew Todd loved her. She would just say Los grew suspicious and ran away. What she feared was another reaction. How worthless was she to Todd after he found Los? She could just be a pawn for the Authority.

Enith stared up into the sky. She had an unobstructed view in all directions. Had she been so wrong about everything? All she wanted was a nice life.

"What must I betray for love?" she asked the empty woods.

Her answer came in the form of an object streaking across the sky. It moved a great distance with incredible speed. Its trajectory was constantly adjusting to the smart guidance system. She never really understood the modern warfare technologies that Los was always talking about, but she did recognize this was a deadly missile. Everything had become so clear. It had all been a mission for Todd. He'd never loved her. Instead, he was just using her to find Los. That realization made her think of the monk's words. Los loved her so much he killed himself to find her in the afterlife. Now, she would give him the chance. If he truly loved her, he would find her in the In-Between.

The missile struck the mountain cliff and exploded in a ball of flames. A confirmation message was radioed back to the command center from a ground crew at the base of the mountain.

Back at the command center in Mount Storm, Authority officials slapped the back of the man who killed Los. Another troublesome rebel was terminated. His death was cheered by the group. The strategy worked. Just give an unsuspecting source a beacon and have them find the hidden rebel. Then, let the technology do the rest. They all agreed the hardest part would be finding gullible victims to lead them to the real target.

"Your mission was highly successful. We want a debrief on how you turned the source," the Authority officer said.

"Will do, sir. It just came down to convincing them I was in love. Not too difficult," Todd replied.

The two men watched a black and white video of the strike from a surveillance plane flying high overhead. The explosion repeated itself on a loop played on a TV screen.

"Our strategy is to penetrate the Kindred at its weakest link. You were the prototype agent recruited for the program. We had the rebel named Los in our prison for almost ten years without knowing his identity. Your source, Enith, I believe was her name, was known to us as having peripheral connection to a Kindred cell. We were all shocked to find out they were engaged to marry," his supervisor said.

"These terrorists are impervious to torture. It's tedious work to be sure, but all those years with her really paid off. I eliminated the entire cell. She gave up names and locations without her even knowing. Los was more difficult. I had to reveal myself to her. It was a gamble but I knew she loved me. She was totally played out as a source. That is why she was terminated. There was nobody else for her to expose from that cell. I couldn't risk her exposing me. I expect to be part of future operations. That is why she was terminated." Todd concluded with a smile.

* * *

Enith's soul flew toward a darkened plane. She was beginning her transit through the In-Between. A gentle but familiar voice guided her toward Los. Back at the farmhouse, the monk began praying his instructions for two souls.

CHAPTER FORTY-NINE

Battletown, VA, December 27, 1974

Bret and Zoa climbed the stairs and walked into her bedroom. Her eyes grew wide with disbelief at the sight. Bret entered behind her.

"Jeez, I thought my room was messy."

"I don't understand. I was just here just yesterday. How can everything change so much?" Zoa asked.

She shook her head and scanned the chaos that was once her room. The dresser leaned into the corner balancing on three legs, its drawers broken open, clothes hung out and spilled upon the floor. Dark mold stained one corner of the ceiling while another corner of the drywall had fallen to the floor. Water dripped through the hole onto the stained carpet. Her windowpanes were cracked and the wooden frames rotted and warped.

"Huh, I forgot to tell you something. I guess it was kinda important." Bret said.

"Did it have anything to do with this?" Zoa asked pointing at her room.

"I think so." Bret replied.

He scratched his head and forced a big smile.

"I can't wait to hear." Zoa said putting her hands on her hips.

"Yeah, hum, Magda mentioned to me that things would not be the same if we came back. We wouldn't recognize our old world or we would forever see it differently. Something to that effect." Bret replied.

He, too, was slowly recognizing the significance of their surroundings and began putting them together with Magda's words.

"What does that mean exactly? The path has changed our lives forever?" Zoa asked.

"I don't think the path changed our lives so much as our experience transformed our vision. We are not the people we were before. Our eyes see different dimensions for what they are."

"Does that mean we are on the path forever?" Zoa asked.

She picked up a piece of a broken doll. It was her favorite memory of childhood. When she left for the dance the night before, it sat pristine and preserved in one piece on top of her dresser. Now, its red dress was frayed and stained, smudged with a dark oily substance. The doll's once beautiful black hair was knotted and tangled. One arm was missing and her left cheek was scratched through the painted plastic. Zoa threw it across the room.

"Magda basically warned me not to leave the path. I didn't tell you that part either." Bret confessed.

"It wasn't my choice to get on the path. It just happened. I really don't want to be on it. I just wanted to run away. Roanoke yes, the path never came into my mind," Zoa stammered.

Bret confronted Zoa and held her hand. He looked at her eyes and spoke softly in a serious tone.

"We entered the path for a reason and I'm not quitting it until I learn why it exists and its purpose. I believe you and I were given a chance to do something special. Please come back with me."

"But what do I tell my parents? I don't want to hurt them anymore." Zoa asked.

"There is nothing to tell them that they would ever understand. Besides, your mother said she had called your father. He will certainly tell law enforcement to stop looking for you because you have come home."

"What is so bad about that?"

"That means the entire law enforcement community is on its way here. They are not looking for a simply runaway. I am worried that we have stumbled onto something much bigger. You might have been a simple runaway before. Once you got on the path, I think you became a threat to them. I don't want you to be hurt by them," Bret replied.

He hugged her and kissed her cheek. Zoa was shocked that this strange boy would be so bold. Then she realized how good it felt to be held tightly. She felt protected in Bret's arms. The world was much stranger and more bizarre than she ever imagined in her wildest dreams. Bret released her and led her by the hand out of her room and down the stairs. The two teens confronted her mother. Zoa fought back tears. She knew there was little time to say goodbye.

"Please don't worry about me. I promise I'll come back. I ran away to be true to myself. I can't come back until I find what I am looking for," Zoa said.

"No dear, please don't leave. You put such a fright into us. Your father will be crushed if you run off again. Please wait to at least see him."

Her mom clutched Zoa's hand and gripped it tightly. They were in a tug of war when an emergency TV broadcast interrupted their struggle. The news program that had been playing softly in the kitchen screeched a blaring signal. A blonde, female newscaster breathlessly reported the evacuation and quarantine of Battletown and the surrounding areas of Clark County. A red banner streamed a continuous message across the TV screen.

Industrial accident at the local chemical plant. Governor declares the entire area a disaster zone. Federal support requested to manage evacuation.

The newscaster explained that all traffic was being rerouted and residents were being relocated to relief centers set up in nearby Winchester. Even the air space of the affected area had been closed due to the industrial accident.

Bret and Zoa exchanged troubled looks. Her mom looked quizzically at the TV.

"Well, that pretty girl has it all wrong. There's no chemical plant in Battletown. They must be confusing it with the lime quarry."

Bret pulled Zoa away from the television and guided her through the front door onto the front porch. Her mother stood transfixed by the TV broadcast. Sirens rang out in the distance.

"Zoa, we have to leave right now. There's no time to wait. I don't know what's going on, but this doesn't feel right to me."

They stepped onto the front yard and scanned the tree lined street for approaching police cars.

"Where do we go?" Zoa asked.

"I'm as confused as you are," Bret replied.

"We can always go back to the place where we came out of the woods. Then, we just find our way back to that scary swamp."

"Can you get us back to the perimeter road?"

"Hey, I know how to sneak around this town better than anyone."

Zoa's next words cut off as the sounds of sirens grew louder and shrill. They crouched low and took cover behind her house. They followed the driveway to the detached garage and, taking Bret's hand, Zoa crossed the small backyard before diving through an over grown wisteria. A short tunnel within let to a latched door in a white picket fence. She opened it. Bret followed. It led them onto a secluded service alley that was invisible from the main street. For the length of the service alley, they paused at every intersection before crossing. Each house they passed was in some state of decay, now even more noticeable in the dawn light. Roof shingles had loosened and fallen off, bricks and mortar crumpled and collapsed. Entire walls of homes lay jumbled.

"Oh, my God. The Culbertson's house used to be the nicest on the block."

Zoa looked in amazement at roofs that had sagged under the weight of their weakened walls and frames. At the end of the service alley, they emerged at the edge of the small central business district of Battletown. Here, they were only two blocks from Main Street. Both Zoa and Bret stopped in their tracks when they passed the local Family Dollar. To their astonishment, it appeared exactly as they had remembered. Bret tugged on Zoa's hand as he ducked behind a parked car. A black SUV sped past them and screeched around a corner. They then sprinted to the edge of town, taking cover whenever the sounds of roaring engines or sirens blared.

As the sound of sirens and the roar of engines grew fainter, they skidded onto the perimeter road. They dove into bushes and hid themselves just in time to avoid a squadron of speeding police cars.

"I didn't tell my mom where we have been or where we are going. A runaway who left a high school dance in a fit of drama shouldn't cause all this craziness," Zoa said.

"I am convinced the government doesn't want us on the path. It must have some quality that is a threat to them," Bret responded.

"Being in another dimension does give us some freedom that we don't have back here."

"Look!" Bret yelled. He pointed to two bent firs across from a street lamp. "Isn't that where we came onto the road?"

It all looked the same to Zoa.

"Maybe you're right. I remember coming out of the woods right across from a street lamp. It was close to an abandoned warehouse or something."

"Look, that's it!" Bret pointed to a warehouse building

"Let's try it."

Zoa plunged head first into the thicket. Bret followed. Bramble was most dense right under the street lamp but they clawed their way inside where thorn bushes tore at their clothes. The sirens wailed, this time much closer than before. The sound of helicopter blades turned their eyes to the rapidly darkening sky. While Zoa traced the helicopter's path, Bret noticed wetness on the forest floor that grew squishy as he struggled forward. Then he noticed the ground becoming drier in patches. He doubled back and found it damp again.

"Hey, over here. Let's follow this water."

They slogged upward into the dense woods to trace its source, hoping to find the bog. The wetness became a flow and then a stream. It spread in width. Soon, it grew to ankle depth. They followed close along its shallow banks. When it widened to its greatest breadth, the pair stopped and stood at the edge of the haunted bog. They peered across in search of the sentinel. He was there, a black hulk patrolling a small island in the middle of the swamp.

"Do you think he'll let us cross?" Zoa asked.

"We don't have any food to give him this time," Bret replied.

"How could we forget? I could have grabbed something at my mom's!"

"We can't go back now. The police are crawling all over Battletown."

Bret scanned the woods around them and nervously peered in the direction of the road from which they had come. Carefully placing one foot ahead of the other, they began to cross the bog one stone after the other. A mist emerged just as they approached the center, obscuring their path forward.

"Halt, who dares approach?" the dark figure probed.

"It's us. Don't you remember?"

"Stop. Come no further!" The black outline was strangely disfigured. It spoke from a tiny throat but wore a huge stomach. "No trespassers. You can't come through."

"Don't you remember us? We passed through here just before," Bret explained.

"We don't have any food to offer you now, but we can bring something back," Zoa offered.

"I must eat. Feed me if you want to cross!"

"If you let us cross, we'll return with baskets of delicious stew and biscuits," Bret promised.

"I must eat now. I am so hungry. I will starve before your return."

Zoa grabbed Bret and whispered in his ear. "How can it exist out here without any food? It must be eating something."

The sentinel splashed toward them baring yellow fangs and glowing red eyes.

"I will eat you and drink your blood!" the creature screamed.

The two cowered as the monster opened its mouth wider than its neck could possibly swallow. A voice shouted from the opposite side of the bog deep.

"Stop hungry ghost! I will feed you if they safely pass."

It was Magda, emerging from the tree line, illuminating the bog with a lantern. Behind her was Tom holding the fire shovel from the chuck wagon. The monster turned to confront them. His unearthly screams were squelched. He saw the large wicker basket she carried heaped with her finest goodies. He sniffed the air and tasted the aroma with a long silvery tongue. Magda approached and stretched out her basket.

"Now let them pass."

The sentinel snatched the basket from her hands and began shoveling food into its grotesque mouth. Just as quickly, Magda turned toward the children.

"You must hurry before he consumes it all!"

It choked on each bite of food as it struggled to swallow through its tiny throat. The pair scrambled past the evil spirit and together, they jumped from stone to stone until they arrived safely on the opposite bank. Magda scolded Bret and Zoa in the same loud voice she used with the sentinel.

"Foolish children. You're better off with the Authority than that thing. It has squeezed many travelers down that narrow throat. Your bodies and souls would have been in that fat belly had I not come!"

"We're sorry, but I just had to see my parents again!" Zoa apologized.

Magda looked at Bret with more anger than any eyes should be able to convey.

"And you took her?"

He nodded his head.

"Oh no. Tell me you didn't go to her house," Magda pleaded.

"Just for a minute. Nobody saw us but my mom. I needed to let them know I was alright," Zoa explained. "Besides, we stayed hidden the entire time we were in town."

"You put your mother and your town in great jeopardy. She must not tell anyone of your visit."

Both Zoa and Bret looked down at their feet in shame. Zoa knew her mother had called her father and felt a hole in her stomach.

"Listen to me carefully. You can never go back again. At least not as who you were before the transit. If you must return, hide your identities. Even then, never visit the people you left behind. The Authority will not stop hunting you. Ever. And they will kill anyone who knows of your transit." Magda explained.

"I never described my experience to her. I just said that I was going away for a little while longer. I wanted her to see that I was safe," Zoa cried.

"But the Authority knows you transited and won't believe anything she says. You must always cover your tracks," Magda explained. She looked beyond them to the other side of the bog and paused to listen to the sound of the sentinel chomping and swallowing.

"We must get away from here. The barrier is much too weak. Anyone or anything could crossover."

"I don't understand. Who does that thing work for?" Bret asked.

"It exists at the threshold of the In-Between and keeps both worlds apart. But it can be bribed." Magda paused in thought. "I must pay more attention to what foolish children speak of on the path. You came very close to spending eternity in its belly." She spat with disgust.

"Couldn't the Authority bribe it with food like we did?" Zoa asked.

"They don't know where to look for access to the path. Every time you use that crossing or any other, you leave a trail for them to follow. Don't ever leave again that way. There are other ways to get back." Magda said.

Bret jumped as something massive moved in the dark.

"Another monster!" he screamed.

"No silly. It's just Kubi and Gangri. Do you think I would confront a hungry ghost all alone?"

The wooly yaks pushed through the underbrush of the woods into the clearing. Magda took turns stroking their long hair.

"Climb on and we'll be back at the camp in no time. The wickiup is up. A fire is going and the blankets are warmed for you. I may even have some fresh baked goods coming out of the oven." Magda winked.

Bret and Zoa realized how much they missed her magic tricks. They eagerly climbed on top of the beasts and grabbed the long furry locks.

Chapter Fifty

Hooves stomped the ground, claws scratched granite boulders, jaws snapped razor sharp across the darkened plain. Fur ruffled in the wind and scales glistened in the moonlight. These were the sounds and sights of the beasts, leviathans, and monstrosities Los navigated at twilight. Screams and laments of terrorized souls echoed all around him. He listened for Enith but didn't recognize her voice among the tormented. Los detected another soul. It had passed this way a long time ago. It was the soul of the Architect of Mount Storm that he was searching for. He followed its imprint for a great distance. Flying at the speed of sound, he arrived within seconds to his location. Before him loomed the familiar outline of two mountain ridges divided by a deep cleft. A river ran between them. Their black mass barely perceptible from the gloomy sky beyond. He recognized one as the Maryland Heights across from Harpers Ferry from the life he just left. In this dimension, everything existed as it did a millennium ago. There was no town just barren landscape. The soul he sought had reincarnated into animal form. Its fears in the In-Between overcoming greater enlightenment. He faced a wall of mountain that rose 1,000 feet from the river. Suspended in air, his conscious soul watched a bear climb up the mountain side until it came to a jumble of boulders halfway to the summit. The bear squeezed through a small cave entrance. Los flew closer. His spirit vision could see what human eyes could not. The bear navigated inside the narrow crevice until it opened into a cave. Los followed the bear inside. It laid down. The long sleep of hibernation was setting in. The bear sensed his presence and stood to face the intruder. Sniffing the air, it could not understand what was before it. It could only detect a blue vapor. Sensing no threat, the bear continued its preparation to slumber. Inside its mind, an ancient language spoke.

"Bear. I need to communicate to a soul. I want to talk to The Architect of Mount Storm. I sense he is within you," Los said.

"Go away and let me sleep," the bear responded.

A growl reverberated within the small cave. The bear laid down its head. Its massive paws extended long claws in preparation for a fight.

"Bear, I only need you to lead me to the cavern within this mountain. The Architect knows the way. There is an entrance that only he knows. The Authority killed him to keep it secret."

From deep within the bear's soul fluttered a memory. It rose to the surface to be recognized.

"I remember now. I was taken to a concrete cell and blindfolded. The sound of a bullet sent me to a horrible place," said the spirit of the Architect.

"Yes, you were killed. I represent the rebels that have waged war against the Authority for over a century. Can you lead me to the entrance?" Los asked.

The bear rose from its dirt bower. It was being guided by the ancient soul of the Architect. Sleep walking its way through a deep vein in the mountain, the bear emerged into a large chamber. Los watched as the bear approached a human artifact. It was a cylindrical cement sewer drain covered with a rusted metal lid.

The bear sat on its haunches having no ability to go further. Los could detect the dull soul of the Architect inside remembering the significance of this object. He alone knew the structure's vulnerabilities and every detail of the subterranean complex. The bear clawed at the metal lid. Los left the troubled spirit and dozing bear behind. His soul passed through the vault door and into the next chamber. Here, the natural rock face was smoothed by a mechanical process and hollowed out into a cavern so large it dwarfed any other he had seen within the Allegany Mountains. It was filled with a complex system of pumps, pipes, and pressure gauges that configured an underground aqueduct.

A large cistern covered much of the floor area of the complex. The liquid it held was unlike anything he had ever seen. It was not water but a blue plasma. Stranger yet, the plasma was circulating with molecules of spirit. Los hovered above the cistern. His soul dipped below the surface. He was immediately submerged within a vortex of spiritual trauma. The overwhelming fear he experienced frightened him. It came from all directions. He whirled around to confront it but there was no beginning nor end to the sensation. He struggled against a current pulling his spirit down to the cistern's depths. Images emerged from the dark waters into view. Generations of souls appeared in translucent human outline. They approached him from every direction, their fearful faces rippling through the water. They wailed in their grief, desperately wanting to escape this watery hell.

One face out of thousands was recognizable. It was Enith's. She was adrift in a gooey pool of ectoplasm deep within the mountain. As her apparition whirled past, he clasped her hand.

"Enith, it's me, Los."

Her eyes looked at him unknowingly. Her face shook back and forth in confusion. Her spirit resisted. The pull of the vortex threatened to break their hold.

"Enith, it's Los. I know you. You are Enith."

Her eyes darted back and forth absorbing the raging torrent of despair that swept her up in its currents. She tried to shake her hand from his grasp and sink back into the depths of the cistern. Los grabbed her hand tightly.

"You must know yourself in order to escape. You died and are free of your body. Know who you are so that you can come with me."

He cupped his face in her hands. Their eyes connected. He felt her fear dissipate. She stopped struggling. Years of confusion and strife that marked their relationship evaporated. A brilliant white light appeared as their two spirits overlapped. Enith briefly recognized her identity before it merged with Los into a single new soul. They embraced. No force could now separate them. For eternity, their love now bound them. Entangled in each other's arms, they rose to the surface of the cistern. This new entity was empathetic to the desperate souls that could not escape the pool. With one voice, the new spirit of Los and Enith thundered across the cavern.

"We will free you. Prepare yourselves. Know who you are. We will come back."

Los had found what he had come for. With Enith secure in his arms, he swam through the cosmic waters and broke the surface of the lake. He brushed the hair from her face. She blushed at the power of his love. Enith sighed deeply and gleamed her contentment with sparkling eyes.

"You love me. You truly love me. I want nothing more," Enith communicated.

"We will never be separated again," Los replied.

He leaned forward and kissed her. She returned the kiss gently. The bliss they felt transformed their physical features. No longer where they separate spirits of human beings. Los and Enith were now one single entity. Male and female were identifiable but conjoined. Together, they rose high above the cistern and flew along the aqueduct for its entire underground tunnel. It finally emerged into yet another large cavern, this one wholly manmade, where they hovered high in its granite dome. They observed large screens placed before another series of pumps that filtered the water before it passed into another series of canals. Grey willowy workers removed the substance from the filters and placed the extract into a nearby containment vessel. With each action of separating the screened substance from the spiritual water, inhuman screams filled the cavern. Los and Enith emanated their wrathful anger at the sight. The workers sensed their rage and gazed with fear toward them.

"Who are you?" boomed Los's voice.

"We are only slaves. We do this against our will," the graylings replied.

Los and Enith had seen enough. The Authority was extracting human misery from the spiritual waters using these slaves. The cavern within Maryland Heights acted as a cistern collecting all the physic trauma leeched from the eastern continental shelf throughout history. It flowed above streams into rivers only to sink into the cistern due to its heavier-than-water weight. It must have seeped here for millennia. Finally, he understood what was happening. The Authority had discovered the cavern. Instead of letting it overflow back into the river and escape to the sea to be dispersed into the planet, they realized the ancient water had useful properties. The spiritual liquid was pumped into the underground aqueduct. It was constructed to divert the water south to a subterranean containment unit deep within Mount Storm. Once there, the psychic properties of the glowing liquid were utilized for their psychological operations. Los realized the Authority, heretofore unknown to the Kindred, was exploiting the spiritual elements they extracted from the liquid. He didn't know how it was being used exactly. He decided he didn't need to know. Clearly, they were attempting to manipulate generations of souls wandering the In-

Between. He suspected the cosmic waters were being strained of anger and fear from past generations who had experienced the violence of the frontier Valley first hand. The Authority was trying to maintain conflict between its citizens by somehow recycling this trauma into future generations. If it could keep them fighting each other, in all dimensions, no rebel army could ever materialize. No wonder they feared the Kindred so much.

The federal aqueduct and pumping system must be destroyed. The Mount Storm processing station needed to be raided as well. The secret passage into the Maryland Heights was their only chance. Invading directly through the hidden train tunnel was impossible. It was too well defended. Thanks to the sleepy bear and The Architect's soul, he would provide the Kindred the exact entrance into the mountain. Lord Jim suspected the hidden cavern was key to something. The processing station underneath Mount Storm was unexpected. They would have to improvise a way to destroy it. No human being could travel through the aqueduct and spirits could not alter the physical world. Luck and opportunity would have to be on the raider's side.

Los locked his spirit closely with Enith's and flew them toward the surface of the mountain, passing through layers and layers of rock. They soared high into the air and over Bolivar Heights. The spirit pair flew above the Shenandoah, across the bottomland, and over the pastures toward a small stone farmhouse in the distance. A candle burned in the second-floor window.

Chapter Fifty-One

Battletown, VA, December 27, 1974

Lord Jim opened the wooden front door and let Wobbly in from the cold. He was shivering as he shook the snow off his coat. His crazy bundle of red hair fell freely once he removed his knit cap. It was a tangled mess. Wobbly spied the roaring fire and rushed to take Lord Jim's empty chair. The blazing fire crackled as he rubbed his hands together. Lord Jim sized up the disheveled young vagabond with a discerning eye. He looked soft. Physically, he was a poor specimen. Overweight and lacking any muscle definition, the boy was not at all intimidating. Clearly, he had no warrior spirit in his DNA. Lord Jim suspected his politics as well. Coming from a long line of communists, Wobbly did not share the Kindred philosophy. The republic needed defenders not mob rule. In the history of mankind, there was no greater experiment in self-government. John Brown was first and foremost a champion of the individual rights. Lord Jim knew the boy's heart was in the right place but not his head. Communism was anathema to the Bill of Rights. The first raid at Harpers Ferry challenged a government that failed to remember its principles. That was how slavery persisted for centuries.

"You smell of alcohol," he accused Wobbly.

"I needed something to keep me warm. It's cold out there."

"How did you make your way to the farm, son?"

"Along the railroad tracks just like I was told. Seriously, how stupid do you think I am?"

"Stupid enough to get drunk the night before a mission. Am I wrong about that?" Lord Jim replied.

"One last party before we all step in the void. Life isn't all doom and gloom, old man."

Wobbly threw out his arms in a grand gesture and sank into the armchair. Lord Jim clenched his fist. He could not reconcile letting the boy into the organization. While he generated much needed cash, he never liked the drug connection. He thought the Kindred were living off the enslavement of addicts.

"You hitchhiked into town from the gap instead of waiting for our driver. You straggled down Main Street smoking pot. You were spotted selling drugs at the high school. Then you made a drunken fool of yourself at Vagaries. You passed out on the pool table with hiker trash sprawled around the place. Why wouldn't I suspect you led the police here?"

"Well, I dragged my ass along the gravel bed of the railroad track for five miles. I got caught in the blizzard about half way. Froze my butt off in the howling wind. At times, I couldn't see my hand in front of my face. It was so bad, I almost missed the rail bridge. I doubt anyone could have followed me even if I was being watched. Just to be safe, I hunkered down inside the old Fairfax church to make sure I wasn't being followed. Then I bushwhacked along the stream until I snuck through the old wood shed out there. I can guarantee I wasn't followed because anyone else would have frozen to death during that odyssey."

"You've got attitude like your old man. That's for sure."

Wobbly's eyes lit up. "You mean that? I'm like my father? I've only ever heard the stories."

"I say you got the stuff of your father. We've just got to put all the pieces together to get the whole man. Just focus on the mission. Let's make your father proud. You'll be with me tomorrow, son. I need you to listen to everything I say and not hesitate a second in carrying out my orders. We're going to need to be decisive and fearless. They'll have us outnumbered and out-gunned."

"I'll do my part. Just don't think I won't."

"Get some sleep. We leave in two hours."

With that, Wobbly went into the kitchen and began rummaging through the refrigerator. Lord Jim heard him cussing the choice of food. He shook his head and took Wobbly's spot in the big leather chair. He covered himself with a wool blanket and went to sleep. In his dreams, an assortment of young fools danced on a battlefield ignoring the bullets that reigned hell all around them.

A full moon rose high and illuminated the winter sky. Wobbly was awoken by a boot kick to the sleeping bag. A gruff voice compelled him to rise and shine. It was a dark solider of the Kindred. He didn't know him but he didn't know most the men in the house that morning. The room was full of them. They rose from underneath bed quilts and sat up on squeaky cots. Within minutes, they were dressed and assembled in the front yard. There were thirty of them in total. Each man had an AR-15 clasped tightly, glinting mechanical blue in the night. Lord Jim was at the front of the group saying something Wobbly couldn't hear. The men broke off and marched in different directions. Only Lord Jim and Wobbly were left standing in the yard.

"Okay, son. Just you and me from now on."

"Why aren't we going with them?"

"Because we're going to strike at the heart of the Authority. At least its beating heart in Clarke County, Virginia. Let's get into the truck and kick this thing off right."

"Okay, old man. Lead the way."

Lord Jim shook his head in both disdain and admiration at the young fool. He obviously didn't understand the sacrifices they were about to make. All the men were, in fact, on dangerous missions but his and Wobbly's was suicidal. With no real purpose but to confuse the enemy, their mission was just a diversion. Without a doubt, they would die this day without a chance in hell of escape.

The old man wondered if he should tell Wobbly the exact nature of their attack that night. After all, he didn't want the young man to be surprised when they stormed into the office of the sheriff and attempted to seize control of the communications system. He wanted the kid focused and not shocked. He still didn't trust him. Operational security was everything. The entire raid depended on their feint. If they were lucky, they would keep all the deputies in the field confused about what was happening. They were going to strike at the serpent's head. Let the tentacles thrash about without purpose. That would give the boys necessary time to act.

Chapter Fifty-Two

Washington, DC, December 25, 1974

The black helicopter flew dangerously low over the capital skyline. It hovered briefly over the Authority headquarters and then dropped down to within feet of the roof. Before touching down, Urizen jumped from the open door and sprinted toward the stairway entry. He bounded the steps with the agility of a man decades younger. Once inside his office, his fist pounded on the door of the metal vault. He peered through its small glass window and shouted.

"Why didn't you see their transit? Twice they went through the barrier! How is that possible?"

He watched a gray image seek cover within the containment vessel. He punched the code to unlock the massive steel door and swung it open. Entering fearlessly into the darkness, he was quickly charged by a dark shadow. A mouthful of razor sharp teeth flashed toward his throat. Without hesitation, Urizen grabbed the creature with one of his massive hands. It screeched in pain under his grasp.

"You mistake me for a normal human. I have no fear of Existents and especially you." He tightened his grip.

As Urizen squeezed, the screech became a whimper until its body fell limp. Urizen loosened his hold until it was released.

The creature scurried back to the corner from where it had come. A wave of empathetic groans echoed through the air. All its fellow Existents sensed the distress of their high priest and vocalized their compassionate suffering in unison. The injured one began communicating with Urizen, but not with words. Its thoughts entered his mind and he responded in kind.

"We came to help this planet and you have enslaved us."

"Your mistake was in thinking that humans deserve to be free."

"Reality is one across all universal dimensions. We share in your experience. A distress call was heard and we responded. Was this a trap you set?"

"I admit your arrival was unexpected, but your innocence is what truly astounded me. Your very existence turned my theorems upside-down. Who could conceive of a multi-dimensional universe? My measurements and formulas became useless. It became imperative to change the fabric of my net. I can't be blamed for taking advantage of your unique abilities."

Urizen stroked his beard as he felt his thoughts penetrated and analyzed by this creature. He was playing chess and needed to be careful least he provide too much information.

"Fear should be relieved, not exploited. How long will you keep us here?"

"Until I develop the ability to detect all transits. Also, I find you empathies interesting. We have not fully exploited your ability to collect cosmic trauma."

Urizen approached the entity and raised his muscular arms as if to deliver a beating. The creature cowered helplessly in its corner.

"Which brings me to the purpose of my visit. Tell me how these fugitives crossed so many times without being detected. By my count, two humans passed through the barrier, twice. Yet, the sensor registered nothing. I find that impossible. Either you allowed this or there is someone within my organization that ignored the alarms. Which is it?"

"The barrier is permeable at certain points. Universes overlap and where they touch, passageways allow for transit. These doorways leave only faint traces. Subtle movements were detected, which were transmitted to the monitoring system. Maybe your agents couldn't interpret what they saw."

"How do I find these points?"

"They move like waves in the ocean or wind in the air. One minute they are there and they are gone the next." The figure rose off the floor and changed colors from grey to white and then blue. "Most important for you, I detect a powerful anger awakening. It emerges from a dark cave. Images of a snake and a boy. They merge and become a foe that will rebel against your kingdom of control."

"All the better to destroy it now. Before it breaks my chains." Urizen responded.

"The universe will not tolerate enslavement. A revolution will bring freedom to humans. You have awoken it yourself."

Urizen turned his back on the creature. He departed the vessel and slammed the door shut. Even through the steel, the creature's thoughts could still reach him.

"This will be a mindful revolution. Your physical powers cannot fight it."

We will see about that, Urizen thought.

He cast one last glance at the creature through the spyglass. He walked across his office, sat at his desk, and picked up the phone.

"I want a complete list of all agents working the monitoring system for the last 24 hours, specifically, the Central Eastern district."

In his mind's ear, he heard the creature whisper.

"His name is Orc. He will vanquish you. We will be free."

CHAPTER FIFTY-THREE

Battletown, VA, December 27, 1974

Suspended outside the second story window, ferocious red eyes watched as the monk prayed over Los' corpse. Suddenly, he stopped and began looking around the bedroom. He sensed an overpowering presence.

The monk recognized the spirits of Los and Enith but they were different. Instead of two spirits, the monk realized that they were now combined into a single wrathful entity. He bowed his head and clasped his hands in prayer.

"I am your humble servant. Speak to me."

A strong wind blasted through the open window and struck the closed window pane at the other side of the small room.

"Let me be your voice. What message do you bear?"

The monk looked to the closed window that again rattled violently in its wooden frame. Through the glass, he saw a ferocious mask with glowing red eyes and a yawning fang-filled mouth. A second pair of eyes pierced the night just below the first. The intensity of their stare frightened the monk. He had never been so close to such an omnipotent force.

"Fearful entity, please deliver your message and leave me. I cannot bear your vehemence much longer."

With a fiery breath, the faces disappeared behind a cloud of condensation that filled the glass window pane. The monk watched as streaks emerged randomly across its surface. He recognized patterns that eventually formed letters and numbers. The message froze as the glass frosted over. He rushed to the window and looked through the clearing window. He saw nothing but dark night. Whatever entity communicated was now gone.

"Los, my friend, you have changed much. Is that Enith with you?"

The monk knocked over a bedside table in his pursuit to grab a pen. The writing was fading, but he copied it exactly as inscribed on the frosted pane. The alpha-numeric scribbling made no sense to him. The writing stopped as suddenly as it started. With tears streaming down his cheeks, the monk double-checked his notes. As he finished the last character, his own excited breath warmed the glass enough for the message to disappear. He flung open the window and stuck his head into the cold night air. He saw nothing in every direction but sensed the presence of a new most powerful spirit. He clasped his hands and offered them a prayer.

Downstairs, Lord Jim had fallen asleep before the fire. He awoke from the racket upstairs. Rising from the chair, he checked his watch. A couple hours till dawn. The sound of footsteps thumping down the stairs made him rush across the living room into the hall.

"Lord Jim, I have something very important," the monk said.

He was trying to catch his breath and say more but simply held out his shaking hand. Lord Jim grabbed the paper he held and started reading.

"We've been visited by the spirit of Los."

"My God, monk, calm down. What are you saying?"

The message appeared to be gibberish. He took hold of the monk's shoulders and held him still.

"Slowly, in English."

"Los has given me a message for you."

"How could that be?"

"He was just here, upstairs, outside the window."

Lord Jim rushed up the stairs into the frigid bedroom. The body of Los still lay motionless on the bed.

"He must have done it. He must have transited and found the Authority's source of fear."

The monk had followed in his footsteps.

"Yes, he and somebody else. I sensed another spirit with him."

Lord Jim stopped in his tracks and looked intently at the monk.

"He was not alone you say? Los was with someone else, outside that window up there?"

"Yes, most definitely. I sensed two souls but together as one."

Now it Lord Jim's turn to have a tear stream down his cheek.

"Well, I'll be damned. Los really did it. He must have found Enith."

Lord Jim took the notepaper and examined it closely. It was not a message at all. Not in the sense he expected. Instead, he was looking at geographic coordinates. I will double check these marking but I recognize this location. I have seen it before. It is Harpers Ferry. Turning to the monk, he embraced him in bear hug. The monk disappeared within a huge black robe.

"Thank you, my friend. Will you continue your prayers? I'm afraid Los isn't yet done with this mission yet."

"Yes, I will but with a much happier heart. They are one strong spirit, and a very good one, too. Best I have ever seen. I sense his despair is now gone. His heart was damaged but no more. Enith is very content. They make a happy pair but I would not want to face their wrath in the In-Between. Woe be to the evil entities that cross their path."

Downstairs, Lord Jim paced back and forth in front of the fireplace. He wanted to soak up as much warmth as he could before he left the farmhouse. Satisfied he was about to catch on fire, he stepped onto the covered porch and into the cold December night. He leaned on the railing and stared beyond the eastern pasture. He raised his eyes to the far away ridge. Something passed overhead and blocked out the stars ever so briefly. It was time to apologize for his sins. He stood straight, faced the dark sky and made his confession.

"So, now you know the truth. I lied to both of you. I made your life together impossible. My lies destroyed your happiness. Worse, I took your son. A guilt weighs on my soul. As soldiers in the cause, I hope you can understand why I did this."

Enith struck Lord Jim violently. She glared at him with hatred in her eyes.

"You son of a bitch! I never thought the Kindred would stoop to that level of subterfuge. I have suffered every day wondering where my child is. Did Los know about? Where is my son now?" The questions came quick and angrily from Enith.

"Your son is alive but on the run. Urizen wants him dead but only because he witnessed a transit. He must not know his geneology. Los never knew. I kept it from him because I wasn't sure he was the father." Lord Jim braced for another slap which came immediately.

"I have to go. Maybe the Authority can help me find my son."

"Whatever you do, don't tell them Orc is your son and Los is the father. Urizen will force you to capture him. Enith, the prophecy has come true. Orc will free us all."

"You crazy old fool. Stop talking about that nonsense. I gotta go and think what to do next."

A gust of wind swept across the lawn. It buffeted the house and rattled the windows. Grabbing the handrail, Lord Jim braced for more and paused his words. He held his breath and pushed out a creeping fear from his mind. He sensed a righteous anger rising-up and spilling over the farmyard. He saw red lights flash on the far mountain ridge. He blinked his eyes at the image. For a second, he glimpsed ferocious red eyes glaring at him. Feeling an urgency to explain himself, his words came out faster.

"As soldiers in the cause, I hope you understand. I justified everything for the Kindred. I am sorry for your pain. For what it's worth, I believe love is indestructible. I knew you would find each other again. Forgive me or not, I will live with my actions for eternity."

Lord Jim felt a calmness pervade his soul. It seeped onto the porch. He felt a transformation in the night air. A bird song broke the silence. He knew the dawn would bring a finality. Like John Brown, he knew the raid would take its own course once it started. He would certainly be martyred. He hoped the Kindred would not die in vain. The In-Between was the next battlefield. At the very least, they would cause a spark that could inflame a rebellion against the Authority. The death of his brothers would not be in vain. He had no doubt that whatever was in those caverns would be destroyed. The mission would hamper Urizen's ability to wage war on souls.

"Time for me to go now. I feel your wrath already. Its source lies in empathy for all souls. I will see you soon. Please have mercy on my soul as I wander the In-Between. Either way, I will be happy to see you together again."

Lord Jim bowed his head in prayer. A gentle breeze softly lifted his hair. A pleasant smell wafted through the air. Memories of better times, summer picnics under the tree-shaded lawn, flooded his mind. They were all together again. Los, Enith and their baby languished in loving embrace on a blanket spread out on the soft green grass. It was a life that never existed. He did not know where the image came from. Maybe from another universe or in a future time where they were reunited. His guilt dissipated with the thought. The early light of dawn reminded him of the mission. It was time to start.

Chapter Fifty-four

Battletown, VA, December 27, 1974

Zoa's mom struggled against the zip ties on her wrist. She yanked her swollen hands against her restraints, trying to peel them from behind her and away from the kitchen chair to protect her face. She could already feel the bruises forming. She looked up at the men and cried quietly. Through her picture window, she could see police setting up crime scene tape across her driveway. Her lawn teemed with police cars. She counted the insignias of at least five different agencies including the Battletown Police, the Clarke County Sheriff's Department, Virginia State Highway Patrol, FBI, and those dark clad men of the Authority whom she had never seen before now. Her husband was sitting in the backseat of a police car.

"Why am I handcuffed?" he yelled.

Police stood just outside the car windows and ignored his pleas.

"You all know me. Let me out."

He banged his head on the glass to get their attention. It didn't work. Their fingers gripped rifles as their feet balanced their weight.

"I am a law-abiding citizen. You have no right to hold me."

Zoa's dad stopped his protests when he finally made eye contact with the officer outside his window. He saw pure fear in his eyes. Looking at the other policemen, he realized they were all scared shitless. He lowered his voice to speak confidentially.

"What's wrong with you guys? My daughter just ran away from home. What are you so afraid of?"

The officers snapped to attention. They all stared stone faced in the same direction. It was then he saw someone who put terror into his heart. The officers cleared a path for a gigantic brute; a strange, solidly built, yet ancient man. Despite his age, he towered over the other officers. His look was furious and deadly.

Zoa's father flashed back to the only other time he had sensed such danger. He was on a summer hunting trip in Canada when a massive grizzly bear wandered into camp. Although they were well armed that summer day, the sheer ferocity of the colossal beast shocked all the hunters. The fear in the eyes of his fellow hunters was identical to this moment. Now, instead of a gigantic bear, a menacing super human appeared before him. Nobody spoke or moved. Zoa's dad sank back into the seat of the squad car. Like the other men around him, he was astonished at the brute striding toward his house.

Urizen stomped across the lawn and up the porch stairs. He sensed weakness and fear all around him. The inferiority of these people made him angry. He stroked his long white beard with one hand and clutched a semi-automatic pistol in the other. Zoa's mom stopped struggling in her chair as he walked through the doorway. She heard agents whisper, "Urizen," as he entered her living room. Her breath caught in her throat. His icy blue eyes told her not to expect any mercy. He circled her chair, stooping low so as not to hit his head on the ceiling. He didn't stare at her but at the agents in the room. They all looked at the floor. Urizen lowered his gaze to meet her eyes.

"Listen to me very carefully," he said in a soft reassuring voice. "I am going to ask you to repeat exactly what your daughter said to you."

She listened to his footsteps make their way around her chair.

"You better not hurt my daughter. She's done nothing wrong except run off from her high school dance. There's no reason for all of this."

"You're not listening. I didn't ask you what she has done, only what she said to you. State terrorism is a serious activity and cannot be tolerated. The danger your daughter caused to our nation, our citizens, your neighbors, and yourself might be mitigated if we acquire certain information."

"You can go to hell. All of you." She glared at each agent around the room until finally fixing her eyes on Urizen.

"That was an unfortunate response. One more chance, the nice way. What exactly did your daughter say to you when you saw her? No detail is too small to mention, so be sure not to leave anything out." Urizen breathed calmly.

He leaned closer to hear her response, but all that could be heard was a collective gasp as she spit in his ear. The suddenness of his strike across her face surprised everyone, including Zoa's mom. The power of his assault sent her and the chair flying across the room.

"Bring him in!" Urizen yelled.

He wiped the spit from where it ran down his cheek. The whole room exploded in activity as some agents scurried out the front door while others picked up the woman and set her chair upright. Within seconds, they dragged in Zoa's father, his feet scuffing the floor.

"What the hell is going on here?"

He saw his wife tied to the chair and bleeding from the nose and mouth. He lunged toward her and shook violently to free himself from the agents who restrained him.

"I demand you let her go. I don't care who you think you are. You are making a big mistake here. This is going right to the top of whatever agency you work for!"

"There is no mistake. We just need some information and we're not leaving here until we get it." Urizen was stoic as he leaned forward and gently lifted the mother's chin in the direction of her husband.

"Please pay attention this time. What you are about to see will happen to every living member of your family, even the most distant relatives. Then we will start with your friends and neighbors."

Without even looking, he fired two shots into her husband's chest. He flew backwards in an explosion of blood. The agents stood confused about whether to pick him up again. Her screams followed the gunshots as they echoed across the empty town. No one was there to hear them except for the prisoners held in the long line of black SUVs. The procession contained Zoa's relatives to the most distant degree. Inside the cars, men tried to wrench the locked doors open, women hugged crying children who desperately clutched them back. All had the same look of fear. They realized a monster was loose in the town. The surrounding agents silently exhaled at the thought of the long day of killing before them.

"Now tell me what your precious daughter said to you. We've got replacements for you husband waiting outside. And I don't think you want to be responsible for the death of your entire extended family. But personally, I think the nation will be better off without your gene pool." He tapped his watch. "Time is of the essence. Your daughter's trail is already getting quite cold."

"Please, I beg you. Don't hurt anymore of my family. I'll tell you what you want to hear!" She took a deep breath.

"Wise decision. I have more bullets than you have family," Urizen purred.

"She said she was alright and that she would come back when she had finished something. That was it. She didn't say where she had been or where she was going."

"That's it?! You stupid woman! Your husband gave his life for that?"

"I swear." She sobbed. "That's all she said! She was only here a minute. She looked around the house, said things appeared odd or something like that, and then left."

"You don't remember anything else?"

"Right after they left. I remember seeing an emergency alert on the television about the chemical disaster. I thought to myself that was wrong because the only plant in Battletown is the lime quarry."

"Why do we even bother with people like you?" He shook his head in disgust. "You don't even deserve the pretense of a republic."

He raised his hand as if to strike again, but instead lifted her, chair and all, closer to his face.

"Now, one last time, are you sure that is all that happened?"

"Yes. She left during the alert with her friend."

Urizen wheeled around at her last words.

"Her friend? Why didn't you mention that earlier?" He thought of the mess at the farmhouse, about the boy who transited and the one who got away.

"I'm sorry. You asked me what she said, not who she was with."

Urizen inhaled sharply through his nose and squatted at her side.

"One last time, and I really mean one last time. Tell me exactly what happened when your daughter was here."

"A young boy, or young man, I guess, was with her. He didn't say much other than kept telling her it was time to leave."

"Think very carefully. Did this boy or young man have a name?"

She looked beyond Urizen to the slumped body of her husband. His blood pooled onto the carpet and reflected the blinking lights of the Christmas tree. She started sobbing but stammered out a response.

"No name that I can remember. He watched and didn't say much at all. He said something about finishing what they started."

"They will never finish what they started," he replied.

Seething with anger, Urizen dropped her to the floor. Urizen stood up and walked out of the house.

"You won't hurt my daughter. I told you everything."

Urizen looked up and down the street and then in to the night sky. He saw stars, but not the moon. He decided the kids couldn't get far in the dark. The monitoring system hadn't detected another transit, so the pair must be in this dimension. Or, could they have found a way back without being detected? The possibility troubled him. The mother had said the daughter was going back to finish something. He realized something was wrong. The girl's initial transit yesterday had tripped the monitoring system. Now, she had come back to her parent's house. That meant she transited back to this dimension. His surveillance system didn't detect her return, or for that matter, her companion.

His conclusion was troubling. There were only two scenarios that could have occurred. His detection system didn't pick up their transit back to this dimension because they found another way to travel. Which meant he had holes in his net that he needed to repair. Or, the system did detect their transit but no alert was issued. Both were equally as troubling, to him. The first scenario meant the Authority's grip was slipping due to incompetence of maintaining its system. He clenched his jaw at the thought of the second scenario. A traitor existed inside his organization.

"I need to return to DC," he barked into his radio.

"Chopper is ready for take-off, sir."

"Bring it to my location immediately, idiot. Land it in the damned street. There's no time to waste."

"On its way, sir."

The thumping noise of a helicopter came from overhead. It engines roared louder as it approached the neighborhood. The propeller wash blew away several hanging plants from the front porch. Agents scrambled to move cars and clear a landing site. Urizen watched impatiently before he realized he had forgotten something. He threw open the door to the house, the gust from the chopper sending old newspapers flying off the porch. He returned to the house where Zoa's mother was still strapped to her chair. He drew his gun. Nearby agents jumped at the flash of its firing.

Emerging from the front door, Urizen bounded down the front steps and into the helicopter that was hovering just a foot above ground. Blood from both of Zoa's parents speckled his coarse robes. The helicopter rose and headed east, gaining altitude sufficient to fly close over the Blue Ridge Mountains. He gazed down from the open door where he clutched the hand railing. He watched as the carpet of trees spread across the ridges. Craggy rock cliffs occasionally broke through the canopy and each cliff brought his gaze intently upon its surface. He wondered which ones were hiding his fugitives. He spied a cluster of oaks and imagined what might lay beneath their broad canopy.

"The damn Kindred must be involved."

"Excuse me, sir?" the pilot said through the headset.

Urizen ignored the question.

"I know you little bastards are down there. You will be found and interrogated. Whatever secret knowledge you possess will be beaten out of you. I look forward to finding out how you're transiting without tripping our system. Go on! Run and hide. I enjoy the hunt."

"Sir, do you want me to land?"

"Did I ask you to land?"

"No, sir."

"Then fly this damn thing to my office before the tear in my net becomes a gaping hole!"

Chapter Fifty-Five

Battletown, VA, December 30, 1974, 3:30 AM

The full moon passed behind sweeping clouds. Men hunched over flickering fires scattered across the front lawn of the stone farmhouse. Some small tents were spaced along the fence line separating the lawn from the pasture. From the front porch, Lord Jim surveyed his assault teams. He felt a mixture of sadness and pride that most of these men accepted their fates so bravely. They were stoic in the face of certain death. Most of them would be dead by this time tomorrow. He knew all of them and their descendants. Lost Mungo confirmed their lineages from the survivors of the first raid on Harpers Ferry. He had personally recruited them but they made the decision to freely join the Kindred. Lord Jim found that once the truth was revealed, people committed themselves enthusiastically to the cause of freedom. Before dawn, these men would launch the second raid. Lord Jim expected success but that didn't mean anyone would survive. In fact, he realized one almost guaranteed the other. For that reason, he had already secured the succession of leadership of the Kindred. His orders would keep certain members from participating in the raid. They would pick up his role should he die. Making life and death decisions was hard but necessary. Lord Jim carefully balanced his selections for the assault teams and the stay-behind cadre. Bigfoot and Whiskeytown were assigned the frontal assault on Mount Storm. It was a mission with no subtlety. Sometimes bravery was the only character trait that factored into his team selection. Both these men were fearless and would ensure the Authority complex was breached. He decided to walk through the lawn and say goodbye.

The stone wall of the old barn blocked the wind while reflecting warmth from the fire back toward the huddled men. Their voices were immediately recognizable to Lord Jim as he approached.

"Gentlemen, you should try to get some sleep," Lord Jim said above the crackling fire.

"The hour is a little too late. Sunrise ain't that far away," Bigfoot responded.

He zipped up the winter hunting parka to his neck and stuffed his hands back in its pockets. Whiskeytown thoughtfully stroked his thick black beard and nodded his head in agreement.

"Well, I know you two will give your all tomorrow. The success of the raid depends on your team breeching the complex," Lord Jim said solemnly.

"They won't know what hit them." Whiskeytown grunted before pulling his hat lower over his eyes.

"I am proud to have served with you. God bless you," Lord Jim said.

He paused to say a silent prayer before slowly walking away to the next fire ring. It always amazed him how bravely Kindred soldiers faced danger. If the mission went as planned, the wave of water flowing from the caverns within the Maryland Heights would flood the underground complex at Mount Storm. When its electrical power station became submerged in water, a massive explosion would rip through to the surface. If the Authority didn't kill these men, the explosion would. He shook his head at the weight of his responsibility. Leading the Kindred all these years left him saddened with grief over the lives terminated or ruined by his decisions.

"Nice speech. What do you think of our chances of coming back?" Whiskeytown asked Bigfoot.

"I don't see my way through this one. We ain't coming back. He knows it. Just don't want to say it out loud," Bigfoot replied.

"Aren't you the negative one tonight. What's got you so spooked?" Whiskeytown asked.

"I had a dream last night. A beer tap at Vagaries was flowing unattended. A large mug underneath it was spilling over onto the floor."

"Sounds like a nightmare. What a waste of good beer," Whiskeytown said.

"It was a vision. The beer was our blood and the unattended mug was this mission not changing a goddamn thing," Bigfoot replied.

"Or, we will be drinking in the halls of Valhalla tonight. All depends on how you look at it. You got to stop being so negative, Bigfoot."

Bigfoot nodded his head and grinned while he wagged his finger as an exclamation point to his interpretation of the dream.

Both men commenced laughing from deep within their throats. The firelight danced off the ice encased stone walls of the barn.

Chapter Fifty-Six

Another long day of walking the path left Bret and Zoa exhausted and starving. Zoa wanted to plop down, but she knew if they didn't set up camp, there would be no supper. Magda's rules. They waited for the food wagon to trundle up the trail, its sight and smell a joy to experience. It appeared magically at dusk, the setting sun glinting off its stained-glass windows. Its pots and pans clanked loudly off the white clapboard siding. Two yaks guided themselves, pulling the wagon without need of a driver. It was as if they were following an old bison track etched eons ago by their animal ancestors.

As it got darker outside, the celestial images in the wagon's windows shined brighter. The illuminated interior filled with aromas that drifted toward their noses. White smoke puffed from its chimney and flowed down the mountain slope. The pair inhaled deeply. They stepped through the wagon's red-trimmed door and took a seat at a small interior table. The kitchen was engulfed in a cloud of steam, which obscured the activity within.

"Hope you two are hungry," a husky voice said.

A set of muscular forearms extended through the fog. Flannel sleeves rolled up at the elbows were the only visible indication that the strong, large hands belonged to Magda. Deep bowls of stew sat before them steaming in the cold night air. Magda's faced followed to wish them good appetites. Zoa and Bret ate until their bellies were full. And then came the steaming cups of cider followed by soft cookies wrapped in brown paper. The two shouted their thanks into the vapor. They heard her wish them goodnight and warned them not to feed the yaks any cookies, even if they asked.

Bret stepped down the ladder stairs from the wagon door. He rubbed his tummy and couldn't resist a small belch. It was so satisfying and worth the distained look from Zoa. It was then he spied a new shelter in the clearing. It was set a little distance from their own.

"Hey, that's my friend! The Shenandoah elder," Bret said.

The figure was turned away from them, facing a campfire.

"We should see if he wants something to eat," said Zoa.

The pair walked the short distance to his camp, their shadows cutting through the glow of stained glass windows. As they approached, Zoa walked into the glow cast from the campfire.

"That's the strangest flame I've ever seen!" she said.

"It isn't a normal fire and my friend is a bit different too."

The Shenandoah Elder was sitting on animal skins spread before the blaze. His eyes were smoky white, obviously without sight. Nonetheless, he stared into the leaping blue flames of his fire. Bret knew he was seeing either the distant past or the far-off future. He was certainly not in the present moment. The fire gave off warmth and smelled of burning wood, though it was silent and smokeless.

"Can we join you?" Bret asked respectfully.

"The Great Way is open to all."

He spread his arms in a welcoming gesture. A gust from the fire blew his long, grey hair away from his face. He appeared to be one hundred years old, at least. They sat down on the blankets next to the fire.

"Do you live here, or are you just passing through like us?" Zoa asked.

"I flow like the great Shenandoah. Even as its water is in motion, the river exists in place. I was here when the first people traveled this way and I am last to leave. Like the great river, I pass through the valley but remain."

"Where are you from?" Bret asked.

"From the Catawba Mountains in the south and the Adirondack Mountains in the north. This valley is only a passage. All people used the Great Valley, but it belonged to none. That is, until the foreigners came. Then it no longer belonged to all people, but very few."

The wind picked up and swept the boughs of a giant evergreen. The dead branches at its crown whistled in the night. Zoa looked up and pushed her long hair away from her face.

"Why are you here?" she asked.

"I miss travelling the way of the warrior, the way of my people. Now, I am free to travel. So, I do." He chuckled.

"Where are you going?" Bret asked.

"I'm looking for someone," he responded.

"Can we help you?" offered Zoa.

"Have you seen Standing Bear. He is looking for his people. We have moved on and he can't find us. He is alone in this world."

"We have not seen any native people since we have been on the path. What do we say if we see him?" Bret asked.

"Tell him that his people are waiting for him. We will be united again and travel the Great Way as it was before. The way it used to be."

With his last statement, the elder, his fire, and his shelter vanished. Only the grass remained with a faint impression upon it. Zoa looked up and saw blue embers rise into the night sky.

Chapter Fifty-seven

Battletown, VA, December 30, 1974

The sleepy hamlet of Battletown consists of five mercantile blocks clustered on either side of the only intersection with a traffic light. Down a nondescript alley of this main street lay the largest building in town. An imposing three-story brick building sat imposingly at its terminus. Flapping in the December breeze, flags marked county, state and national authority of its occupants. The sun was just peaking over the Blue Ridge Mountains. The parking lot was full of empty police cars. The officers had yet to arrive to work. Inside, a skeleton crew of employees were ending their night shift. The lobby floor shined under the fluorescent lights. Lord Jim and Wobbly burst into the brick office building wearing small backpacks and bearing weapons.

"Hands up!" Wobbly yelled.

Lord Jim pointed his shotgun as Wobbly quickly disarmed the deputy.

"What is this?" the Deputy responded.

"Who else is here?" Wobbly asked.

"Jim is downstairs at the holding cell and Frank is upstairs monitoring communications."

"Cuff him Wobbly," Lord Jim instructed.

"We don't have any money here and the guns are locked up. Not sure what you boys hope to get out of this," the deputy calmly stated.

"This is about liberty, not money," Lord Jim replied.

Footsteps could be heard coming up the stairs from the basement. Lord Jim whirled around to confront the newcomer. Another Deputy went for his holster to withdraw his service weapon.

"Don't do it! Hands off your weapon!" Lord Jim yelled. "Put your gun down."

The deputy raised his weapon. The blast from Lord Jim's shotgun thundered through the empty building. The deputy flew backward onto the stairs. His blood washed the floor. Wobbly looked on in horror. Lord Jim went to the front door and dumped his backpack on the floor. He withdrew a metal chain that he roped through the handles of the glass double doors. He pulled the chain tight and secured it with a large padlock.

"Boy, grab his gun and follow me."

Wobbly did as he was told and followed Lord Jim upstairs. The pair ran down the brightly lit corridor. Their boots left a bloody trail to the door above which hung a communication center sign. Lord Jim slowly opened the door pushing the barrel of his shotgun in first. A deputy sat before a large console of radio communication equipment wearing a pair of headphones. Lord Jim tap his shoulder with the barrel of his shotgun. The deputy took off his headphones and rose from his chair.

"What the hell are you doing up here?"

"We are starting radio Kindred," Lord Jim replied.

Wobbly quickly cuffed him from behind.

"Put the two of them in the basement holding cell and then station yourself inside the front door. Take this walkie-talkie. We can expect a lot of company soon." He handed Wobbly a revolver from his knapsack. "When they show up, wave that gun around."

"Do I shoot?" Wobbly asked.

"If they come in, shoot."

"If they retreat?"

"Haul ass back here and we will lock ourselves in."

Wobbly escorted his prisoner out of the room awkwardly clutching the pistol. Lord Jim sat down in the chair. He held one earphone to his head. He brought the microphone to his mouth to speak but paused.

"I pray for the souls of our soldiers. Give us strength. Our struggle is begun. A wrathful empathy is about to be unleashed. A wave of spiritual water is going to wash clean this land. The Authority will take its vengeance. Many souls are going to crossover this day. Grant them safe passage."

Lord Jim once again brought the mic to his mouth. He began reading a short message, repeating the words over again. It was the pre-arranged signal to start the second raid on Harpers Ferry. Small groups of men and women, black and white, would emerge from shadows. Their assaults began in stealth. Penetrating the Authority complexes required the element of surprise. Lord Jim's goal was to give them as much time as possible. To do this, he needed to convince the Authority that his seizure of the Battletown municipal building was the main strike. The Authority was already taking the bait. While his small action was about to be crushed, Kindred at this very moment began infiltrating their targets. Lord Jim wanted to sow as much confusion as possible about their intentions and movements.

"Group A has commandeered the Battletown municipal building. We are under assault. Reinforcements are needed here. Group B is seizing the armory in Winchester. Group C is blocking Route 340 north and south."

Sooner than expected, large contingents of law enforcement from the county sheriff's office and the Authority arrived in the parking lot and quickly surrounded the building. Without hesitation, a SWAT team began ramming the glass doors. Deciding it was worthless to wave his gun, Wobbly pointed his revolver, closed his eyes and pulled the trigger. To his astonishment, the hammer just clicked. There was no ammunition in the gun.

"Old fool. This whole thing is a set up," Wobbly cursed.

Wobbly threw down the revolver and ran upstairs. He heard the front glass door shattering. Shots rang out and bullets flew just a few feet behind him. Turning the corner, Wobbly ran down the hall and dived through the open door of the communication room. Lord Jim slammed the door shut behind him and pushed a desk up against it.

"Jesus Christ, what kind of raid is this?" Wobbly yelled.

"We are just a diversion. This isn't the raid at all, son," Lord Jim replied.

"Now you tell me. Maybe that is something I should have known before volunteering," Wobbly said.

"Wobbly, you didn't volunteer. I gave you an order. You followed it like the rest of them."

The two men ducked down underneath the communication desk as bullets ripped through the door and sent shrapnel and debris flying across the room. Lord Jim rummaged through his knapsack one last time.

"I brought something that might get us out of here." He pulled out a stick of dynamite.

"Get us out of here alive?" Wobbly asked.

"I saw rain slickers hanging in that closet. We need to put them on and hang outside those windows."

In one last desperate attempt to right a wrong, Lord Jim executed their escape. He fired his shotgun through the barricaded office door. Wobbly grabbed the long black raincoats. The words, *Sheriff Department,* were emblazoned across the back. He then set a timer on the bomb and placed it next to the door. Wobbly donned one coat and threw the other to Lord Jim. He quickly pulled it on. Both men ran to the nearest window. Lord Jim lifted the glass pane and helped Wobbly through.

"Hang there until the blast then climb back in. Follow me out of here. We need to exit while everyone is still confused by the blast." Wobbly instructed.

"This is the plan? Blow ourselves up?"

"Shut up and do exactly as I say. Hold on tight."

Lord Jim had just barely shimmied through the window and lowered himself when the explosion rocked the building. The percussion came with a rush of flames. His hands burned with the heat. As soon as the force diminished overhead, he pulled himself up. Wobbly was struggling to climb back in. Lord Jim helped him through the window. Lord Jim led them past the blown office door. Three Authority agents lay bloodied in the hallway. Their bodies were still. A wounded agent was crawling toward the lobby stairwell.

"Lift up his other arm. We are going to carry him out and hope they let us pass," Lord Jim said.

"This keeps getting better," Wobbly replied.

The building was full of dust. They past two other agents limping back down the stairs. A new SWAT team rushed toward them pointing their weapons wildly.

"This is a restricted area. Authority agents only. Make your way to Main Street. There are ambulances there," an officer ordered.

Wobbly and Lord Jim carried the dying agent through the lobby and outside the building. Other dark clad agents of the Authority waved them past.

"Just some deputies coming through," one agent yelled.

Beyond the Authority perimeter but before the sheriff's blockade at the end of the lane, they laid the agent down onto the parking lot. He was already dead. Lord Jim grabbed Wobbly and pushed him toward the row of Battletown police cars parked along the far corner of the lot. They climbed in the first one. Lord Jim pulled a ring of keys from his pocket.

"I grabbed this from the front desk. Was going to lose them so they couldn't patrol the back roads. Never thought we would have a chance to escape."

He began trying each one in the ignition. On the seventh key, it the engine turned over.

"Hold on boy."

Lord Jim accelerated forward over the curb. He sped across the town commons weaving around park benches and in between towering elm trees. Roughly following the brick nature path, he steered for the far end of the grassy square. The car burst onto the perimeter street.

"We can't go through the road block. The sheriff will know we are not his deputies," Lord Jim said.

"Where do we go from here? Is there, like, a safe house or something we can use?" Wobbly asked.

"If we can get to 340, we might be able to pass blockades if they're run by the Authority. We just can't look too desperate," Lord Jim replied.

"I have never felt so desperate in my life," Wobbly confessed.

Lord Jim circumvented houses, plowing over shrubs and children's playsets. He finally turned onto the road leading out of town. Accelerating, they reached sixty miles per hour. Wobbly thumped the car's dashboard in celebration of their escape. Lord Jim was tempted to smile until he saw cars slowing down ahead, their brake lights signaling danger.

"It's a checkpoint," Lord Jim said.

"Fuck, we were so close," Wobbly replied.

Waiting in line, Lord Jim calculated the option to drive across the pasture to his right. It stood between them and the Shenandoah River. If they could make its banks, they could ditch the car and swim for the other side. Then, they would climb into the Blue Ridge Mountains.

"Your call, boy, should we take our chance with the checkpoint or make a break for it?"

Creeping forward, the cars approached the blockade. Ahead, they saw the uniforms of the Battletown Police Department and Clarke County Sheriff patrol cars.

"Were fucked," Wobbly said.

Lord Jim gunned the engine and veered across the adjacent field. The car weaved between large protruding rock formations. A barrage of bullets struck the rocks to either side of the car.

"Finally, those damn rocks are good for something," Lord Jim cursed.

"It's like we're being protected by a dragon that is rising up from deep underground," Wobbly shouted.

Black SUVs appeared suddenly to either side. Agents in the back seats leaned out open doors. Their machine guns emptied magazines of automatic fire into the escaping vehicle. The back windshield exploded in a shower of glass. Lord Jim could feel the wheels flattening. He was losing control of the car. An explosion in his review mirror offered some relief. An authority chase vehicle had smashed into a large rock and exploded on impact. A helicopter joined the pursuit. Agents fired down through the car roof. The front windshield shattered and broke apart showering them with glass. The car raced toward a line of trees at the far end of the field. Lord Jim turned sharply toward a barbed wire fence that ran along a rural lane. He accelerated and crashed through the fence but crossed over the road into the ditch on the other side.

"Get out, boy! Run like hell to the river!" Lord Jim screamed over the racing engine.

A line of agents leveled rifles at them from all directions.

"It's over," Wobbly said.

Both men fell to their knees in exhaustion. Lord Jim smiled at the sheer number of agents surrounding them.

"We've done it boy. Look at all these bastards. We tied them up for a couple hours. Gave our men the diversion they need.

"Yeah, for once being a failure is winning," Wobbly laughed.

The whirling blades of a helicopter descended to the field. It hovered just above the ground before Urizen leaped off.

"What a pitiful pair!" he exclaimed.

He approached the kneeling men and withdrew his pistol from its holster.

"I will enjoy this execution. Men, gather around and see what we do with rebels."

"Are they really going to kill us? Why not take us prisoner?" Wobbly asked.

"I am sorry I called you, "boy." You did a man's job today. I am very proud of you."

Urizen fired a shot into the sky, relishing the fear he sensed from Wobbly.

"I don't want to die. I am scared," Wobbly admitted.

"Don't be. It will only cause you problems as you enter the In-Between," Lord Jim admonished him sternly.

Urizen brandished his pistol to the audience of smiling agents. They gleefully await the execution.

"I am scared," Wobbly repeated.

"Get hold of yourself. Focus intently. You must travel bravely now."

Urizen yelled at both men to shut up. The fear he sensed seconds ago was dissipating. That was unacceptable.

"I don't want to die," Wobbly cried.

"Look me in the eyes Wobbly. There is another realm, greater than this life, but it can only be grasped if you have no fear. You must have control."

"Too late for that, I just soiled my pants," Wobbly smiled.

Lord Jim and Wobbly began laughing.

"Let's go together. We still have more battles ahead."

"I can't wait. I guess I won't need clean underwear where we are going?"

Their laughter became a roar. The surrounding agents became nervous at their lack of fear. Urizen became enraged.

"Enough!" he screamed.

He pointed his pistol at their heads. Two shots ring out. Lord Jim and Wobbly fell forward into the roadside ditch. Their brains splattered everything nearby. Agents scurried to drag away their bodies to a nearby SUV. The cars sped away with their trophies. Desolate once again, the rural asphalt lane glistened in the noon sun. A streak of blood trailed from where the SUV had been parked to a much larger pool at the base of a wooden post affixed with a Virginia Department of Transportation sign. As the blood of Lord Jim and Wobbly dripped over its lettering, the words, *End State Maintenance,* became illegible.

CHAPTER FIFTY-EIGHT

Battletown, VA, December 31, 1974

As the entire law enforcement community of Clark County descended upon the brightly lit municipal building, raiders of the Kindred began their simultaneous assault at two other locations. These raids were just as desperate as the first led by John Brown. They faced overwhelming odds. Once detected, the crushing power of the Authority would be directed against them. Their only hope for success lay in the element of complete surprise. Lord Jim and Wobbly provided each team precious minutes to strike. Like a snake thrusting up from the forest floor, their fangs had but one chance to penetrate the prey.

At the designated time, a dozen men rushed from the darkness of the C&O canal and over its embankment. They immediately began climbing the steep rock face of the Maryland Heights. Sleet from the raging blizzard smacked them hard in the face as their hands gripped granite outcroppings. Ropes looped around their waists secured rifles and flashlights. The mountain's western face was still dark as dawn broke. From the opposite bank of the Potomac River, anyone waking up in Harpers Ferry would not distinguish the bodies against the wet rocks. Skilled and determined climbers, they inched toward a dark cleft in the center of the cliff face.

Another dozen raiders slithered through holes cut in the perimeter fencing of Mount Storm. The high grass provided them some cover as they crawled toward a metal hanger building. They waited in the shadows until its large doors retracted to let a semi-truck exit. Bigfoot and Whiskeytown had trouble squirming through the wire.

"God, damn it. Cut a man-size hole next time," Bigfoot swore.

"Seriously, we need to give the wire cutter to someone who at least wears size XXXL," Whiskeytown added.

Once through, the team formed a firing line that advanced toward the main complex facility with the two big men at either end. They rushed forward firing their rifles at the Authority guards stationed outside the main doors. The guards only managed to fire off a couple shots in response before falling under the withering barrage of bullets.

"Now shut those doors!" Bigfoot yelled. "Everyone take cover. I am blowing the motors that operate the chain driven doors."

An explosion sent shrapnel flying through the cavernous warehouse. They were now sealed inside the complex itself. Nobody could escape including themselves.

"They will blow the doors open from the outside but that will give us some time," Bigfoot said calmly.

"Before that can happen, the Authority will need time to concoct a cover story for these explosions," Whiskeytown added.

They knew locals were surely awake now with the sound of the blast and calling media outlets for information. The fake script describing the chemical accident would take several minutes for the Authority to write and more minutes to distribute. While the media was compliant, they all knew it lacked the creativity to produce its own lies. Meanwhile, the raiders began planting bombs in the large elevator room. It contained the motors and cabling systems that hoisted elevator cars up and down from the depths of the complex. They would then descend the narrow staircase to the subterranean levels of the complex. They were in search of the massive underground transformer vault. Timing was critical to open-up the secure doors that protected them from underground flooding. Once open, the team was instructed to run like hell to the surface. They had not been provisioned to plant bombs at this point. Whiskeytown suspected a cataclysmic event would occur. If the transformers exploded, it would not be by their bombs.

Back at the Maryland Heights, the lead climber kept stopping on each ledge with sufficient horizontal surface to free his hands. He would glance at his compass and map and then squint upwards. His eyes would follow an invisible line that projected from his mental calculations. He was triangulating the exact spot of the hidden cave entrance. Assured of its location, he began climbing again. The raiders below followed his route uphill. Traversing the final overhang, the team assembled outside a small crevice invisible from the ground. They filed into its narrow passage. Now each hand was free to hold a flashlight and rifle. Dirty and soaking wet, the raiders emerged within a larger cave that contained an iron gated cylinder concrete drain. They immediately began cutting through the metal bars with diamond tipped metal strings. When enough had been severed, they used brute strength to force the bars open. One by one, they slipped through the entrance and slid down the drain several yards before dropping down into a cavern. Casting aside their flashlights, they adjusted their eyesight to the bright artificial lighting that illuminated the interior. Several men could not maintain their silence at the bizarre sight before them. A large cistern swirled with a luminous water. Apparitions swam within its current. Two men fell to their knees and made the sign of the cross. They were in the presence of the supernatural and it frightened them more than the Authority. Each raider unpacked bundles of dynamite from their knapsacks and began setting explosives around the cistern's retaining walls. The plan was to send a tsunami wave along the interior aqueduct to flood the lower levels of Mount Storm. In the process, they would also destroy the cistern itself and the pumping station.

Further to the south, the second team was already shooting its way past the subterranean level security posts. The objective of their mission was to open the doors to the massive transformer vault. If they could expose it to the coming wall of water, a massive explosion should rip through the subterranean complex and destroy the broadcasting system that the Authority used to implant fears in the citizenry.

"Those must be the doors," Bigfoot said pointing ahead.

"What if they are locked?" Whiskeytown asked.

"We'll use our guns to shoot them open. We can't explode them ourselves or we stand no chance of getting out," Bigfoot answered.

Automatic gunfire echoed through the subterranean complex as the door lock was shot to pieces. The team carefully opened the huge doors wide. They plugged the large drains at the base of the transformer vault.

"Now, let's get the hell out of here!" Bigfoot yelled.

The team heard a muffled boom. The sound came from deep within the entrance of a tunnel at the far end of the cavern. An aqueduct disappeared into its darkness. Bigfoot squinted to determine what flowed within it. Whatever the liquid was, it was not water. It glowed faint green. Its surface rippled slightly with the far-off sound.

"They must have blown the other complex. We got to get to the surface and fight our way back out through those doors." Whiskeytown ordered.

The team now started climbing the staircase. They were seven stories underground. At each floor, they met a blaze of gunfire from the landing above. Returning fire, they advanced upward. It was a matter of attrition at this point. They lost at least one Kindred per floor. The progress was costly and time was running out. The running gun battle was taking too long. Just one level from the surface, Bigfoot was shot in the upper chest.

"Damn it. We were so close," he said

"Mere flesh wound for the likes of you," Whiskeytown replied.

He sized up the entrance wound. The entrance hole was small but the exit had blown away a large part of his back. He grimaced and pulled up Bigfoot with one arm while he fired several shots with the other.

"We will get you out of here buddy. Someone has to turn off that beer tap."

"I think I like your idea of just drinking the keg dry," Bigfoot replied blinking in and out of consciousness.

"You better save me some you bastard."

They were the only two left. Whiskeytown dragged Bigfoot up the last flight of stairs. A trail of blood marked their ascent. Finally, the last landing appeared. Whiskeytown sat Bigfoot down in the stairway and peeked inside to the main warehouse where they had first entered. They were on the surface now but Authority agents were everywhere. He went back to Bigfoot and sat down exhausted from the climb.

"Well, we can't go down and we can't go out. And there sure in the hell is no chance of rescue," Whiskeytown said looking down at his friend.

"In my pocket. I brought some rescue." Bigfoot pointed at his parka's front pocket.

Whiskeytown reached inside and pulled out a small mason jar. He opened it and tasted the clear liquid.

"You are a bartender to the very end. Have a little bit of heaven."

Bigfoot tried to swallow some moonshine but spit up blood.

An explosion rocked the entire complex and a wave of heat and light seared through the stairwell.

* * *

Los witnessed the attack on the cistern, flying above the wall of water surging through the tunnel. It splashed into the lowest level of the Mount Storm complex and rapidly filled up the basement. Within seconds the transformer vault was engulfed. With Enith clutching tightly to him, their spirits flew unaffected through the flames, even as Kindred and Authority agents alike were incinerated. Passing toward the surface, Los sensed a strange presence that was completely alien to him. He veered toward another tunnel where the sensation was strongest. It led to yet another large pool inside a windowless room. Inside, he spied gray figures furtively moving about in the darkness. They were not human. He sensed a great sadness or despair emanating from them. Then he realized the creatures were drawing psychic trauma from the water and ingesting it. None of it made the least bit of sense. They detected his spirit and approached. Voices were entering his mind, pleading with him to free them. Again, it made no sense to the last bit of his conscious mind. He wanted no part of these things and flew away. Enith could sense his apprehension and clutched him tighter.

CHAPTER FIFTY-NINE

Bolivar Heights, WV, December 31, 1974

A Tibetan singing bowl hummed in the broadcast booth of the empty college radio studio. Its hum marked the end of a silent moment of meditation. Standing Bear leaned forward and spoke softly into his microphone.

"This next song goes out to all the wrathful empathies tonight. Whether they're hiking the GT, travelling the Golden Path, or patrolling the In-Between, let's keep these intrepid warriors in our thoughts. Most are striving for understanding, some journeying through time and space, and a few very special ones are saving lost souls. They're all out there battling against oppression in its many forms."

Standing Bear fell silent for just a moment. The dead air across the radio caught the attention of listeners.

"I'd like to say a prayer for a very special brother out there. He crossed over tonight. His flight in to the darkness is especially perilous. I'm thinking of you, brother Los. I can't say too much. Just remember, listeners, that while you're warm and safe, with your belly full of food, monsters roam out there in the shadows. The only reason they don't come into the light and take control of this world is because a few souls put themselves between them and us. Against impossible odds, outnumbered and outgunned, these heroes of the universe are, at this very moment, standing up. Sorry, listeners, to be such a bummer at this late hour. It's a dark and cold wintery night. But the darkest night heralds a new dawn. To the brave souls, you are not forgotten. Here it goes. A new song by Bob Marley."

He placed the needle on the record and the anthem "Get Up, Stand Up" scratched to a start. The song wafted from the studio speakers. It was midnight and the small campus was abandoned. Most students had gone home for the holidays. A lightly falling snow quieted the campus even more. Standing Bear was the DJ of last resort for this lonely shift. No students ever volunteered to run the boards on the late Saturday night and early Sunday dawn shift. He didn't mind since he had no place to go. He was alone anyway. He had no relatives in the area and no social life, so he enjoyed broadcasting through the night. He imagined a vast audience of solitary listeners across the Eastern Panhandle to whom he felt connected invisibly. They tuned in to his program for spiritual companionship as much as for music and information.

Standing Bear listened to Marley's lyrics. He wondered why so few heeded its words. He shook his head and decided to get a cup of coffee before the track ended. He left the recording studio and headed toward the kitchen. As he filled his mug, he thought he heard something out in the hall. But the janitor had certainly already left for the night.

"Hello?" He opened the studio's door.

The corridor was dark except for the emergency lights. A heavy metallic clash made him jump. Banging came from all directions. A dog or hound barked somewhere in the building. He ran back into the studio and locked the door behind him. In his hurry, he had spilled coffee all over his pants. He was on his way to the kitchen to wipe off with a towel when he heard the small transistor radio come on by itself. It broadcast an emergency alert. The announcer's voice was compelling and his message urgent.

"Battletown, Virginia, is under a mandatory evacuation and will be quarantined for public safety. An explosion at the chemical plant is spewing toxic fumes into the air, making it unsafe to breath. Emergency crews are on the scene trying to eliminate the leakage. Law enforcement has secured the perimeter. Some citizens have been attempting to re-enter the town by crossing the Shenandoah River. They have been blocked and are now evading arrest by hiding in the Blue Ridge Mountains."

Standing Bear knew a lie when he heard one. This must be what Los had warned him about. It was the sign. He knew now what he had to do. He ran back to the broadcast booth and pulled the needle from the record. He spoke in a loud but somber tone to his listeners.

"I interrupt this broadcast with a very special message." He pulled the cassette that Los had given him from the top right drawer of his desk.

"Please listen to this taped message. Record it if you can. Rebroadcast it if you do."

Standing Bear inserted the tape into the radio deck. Its tape reels whirred to life. The narrator's voice had a strong accent, Russian probably, but his speech was slow, deliberate, and understandable. The somber tone of the recording only intensified the urgency of its message. While the recording played over the airwaves, Standing Bear picked up the phone and dialed all the other college radio stations in the listening area. He implored each broadcaster who answered to pick up his broadcast. Most agreed to his request, pushing the message further. He worked his way outwards geographically in an expanding circle and when the tape ended, he simply rewound it and played it back. After fifteen minutes, his broadcast spread further and further across the country. He tuned an AM radio to stations as far away as Newark, Columbus, Nashville, Chicago, St. Louis, Ann Arbor, Madison, and Phoenix. He was dialing Oakland when a loud knock erupted on the studio's door. He remembered that he had locked it and thanked himself for being paranoid. Was it the Sunday morning student already? No student could strike the door that hard. He was worried.

"Just a minute, I'm coming," he called out.

The knocking was urgent and thunderous, not the sound of a coed student sleepily showing up for their morning shift.

"Who's there?" He stopped in his tracks.

The possibility of the door exploding open seemed like a very real one. The pounding stopped and all was silent.

"I'm not opening the door until you identify yourself!" He yelled through the barrier.

Bullets dented the fireproof metal door. Standing Bear wheeled around, ran back into his sound booth closing the glass door behind him. The sound of iron against steel hurt his ears. He recognized that grating sound. It was a crow bar prying open metal.

It must be the Authority, he thought to himself. They heard his broadcast, tracked him down, and were intent on stopping it. The studio was filling with the Sulphur smoke of gunpowder. Standing Bear stood before his microphone for the last time, stopped the tape, and spoke his final words.

"Each act of defiance must eventually meet a response. Mine has come, and I am resigned to my fate. Please continue the struggle, brothers and sisters. I'll continue the struggle on the other side. I go without fear. We will triumph in the end. I am standing up now looking for my people."

His final declaration was punctuated with the staccato sound of automatic weapons firing over the radio. Stunned listeners heard muffled voices, then a stern voice shouting commands until the broadcast was yanked silent. When it started again, the samizdat narrator was no more. Instead, a bland voice repeated an alert of the Battletown chemical spill.

Chapter Sixty

Linden, VA, December 28, 1974

Lost Mungo had a message to deliver. It had been passed between Kindred hands for generations. Even before the first raid on Harpers Ferry, the message existed. It was entrusted to John Brown who carried it for years. He never spoke of who gave it to him. Before being hung at the gallows, he revealed the message to a trusted confidante. It was then secreted through his funeral attendees until it reached the hands of an escaped raider. It disappeared with him into the mountains. Despite its couriers being hunted, imprisoned or killed, the words of the prophecy survived. The Authority feared rebels not their thoughts. That was their mistake. The truth was a weapon. It was whispered by fugitive voices around campfires under starry nights. Like sparks released by the flames, the enigmatic words rose to the heavens and took refuge among the angels. Thus, the hidden knowledge was repeated and remembered. Across time and space, the Kindred watched for signs of the prophecy. Descendants and their names were duly recorded. The predicted patterns were patiently awaited. It was a riddle until now. At first, the prophecy seemed too vague. At times, Lost Mungo even doubted its precision. Had the exactness of its parts been altered over so many recitations? Until now. The signs were now unmistakable. A great event was in motion. A cataclysm was approaching. The universe would call forth heroes to confront a great evil. His genealogies revealed the names.

Lost Mungo had spent years preparing for this moment. He felt a relief that the burden of securing, protecting, and delivering it was finally at hand. It was time to meet the recipient and deliver the message. Turning it over would feel as good as taking off a heavy backpack after miles of hiking. He was tired but wanted to see it through. His time for rest would come soon.

Upon receipt, it would initiate a chain of events. Unless, of course, the recipient did not understand the message, or worse, rejected his role. That was a possibility Lost Mungo had not thought of until now. He couldn't blame him for refusing. Who among us could accept such a challenge at sixteen years of age?

He stared at the young man before him in the clearing and knew he could not deliver the message and leave. He knew in his mind and in his heart that he must stay with the boy until he was no longer needed. After all, he was about to place an enormous weight on this young man's shoulder. The future of the coming revolution, one that would shake the universe across all its dimensions, would be in his hands. Lost Mungo sighed at the thought. His decision to join the Kindred had been less demanding by comparison. He didn't want any part of what lay ahead if Orc accepted.

For years, he had sensed the tension building across the great valley. The signs were there. His vision was certain now. The pressure of the universe was focusing, its frequency increasing, the alignment of its force approaching. He saw the suspended mountains shudder in the sky, the rocks on its valley floor slither. The deepest river pools grew ever darker. Orc would unleash these natural forces against the Authority. He and Urizen would battle to the death. The apocalypse was near.

Lost Mungo felt old and tired. Just the thought of explaining it all to Orc fatigued him. He couldn't image what fighting alongside him would do. He reminded himself that unity was fundamental to the Kindred philosophy. Their motto was simple: *remember the past, know who you are, act your conscious, and never, ever abandon a member.*

They were a mismatched pair. He felt as ancient as his beloved mountains and the teenage boy appeared as green as a spring flower bud. The men faced off in the clearing. Lost Mungo raised his open hands to show he was no threat. He led Orc to a spot in a nearby oak grove. He sensed the boy possessed revolutionary anger about to explode. They took seats on a large sculpted stone underneath towering oak trees. Lost Mungo peered upward and nodded his head in agreement. The forest canopy blocked aerial surveillance. For the first time, both had room to breathe and relax. Lost Mungo slid his backpack off. It thumped to the ground.

"That's a heavy load mister," Orc said.

"You have no idea," Lost Mungo replied.

"Have you come a long way to get here?" Orc asked.

"You could say that."

"You seem awfully familiar. Do you know my people? We're from near Sky Meadow." Orc caught himself.

He wanted to change his words since his people were probably all dead now. Lost Mungo stopped searching his pack at the question. The question was a good one. The boy was smart. He had already jumped his explanation. He decided not to answer just yet. Besides, the boy was still coming to terms with the Authority and its deadly assault. He didn't know the half of it yet. Considering his pack again, Lost Mungo continued rummaging through its messy contents. The sight distracted Orc from his thoughts. He watched the eccentric but obviously harmless old man with a mixture of curiosity and skepticism.

"Where is it? I saw it here just yesterday. Let me see where I put it."

Lost Mungo shuffled wrinkled parchments back and forth. His wrinkled and freckled hands shook with infirmity. Orc let loose a little chuckle at the sight. Lost Mungo returned a scowl that quickly turned into a big smile.

"I found it!"

Lost Mungo held the document to his face. He brought it close to his eyes to better scrutinize the script. He mumbled its words. When he was satisfied of its content, he peered over the top of the document at Orc. He sighed.

"I have been carrying this for so long." Lost Mungo began.

"It looks older than me." Orc replied.

"That's why I must start at the beginning. Well, at the beginning of your story. There are so many beginnings, it's hard to know where to start." Lost Mungo appeared every bit the senile old man.

"My story?" Orc asked.

"Yes, your story. It starts before you were born. I mean in that one story emanates from another, and so on and so on. We don't have time to go back to the very beginning. Let's start with your story and its beginning."

"Whatever story you tell me, it has to be fast. I have been running through the woods for over a week. There are people hunting me and I expect them to come over that mountain ridge anytime now."

"To survive, it's essential to know why they are hunting you."

"I saw them kill my step mom and aunt," Orc replied.

"You saw something else too."

"You mean my cousin Bret? Yeah, that was weird."

"That was enough for them to kill you and anyone else that was nearby."

Their heads turned toward the distant sound of gunshots, reminding them of how little time they had.

"I don't understand why they would kill us over my cousin disappearing," Orc replied.

"He didn't simply disappear. He transited to another dimension. Your cousin has special powers, which makes him a direct threat to the Authority. Whether it was intentional or not, he is now part of the struggle."

"What struggle?"

"One you know nothing about. Nobody does for that matter. It has been hidden by the Authority for decades. There is a conspiracy so great that it is almost unimaginable. Nothing is as it appears. History itself has been manipulated. Even current news is fake. No one can see the truth even though it is in plain sight. People are asleep. Only a few are awake. This minority is fighting back."

"You mean my uncles?"

"No doubt they are taking their revenge but I am speaking of a group that is deeper and darker."

"I am confused. Is Bret part of this group fighting back?"

"He is free to find the truth on his own and will be among others who are awake. I cannot say if he will join the cause. He will pose a grave threat should he decide to. The Authority cannot track him while he is in the other dimension. That means he can strike from any direction with no warning. When I say any direction, I mean any time in history. That is why they want to destroy anyone near a transit. They are afraid you may have similar skills."

"Well, I can't disappear or I would have done it by now. It sure beats running over these mountains," Orc said.

"You are unique in another way. If the Authority finds out what I am about to reveal they will send an army after you."

"So, I may not have any choice but to join this deep dark group?" Orc said.

"They are called the Kindred. I don't mean to scare you but they have been waiting for you for a very long time. Let me try to explain."

Orc hunched over Lost Mungo who traced his finger across the parchment. It showed an elaborately decorated family tree. He started at the first generation. It was a combatant who escaped the first raid on Harpers Ferry. He went on to the next generation and the next, his finger tracing each generation through time. The tree broadened. He came to the names Los and Enith. A blank space was below them.

"What does any of this mean?"

"It means you are a child of the Kindred. But there is more. There was a prophet who foretold that the son of Los and Enith would rise and battle Urizen.

"Who is Urizen?" Orc asked.

"He is the controller for the Authority. He is the one who tracked Bret's transit. He sent the death squad that killed your step mom and aunt. He is the one hunting for you. I am sure he knows of the prophecy. Let's hope he doesn't know that you are the fulfillment of the prophecy."

"Who is this prophet and what did he say?"

"His name was William Blake," Lost Mungo said.

"I've never heard of him."

Lost Mungo laid *The Genealogies* onto his lap. He studied the low clouds racing overhead. He stretched his legs out to fight off the pain in his knees.

Orc stood up and began pacing to the edge of the clearing and then back to the boulders.

"That's easily explained. The Authority doesn't want anyone to know of his prophecy for America."

"How long have they kept it secret and what did he say?"

"Since 1793. He predicted the American experiment with liberty would struggle and fail. Instead of a republic governed by the people, he warned that a great new master would usurp them and rule. This new king would cover his true power, surreptitiously converting everything and everyone into cogs in a gigantic mechanism. Urizen was the creator of the enslavement machine. He left no room for independent thought. Despite its encompassing structure, people still fought for freedom. They searched for escape from their slavery. Urizen fought back. He made them fear what lay beyond the mechanism. Fear, instigated and manipulated by the Authority, pervaded the void that people sensed was out there. In this darkness, Urizen unleashed monsters. It worked. Most citizens submitted to this subconscious control and stopped searching for the truth. The evil system Urizen put in place so long ago persists and grows even today."

Orc stopped his pacing and marched up to Lost Mungo.

"What do Los and Enith have to do with this?"

Lost Mungo grabbed his pen, hesitated, and filled in the final name on the family tree, *Orc*. He then folded up the parchment and gently wrapped it up within the leather cover. Placing it securely inside his backpack, he slowly stood up.

"Please help me put this on. I can never pack light even after all these years."

Orc rushed to his side and lifted the pack while he strapped himself into his shoulder, waist, and chest harnesses. He turned solemnly and faced Orc.

"The prophecy says a man and woman would give birth to revolution itself. Each parent possesses powerful forces that combined to produce a fierce creature. In the meantime, people once again fall into slavery, possibly forever. The prophecy names the man as Los and the woman as Enith. Their son is named Orc. He is the embodiment of chaos. His rage is uncontrollable. His awakening will unleash a universal rebellion. I believe you are that person. Only you can destroy Urizen."

Lost Mungo paused and turned toward the trail he knew was just beyond the tree line.

CHAPTER SIXTY-ONE

Near Strasburg, VA, December 31, 1974

Crouched in a small cave just below Signal Knob peak, Orc surveyed the expansive view of the northern Shenandoah Valley framed by the damp rock entrance of his hideout. He chose this craggy precipice for the same reasons both Union and Confederate armies fought over it during the Civil War. It offered an excellent vantage point to observe movements across the Valley floor. The town of Strasburg lay 2,000 feet directly below. The steepness of the elevation meant nobody would be climbing up from the small town. Hikers reaching the summit would arrive slightly above and behind his cave entrance and only after an exhausting four miles up a winding trail starting deep within Fort Valley. Orc knew this area well. This fortress valley surrounded by steep ridgelines had offered protection from enemies for centuries. His uncle told stories of how George Washington planned to retreat to this hidden valley should the Continental Army be defeated in New Jersey. Now Orc was repeating what his ancestors had done when faced with danger. Like his kin, he retreated into the mountains to catch his breath and collect his thoughts.

Orc pulled up the zipper of his camo hunting jacket. He wrapped his arms around his torso to trap his body heat. He ripped the cardboard box scavenged from the dumpster behind the grocery store in Strasburg. Tearing off two pieces, he placed one underneath him to take the chill off the cold rock floor and began stuffing the other piece into the small cave opening. The wind chill would only get worse during the night. The cave became darker. A sudden burst of light shown around the edges of the cardboard and illuminated the cave interior. Orc ripped away the improvised door and knelt at the edge of the entrance. His retina closed tighter as a second fireball erupted from a mountain ridge east of Battletown. The flash of light turned night into day. Violent concussions boomed across the valley. He reached for the hunting binoculars that his Uncle Jubal had given to him. Scanning the ridgeline, he focused the viewfinder at the burning fires. They were scattered across the entire Mount Storm complex. A dark blurry image in the center of the complex was obscured by smoke. He waited for the wind to clear it away. This gave him time to emerge from the cave and climb up several boulders to get a better view. Adjusting the lenses, he watched as a large crater came into view. It emitted a blue flashing light that reminded him of lighting. Orc heard stories about this strange federal facility. His uncle said it went deep within the mountain.

Orc could see debris raining down over the sprawling campus facility as a roiling cloud mushroomed into the night sky. The violence of the explosion ignited fires around the perimeter of the crater. Orc watched as an eerie glow grew in intensity from its depths. Injured employees of the Authority escaped from the gaping hole and scrambled through the wreckage to safety. They fled across the surface of the mountain even as new federal agents swarmed toward the blast site from surrounding buildings. Orc found the chaos he saw through the binoculars exhilarating. He didn't know why. He couldn't imagine his uncles doing this much damage. That meant someone else was involved in the battle. Whoever blew up the mountain was on his side of the battle. The strange old man who called himself Lost Mungo had mentioned something that suddenly made sense to him.

"A second raid would cleanse men's souls," Orc muttered.

The wind slapped his back. He turned and saw nothing but the silent dark tree line. The wind slapped his face. He stumbled back and nearly fell off the boulder. The gust was like an invisible ghost trying to push him off the mountain. Or, he thought, goad him into action. He felt the world swirling around him, silently screaming to act. Orc realized what he saw through the binoculars was the rebellion he needed to be part of.

Orc scanned back to ground zero. His eyes adjusted to the dark as the flames died down. After several minutes, only a strange blue glow emanating from within the crater remained. Suddenly, the agents retreated in unison from the impact zone. The illumination glowed brighter in the dark night sky. At its peak intensity, Orc saw a large creature step over the rim of the crater. It was a giant man. His form was transparent and radiant. A small woman clung to his chest, both arms and legs wrapped around his torso. Together, they appeared to make a single creature. Their faces looked strangely familiar, but were twisted with fearsome expressions.

"Where have I seen them before?" Orc asked himself.

Orc thought back to the clearing when he met Lost Mungo. The old man claimed first-hand knowledge of his parents. He produced an old Polaroid from his dirty leather-bound manuscript. Orc had stared at the images that emerged from the faded and creased photo. Now, he closed his eyes to remember their faces. There were similarities between the couple in the picture and the faces of the creature he saw through the binoculars. He knew his aunt and uncle were very secretive about his real parents. The circumstances of his abandonment were mysterious. He didn't care anymore. They never came back for him. He was alone now.

As the creature walked through the perimeter fence, the steel razor wire reflected its blue light. Everything it passed gleamed briefly before fading into darkness. Orc heard the distant sound of gunshots. The fierce entity turned to glare at the agents with no indication of being harmed. It let out the blood-curdling scream of an angry monster. Agents fell back and then recovered their composure and began firing at the escaping creature.

Something about the pair made him very emotional. Their forms were separate but unexplainably immersed. They were distinct yet one entity. He wondered if his parents had finally found each other. If so, would they finally come looking for him? As the bizarre entity clambered over the fence, gunfire intensified into frenzy. The bullets again appeared to have no effect. These were not humans, but spirits trespassing through the material world. The female figure was desperately clutching the male. Theirs eyes seemed frenzied but defiant. As the ghostly apparition strode away from the perimeter fence and into the woods, a glowing radiance followed it through the darkness. He watched the moving light grow fainter as it disappeared into the cleft of the mountain. To no avail, the agents kept firing at the fading image. Eventually, the light source disappeared completely, leaving only the dark mass of Mount Storm in the binoculars.

Orc dropped the binoculars to his chest. He shook his head in disbelief.

"What the hell was that?" he questioned.

This time the wind whistled a reply. The branches from all the trees on the summit clashed together in one great shriek as a mighty squall animated the forest canopy.

"Jesus, this is a weird night."

Orc was sure he just witnessed something supernatural. Whatever it was, he realized it had something to do with the blast. Lost Mungo had mentioned the Kindred and explained his connection. Clearly, the Kindred had just blown the shit out the complex. He knew his uncles were probably shooting the hell out of whatever agents crossed their paths at this very moment. The Blue Ridge Mountains were full of death tonight. The creature scared him but in a strange way. He sensed its awesome anger but didn't feel it threatened him. For some reason, he felt it emerged to protect people against the Authority.

"But why did you run away into the forest?" he asked the vanished image. "We need you."

Orc retreated into his cave and grabbed the knapsack Lost Mungo had given him. He packed up everything, carefully folding the cardboard and stuffing it inside.

"There is no time to sit around. I've got to get moving," he said to the empty cave.

Hiking down the eastern side of the mountain, he began crossing the ridge and valley geography of Appalachians. Orc contemplated the significance of what he witnessed. He was thrilled to see the Kindred in action. They had obviously struck deep within the complex. The Authority would be hopping mad and swarming over the mountains looking for rebels and that spirit thing. The creature intrigued him. He looked at either side of the dark mountain trail. His headlamp shined on through into the forest. Was it out there tonight? He sensed something following him. Stopping to listen to the silence, he heard footsteps stop a second after his.

"Who is there?" He yelled out.

An owl hooted in reply. He began hiking again. The sound of footsteps paralleled him just beyond sight. Orc felt no fear of the presence. Whatever it was posed no threat to him.

"There was no way people could deny the Kindred now." He thought.

Clearly, these warriors had emerged from the misty hollows and shrouded river banks into full view. Everyone up and down the Valley must have seen that explosion. Unlike the murder of his mother and aunt, this attack could not be kept secret. Its murderous evil had been slapped in the face. People of the Valley would rise and join the rebellion. Orc wanted to enter the fray. He clenched his fist as he descended the trail. If an Authority agent were to cross his path, he would grab a rock and crush his head in. Orc's rage threatened to take over his mind and soul. He struggled to regain control.

CHAPTER SIXTY-TWO

Harpers Ferry, WV, July 17, 2016

D B snuck his way down the main street of Harpers Ferry. His pack, however, was fully loaded and its weight exaggerated his movements. Instead of sneaking through the darkness, he staggered awkwardly around obstacles. Anyone who caught a glimpse of him assumed he was just another drunk thru-hiker. His ungainly escape would have garnered more interest had townies not been so familiar with inebriated trekkers. His cover was therefore perfect and nobody thought otherwise.

DB didn't know exactly who his pursuers were or from what direction they would confront him. They could be anywhere and everywhere. Before he escaped, he donned Lost Mungo's pith helmet hoping it added some necessary eccentricity of his disguise. It was now securely strapped under his chin. No federal agents would be searching for DB Cooper wearing an eccentric tropical sunhat, especially in the depths of winter.

The sound of sirens sent him stumbling down a darkened stone staircase into a dark alleyway. Once the sirens roared away, he again took to the main street and headed down to the river. His plan was to follow its banks until he came to the bridge across the Shenandoah. Only then would he again expose himself to traffic. If he were spotted, he would be hard to catch without blocking off traffic in both directions. He had been as surreptitious as possible, comically so, he was sure. It must have been effective; the river road was just one block away.

He was close to the armory where John Brown had made his famous last stand. DB now felt a strong connection to his maligned hero of history. The faint sound of whistling suddenly reminded him of Brown's tragic fate. It was coming from the darkness of Pig Alley. He squinted his eyes to see through the pitch blackness. He already knew what would be there. He froze. Getting to the river meant walking past the sound and whatever was making it. He sucked up his courage and continued walking. What was worse, the specter, or the murderous agents?

Again, as before, the ghostly specter hobbled into sight. It was the same African American male with a deep wound in his neck. As the wound whistled air through its gaping hole, the ghost motioned to DB. As much as he wanted to run, he simply couldn't move. The figure approached and the whistling grew louder. The ghost looked at DB and then pointed toward the river. DB saw pleading in its eyes. He finally got the nerve to move, but the ghost rapidly blocked his path, pointing insistently to the river. DB could go no further. He backtracked one block and climbed up a side street perpendicular to Main Street. At the top of the lane, he saw a white blaze. He realized he was on the Great Trail where it passed through downtown Harpers Ferry. He had unknowingly bisected its path. The white blaze reflected the moonlight and beckoned him. DB realized if he followed the trail another mile, he would end up right at the base of the bridge over the Shenandoah. It was perfect. The woods would cover his escape.

A prominence of manmade rock gave him the vista to see the river road below. He walked to its edge and scanned the lower town. Instead of the specter, he saw two police cars blocking traffic into the historic center of Harpers Ferry. One of the policemen swept a spotlight through the woods and up the ridge. DB stumbled backwards to get out of sight. He took off down the trail. As he walked, he realized the ghost had been uttering a silent warning: Do not advance any further. This ghost had appeared to both himself and Lyn. It had tried to warn her, too.

"'Did she listen?" DB asked the empty night sky.

He ought to have figured this out before. Instead of reacting with fear, he could have simply tried talking to the spirit or at least listening. Ghosts are trying to communicate not haunt he realized. He reached the bridgehead and began walking along its pedestrian walkway. This gave him a moment to ponder the fact that Lyn's chance at survival depended on her listening to the supernatural universe. Why should he escape and not her? All this mess was his making. He had taken the internship to scan the trail journals. He was the one who found evidence of the Kindred. He was the one who told

Leo Davis about the secret communications and conspiracy. Now Leo was dead and Lyn was missing. His curiosity was at fault. The bright headlights of oncoming cars broke his train of thought. He hurried to cross over the bridge and started climbing up into the Virginia mountains.

The root choked trail tripped his every other step. These subterranean skeletons reached out from their dirt graves and grabbed his mud soaked boots. He fell more than he hiked. When the trail finally leveled out, he tiptoed across boulder fields that had avalanched across the trail with the deluge of rain from Hurricane Agnes. Once, his boot slipped into a dark hole between two large rocks. He pulled and twisted it free but not without feeling a painful strain. As the dawn greyness emerged, frost illumed everything in the forest. Despite the chilled air, he mopped his face with a bandana. It failed miserably to stem the flow of sweat blocking his vision. Checking his map, he shook his head in disbelief.

"That's impossible. I only hiked 9.7 miles?"

It was a reality check that his night long odyssey was, in fact, so short geographically. In his mind, he traversed a great and dangerous sea, hopscotched across dangerous islands, and brushed against the very gates of hell. The fact that he was less than ten miles from Harpers Ferry was shocking. He needed to move faster but the terrain was challenging. Not a single footfall landed with assurance or precision. It was as if he had forgotten how to walk under the weight of his pack and the uncertainty of the trail's surface. The dark woods, however, allowed DB to shed his fear of pursuers. In the fading sounds of the bridge traffic, he found solitude and a sense of protection. The contours of the mountain sealed his escape by enfolding him in its embrace. He was disappearing into oblivion and it felt good. A blue blaze signaled sanctuary was nearby.

DB collapsed, exhausted, into the Pine Bluff shelter. The unfamiliar weight of his pack added to the friction on his feet inside his boots. The hotspots on his feet were no doubt large blisters now. He glimpsed the shelter at the bottom of a narrow hollow between two parallel ridges. The pack's contents hung heavy on his shoulder but his hips took the brunt of the pain from his waist belt. He thought about what weighed so much. Certainly, *The Genealogies* weighed him down. He thought of Lost Mungo carrying this burden for decades and doubted he would ever be so strong. The empty shelter cast a faint shadow in the morning light. Its changeless rectangular geometry contrasted with the broken, bending, and swaying forest. DB sat at the ledge of the shelter's opening and didn't have the strength to remove the shoulder straps of his pack. Instead, he balanced its weight to relieve the pain. He realized he was also balancing another decision. Too tired to admit his fate, he kept the pack on.

He thought of Lyn and the normal life they would never share. If she was still alive, they would live on the run for the rest of their lives. Like the morning sun, it dawned on him that she may not want to share such a life. He cringed at the thought of her realization that she had no choice. The killers chasing them would kill her if she came back into public view.

"Oh Lyn, I am afraid you are stuck with me whether you like it or not," DB murmured.

He didn't want to be within striking distance when she had this epiphany. DB then felt guilt over Leo. He would still be alive if the trail journals were never analyzed. The sound of a breaking twig caused him to glance out into the woods. He quickly looked upwards to the trail. Nothing moved in the forest. Something was out there but it was probably just a squirrel. The killers back in Harpers Ferry were certainly still hunting him. He felt relief that his trail was probably too cold to follow. They wouldn't think to look for him here. At least, he hoped not. The thought of them pursuing him through the night on the same difficult trail made him shiver. He remembered his portable radio and pulled it from his pocket. He searched for a news station. A series of repeating claxon sounds indicated an alert. He listened as a somber voice reported on a murder and disappearance in sleepy Harpers Ferry, West Virginia. A young female college student was missing. An employee of the GT visitor's center was found dead. The police were asking the public to locate a person of interest to the investigation. He was a young man who knew both individuals and had fled the scene. Anyone knowing of his whereabouts was to contact the authorities immediately. This person of interest was not suspected of murder at this point. He was, however, a fugitive and considered armed and dangerous. His name, David Cooper.

DB dropped the radio into the dirt. He slid the backpack off his shoulders. It hit the mud stained wood floor of the shelter with a thud. Free of the heavy, sweat-drenched pack, DB clutched his knees. He rocked back and forth as he stared into the gloomy forest. The void stared back. There it was. He was a suspected murderer. Was it only a matter of time before he would be dead too? Obviously, somebody was threatened by his research. They would even kill to get hold of it. He stopped rocking and stood up. It became obvious now. He had unknowingly stirred a secret force into action. Suddenly, airbrushing history seemed innocuous compared to spilling blood.

"The Kindred!" He yelled. "They are the key."

Obviously, the murderous force that he had attracted into the light was still searching for the Kindred. They knew of the secret government and wanted desperately to crush it. Now, he possessed the entire organization in his backpack. No wonder they acted with such violence.

"How big is this conspiracy?" DB said to himself.

He realized that nobody but the Kindred could be trusted. His only contact with the underground had been Lost Mungo. The men in the woods said they would be in touch. DB wondered where to wait for them. How could they find him deep in the woods he wondered? Clearly, he did not have the luxury of waiting around for them to make contact. Clearly, the bar in Battletown was important. It had been mentioned in the shelter journal as a favorite watering hole. He might just find a bunch of thru-hikers filling up on alcohol. It also might serve as a secret meeting place for the Kindred. It was a chance he thought worth taking. He hoped Lyn was waiting for him there. DB stared up at the stars. He searched for the North Star but couldn't find it.

Eventually, the biting wind made him focus on warming up. He inflated his sleeping pad and positioned against the back wall of the shelter. He spread out his sleeping bag over it careful to keep far away from the opening. It was only a thin separation from the cold shelter floor, but it was warm. Keeping to the rear of the shelter would help cut down on the wind and any rain spray that may blow in. He grabbed *The Genealogies* from his pack and hunkered down within his bag. His headlamp cast an arc of light onto the weathered pages. He sketched his fingers over the elaborately drawn family trees and Lost Mungo's coded notations. He listened to the wind and the dead leaves on the forest floor and began to nod off, *The Genealogies* slipping from his fingers. In his daze, a slipstream carried his thoughts from the shelter into the sky high above.

Images of Lyn and Leo passed before him. In his dream, another strange apparition made an appearance. It was standing at the edge of the shelter. The specter took the form of a man wearing a pith helmet and backpack. The ghost was solid in mass but vacillated at the edges between existence and apparition. DB blinked to see more clearly, adjusting his head within his mummy bag. A projection of Lost Mungo flickered before him.

"Wake up. I need to talk to you. Listen to me. You fear open doors, but they are not as you think. There are no monsters on the other side. Nothing is coming through. It's the exact opposite."

An owl hooted in the wind-swept clearing and tree branches swept against the shelter roof. The dream continued.

"The universe is calling. It waits on the other side. You must walk through the door. Don't be afraid. *The Genealogies of the Wrathful Empathies* exists in multiple dimensions. We exist in worlds everywhere, evolving into everything. Do not fear the external beyond the door. It is but the internal within you. They are the same. We are within everyone. We, Wrathful Empathies, escort those woken from eons of slumber. It is your life that is ephemeral. We are the eternals. We evade the watchers. We escape. Slip through your mind-forged manacles. Walk through the door. Join us."

DB woke from the dream in time to see the image of Lost Mungo evaporate. He rubbed his eyes, trying to understand what he had just seen.

CHAPTER SIXTY-THREE

As the sun rose that morning, so did the travelers. They were beginning another day of hiking. Zoa sat on the ground next to Bret. She brushed silver dewdrops off blades of grass. As they fell, they reflected the light like millions of tiny prisms. They reminded her of signals from across the universe. She sensed motion and looked up. People already journeyed the golden-hewed path that stretched toward the horizon in both directions. She saw Magda and her wagon, its white plume of vapor streaking steadily from the kitchen smokestack. Magda was somehow everywhere at once, dishing fried apples into hiker's tin cups.

Zoa gathered her things and placed them in her small backpack. She adjusted the shoulder straps and cinched the waist belt. As the pack contoured to her body, its weight disappeared. It felt familiar and comforting to carry all that she possessed. Magda and her magical wagon would provide whatever else she needed somewhere up the trail.

She stepped off the clearing and onto the trail. She wasn't sure of their destination, but the journey seemed more important. The sun warmed her brow and a gentle wind lifted her hair. She was happy to be moving again. Bret and Tom were already deep in conversation. She quickened her pace to listen.

* * *

"Tom, I can't help but notice that you seem to age every day. Why isn't that happening to us?" Bret asked the middle age man before him.

Zoa tugged on his pack and glowered at his question.

"Don't bring me into this. I am perfectly fine with my age," she said.

"That's simple. We came to the path from different doorways," Tom replied.

He waved his white ash hiking staff at the bordering mists.

"Is that why you seem to hike more purposefully than us?" Zoa asked.

"You could say that," Tom winked.

"Does that mean you have limited time on the path?" Bret asked.

Again, Zoa tugged on Bret's pack and scowled.

"Geez, Bret, what is with all the personal questions?"

Bret looked genuinely surprised she found his questions inappropriate.

"We've got to talk about something. Besides, don't you want to know his story?" Bret responded.

"I take no offense, Zoa. He is simply a curious boy. That is a good trait in my book," Tom responded.

"So, can you explain the different doorways?" Bret continued.

"Picture a sanctuary with an outer and inner room." He waved one hand in a wide arc. "Lifetimes can be spent waiting in the outer room."

"I don't understand. Why would you have to wait?" Zoa asked.

"There's a riddle that must be solved before one is allowed entrance into the inner room," Tom replied.

"Did you solve it?" Bret asked.

"The very moment I crossed over! Being on the path means I can set some things right. There's no time to waste. Your little adventure last night should have opened your eyes. The existence of the path threatens the Authority," Tom stated.

Tom whirled around and confronted the two. "You threaten the Authority," he clarified.

"Maybe that explains why your town looked like a warzone." Bret said to Zoa.

"You're not safe out there. You might not even be safe here anymore." Tom thumped his staff into the hard ground for emphasis.

"Did we solve the riddle without knowing it? How else would we have gotten here?" Zoa asked.

"You two have a rare combination of powers. You were brought here for a reason. Your life off the path will never be the same. It doesn't exist anymore, or more accurately, it never existed the way you experienced it. You were asleep before and now you are awake."

"Magda tried to warn us but I still don't understand what we saw." Zoa said. She threw up her hands and shook her head. Bret nodded his head in agreement.

"Yeah, I don't understand how people don't see the decay."

"Your presence on the path changed your vision," Tom answered.

"Those people back there need to know of this dimension. How else can they understand the peril they are in?" Bret said.

"I'm afraid people have to solve the riddle for themselves. It's within all of us to understand. We just spend most of our lives avoiding it."

"But what can we do to help them?" Zoa asked.

Tom stopped hiking again and faced them.

"You have many choices. None are safe, but some more dangerous than others. The world needs teachers. You can return to instruct those who are curious and seek knowledge. There are also more active roles...."

Tom paused to gage their interest.

"I hesitate to tell you anymore."

"Please tell us," Zoa and Bret said

"There are secret societies, groups that operate in the shadows. Some have existed for centuries. I know of one that operates in the Shenandoah Valley and its surrounding mountains. It is called the Kindred."

"How do we join them?" Bret asked.

"You don't join them. You're either one of the Kindred or not. If you have the right ancestry, they'll find you," Tom explained.

"That's not much of an option. You made it sound like there were more." Zoa replied.

Angry baying of a large hound echoed from somewhere beyond the mist. The three hikers stopped in their tracks. Bret exchanged a nervous glance with Zoa. The mist swept across the trail. Answering from the other side of the trail, came a furious bark and gnashing teeth. Zoa edged closer to Bret. Tom circled around the two as he peered into the mist. They listened to the sound of something crunching its way toward them. Tom leveled his staff in defense. Bret stepped in front of Zoa. She turned to cover their backs and raised her fists. The three stood in defiance; ready to fight whatever came through. The mist retreated and the trail fell silent. Tom motioned them forward. He wiped sweat off his face with a silk handkerchief he pulled from his waistcoat.

"You could travel the path with me. I could use some help," he said.

"What will we do besides hike every day?" Zoa asked.

"Yeah, this is pissing me off. It seems like we are just running away. I want to do something," Bret said.

"I have a destination in mind. It is not only a place but a time. When I get there, I plan to leave the path and try to persuade an old friend of something very important. At the very least, he must be warned," Tom said.

"So, this path is some kind of conduit that we can manipulate?" Bret asked.

"Very smart boy," Tom replied.

"I figured that out already. Does that mean all these hikers are doing the same thing you are? Zoa replied.

She squinted her eyes and smirked at Bret. He looked astonished at the significance of her question.

"You are even smarter," Tom responded with a loud laugh.

"Can the Kindred still find us on the path. If we have the right family or whatever?" Bret asked.

He thought about his question and clarified it.

"I mean we are not really closing that option, right?"

"The Kindred will find you if they want to. Don't worry about that," Tom explained.

"Sounds like we can either sit here and wait for the Kindred to invite us into their brotherhood...." Bret said.

"Or sisterhood," Zoa added.

"Whatever. Or, we can hike with you and they will find us no matter where we are," Bret finished.

"I am not sure what my ancestors did back then. I may not even be part of the Kindred," Zoa offered.

"Right, I don't know my ancestry past my mom and dad. Embarrassing to admit but true," Bret confessed.

"Well, if you stay with me, you'll see Battletown again, but about 300 years earlier," Tom chuckled.

"Well, I've got nothing to go back to. My mom can't stand me and besides, I think you guys are my new best friends." Bret cast a glance at Zoa.

She nodded her head in agreement and blushed. Tom pointed his staff toward the horizon where the path disappeared into the sky.

"It's agreed," he announced with officialdom. "We hike together across time and space."

"I feel like we should we do a group cheer or something," Zoa said.

"Yeah, like put our hands together and shout something on the count of three!" Bret proposed.

"But of course!" Tom agreed. He stopped and tied the silk handkerchief around his neck. He adjusted his slouch hat into a tricorne. He buttoned up his coat and solemnly raised his staff. He tapped it three times on the dirt. On the third tap and before anyone could respond, Tom let loose an unusual cry.

"Huzzah, Huzzah, Huzzah!"

Bret and Zoa didn't join in but looked at each other in confusion.

"What the hell does that mean?" Bret asked.

"It's an exclamation, my boy! Let's try it again!" Tom said.

All three joined in this time.

"Huzzah, Huzzah, Huzzah!"

Bret and Zoa laughed together at the word. They made an unlikely, but ideal, trio. Tom was now a middle-age man, outfitted in knickers, buckled shoes, and a wool jacket with a cotton shirt underneath. His newly formed hat and silk scarf added to his colonial flair. Bret studied Zoa and realized she looked like a teen actress from a slasher movie.

"What are you looking at?" She challenged his stare.

Zoa pulled on her trucker cap and oversized jacket. It hung below her waist. Her high school dress was shredded and dirty. The cowboy boots were covered in mud.

"Are you going to bring the preppy look back through time? That is a big responsibility." She added.

Bret adjusted his oxford shirt and rolled up his chino pants above his ankles. He adjusted his madras pattern belt and checked his rope watch.

"Better than hunting camo," he responded.

"Enough. We have miles to travel. Let's get moving," Tom chided.

Bret glanced again at his watch. He tapped the dial. It had stopped working since he got the path. He looked up. His friends had gotten a few paces ahead and he two-stepped to catch up.

Chapter Sixty-four

Loudon Heights, VA, June 25, 2016

In the glare of artificial lights, a group of nervous black clad agents sat around a folding table covered with maps. The large canvas tent pitched above them had its lower sides fastened tightly to the ground. A hulking figure bent low to enter. His massive head scraped the ceiling and shook vigorously to clear the long white hair from his eyes. He pounded the table with his fist.

"What do you mean he got away?" Urizen thundered.

The agent looked down at his feet, too embarrassed to admit an apparent imbecile escaped his death squad.

"Sir, we searched multiple locations and interrogated the informant who reported him. We found no manuscript of any kind. The informant died abruptly before revealing useful information."

"You killed him prematurely," Urizen clarified.

"Sir, a search of both the employment location and the citizen's residence revealed no intelligence material, at least none of interest."

"*The Genealogies of the Wrathful Empathies* is the key to identifying the entire Kindred organization past, present, and future. I have been searching for it, or its author, for longer than you can realize."

"Sir, we have a dragnet of the area. It's a matter of time before…."

"Silence!" screamed Urizen. "This subject will disappear into the shadows just like the rest of this freedom cult."

"Sir, we have the entire law enforcement community conducting overt and covert surveillance. There is no possibility of escape." The agent regretted his choice of words as soon as he uttered them.

"Obviously, you do not understand what you are up against." Urizen made a mental note to schedule the agent's execution along with his entire team. He would have done it immediately, but wanted a larger audience. Too much was at stake. A mere college student had deciphered easily available trail journals and discovered critical information about the Kindred. The more he thought about it, the angrier it made him. With no technological resources or intelligence material, he managed to unravel layers of secrecy within which the most dangerous threat facing the Authority had successfully operated since 1859. This person could not be as stupid as his staff reported. He must either be smart or extremely lucky. Otherwise, he would be dead.

"Give me a name," Urizen ordered.

His assistant pulled up information on the screen. The Lord of Death scanned the report and pounded his fist on his desk at the description of the target's mediocrity. His grades were average both in high school and college. Poor job performance reports. Psychological evaluations categorized him as a passive aggressive, egoist, with tendencies to believe in conspiracies. Subject also suffers from attention deficit disorder and possibly bi-polar. Urizen wondered if DB Cooper was indeed lucky. He did not see the makings of a genius in the report before him. Oh, yes, he thought to himself, the unit would pay dearly for their incompetence.

"I want you to speak to the lead agent in charge."

"Sir, they are in active pursuit."

"Do what I say."

"Yes, sir."

Within minutes, the supervisor had the agent on the communication system.

"Are you with others?" Urizen calmly and quietly spoke into the phone.

"Yes, sir. I'm with my pursuit team."

"Good. Would you please hand your phone to the nearest agent?"

"Yes sir." Urizen could hear the phone shuffle from one agent to another.

"Who I am speaking to?"

"This is Special Agent McCafferty, sir."

"Are you armed Agent McCafferty?"

"Yes, sir. I have both a semi-automatic handgun and an AR-15."

"The long rifle will be a bit of an overkill, but the handgun will do nicely."

"Sir, I don't understand. What are my orders?"

"I order you to withdraw your handgun and shoot your supervising agent in the head, quickly or he have time to shoot back. If you hesitate, I will see you shot as well."

"Sir, requesting confirmation of that order."

"Don't lose the element of surprise Agent McCafferty, or you will be the one with a bullet to the head."

Agent McCafferty duly withdrew his handgun from its holster, pointed it at the lead agent and pulled the trigger. Urizen listened to the gunshot blast before placing the phone back in the receiver. He turned and confronted the supervisor in his office, who turned to ensure none of his agents were standing behind him.

"What does law enforcement know about the situation?" Urizen asked.

"Sir, nobody knows of the Kindred and our quest for *The Genealogies*. Apparently, two FBI agents were previously investigating DB Cooper and conducted an interview."

"You had DB Cooper in custody and let him go?" Urizen stammered.

"Sir, they were investigating a lesser harassment charge. Just a couple of White Hat FBI agents who are not read into the Authority activities. We will call them off."

"No, keep them on the case. Tell them Cooper killed Leo Davis and a federal agent. Make sure both bodies are left on the scene. Also, accuse him of collaborating with domestic terrorists," Urizen ordered.

"Yes Sir. And what about the girlfriend?"

"Let me guess, she escaped too?"

"She was not at the residence when it was searched."

"Add a kidnapping charge to Cooper's arrest warrant."

"Yes sir." McCafferty terminated the call before Urizen could ordered someone to shoot him.

Urizen un-holstered a pistol, loaded six rounds in the chamber and exited the tent. Urizen stalked across the parking lot pistol in hand. Nearby agents stopped in their tracks when they recognized him and quickly stepped aside. Urizen glared at them. Several held their breath and looked away. A cold current of air trailed behind Urizen as he strode past. He made a mental note to execute Agent McCafferty. What incompetent leadership to let the suspect escape, kill an informant before getting information, and not secure *The Genealogies*. Most egregious, his agents underestimated this DB Cooper. The name sounded familiar and that angered him too. Who was this person exactly? Maybe he was a genius. A fugitive hiding in plain sight, even. Urizen stopped to study a large area map tacked to a portable desk near the helicopter landing area.

"Where have you gone young man? Urizen traced his fingers across the topographic lines. "Are you safe with the Kindred yet? I don't think so."

A smile displaced the grimace on Urizen's face as he answered his own question. The Authority employees fidgeted. They wanted to move away from Urizen but were afraid to draw his wrathful eye.

"No, I sense you are still alone," Urizen whispered. He stopped his hand at a dense concentration of lines around Harpers Ferry.

"I think you are in the dark night, afraid, and struggling to escape through the mountains. No, you are not safe yet, DB. I will find you and I will kill squeeze information out of you, one way or another."

To the relief of everyone in the hallway, Urizen punched the map and made his way to the helicopter pad on the roof.

Chapter Sixty-five

Morgantown, WV, June 25, 2016

A bright artificial light cast a cool blue sheen over the sterile windowless office. Sitting before a steel gray industrial desk, one FBI agent poised his fingers over the keys of his computer keyboard. A second agent adjusted the leather shoulder harness of his service revolver and pointed at the blank electronic template flickering on the monitor.

"So, what are we going to say?" Agent Smith said.

"Well, I have been sitting here for ten minutes and don't know where to begin. This is a strange case." Agent Sparks replied.

"That's an understatement. Somehow a simple anti-government whacko airing his grievances to a park ranger has ended up with multiple homicides."

"And got the attention of the Authority back in Washington. How did this freak become a national security threat?"

Sparks took a deep draw from his coffee cup and rocked back and forth in his chair. The motion did not jar lose any ideas.

"So, what do we even call this guy? Suspect or next victim?" Agent Smith asked.

"Let's start with the facts," Sparks replied. He read aloud as he typed the basic information into each empty field of the all-points bulletin report.

"Issued June 25, 2016. FBI West Virginia Panhandle District Office. Be on the lookout for fugitive David Bartholomew Cooper, AKA, DB Cooper, who is known to be in the Appalachian Mountain areas of Georgia, North Carolina, Tennessee, Virginia, West Virginia, Maryland, Pennsylvania, New Jersey, New York, Connecticut, Massachusetts, Vermont, New Hampshire, and Maine. Cooper is wanted for questioning in the murders of two persons in Harpers Ferry, West Virginia and is believed to be armed and dangerous. He was last seen travelling on foot and may be headed either north or south along the Great Trail."

Agent Smith threw his arms in the air and paced around the desk.

"That's it? I could have said that. We're going to look stupid issuing a APB like that," Smith said.

"Not following you exactly. I listed all the facts and nothing but the facts."

"Exactly. We need some nuance. Think about it. This stupid kid has the same name as the most infamous hijacker in U.S. history, who, I might add, the FBI never caught. Just like his namesake who was on foot in the Pacific Northwest forests, we've narrowed our suspect's known area to be anywhere along the eastern continental divide!" Agent Smith slammed his coffee mug onto the desk.

Sparks turned his frustration on Smith. "So, what's your bright idea?"

Agent Smith sat down at the computer and read aloud as he typed his version of the APB.

"The FBI is issuing an all-points bulletin asking law enforcement officers in West Virginia, Maryland, and Virginia to be on the lookout for David Bartholomew Cooper, a white male, age 21 brown hair, green eyes, five foot nine inches tall, last seen leaving Harpers Ferry in an unknown direction." Smith glared at Sparks. "Suspect is reportedly on foot, carrying belongings in a backpack. He has been seen reviewing documents of an unknown nature enclosed in a leather binding. Local law enforcement should not attempt to arrest Cooper, but alert Special Agents in charge, Smith and Sparks of the Martinsburg District Office of the FBI, of his whereabouts. The suspect is wanted for questioning in the deaths of two persons in Harpers Ferry. Cooper is mentally unstable and known to possess information critical to the FBI. His esoteric knowledge of historic events suggests his propensity to visit popular landmarks and/or National Park Service visitor centers. This information is key to his potential whereabouts. Visitors meeting his description and asking unusual questions should be considered suspicious and be reported. Cooper has been employed with the Friends of the Great Trail as an unpaid internship, yet has means, either financial or otherwise, to elude capture. He is possibly affiliated with local anarchist groups who distribute free food and sodas. Suspect has fantasies of being infamous hijacker DB Cooper and is known to mock law enforcement. He has possible ties to known secret cult or militia organizations, e.g., Ku Klux Klan."

Agent Sparks interrupted Smith, "Seriously, the KKK? We have no evidence of that connection."

"I know but we have to demonize him. God knows these mountain people may actually feel some kindred towards an anti-government rebel." He continued reading his report.

"Currently the object of FBI investigation, Cooper may be in the company of persons who are armed and dangerous. Suspect has no known tactical or survival skills and is therefore expected to seek urban areas where he has access to preferred amenities such as pizza and beer."

"I think you nailed the little bastard. I mean, how many crackpots fit that description?" Sparks responded.

"Exactly. We capture this little smartass and drill a new hole in his head for information. I don't think he's capable of killing a bug, let alone two people, but it's always the little weirdos that surprise you." Smith said.

"Let's issue it in the electronic bulletin system with instructions that posters be placed at every trailhead along the Great Trail from southern Virginia to the Mason Dixon. Should be able to pick up the little shit in no time." Sparks added.

Smith entered several more key strokes and then punched the submit button at the end of the electronic form.

"Its official. 4:16 PM Thursday, bulletin alert issued. These posters should be up by Sunday at the latest."

The two agents called it a day. Putting on their black suit coats, they turned off the lights on their small office and left the building.

"I am off tomorrow. Have a good weekend," Smith said.

"Good team work today. Let's inspect the posters Monday morning. Meet here and drive together to Snickers Gap where highway 340 crosses the mountain." Sparks replied.

"Ok, let's hit that service station at the base of Loudon Heights just before the bridge into Maryland for some coffee on the way up," Smith added.

* * *

At the start of the new work week, they drove together for the inspection of their first trailhead poster placement. They parked their car and carefully sipped very hot coffee from small plastic holes in their Styrofoam cups. Emerging from the black government leased sedan, they walked across the gravel parking lot searching for a white blaze to indicate the presence of a trailhead. About ten yards to the left of the Great Trail was a black and white portrait. It pictured a thin man with a receding hairline wearing dark sunglasses. His pointed chin looked familiar to Agent Smith.

"Wait a minute! This is the wrong DB Cooper!" Smith yelled.

"What are you talking about?" Sparks responded squinting his eyes.

"This isn't Daniel Bartholomew Cooper, our dipshit college student," Smith said with growing outrage.

"Ah fuck, you're right. This is the original DB Cooper!" Sparks yelled.

"If they put up the wrong poster here, do you think it went up everywhere?"

"I told the secretary to attach the photo to the APB." The two agents exchanged nervous looks.

"These posters have to be removed," Smith said.

"Across three states, replacing them with the right one? That will take at least 24 hours," Sparks replied.

"Giving our suspect another day to travel and cover his tracks."

"You know, I am really starting to hate that smirking little smartass."

"I bet he's out there somewhere right now laughing his ass off."

Agent Sparks looked up at the forested ridgeline. Agent Smith tugged at the laminated poster, but it had been firmly affixed to the tree and did not come off. Both agents grabbed and started pulling.

"Hey man, isn't it like, a crime, to you know destroy federal property?" came a squealy voice from behind them.

Agents Smith and Sparks wheeled around to see a pair of hikers. One was tall and thin with dreadlocks while the other was short and stout wearing a slouch beanie.

"Yes, it would be if we weren't FBI agents. Please stand back and mind your own business." Agent Sparks was growing red in the face from both his exertion and embarrassment.

"Hey, that guy looks really familiar," the tall hiker said to the other.

"Who are you exactly and what are you doing here?" Agent Smith said over his shoulder. He was still pulling hard on the poster corners.

"I'm Stash and this is Jelly Bean, aka, the Mother Lode. That's with an 'a,' not an "e." Do you get it? Anyway, we're about to be, like, in absentia in your jargon." Stash responded pointing to his oversized friend.

"I don't understand. Are you due in court?" Agent Sparks turned to confront them. "Missing a court date is a serious offense."

"He meant we're going hiking for a couple days," Jelly Bean clarified.

"Well, Mr. Dumbass Stash, I hope you packed enough weed for yourself and food for Fat Face." Agent Sparks was growing increasingly angry at the two interlopers.

"We were just, like, doing our civic duty, man. What's with all the hostility?" Stash replied.

Agent Smith pulled his service revolver and pointed it in the air.

"I was being nice, this is hostility. Time to move on, gentlemen, before I lose my temper and have to bury your bodies somewhere."

"The trail is a violence-free zone, man," Jelly Bean replied.

Both hikers walked toward the trailhead.

"Dude, that's DB Cooper, the hijacker," Stash started up as soon as soon as he thought they were out of earshot. "Can't believe I remembered that, man."

"How cool is that? I thought he was like, way out in the Pacific Northwest though?" Jelly Bean replied.

"He's one trucking dude. Amazing distance to travel. All under the watchful eye of the man." Stash shook his dreadlocks at the awe-inspiring accomplishment.

"Okay, we can still hear you! Now fuck off up the trail or be placed under arrest for obstructing a federal agent." Agent Smith had torn down half the poster and shook it in his raised fist.

"Chill. We're leaving. Happy trails," said Stash.

"If we see DB, we'll him you're looking for him," offered Jelly Bean.

The disheveled hikers laughed at their joke and staggered out of sight up the Great Trail.

The agents finished stripping away as much of the poster as they could. Two nails still affixed at the top and bottom would not release the entire poster. To their amazement, the remaining strip formed a perfect vertical trail blaze. Only upon close inspection did it show a very narrow portrait of DB Cooper.

"Fuck, is it me or does that look like a fugitive trailhead sign." Agent Smith threw his arms in the air.

"Sure does. Do you think this will confuse anyone?" asked Agent Sparks.

"If someone does try to follow it, they'll find out pretty fast it doesn't go anywhere. It's a dead-end."

"Yeah, probably, but I don't want those Park Service weenies complaining. Wouldn't want it going up the chain that hikers are disappearing because of our poster mishap."

"People might get a little disoriented, but they should realize the trail peters out within five or ten yards. Anyone who goes further wants to get lost," Sparks noted.

"Let's go. We've got to pull down all these posters and replace them before it gets noticed by the press."

"You mean before we become a national joke," Smith stated.

They exchanged nervous looks again and began picking up shredded bits of poster off the ground. The agents hurriedly climbed into their car and accelerated out of the parking lot. Within minutes, the sounds of nature began filling the void of their fading engine noise.

* * *

The sun rose above the mountain ridge, fully exposing the trailhead and the DB Cooper blaze image to daylight. If one were to enter the forest at this new trail sign, they might see the faint trace of a ghost trail. While no hikers tread this path, and hadn't for years, it was still detectable to the sensitive eye. Decades ago, the Great Trail was rerouted to take advantage of newly acquired public land, which offered a much more scenic route to the cliffs above. Seasons of uncleared blowdown had obscured the trail's silhouette. Its blazes had faded to the point of near invisibility. Yet, its memory remained. It just happened to be directly behind the remnants of the DB poster. It climbed up the mountain, winding back and forth along forgotten switchbacks toward the summit. Following this path far enough, one would arrive at an isolated summit. This particular morning, a hiker would see a solitary figure slipping out of a backpack and removing a sweat stained pith helmet. If the hiker was stealthy enough to approach within earshot, the figure could be overheard talking to the sky.

"Lyn, I will find you."

Chapter Sixty-six

Linden, VA, December 30, 1974

Orc was sitting atop a large boulder at the edge of the darkening forest. Shadows cut jagged angles in the setting sun. He had spent the day climbing and descending steep ridges. His arms and legs were scratched and bleeding. Razor-sharp briars had ripped his clothes. He had tried to stay on the trail but deadfall blocked his movement. Bushwhacking across stretches of the forest brought pain and misery. His current resting place was a refuge from the bugs and exotic clutter of the woods. He heard gunshots echo across countless mountains to the north. He knew his kinfolk were fighting and killing in dark hollows. He felt no pity for those black clad men on the receiving end of their bullets.

Seven miles away, Orc's uncle stalked his prey. He was out for vengeance. The Authority had no chance against him, not on this ground. This was his wood.

"Fan out along a skirmish line," Jubal Mosby whispered.

The seven-man team moved in concert, forming a V shaped line. Mosby took point. They stepped over the bodies of a federal patrol.

"Let's get ready for the patrol ahead to reverse and come back to the sound of our gunfire."

The men around Mosby had fought in the same jungles in Vietnam. Their special forces training, combined with their years of hunting in the Blue Ridge, made them a lethal force. While the country had forgotten their sacrifices, they struggled to survive in an economy that didn't need killers. He and his men were once again battling. This time in their homeland.

Upon returning home and seeing his fellow vets abandoned, Mosby decided to live by his own laws. He had no qualms about how he fed his family, regardless of how the money was earned. Who cared if the product was heroin smuggled in from his network overseas? Mosby had crossed over into a hardscrabble existence just as rocky and barren as the Appalachians that held his ancestors.

Though his team looked rag-tag wearing a mix of military uniforms and hunting camo, their weapons were lethal. These men knew their welfare depended on their guns and plenty of ammo. Nobody was better at waging war. The tribal fighters of Indochina could affirm this. The United States fought to a standstill against these peasant warriors. All the technology in the world was no match for devoted armed guerrillas in mountainous highlands. They fought desperately for their ancestral lands and for their people. Mosby could relate.

After setting up an ambush, Mosby surveyed the bodies. He brought the walkie-talkie to his mouth and spoke clearly and confidently in a measured pace and cleared the channel.

"Break, break."

Once silence fell over the radio, he continued.

"Ghost Two, Ghost Two. This is Ghost One. Over."

"Ghost One, this is Ghost Two. Copy," Replied Jubal.

Loud static and sporadic radio traffic punctured the silence of the forest. The air itself was still, loaded with gunpowder smoke.

"Ghost Two, what is your position? Over."

"Ghost One, we are to your west one half kilometer. Taking position on top of the lower ridgeline. You are in our sights to the east and the Shenandoah to the west. Over."

"Ghost Two, copy. Are there any federals in your area? Over."

"Ghost One, motorized traffic on the river road but no deployment. Over."

"Ghost Two, block westbound and take care of any stragglers fleeing our assault from the east. Parallel our movement south to the designation area. We will move between the two ridges. Confirm order. Over."

"Ghost One, WILCO. Over."

"Ghost One, Ghost One. This is Ghost Three. Over."

Mosby swung his binoculars from the west to the eastern ridge that rimmed his hollow.

"Ghost Three, this is Ghost One. Copy," Mosby replied to his cousin Jed.

"Ghost One, we're on the higher ridge west of your position. Will block intrusion from the east and neutralize any poor son of a bitch that escapes your team in our direction. I don't expect any. We met one Authority patrol member and neutralized. This is a turkey shoot. Over."

Mosby fine-tuned the lenses and searched for a sign of the third team. He smiled to himself when he didn't see anything. These boys are good he thought to himself.

"Ghost Three, Ghost Two, move south and keep parallel to our position. Terminate mission at designation area. Break off operation."

"Ghost One, WILCO. Over."

"Ghost Two and Three, this is Ghost One. At the designation point, break off engagement, disappear and leave no trace. Meet at the third rendezvous point for post-operation debrief. Over."

Both teams acknowledged his orders and the radio fell silent again. Mosby knew it was just a matter of time before air support would arrive. The reason it had not come sooner was simple. The Authority needed to keep their search and destroy operation covert from the public. He suspected it would take a little time to set up a cover narrative. That time had surely passed and his men needed to extract from the field soon. Mosby took the wrinkled photos of Bret and Orc from his front jacket pocket that he carried for years as gifts from his aunt. He grabbed his walkie-talkie and issued one more communication.

"Ghost two and three, this is Ghost One. Over."

Both teams replied in whispers. Mosby issued his final orders of the day.

"Don't forget our two friendlies. One may be captive. If so, attempt rescue and rendezvous at secondary, not primary site. The other may not be in the field." *Not ours anyway,* he thought to himself. "If you find their bodies, attempt extract back to third rendezvous. Be advised, it's a matter of time before they ratchet this with air support. Ghost One. Over and out."

Mosby looked to the woods. He knew the Kindred were out there, watching and assessing his actions. They had to be. Someone was killing federals besides his crew. They had come across several bodies they had not killed. The cause of death was unfamiliar to Mosby and his men. The Kindred had ways of handling things to make them look natural, but this was different. It looked like some badass snake was taking out Agents by way of the jugular vein. The dead men didn't stand a chance. It would have been almost instantaneous death.

As he hunched behind a tree, Mosby wondered what kind of snake could attack and kill so many men? He looked around at the brush at his feet. Death could come at any time. He shrugged his shoulders and began scanning the clearing before him. *Don't go into the woods if you are afraid of dying,* he thought. They got what was coming to them. No tears from him. The government could push people only so far until they revolted. Mosby was sick and tired of struggling to survive. Now, they murdered kinfolk for no reason but living. Yep, the government lit a fire this time. It would consume these mountains before burning out. Bodies would be stacked up like so many cords of wood. He knew his team didn't stand a chance facing the full force of the Authority alone, but just like the VC, he could fight a long, dirty, and bloody guerilla war.

* * *

Back at the old stone chapel where Lord Fairfax himself had worshipped, the Mosby Raiders shuffled in and seated themselves in the dust covered pews. Boarded and locked, it sat in a small depression several miles beyond the city limits of Battletown. Its overgrown cemetery contained the earthly remains of distinguished Virginians dating back to the 1700s, and, later, heroic sons of the Confederacy. A nearby stretch of road carried people past the chapel at a posted speed of 55 miles per hour. A rusted signpost summarized its historic relevance. Most drivers barely had time to glimpse the slate roof before the stone walls quickly passed through the rearview mirror. Just another abandoned memory of the area's historic past. There were so many scattered across the Valley.

The small, historic church no longer saw Sunday worship. The mice were its only regular congregation. But tonight, the church held two-dozen men, their faces lit by the soft glow of candlelight. They no longer wore their camo fatigues or sported assault rifles. They were indiscernible from the rest of the county residents except for their willingness to die for liberty.

"So, we got the entire Authority coming down on us. Can we expect any help from anyone?" asked a man in overalls.

"What about the Kindred, where were they today?" asked another.

Jubal's face grew serious. He stopped his pacing at the front of the church.

"Just assume the Kindred are always there." He glared at the men before him.

"Nothing moves in those mountains without the Kindred knowing it. Who do you think funneled those agents our way? The agents feared what they saw in those woods more than they feared us, and they chose the safer confrontation. At least with us they stood a chance of surviving the fight. I, myself, saw things out there I can't explain. Some of those agents died unnatural deaths. Something evil was afoot and I don't want any part of it. Let's just hope the Kindred stays on our side and they keep a safe distance between us."

"So, what's next? Where do we engage tomorrow?" Seth asked from his position guarding the front door.

"We find the boys," Mosby replied.

"The boys are either dead and buried or captured and held somewhere. They aren't in those hills. That's for sure," Seth countered.

"I don't believe they're dead. Those agents wouldn't be out there if they'd caught the boys. That means they are still on the loose. We've got to go out every day until we find out for sure. I'm not going to leave them on their own. Their parents deserve that from us. God rest their souls."

Mosby bent his head in remembrance. The chapel fell silent before a voice hollered out.

"I say we keep kicking the federals' ass until they back off our mountains. They only come here to smack us down. Where are they when we need decent jobs?"

The other men erupted in shouts of agreement. Mosby quieted them down.

"We'll strike when they least expect it. We'll stay mobile, never defending a fixed position. We'll hit and withdraw. Move to another position. Repeat. Then we'll vanish altogether. They'll never know we're coming for them, and by the time they respond, we'll evaporate like spirits. It worked for our ancestors and it will work for us. We'll just keep doing what's in our blood."

He knew that was the weakness of the Authority. They had always underestimated the men of these hills. Mistook their economic status for a lack of intelligence and aptitude. Mosby thought of the dead federal agents as a testament to that failed logic. He was proud of his men. The only thing that surpassed their skills at bushwhacking was their secrecy. It was endemic to the region. Might even be an inherited trait. These men knew instinctively how to cover their tracks. Some had walked miles across pastures just to reach the chapel, their pickup trucks parked behind hay bales stacked alongside desolate roads. Others had crossed fields, waded streams, and navigated woods to covertly arrive at the chapel. It felt familiar and welcoming, like a deer following the same animal track travelled generations before it. It was ancestral—primal—for these men to be in this valley. They would defend it to the death, and even then, refused to be laid to rest.

A train whistled its approach to the chapel, which sat near the tracks. The men fell silent. The growing rumble would soon rattle the church itself. Mosby sent the men away with his final instructions.

"Now, go on about your lives. Act normal like everyone else. I want to see you at the Fire Station Pancake Breakfast. We can ride in together during fox chase season, bring in the hay, and I damned better see you at the Blue Grass Festival along the river come the fall. Keep your mountain legs. Get out and hunt. You'll be called when the time comes. We've inflicted damage today. Now it is time to drink some moonshine."

A roar of laughter followed Mosby's final words. He finished his instructions when the men quieted down.

"Tonight, you all know to disband alone or in pairs, but no bigger numbers. Take the backwoods or cut across the fields. The more hidden your path, the better. May God bless."

Mosby concluded the meeting and popped the cork on a clear jug. The men lined up to take a swig before exiting the door. Silently, like shadows, they spread out across the valley and disappeared in to the night.

CHAPTER SIXTY-SEVEN

Battletown, VA, June 25, 2016, 7:00 PM

The taxi slowed before the flickering porchlight of Vagaries. The driver turned to Lyn and motioned toward the tavern.

"This is it. If you still want to get out, then the fee is $31 exactly."

Lyn looked through her passenger window and grimaced. The tavern was at the end of a dead-end lane. Half the street lamps were burned out. The few that were working cast a yellow glare onto the sidewalk leading up to the front door. Empty beer cans were strewn across the front yard. Barely visible in the light, she saw half a dozen grimy backpacks lined along the front porch. A glimmer of hope lifted her spirits when she noticed one was purple and sported a flower. At least I can expect to find a single female inside she thought.

"Here are two $20s. Can I have, like, $5 back? You can keep the change."

"Thank you. I will wait outside for a couple minutes in case you change your mind."

"That's very kind. I am not quite sure what to expect."

Lyn took back her change and got out of the taxi. She walked up the sidewalk and stepped up to the porch. She paused before opening the front door. Boisterous voices came from inside and she tried to listen to their conversations.

"Last call!" a deep voice boomed.

Angry muffled voices responded to the notice. Lyn slowly opened the door and peeked inside. A group of men crowded the bar, each one holding beers in both hands. She had never seen a more disreputable group of ruffians. They were all bearded with long straggly hair falling freely from under trucker caps. The song on the

346

jukebox ended and the door creaked as she pushed it open. The bartender was an elderly woman. She peered past the men and was the first to see Lyn.

"Come on in dear," she croaked.

All the tavern denizens turned around and stared at her. Lyn assumed their stupefying appearance was a combination of drunkenness and the sheer disbelief that a young woman was in their midst.

"Hi ya'll. I am Lyn."

"You thirsty?" the bartender asked.

"A little drink might help my headache. I am afraid I don't have much money."

A man stepped forward and offered her a barstool. The crowd made a path for her to sit down. Lyn took a seat on the tattered nylon cushion. A tall can of Pabst Blue Ribbon was placed before her. Lyn took a sip and then another. The cold beer tasted so good going down her parched throat. She realized the pain in her stomach was raging hunger.

"Is there a menu I can look at?"

"Well, that all depends on what you consider food," another man in the bar said.

All the customers joined in the joke and soon everyone was laughing but her.

"I am sorry if I intruded on something but I have a bit of an emergency. My boyfriend told me to come here and ask for Lord Jim. Does that make sense to anyone?"

A hush fell over the bar, men nodded their heads and shuffled back to their chairs. The bartender leaned closer and offered her hand to shake.

"You are in the right place dear. We go by trail names here not real names. The name you gave carries a lot of weight here. Do you have a trail name by chance?"

"I am afraid not. My boyfriend goes by DB, which is kinda a trail name, I guess," Lyn said.

"Just call me Escape Goat or Scape Goat for short. Lord Jim was my old man. I lost him in the second raid on Harpers Ferry back in '74. We still get refugees straggling in here bearing his name. Nice way to keep his memory alive I guess."

"My boyfriend talked about him I think but I can't be sure. He studies History in college. I mean was studying in college. I am not sure what we are going to do now," Lyn replied.

"If you have made your way to Vagaries, things must have gotten pretty bad. Consider yourself on the run now."

Lyn was shocked at hearing her predicament summarized so concisely. Tears welled up in her eyes and she began to cry.

"I don't think I have a place to stay tonight and I am all alone."

"You will never be alone anymore dear. This is your new home. We protect our own."

Lyn looked around at the patrons. She wasn't sure these were her kind of people. They looked like throw backs to another era. They did appear concerned and focused on her plight. She noticed one was watching the lane through the window next to the front door. Two others had gone into the kitchen and were noisily preparing something. Another pair of men were leaving the fire exit door at the side of the bar. The sound of a car engine roared to life outside after they closed the door. She cringed at the décor of the bar's interior. She could think of much better places to be stranded than Vagaries. The bartender seemed nice enough but Lyn caught her talking on the phone behind the bar, obviously about her. She hung up and began wiping off the bar.

"Everything will be okay dear. Those two men are going to look for your boyfriend. We were expecting you but not tonight. If he is out there, they will find him. We are already fixing the room upstairs for you. Stay here if you like. When you feel up to it, you can help around the place. No saying when your boyfriend will make his way here. Sounds like he is travelling the hard way through the mountains. There is a pretty purple backpack on the porch for you in case you must skedaddle. It's already packed with clothes and gear. In the meantime, let's just take this one day at a time. I find that is always the best way to live life. Always be in the moment. Now, I want you to eat something"

A plate of steaming pasta arrived and was placed before her stool at the bar. The sauce was homemade and delicious. Another cold can of Pabst slid toward her from the bartender.

"I am afraid I can't pay for any of this. I left in such a hurry." Lyn said flustered by the service.

"You have no tab here dear."

Lyn ate with gusto and gulped down the refreshing beer. A country song started playing softly on the jukebox. Its steel guitar twanged out a relaxing vibe. Exploring the peculiar establishment between bites of food, Lyn took in its many oddities. There were lots of antlers mounted to the walls. More than a dozen old license plates from up and down the East Coast. For some reason, many pairs of boots hung from their shoelaces above the bar. She then noticed a brass bell affixed to the wall and wondered what purpose it could possibly serve.

CHAPTER SIXTY-EIGHT

Washington, DC, December 31, 1974

Agent Valle looked over the office through his vapor mask. They made him wear it to avoid contamination. He never believed in their mental viruses. Now, his hot breath fogged the glass. With his eyes forward, he tried to insert the documents into the burn bag without drawing attention to himself. His protective gloves did not allow for a good grip. The papers slipped through his hands and spilled onto the floor scattering everywhere. He bent down and clumsily picked up individual pieces but only dropped them again. He looked up to see if anyone noticed only to see his supervisor walking toward him.

He had just finished the third shift at Mount Storm. Shortly after coming on duty, he intercepted a rebel radio broadcast. Its contents seemed initially treasonous. He sounded the alarm. Then a pair of transits blipped on his screen. Being a new operational agent, he didn't want to overreact. These ones were very faint. He cringed at the reaction of the Authority. He knew the broadcaster would be raided. Violence and death would be the result. The transmission stopped within fifteen minutes of his alert.

It was during the translation of the content of the broadcast that he realized what was so unnerving about its message. His fingers paused as he typed the words. The audience of the message was not the general citizenry. Instead, it was an urgent appeal to those actively supporting the propaganda lies of the Authority. Specifically, it was directed to government agents, including himself. He rushed to finish the translation. He found the petition strangely compelling. It was accusatory toward anyone who contributed to the oppression. Agent Valle knew the Authority depended on the willingness of key members of society to maintain its narrative of control. It's true weak spot—the enormity of the lie—required a vast complicity. Its saving grace—the failure of anyone to expose it. Until now. He never believed the lies himself but thought it worthless to protest. A vision formed in his mind. If people knew of a swelling action to stop the deceit, enough might speak the truth. All that was needed to tip the balance in favor of truth were a few early voices.

The broadcast played over and over in his mind. The voice now inside his head. He felt remorse in his gut for oppressing its transmission. Worse, he felt guilt for the certain death of its broadcaster. It was then the second pair of transits signaled on his screen. This time he ignored them intentionally. These would be missed. After all, he was the detection system. The transits were just blips on a screen. If he didn't react and sound the alert, nobody would be the wiser. He had not risked much yet. For the first time, he felt connected to the transits. He envied their courage. He desired their freedom. He hoped they made the best of it and silently wished them success. It was then he proceeded to print out the document but hesitated to take it to the burn room. He thought others should read it. Now the contraband lay sprawled before him in the Surveillance Division of the Authority's fifth floor headquarters.

Agent Valle hurriedly scooped the transcription into a red burn bag. By the time his supervisor was at his desk, he was securely tying the sack shut.

"You did great work this morning," his supervisor said.

"All in a day's work, sir. Do we know if the threat was contained?"

"I believe so. There were some rebroadcasts, but we're tracking those down. You caught it just in time. Any longer and it would have been very difficult to put the genie back in the bottle."

"Just doing my job, sir."

"We still have some work to do. Keep an eye out for secondary communications. That message was extremely dangerous and diligence is our best defense. It would only take a few leakers to expose the Authority. The republic would have to be officially terminated. We couldn't operate from subterfuge anymore. We wouldn't want that, now would we, Agent Valle?"

"We are all part of a machine sir; no individual should ever think beyond his role."

"Just keep an eye out for your coworkers. I heard the broadcast is being reproduced and passed from reader to reader. It's a grassroots practice to evade our censorship that will be met with harsh punishment."

Valle could feel the weight of the bag against his thigh. "Yes sir. The broadcast seemed dangerous. Otherwise, I wouldn't have reported it. I know what it is capable of."

"Why is your mask fogged up?" His supervisor asked peering through his clear visor.

"Just a little over heated with excitement I guess." Valle replied.

"I use those anti fogging wipes. Works great. Looks suspicious otherwise. Walking around in a fog all day."

"I will try them sir, Thank you sir."

"You didn't digitize it yet, correct?"

"I was about to start that process when you came over, sir."

"Well, don't. I want no records. Erase the original recording as well. As far as we're concerned, the broadcast never happened. That rebel letter doesn't exist."

"Understood." Valle nodded his head in agreement.

"Another thing…it appears we missed several transits today. Did you see anything?"

"No sir. I didn't detect anything beside the broadcast."

"Well, someone missed it and there's going to be an investigation. It certainly looks questionable that the missed transits and the broadcast happened on the same shift."

"Do we know what sector, sir?"

"I expect to get that information shortly. In the meantime, keep an eye out for any staff that acts suspicious or tries to leave the complex. We're on lock down. Make sure you report them to me directly."

Agent Valle's heart drummed in his ears, "Why are we on lock down sir?"

"I guess Urizen himself suspects traitors inside the organization. These transits should have been detected. A full-scale investigation is under way."

His sweaty palms slipped inside the protective gloves. Agent Valle was sure his supervisor would see sweat dripping out on the floor. His mask clouded over even worse than before.

"Make sure you burn the contents of that bag Agent."

His supervisor patted him on the shoulder and walked away. Agent Valle was now sweating through his bio-containment suit. The broadcast had reached his soul. When two faint transits had come across his screen, he ignored them. When the pair transited again, he covered it up.

"How did the Authority know about them if I didn't sound the alert?" Agent Valle mumbled to himself.

He was caught. It was only a matter of time…hours, maybe minutes, before the data traces revealed his betrayal. What to do? He asked himself. One thing for certain, he would distribute the transcript of the broadcast. He answered his own question. What did he have to lose? The punishment for treason was death. Urizen would be the one to put the bullet through his brain.

He hurried down the corridor to the Records Disposal Center but passed the entrance. A sense of desperation overcame him. The Authority eviscerated the essence of life by thwarting the very ability to think clearly. Constantly probing their fears and feeding them false narratives, the Authority chained people mentally. He could no longer be complicit in this institutional slavery.

Instead, Agent Valle advanced to the next office doorway. He peeked inside the copy center to ensure it was empty. Once he confirmed he had the room to himself, he placed the manifesto in the document feeder of the machine. He keyed the number 100 and hit the copy button. He found an empty box behind the room's door and he started packing up the copies.

Shouting and screaming erupted down the hall made him jump. He ran to the hall and looked toward the noise. To his horror, there was a squad of armed agents at his desk.

"Fuck, how did they get here so fast?"

He realized he had precious little time and went back to the printer and cancelled the copy command. Instead, he selected the transmit service. He typed in the organization directory and pushed the transmit button. He smiled at the thought of using the Authority's equipment against it. A burst of machine gun fire perforated the room. His body took most of the bullets. He collapsed against the machine. It kept functioning long enough to electronically transmit the patriotic message to over 114,000 Authority employees including key controlled media reporters.

As his life force ebbed, he sensed his soul release from his body. It passed through a portal where it was suddenly alone on a darkened plain. No more agents or office building, but instead, vague but fearful images converged around him. Evil spirits and hungry ghosts emerged from the darkness. They bayed and threatened to devour his soul. Disoriented, fearful, and desperate, he started to flee. Suddenly, from within a brilliant whiteness, emerged a wrathful deity. It was a strong, towering male embraced by a beautiful female consort. The pair raged at the evil spirits and cleared a space for his soul to move forward. The great empathy stayed by his side and kept the angry beasts away.

CHAPTER SIXTY-NINE

Battletown, VA, December 31, 1974

The tailgate door dropped with a thud. The Buddhist monk tiptoed in his sandals behind the bearded men carrying Los across the frozen front yard of the farmhouse. Tears streamed down his face as the body of his friend was loaded into the truck bed. Canvas was draped over his body. His guidance prayers for Los stopped when the image appeared outside the open window. There was no reason to continue. His friend had emerged from the In-Between as a powerful entity. The monk now needed to mend the wounded warriors. He prayed now for the many Kindred who died in the second raid on Harpers Ferry. He was no strategist and did not want to judge its success. Certainly, he anguished over the sacrifices made. So many Kindred were gone. Many were nameless, faceless, and unknown to him. They had bravely stepped forward from the shadows and into danger. Their forefathers had raided Harpers Ferry and just like in 1859, most of the leadership had not survived. The monk bowed his head with each prayer for Los, Lord Jim, Bigfoot, and Whiskeytown.

And then he said a special prayer for Wobbly. He worried this young man was unprepared for his journey through the In-Between. They all were shocked at the news of his death. Why had Lord Jim taken him along? The monk remembered him fondly. He wasn't suited for fighting. He'd been fun-loving and generous, his infectious laugh kept their hearts from hardening. He wasn't part of the Kindred by blood, but a member in spirit. Where would they possibly discover another like him? He'd never had children, so there was no lineage to take his place. Maybe another would step forward to fill his shoes. It was unlikely; he was truly one of kind. A good soul who struggled to know himself right up to the end. The monk wondered how the Kindred would survive without this jolly soul. Maybe Vagaries would finally turn a profit he chuckled to himself.

The monk thumbed his prayer beads and reflected on his role in the raid. It started when a letter had come in the mail. By the time it reached the monastery, the sturdy envelope was worn and dirty. He recognized immediately the Virginia return address. His friend Los was calling in a favor. Thus, he travelled out of the highest mountains in the world. First, by foot, then bus, until he finally boarded a plane. He found his way to the great Shenandoah Valley. But it was too late. Upon reaching the farmhouse, Los had already committed suicide. His mission started sooner than expected anyone had expected. Something had happened to accelerate Los's venture into the spirit world.

He prepared the body and began the death prayers. He guided Los's soul to the very end and only stopped reciting prayers when Los rescued Enith. In that moment, to his awe and amazement, he sensed them transform into a new wrathful deity, something great and powerful. Los no longer needed his guidance. He would patrol the In-Between for eternity, and together with Enith, would protect souls from evil spirits sent by the Authority.

So many good warriors had fallen, but now he could feel their presence surging through the In-Between. Their heroic spirits didn't need any help from him. These travelers felt no fear. Most would reincarnate easily into higher life forms while others, like Los, would never return to this earthly existence. The world needed his fighting skills in the spiritual realm. The monk felt the transformation painful but necessary. Off in the distance, he heard a train whistle. It reminded everyone of Wobbly. Would the absurd happy hour at Vagaries ever be the same again, he thought? No more dancing and spilled beer at the sound of that train whistle. The monk looked across the pasture that stretched to the river. He thought the Shenandoah Valley looked cheerless and the surrounding mountains despairingly dark.

Before climbing into the back of the pickup, the monk glanced back at the stone farmhouse. It promised Los happiness but had only witnessed his sorrow. Hopefully, another family would enjoy its potential. The view toward the Blue Ridge was stunning, like a portal to another world. Driving up its rough, rock-strewn path was an escape into a wondrous universe. The old stone barn stood sentinel, guarding the stone farmhouse from harm. Together, the pair had witnessed centuries of history. The monk doubted if it had ever seen such heroes before.

There was nothing left for him to do except pray at their funerals. The truck led a ramshackle funeral procession one last time along the dirt river road. After pausing at their favorite spot along the riverbank, the convoy turned onto the highway and climbed up to the mountain gap. The monk pulled his wool cap tight over his head and wrapped his golden robe around his neck. The pickup truck slowed and turned onto a hidden gravel road. The rest of the trucks continued up and over the summit. Quickly disappearing into the woods, the truck creaked to a stop at a small trailhead parking lot. The monk climbed down out of the truck bed and watched the Kindred unload the canvas wrapped body of Los. He followed the men who shouldered the corpse and marble urn onto the trail. His sandals slipped on the stones and roots. Despite the cold, he took them off and walked barefoot along the trail. His calloused feet did not feel anything. The bearded men carried their precious load to its final resting place. It was the same narrow ridge where the two young sweethearts ran, laughed, and fell deeply in love. It would be their mortal resting place.

He watched as a large bonfire was lit. He prayed for hours as Los's body was burned and reduced to ash and bone fragments. They waited as the fire died and the coals were cool to the touch. The monk opened the urn and poured out Enith's ashes. He then mingled them together with a white ash staff. The small party scooped up the ashes and carried them along the narrow ridge to its rocky end. They spread the ashes out as they walked. The monk prayed again as he watched the ashes swirl and settle upon crowsfoot, fern, and trillium. Los had told him how they collapsed together onto this heavenly bed that very special day. Now, their ashes would rest together for eternity. Each spring new trillium would sprout from the floor of the rich, mixed upland forest. Its three-petaled white flowers would open anew, rising above a whorl of three, leaf-like bracts. His last prayer was that from this natural bedchamber, Los, Enith, and eventually Orc would be together forever even if it was simply as a forest plant.

The same battered pick-up truck drove him to the airport. The monk boarded a plan to his homeland. He laughed softly when he spied the snow laden peaks of the Himalayas outside the airplane window. He remembered how he gently reminded Los that they were the highest mountains in the world. Los' reply was wise. They were also the youngest mountains in the world. They, too, would be small like his Appalachians once time had worn them down.

CHAPTER SEVENTY

Clarke County, VA, June 30, 2016

T he lights of Battletown twinkled below him. Standing on the
edge of Bears Den Rocks, DB took in the view and sighed with relief.
He just finished hiking 20 miles from Harpers Ferry. True, he stopped
to rest at a shelter halfway through the hike. The strange sounds of the
forest kept him awake. Every twig snap alerted him to his danger. He
was sure the swaying trees were allowing murderous agents to slowly
creep toward him. After a couple hours, he gave up and night-hiked to
this vista. Now, at least, he could see his destination. He mulled over
his next decision. Should he risk hitch hiking into town or bushwhack
there?

"I have come too far to get caught now," he thought out loud.

Jumping back down off the rocks, he plunged down the steep
ridge. It was easy going if he didn't lose control and fall head over
heels. He made good time and soon enough emerged near a cabin in
the woods. It looked empty, maybe even abandoned. A rusted real
estate sign testified that nobody had any interest in the place. He
pushed on through the forest, circumventing anything that blocked his
way, which mostly consisted of fallen trees and briar patches. He hit
the base of the mountain, crossed the small hollow and climbed the
last small ridge between him and the Shenandoah River. He made a
quick dash across a rural road that ran the length of the riverbank.
Pausing to judge the depth and current of the water, he finally waded
in.

He quickly lost feeling in his legs but felt lucky it never got
higher than his waist. Until it did. Halfway across, his head was
suddenly below water as the river bottom disappeared. Panicked at
the thought of drowning, he kicked his feet vigorously. To his
surprise, he struck rock bed only a couple feet away. He was able to

walk along a rocky spine protruding from the riverbed all the way to the other bank. He emerged dripping wet and shivering.

"He remembered watching a TV show about a drunk Russian who fell off a train in the middle of a Siberian winter. The guy only wore long underwear or something. He didn't freeze to death simply by running mile after mile until he made it back to civilization. He looked and felt stupid when rescued but lived to talk and laugh about the experience. DB climbed the riverbank and started jogging along a dirt service road. When it started to veer away from Battletown, he simply hopped a fence and struck out across open fields. He could see the big blue water tower that bore the town's name. Like the crow flies, DB made a beeline for it.

An hour later, DB crossed a perimeter road that appeared to skirt around the edge of Battletown. He waited in the woods for the sun to set before stepping onto it and walking the last couple blocks to Vagaries. The town was eerily quiet except for barking dogs and the occasional passing car. Nobody was out walking the streets. He didn't have to worry about talking to anyone. He reached the lane that matched the address Lost Mungo had giving him. Turning the corner, he saw a dismal looking building at its terminus. Someone had scrawled the words, *The Vagaries of Life Tavern,* across it with an apparently unsteady hand. DB walked up its porch steps and opened the door. A cheer went up when he walked in.

"We got our twelfth person!" a drunk man yelled.

Everyone patted him on the back for reasons that eluded him. DB wondered if they were celebrating him specifically. He felt like a returning hero. Suddenly, a bell on the wall starting to vibrate with the sound of a passing train. The patrons started jumping up and down in anticipation of something happening. The jukebox belted out a rock song he didn't recognize. The bell clanked and the crowd carried him with their surge to the bar.

"Absurd Happy Hour!" they chanted over and over.

"What the hell is going on here?" DB shouted over the noise.

"Free drinks dumbass," replied another tottering drunk.

DB was now trapped against the bar with the weight of the surging crowd.

"What are you drinking?" asked a familiar voice. "Oh shit, forget it, we've only got Pabst."

DB turned in time to find Lyn pushing a beer across the bar.

"You're alive!" DB shouted.

"It took you long enough to get here?" Lyn responded.

The two reached over the bar to hug but couldn't quite close the distance.

"I will hug you in a minute. We got an Absurd Happy Hour happening. This is a fucking amazing moment of chance. Hop back here and help me serve some beers," she yelled over the roar of the celebrating drinkers.

DB went around behind the bar and hugged her tightly to the amusement of the crowd. They stared at each other closely and kissed passionately. The joyful mood of the patrons quickly turned to shouted complaints when they realized the romantic reunion was impacting their alcohol consumption.

"What are we going to do now?" DB asked.

"I am drinking a beer and living in the moment. We can worry about tomorrow, well, tomorrow," Lyn responded with glee.

* * *

Closing Vagaries for the night was no easy feat. After shooing patrons out the door, Lyn got the feeling they were just moving the party somewhere else in Battletown. One large patron was curled up on the pool table snoring loudly. DB laid a blanket over him and turned out the lights. Lyn locked the front door and peered out the front window. It was instinctive. She didn't know what she was looking for or expecting to see. The pair climbed the stairs and collapsed into a deep sleep.

DB woke the next morning to find the entire tavern vibrating to the thunderous sound of a train passing. He found Lyn snuggled warmly in his arms and wanted little else from life. A sudden fearful thought surged into his consciousness through a haze of alcohol.

"*The Genealogies!*" he shouted.

"What is it?" Lyn muttered without opening her eyes.

"I don't see my backpack," he said.

"Check downstairs behind the bar," she answered.

DB jumped out of bed and crashed down the stairs. Each step made his head pound worse. It was not behind the bar. A frantic search of the entire bar proved fruitless. He stepped out onto the front porch and saw it hanging from a clothesline. It was empty.

"Don't worry about *The Genealogies*. I dried them out for you," a graveled cigarette voice said from behind him.

DB whirled around. An elderly woman was holding *The Genealogies* in her out stretched hands. He accepted them, carefully evaluated their condition, and then stowed the leather-bound treasure protectively under his arm.

"Thank you so much. These are precious," he said

"You must be DB. I am Scape Goat."

"Nice to me you," DB responded

It was at that moment he realized he was naked. He looked nervously around for something to cover himself. Seeing nothing, he hid behind the leather manuscript.

"Welcome to Vagaries. Sorry I missed you last night. Looks like you had a good time. Your pretty little girlfriend was relieving me behind the bar. I think she has a job here if she wants it."

"I will be sure to tell her," DB said looking at his wet dripping pack.

"I helped Lost Mungo out more than once. Shit happens. Now, go back upstairs. I think Lyn wants to know what's next."

"Right. Wish I knew myself." DB climbed the steps.

When he entered the room, he found Lyn arranging gear and clothes on the bed.

"From what I understand, you will be doing some hiking. Records must be maintained. Funny, how you are coming full circle. First, you read shelter journals for clues you didn't know existed and now you are looking in the same journals for clues you know are there. All to maintain *The Genealogies* no less." Lyn said as she folded clothes.

"It's more than funny. Fantastically impossible. It's like the universe set me on this path." DB replied running his fingers over the cracked leather.

"Well, you can take me with you or I can wait here for you to return from each trip. Either way is fine with me."

"Not a bad way to keep a low profile until things blow over with the FBI," he said realizing immediately how stupid it sounded.

Lyn stopped folding and turned to face him.

"DB, it's never going to blow over. If we want out, Scape Goat said these people will help us start a new life under new identities. I believe her. I also believe we should help with their cause. Actually, I believe it's as much ours as theirs."

Lyn paused and smoothed the creases off the clothes on the bed. She began folding them tightly and placing them in plastic bags.

"Next time you fall in the river, try not to get everything so wet. Or, better yet, don't fall in the river," she said. "Anyway, all those times you talked about some big government conspiracy, I thought it was some sophomoric phase you would grow out of. Now, I realize it is true and bigger than ever."

"I have to admit, I doubted myself sometimes. It is like we crossed over into another dimension or something." DB paused trying to express his thoughts.

"Oh, DB, you have no idea," Lyn said cryptically.

She pulled out something from under the bed and placed it next to his supplies.

"I think you are going to need this."

DB picked it up, placed it on his head and adjusted the chin strap.

"Well, I declare, DB Cooper, you look dashing."

They both laughed and fell back on the pile of clothes and gear.

"Ouch, that hurts!" Lyn yelled.

DB pulled out *The Genealogies* from underneath them and set it down by their feet.

Chapter Seventy-one

Battletown, VA, Spring 2017

The stone farmhouse once again echoed with the noise of human occupants as Bret and Zoa dropped shipping boxes onto its cracked and scratched pine floor. They were its proud new owners. The moving truck was waiting for them in the front yard when they returned from signing paperwork. By the time they got home, it was already filed away into dusty metal cabinets at the 260-year-old Thomas Hamilton and Sons title office in Winchester. Of course, they used fake identities supplied by the Kindred on all the documents. Bret was constantly amazed at how many of its members worked diligently in artificially lit, barren bureaucratic offices. Their lineage demanded action but not all its members were capable of roaming natural wild places and fighting violent pitched battles under the light of a full moon.

The glorious spring morning swept a fresh cool breeze through the open windows. The day was full of possibilities. Their adopted child followed them into the small house. Her name was Othona. She was a beautiful nine-year-old. She ran through every room of the small, cozy farmhouse within minutes. Each room had its own fireplace and the walls dividing the rooms were at least two feet thick. There were only two bedrooms on the second floor. One would have a queen size bed for the happy new couple. They loved the place. A screened porch out back would allow them plenty of bug-free evenings and a view across the expansive rock-strewn cattle pasture. Its tranquility was intoxicating. Zoa led Othona to the room she could call her own. The little girl gazed up the absurdly twisting and narrow staircase to the second floor. Her room was at the top and to the left. The little girl hopped two steps at a time while Zoa followed with an armful of pillows and blankets.

"And this is your room. We'll put the bed against that wall under the window. You can fall asleep under the stars and cool off this summer with the breeze at night. When winter comes, we can warm up the room by lighting a fire in the fireplace. The other bed will go against that wall."

"Why do I need another bed?" Othona replied.

"Oh, who knows, you may have a little brother or sister before too long. Your father and I have an appointment with some people next week."

She thought of using the word orphanage but chose not to. For some reason, travelling the Golden Path precluded them from conceiving their own children. It was a tradeoff they never regretted.

"We can play together outside and explore the woods." Othona giggled as she ran out her bedroom door and leapt down the stairs.

Bret was in the front yard talking with Tom. The moving crew cast quick glances at the pair while they carried boxes down the ramp of the truck. They closely eyed the eccentric elderly man who sported a long, grey ponytail and spoke with a strange accent. He carried a shovel but didn't appear to be a farmhand. His shoes were too impractical—leather with shiny buckles. Zoa held Othona's hand as they descended the porch stairs and crossed the soft green grass that was sprinkled with white flowered clover. When they got closer, she overheard Tom say something about a menace in the barn. Her eyes darted in its direction.

"Tom, I don't want the snake killed. It maintains a balance," said Bret. Tom stuck his shovel into the ground.

"One must weigh its potential for good as well as evil. You are the Lord of this manor and I respect your authority. I equally advise you not to let your daughter wander those fields without the proper high boots." He looked at the girl's bare feet.

"She'll be alright. In fact, she's already had an encounter with that scary snake. Isn't that right, Othona?" Bret looked at his daughter.

"That's the menace?" She wriggled her mouth at the word and nodded her head in confirmation. "Yes. I was in the barn this morning and saw a monster snake skin hanging between the rafters." She described the incident catching her breath as the words tumbled over each other.

"It probably went in there to shed its skin. Nice warm place. We should be careful renovating in there. After all, it would be bad for business if my guests got bitten by a rattlesnake," Bret laughed.

"It'll take a lot of blood, sweat, and tears to convert that old barn into this hiker inn you describe," Tom chimed in.

"The term is hostel. I am not running an inn but just providing a place to lay down a sleeping bag and take a shower. We are not hostellers for pete's sake," Bret corrected.

"But, you are servicing pilgrims nonetheless," Tom winked in reply.

"We have some inheritance money that will go toward the project. You can help by keeping your trained eye on our guests, invited or not." Bret suggested.

He put his hand on the old man's shoulder, which felt surprisingly strong.

"We've got to finish unpacking and then focus on getting some firewood delivered and stacked. I have a feeling this house is going to be freezing this winter." Zoa shivered with mock coldness.

"People were a tougher breed when this place was built, you know," Tom replied.

"This is 2017, not 1795, and we're tougher in different ways," Zoa started to explain, but Othona was tugging on her sleeve.

"Mommy, I think I just saw something in my bedroom window."

Zoa knelt to hold her daughter's hands and looked into her eyes.

"Tell us what you saw, dear."

"It looked like a ghost."

"What did this ghost look like?" Bret exchanged a concerned look with Tom.

"A strange ghost because it wasn't just one person...," she paused, puzzled at the sight. "It was as if a man and a woman were together, looking out."

The adults let out a collective breath.

"Othona, there are a lot of things to be afraid of in this world, but what you saw is not one of them. In fact, I don't think it was a ghost at all, but a very special angel." Zoa stood up.

"I think we may have to discuss Wrathful Empathies sooner rather than later." Bret nervously glanced at Zoa and Tom.

Tom leaned forward and whispered in Othona's ear, "Just tell your parents if you ever see a giant man with white hair and a long beard."

"Yes sir," Othona replied peering around the farm yard inspecting its activity.

"Don't let him scare you with talk about this old evil man," Bret said.

"That's not scary to me," Othona replied.

Loud voices interrupted their conversation. They all turned in the direction of the noise and saw two male backpackers walking up the rough drive. They had just emerged from behind the stone barn and waved their arms in greetings. Zoa and Bret looked at each other incredulously.

"Hello. Is this the hiker hostel?" shouted the tall one with dreadlocks.

"Well, yes, except that we've not exactly opened yet." Bret cupped his hands around his mouth to project the sound.

The two hikers rambled over to the group standing under the giant oak tree in the front yard. The shorter, stout hiker lumbered a few steps behind the other and joined the conversation.

"Sorry if we're early! What time do you open today?" he panted.

Bret paused and exchanged looks with Zoa. "What I mean is, the hostel may not be open for a year. We haven't even started renovating the barn. I'm afraid you came all the way out here for nothing."

"Bummer man. We heard you were opening today. We met this crazy-looking guy in a pith helmet at the shelter last night. He gave us directions here. Anyway, sorry for the surprise. I'm Stash, by the way, and this is Jelly Bean, AKA, The Mother Load. That's with an "a," not an "e."

"Well, it's certainly nice to meet you guys. In recognition of your effort to be our first customers, and since it's getting late, I'll offer you free tent sites in our yard," Zoa nodded.

"Free water from the house, as well," Bret offered.

"Cool, we're in."

Tom scratched his head with one hand and leaned on his shovel with the other.

"Now tell me, exactly, who told you to come here?"

"Said his trail name was Lost Mungo. He was curious about our family history. Kinda weird, but whatever. Kept squiggling in a note book or something," Jelly Bean replied.

"Yeah, that was a couple weeks ago. Some way or another he knew my dad had died even before I did. Turns out he was killed in some bullshit traffic stop. We're suing for release of the records, but it seems to have all gone down the memory hole. The Authority just keeps saying it's national security, blah blah," Stash explained.

"Why did he tell you to come here?" asked Zoa.

"He said there was a job here for me. We would find kindred souls or something like that. Mentioned the hostel had some kind of Tibetan Buddhist vibe. Sounded awesome to us, so we're here. But here's where it gets weird again. He even knew the name of a place but you said it isn't built yet. He called it the "Singing Bowl Hiker Hostel." Me and Jelly Bean came here right from my dad's funeral. We're kind of on a suspended thru-hike," Stash said.

"Sounds like we got a name for our hostel," Bret mused.

"I like it!" said Zoa.

"What on God's Earth is a singing bowl?" asked Tom.

"It's like, a metal bowl that produces a tone that Buddhists use to signal the beginning and end of a meditative session," Jelly Bean explained.

"I think the name works. The Hiker Hostel is a break from the Great Trail, which is itself a long-distance meditation," added Stash.

"Looks like Lost Mungo might have been right. How about I offer you jobs working on the renovation of that old barn there?" Bret pointed across the field. "You can camp through the spring and summer and then move indoors in the fall. If that's okay with the missus?"

Bret looked to Zoa and she nodded.

"It's a deal."

"He is saying you're hired," Tom summarized. "When can you start?"

The hikers looked at one another. Stash scratched the back of his neck.

"Tomorrow, if that's okay. We just hiked about seven miles and could use a break," he grinned.

"Tomorrow it is. I have to warn you though. There is a snake prowling these parts, but you're not to kill it per the management." Tom jerked his thumb at Bret.

The little group all turned their heads toward the sound of barking dogs coming from beyond the barb wire fencing that separated the yard from the pasture.

"Would you cut down on that racket?" A woman's voice boomed from behind a copse of trees.

Seeing nobody, they looked at each other quizzically. The voice boomed again but much closer. It came again from across the pasture. When they turned toward the mountains, they saw her. She was a short squat woman with long black hair speckled with gray. A colorful bandana tied it up at her wrinkled brow. She slung a cotton bag full of saplings over her shoulder. A pair of obese brown Labrador retrievers struggled over the rocky terrain with her.

"Hello camp!" she yelled as she closed the distance.

"Magda!" they all yelled at once.

"I couldn't help but notice your fine stone house and this little gathering here. Can I join you?"

"But, of course! Come on over. What are you doing out there?"

"Oh, I'm on contract to plant a hillside a couple farms over from here. Trees help to cut down on erosion, you know. We," she pointed to her labs, "got to wandering and I got a little turned around."

"Tree planter and chuck wagon cook. What a resume," Zoa responded after hugging her tightly.

"Besides there's a big black bear just over that rise. He was standing up looking at you guys. Then he saw me and the dogs. Couldn't figure out what we were. Thankfully, he took off. Still out there somewhere though I figure. I could outrun him but High and Lonesome here would be in trouble." She scratched the panting dogs.

"Do you need a place to stay?" asked Bret.

"My truck's parked about two miles away, at least I think it is." Magda shrugged

"Not a problem. You're welcome to spend the night here," Bret offered.

"I'm a still a pretty good cook. I can earn my keep if you let me lose in the kitchen," Magda offered.

"Yes, absolutely! We got spoiled by your cooking," Zoa said.

"We might even need a permanent cook come next spring," Tom suggested.

That evening, the eccentric but happy band sat around a great bonfire Tom built in the backyard. They toasted their new endeavor, the Singing Bowl Hiker Hostel, and devoured a thoroughly delicious meal beneath the stars. Bret stared off at the Blue Ridge while Othona cuddled in Zoa's lap.

"Mommy, why do you and daddy always stare at those mountains?" Her eyes fluttered with sleepiness.

"Because, dear, we have wonderful memories of our adventures along the Great Trail along those ridgelines." Zoa stroked her daughter's hair.

"If she ever disappears, we'll know where to find her," Tom said.

The bonfire was in the corner lot behind the farmhouse. A ring of stony ribs broke through the surface of the lawn forming a natural seating area for the group as they warmed themselves by the fire. An ancient hemlock towered behind them. As the evening settled in, a high wind whistled through its bare upper branches. Bret, Zoa, and Tom exchanged glances at each other and then up to the hemlock as if looking for an old friend.

"Look at the fire!" said Othona.

"What about it, dear?".

"The flames. They're turning blue!" She looked at them intently. Her face reflecting the awe and wonder of her vision.

"Far out!" Stash and Jelly Bean said in unison.

The blue flames blended with the Blue Ridge Mountains beyond. The dogs snored noisily as Magda stroked their heads. She then started humming an old gypsy song. Tom paced around the edge of the group with the shovel in his hand. Othona fell asleep in Zoa's lap. She dreamed of a golden path that was enchanted with heroes, monsters and gods.

CHAPTER SEVENTY-TWO

Shenandoah Mountains, VA, January 1, 1975

O rc hiked alone up the mountain. He left the eccentric man behind once they found the Great Trail. Lost Mungo's backpack was now strapped to Orc's shoulders. The old man said it was full of supplies and gear. He also clutched a list of names, times, and destinations scribbled into a spiral notebook. Lost Mungo had instructed Orc to use the information when he needed support of any kind. The battle his uncles waged in the woods had distracted the black clad killers. They were fighting for their own lives and would be lucky to survive the night. Orc was on his own now since Lost Mungo had put him on the Great Trail.

They parted company three miles ago. Orc stopped to drink from his canteen. He stared at the dark mountain before him and remembered Lost Mungo's final words of warning, "If it is big and in front of you, that's where the trail is going." Sure enough, Orc climbed for another three miles, each step higher than the last. His legs ached and sweat dripped from his face. He dreaded looking too far ahead. If he kept his eyes focused only on the next white blaze, he could pretend the climb was almost over. It didn't work for long. After a few feet, he would glace too far ahead and see a dozen blazes ascending the mountain then quickly look down at his boots and try to forget what he had just seen. Instead, he concentrated on his foot placement. Rock here, root there, step up, hold onto boulder, grab tree branch—whatever assistance was available to pull him up the mountain. He couldn't believe people did this kind of hiking for fun. It was another hour until the next white blaze was not above him.

At last, he reached at point where the next step fell flat. The ascent was complete. As the trail traversed the mountain plateau, his heart stopped pounding in his ears and his breathing became less labored. The numbness in his legs eased and the breeze dried his sweat. The trail was now flat dirt with grass at its edges. Knowing his next footfall would not result in a painful twist of the ankle, he could safely look around to the forest on either side of the trail. Much to his relief, Orc saw the white blazes ran flat as a pancake until the path disappeared.

The climb up the eastern slope of the mountain protected him from the western airstream, but the summit left no place to hide. The breeze quickly turned into gusts. The sweat on his skin suddenly felt cold. His clothes were soaked through with perspiration. They now felt like a cold wet blanket. Orc stopped and dropped his pack. The wind whipped his shirt sleeves and flapped open his pants pockets. He pulled a jacket from his pack and put it on. It was made of goose feathers and warm despite its lite weight. As he knelt to dig through his pack for hat or gloves, a movement up the trail caught the corner of his eye.

It was a flash of colors low to the ground, its movement fluid and sinuous. The sound of rustling in the brush alerted Orc just in time to avoid a flash of fangs. It was a monstrous rattlesnake; the biggest Orc had ever seen. He had not even heard tales of such a creature. He swiped it aside with the long white ash hiking staff given to him by Lost Mungo. The snake coiled itself and poised to strike again. It hissed and spit and rattled its tail in a whirl of vibration. The effect mesmerized Orc for a moment until he stumbled backward and pulled himself from its trance. It followed him, inching forward while maintaining its coil, its red eyes blazing as if it came to settle a personal score.

"What are you doing above ground, snake? Don't you know it's winter?"

The snake increased the intensity of its rattle. Its head moved side-to-side. It kept Orc in its sights and lashed its tongue every second to taste his scent. Orc realized it wouldn't stop until it drew blood.

The snake was conscious of something before it. This entity was different than its other prey. The snake craved human flesh, but before him was no mere mortal. The snake tongued the air again, this time with confusion. It grew angry and struck out again, this time nearly biting the creature leaping before it. Recoiling for another strike, the snake felt drained of energy. It doubted it could strike again. Something was wrong. The strength it had just moments ago was draining. It inched closer and recoiled tighter.

"That's right. You're cold-blooded snake. Every time you strike, you lose power. Why don't you go below ground where you belong?"

Each strike, ever weaker, was met with a blast from the wooden staff. In a few minutes, the snake was exhausted and slipping into a cold-induced slumber. It attempted to slither away in search of the hole from which it had come, but it had no strength to move. In its desire to kill, it had forgotten its limitations. It lay at his feet, defeated and deflated. The creature suddenly appeared pitiful to him. For some reason, Orc was overwhelmed with a sense of empathy for the creature. He felt some kindred to it. The feeling confused him but didn't stop his next action.

Orc struggled to pick it up, its massive size almost more than his strength could handle. He held its limp body out in front of him. He opened his jacket and stuffed the snake inside. It lay coiled, unmoving and near death, absorbing his warmth.

Once again, Orc began his hike with the creature as his companion. He put the white staff under his arm and retrieved the small spiral notebook from his pants pocket. Lost Mungo's instructions led him south to the Iron Mountains. It would be at least five days before he arrived. Once there, a rough map indicated where he could hide among craggy summits in the Grayson Highland, one of which contained a small cave. Lost Mungo told him the black clad killers worked for something called the Authority. Orc should stay in the cave where this organization's surveillance wouldn't be able to penetrate his rocky sanctuary. He was told to expect help from the local mountain people. Lost Mungo said they were his distant relations and this connection carried some sort of unspoken protection. His father and uncle were supposedly part of this group. Lost Mungo had called them "the Kindred." These were the people who had supported his aunt with money, food, clothes, and just about whatever she needed to raise him. In fact, Lost Mungo had said Orc himself was even part of the Kindred. The group was particularly strong down in the Iron Mountains and he would be safe there.

He followed the ridgeline for miles until it finally descended into a stream valley. As he approached a road crossing, he prepared to hitchhike. He ran his hand through his hair and went to smooth out his jacket when he realized his coat was noticeably bulging from the coiled snake within. Reluctantly, he decided to hike on. He drained what remained in his water bottle and filled it in the stream before hiking up the next ridge.

He could feel the snake warming as he started his climb. It slowly uncoiled and began to search for a way out of his jacket. Eventually, it circumnavigated his waist and coiled around him, its head meeting its tail. Fearing a bite to the stomach, he withdrew the snake and placed it on the ground. It lifted its head and tasted the air. Its tongue darted back and forth. Orc's odor was unfamiliar. This is no human the snake determined. It hesitated to attack and instead circled in confusion. It had never felt a presence more dangerous than itself.

"What's the matter, snake? You don't know yourself anymore? Look around, there's nothing here to kill. Bite yourself and spare the world your poison."

The snake spun around and struck a new victim. Its fangs sunk deep and pumped venom until dry. Orc watched in disbelief. He'd heard mountain folk tell tales of such bizarre behavior. It was a sign that his uncles said would foretell the end of the world. A great serpent devouring itself. He never understood what it meant until now. Had it followed his command or did it choose to hurt itself? What would happen if it kept swallowing? Would it disappear completely or emerge larger and more powerful? He didn't have time to ponder it much longer. Those murdering agents would be looking for him. Lost Mungo warned him to never stop moving, never think he was safe, and never, for even a minute, come out of the mountains. He had faced a monster, saved it from certain death, and then watched it disappear into itself. Strange times, he thought, strange times indeed.

He looked to the bare winter sky. He needed to open some space between him and the Authority, not to mention the disappearing snake. The Iron Mountains were as far away as he had ever been. After he hiked about a hundred yards down the trail, he stopped and took off his pack again. He looked inside for something to eat. He found something that looked like a candy bar but tasted like oatmeal. It was hardened into a rectangle.

"Not too bad but dry as hell," Orc said to himself.

He swigged some water to wash it down. He looked at his map and figured his destination was at least 150 miles to the south. Orc was familiar with the woods and didn't fear sleeping outside but he had never hiked with everything on his back. He would just take each mile as it came. Lost Mungo said trail angels would help him out along the way, but that he should only leave the trail at night. He had given him a map marked with deserted trailheads. He was to wait there after midnight. If nobody met him within 10 minutes, he was to keep moving to the next destination. Lost Mungo told him to trust whoever showed up. They were his Kindred. They would ensure he got the necessities to keep going. If he had to go into town for a shower or something critical, they would arrange to bring him back before dawn. It was all well practiced. The Kindred had been doing this for a very long time. He would finally meet, face to face, all the people who had helped to raise him from a distance. It was his turn now to carry on the fight. His uncles should have given him a gun and let him join them. He felt like a man even if nobody else saw him that way. His uncles just wanted him out of the way. Now, he was depending on total strangers. Suddenly, tears flowed down his dirt stained cheeks. He wanted to go home to his step mom but realized that was something he could never do ever again. Maybe he wasn't a man after all he thought.

He was stuck with the Great Trail for now. It made Orc angry that so many people seemed to know so much about his parents. They had abandoned him. His father would rather fight instead of raising him. His real mother just disappeared. He wondered how such people could be loved and respected by so many others.

Orc hiked another twelve miles until he finally sought reprieve in a dirty wooden shelter stuck back all by itself in a creepy dark hollow. He sat down inside and dropped his pack. He studied his map intently. He traced his finger along the Great Trail until he found another shelter close to a road. It was about 20 miles ahead. Tomorrow, he would time it right to be there at midnight. For now, he would get some rest. He opened several bags in his pack until he found a sleeping bag. Again, it was made of goose feathers that made it just as light. He took off his hunting boots and rubbed his sore feet. Hopefully, Lost Mungo had packed some extra socks. He climbed inside and felt toasty warm. He put his arms behind his head and stared out into the darkening woods. He wasn't scared but wished he had his .22 rifle. It would at least provide some noise should a bear wonder out of hibernation and try climbing into the shelter. He turned on his side and fell immediately asleep.

He dreamed of giant serpents and raging black wolves. He fought off their assaults as he trekked across a darkened plain. Then came other monsters. These had gnashing teeth and screamed horribly. They drank blood from human skulls. Their eyes glared at him from the dark and threatened to add his skull to their necklaces of defeated foes. Flashing lights lit up the dark sky and thunderous clashes rocked the ground. He was on the brink of defeat when he recognized these wrathful deities for what they were: harmless images. He turned his back on them and walked away. They pursued but he did not turn around. Without his fear, they evaporated into the night.

Orc awoke from his dream and stared into the gray light of dawn. Two muffled voices came to him as the dream faded.

"You will destroy him," the first voice said.

"The caverns, the caverns," the second voice repeated.

Orc got out of his sleeping bag and walked onto a rocky cliff to watch the sunrise. He looked toward the blood red dawn and answered as if in a trance.

"I am Orc. Wreath'd round the accursed tree:

The times are ended; shadows pass, the morning 'gins to break;

The fiery joy, that Urizen perverted to ten commands,

What night he led the starry hosts thro' the wide Wilderness:

That stony law I stump to dust"[2]

His eyes glowed red in a mirror image of the sunrise. The words he muttered were foreign and strange. He didn't know their meaning. Now, he saw a white-haired giant lurking behind the far ridgeline. His head and shoulders appeared and disappeared with the elevation change. The hulking titan glared toward Orc as if challenging him to battle. It was then that Orc summoned a primal scream from deep within him. The mountains shuddered and shivered at his voice. It happened in a second and then was over. The monster was gone. Orc was dizzy and weak. He looked again to make sure he didn't imagine it. The mountains were once again motionless, stoic in the face of time. Squinting his eyes, he sensed the immense forces pent up inside them. His mind unleashed them from their chains. One ridge after another began undulating like waves rolling in from the sea. Each a

---

[2] Blake, *The Complete Illuminated Books*, 421.

different shade of blue. He then stopped their motion with another thought. Everything was now back to normal. He was fully awake. The mountains were still. He spun around to return to the cave when a far-off wisp of smoke caught his eye.

"Either we got the beginning of a forest fire or someone is having a bonfire on top of that mountain," Orc muttered to himself.

He noticed the smoke from the fire spread horizontally before settling down into the valleys. Something about the view saddened him. Crawling back into the cave, he bundled up his belongings. He emerged back into the morning light, strapped on his pack and began hiking. He glanced back at the dark opening of the cave. It was a place of refuge that he would use again.

The trail snaked away from the summit down through a tunnel of rhododendron. The skeleton branches formed a cathedral overhead that blocked the cold wind. Inside the warren of evergreen, he noticed scaly undersides of the leaves. He imagined himself walking under the wings of a giant dragon. The path was littered with clumps of white flowers that had fallen to the ground after their bloom. He trod over them and relished the softness of the path. He cinched the straps of his pack tighter and advanced around each turn and twist of the trail. He was almost having fun. The trail was changing him for the better. There was nobody but himself to depend on. He no longer felt afraid of being pursued. Walking with a bounce in his step, Orc felt the same now as he did when tearing across the mountain trails on his ATV. Far from being scared, he felt thrilled to test himself.

Passing out of the tunnel, he hiked past a small rocky vista. He paused and looked far off to the south across a sea of ridgelines. For the first time in his life, he felt surrounded by kith and kin, except these kindred were not people but mountains. And that was enough.

The End

Mark Ewing is an avid backpacker who has explored the Blue Ridge mountains from Pennsylvania to North Carolina. He is a refugee of the Scotch Irish diaspora who is still looking for that perfect mountain home where he can live free and clear. To this day, he searches any rock laden dirt road that lies just beyond End State Maintenance signs that he comes across in his travels. He drives up each road looking for an old stone farmhouse at the end. Of course, it must have a view of the mountains, be haunted by ghosts with a tall hemlock nearby. He will pause to listen for the wind to whistle through its bare top branches.

The 2nd Raid on Harpers Ferry is the first book in his Wrathful Empathies trilogy.

For more on his thoughts and fears (not to mention work) visit:

www.wrathfulempathies.com

lostmungo2@gmail.com